New York Classics
FRANK BERGMANN, SERIES EDITOR

OTHER BOOKS BY HENRY W. CLUNE

HENRY W. CLUNE

The Genesee

Foreword by ROBERT KOCH
Illustrated by DOUGLAS GORSLINE

SYRACUSE UNIVERSITY PRESS

Foreword © 1988 by Syracuse University Press
Syracuse, New York 13244-5160

Syracuse University Press edition 1988
95 96 97 98 99   6 5 4 3 2

This edition is reprinted by arrangement with Henry Holt and Company, Inc.
The Genesee was originally published in the Rivers of America series.

The paper used in this publication meets the minimum requirements of
American National Standard of Information Sciences—Permanence of Paper
for Printed Library Materials, ANSI Z39.48-1984. ∞™

Library of Congress Cataloging-in-Publication Data

Clune, Henry W., 1890–
The Genesee/Henry W. Clune : foreword by Robert Koch :
  illustrated by Douglas Gorsline.
        p.   cm.—(New York classics)
    Reprint. Originally published : New York: Holt, Rinehart and
  Winston, 1963.
    Bibliography: p.
    Includes index.
    ISBN 0-8156-2436-0 (alk. paper)
    1. Genesee River (Pa. and N.Y.)   2. Genesee River Valley (Pa. and
  N.Y.)—History.   I. Title.   II. Series.
  F127.G2C5 1988
  974.7′88—dc19   87-33582
                                                   CIP

Designer: Ernst Reichl
Manufactured in the United States of America

For ROBERT G. KOCH

with deep appreciation

HENRY W. CLUNE was born in Rochester, N.Y., in 1890. At 20 he began his life-long career as journalist and writer. "Seen and Heard," his regular Rochester *Democrat and Chronicle* column on diverse topics, made him one of the most regularly read American journalists for sixty years. His published books include six novels, three collections based on the column, *The Genesee*, and three reminiscences. He still occasionally publishes lively commentaries, and he continues to write new short fiction.

A Rochesterian and long-time reader of Henry Clune, ROBERT KOCH taught English at the Rochester Institute of Technology before becoming Dean of the University College at the University of Rochester. There he also directed the summer Writers Workshop for fifteen years. He is a former theater reviewer and a regular arts and cultural interviewer on WXXI-FM since 1976. Now Dean Emeritus, he is writing full time.

FOREWORD

Early in *The Genesee* Henry W. Clune recalls his visit to the
river's source near Gold, in Potter County, northern Pennsylvania. He asks Merle Hosley, the farmer on whose land the
spring gushes, why he hadn't erected a marker to identify the
spot.

"Oh, I don't know," he said, with a little shrug. "Guess I never thought
about it."
"But there's a marker—there're two markers—at the [nearby] beginning of the Allegheny."
"Well, it's a longer river."
It is a longer river by nearly two hundred miles, to its point of confluence with the Monongahela at Pittsburgh. But length isn't everything. I
told Mr. Hosley that I had lived for a total of sixty years never farther
than three-quarters of a mile from the channel of the Genesee; that I had
paddled a canoe on its waters and swum in them in the summer; skated
on its ice, picked chestnuts along its banks, more or less found my wife

[a championship swimmer] in it, and yet, until now, I had never taken the trouble to look out its source.

He said simply, "Well, you've seen it today."

The river lacks the fame of the Mississippi, Missouri, Ohio, Colorado, or even the Allegheny, among the more than fifty waterways celebrated in the "Rivers of America" series of books. Of the other New York State rivers represented in the series, certainly the Hudson and St. Lawrence are better known than the Genesee, and probably the Mohawk is as well. As the author reminds us, the Genesee has nevertheless, "in the face of great obstacles, flowed north with a contrariness reflected in not a few of the people who have lived adjacent to it." Their story has encompassed a surprisingly broad slice of American history, from the height of the League of the Iroquois to today's high-tech society. Aspects of the valley's story have attracted the literary skills of Samuel Hopkins Adams, Carl Carmer, Paul Horgan, Jerre Mangione, and others. But the valley's most devoted literary talent has been Henry Clune.

Only Henry Clune could have written this wonderfully personal book. His colorful portraits quicken the history of *The Genesee*. When he wrote the book twenty-five years ago, Clune had been a reporter and columnist for half a century, already published five of his six novels, and spent an active lifetime beside the Genesee.

He has personally witnessed nearly a century of Genesee valley history. Born in Rochester, N.Y., on February 8, 1890, Clune was raised about a city block from the river. His schooling cut short by an itch to get on with the rest of life, young Clune began his real education as an unpaid "sub" reporter on one of Rochester's daily newspapers. He soon established a paid niche in local journalism with his "Seen and Heard" column, and over the years he became arguably its leading practitioner and spirit. He has been characterized in the *Saturday Review* as "one of a distinguished breed of men that may be vanishing from the American scene—publishers, editors and columnists who stayed home and made good." He has stayed home, except for a stint with the *Stars and Stripes* in France during World War I, and brief flings at the journalistic life in New York City and Detroit. As a track enthusiast and aficionado of the mile run, he has written from three continents, but Rochester has always been his home base.

During most of these years, the newspaper offices of the Rochester *Democrat and Chronicle* were on the Main Street bridge that spanned the Genesee. There he tapped out amusing, sympathetic, sometimes skeptical bulletins from his "Main Street Beat," as a published memoir based on the pieces was titled. Along the way he interviewed the prominent and notorious—from Winston Churchill and W. Somerset Maugham to Babe Ruth and Tallulah Bankhead.

With champion swimmer Charlotte Boyle Clune, he raised four sons and five bull terriers at Scottsville, ten miles south of the city. The family occupied a house overlooking both the alluvial fields that border the river and the site of the first house built west of the Genesee. He and Charlotte still live there.

Along the way Clune squeezed out time to write his six published novels, all of which reflect in one way or another the rich harvest of human experiences on which he has reported. He continues to write peppery commentaries and sprightly short stories. For most of this century, he has commented on much of the impatience—from jitney to jet—that passes for progress beside the (usually) patient Genesee. It is not, however, the length of his residence but his friendships and interests, sharpness of eye and ear, and keen appreciation of a good tale that make *The Genesee* so lively a book.

Clune introduces us to the river on one of its springtime rampages, a time during which it remains seductive even while flooding out its loyalists. The Iroquois, who named so many sites in the Genesee basin, called it "the beautiful valley." The Senecas, aggressive keepers of the western door to the longhouse of the Five Nations, found their own heartland in the rich soil and abundant forests of the valley long before French missionaries and soldiers "discovered" it in the seventeenth century.

French, British, and American incursions are the subjects of exciting and revealing tales of the Marquis de Denonville, the Jesuit René Frémin, the Indian captive Mary Jemison ("the white woman of the Genesee"), Ebenezer ("Indian") Allan, Moses Van Campen, Horatio Jones, and many others whose lives were intimately entwined with the Genesee. Historical facts about these and other colorful lives are insinuated into the leisurely yet forceful narrative as subtly as the Honeoye, Canaseraga, Oatka, and two Black creeks contribute run-off from the river's basin.

The Genesee was never a major waterway, but waterpower at its falls spawned and sustained flour mills which, with the deep soil upstream, made the valley for a time the breadbasket of the young republic. When the Erie Canal crossed the Genesee on a long aqueduct which, a century and a half later, still carries one of Rochester's main streets on its back, the valley's major city became the brawling "young lion of the west." The intersection of these waterways was the focal point of its development as a major milling and manufacturing center.

Up the valley, nearly to the river's source, Wellsville continued to flourish later in the nineteenth century by replacing a diminishing timber supply with oil's black gold before that resource became the province of Western states and Middle Eastern sheikdoms. Between these two boom towns, where the present Letchworth State Park straddles the river, the determined Genesee carved the Grand Canyon of the East. Here Mary Jemison lived and is remembered. After later exploitation of its natural resources, this dramatic site was saved by the conservation efforts of William Pryor Letchworth, an important reformer of orphanages and prisons.

Downstream a few miles the sprawling Wadsworth family fiefdom attested to a different pioneering spirit, taste for cultivated affluence, and a considerable sense of civic responsibility. This enclave—and a nearby fortune founded on JELL-O—supported the third-oldest fox hunt in the U.S., which survives as a horse show that Henry Clune still attends. His interest is in the stories that equestrians and plain folks tell. His fascination has always been people, especially those leading the parade or darting in and out along its edges.

Clune's tales of the frequently lethal encounters between the Iroquois and their contending European and American invaders set the stage for the prime legendary figure of the region, Mary Jemison, a captive of the Indians who later freely chose her captors and rose to influence among them. His novelist's sense and reporter's skepticism shape a shrewd narrative of this complex and remarkable woman. He is equally astute in reconstructing other Iroquois-American encounters, especially those involving land developers, with their cynical use of firewater and tribal politics to win crucial treaties that promised "nevers" and "forevers." As Clune writes, "the poor Senecas did not realize how short a time 'forever' could be." His narrative contributes useful perspectives for modern white-Indian conflicts, including the Kinzua Dam and the Niagara Power Project.

In *The Genesee* too are comic tales of military bravado in the War of 1812, of Sam Patch's celebrated leap to his death at the Genesee Falls, of fighter John L. Sullivan's training camp at Belfast, and others. And there are stories of heroic efforts by imaginative entrepreneurs to make the well-endowed valley even more productive, including Seth Green, the founder of fish culture through hatcheries and stocking; Elisha Johnson and the short-lived Genesee Valley Canal; George Eastman and his contributions to the development of photography and motion pictures through the Eastman Kodak Company; and as many more as the "Rivers of America" format allowed. Pen and ink sketches by his friend, illustrator Douglas Gorsline, highlight the tale.

The quarter century since *The Genesee* appeared has confirmed and extended the story that Henry Clune fashioned. Even as he was writing, the remarkable development of the Xerox Corporation in Rochester was just picking up speed. The educational and high-tech life of the region has continued to burgeon, as have its fields, orchards, and vineyards. The Mt. Morris Dam has controlled flooding in the lower valley, and there is a controversial proposal to generate hydroelectric power in connection with it, but the river's Lake Ontario port has languished. The Genesee River remains the picturesque spine, attracting new admirers, of the dynamic valley that Henry Clune portrays in this lively, accurate, yet warmly responsive book.

It is also an artful book that keeps things in perspective while listening for resonances, as when, in closing, he notes the arrival of a large Japanese freighter at the river's mouth, then adds: "It might have been a novelty to Ed Morley, down in Potter County, Pennsylvania, whose father used to stretch a potato sack across the breadth of the Genesee, as it flowed through the Morley farm, and catch a mess of brook trout for supper."

In short, this is an enjoyable book that will continue to shape and give timbre to lives along and well beyond this modest but historically important New York State river, for its story is quintessentially American, and Henry Clune is deeply receptive to its flavor and meaning. In this New York Classic he has placed markers for us all along its course.

September 1987   ROBERT KOCH
                                 Rochester, New York

THE GENESEE

1

THE Genesee River was on its springtime rampage. It had overflowed its banks and flooded the cellars of houses in three small communities a short distance south of the city of Rochester, New York. It had washed over porches and eddied into the downstairs rooms of dwellings in the most depressed areas of these settlements. It was creeping higher by the hour.

This was an old story to the residents of Riverdale, of Ballantyne, an adjoining community to the north, and to a handful of suburbanites on the east side of the river. With the certainty of the vernal equinox, they expected, sometime each March, to be menaced by floodwaters or actually flooded out. They were fatalists. Eleven months out of the twelve they lived in peace and security; then, with greater resignation than Job, they suffered not only the inconvenience of having to store their household chattels in places beyond the river's highest reach but often the indignity of being rescued by police boats.

Their philosophy about all this was perhaps best expressed by a middle-aged widow who, as the *café-au-lait* waters moiled and boiled about her calves, waited on the doorstep of her house for deliverance by a sheriff's deputy in a skiff. She was not, in truth, in panic; this was too common an experience to excite that sort of emotion. But with a lack of selectivity often displayed by persons in a panic, she had salvaged three household articles that were of little use to her in this emergency. In one hand she carried a cut-glass fruit bowl and in the other an empty bird cage. With chin and elbows she pressed to her ample bosom an embroidered legend, held in a scrolled wooden frame, *God Bless Our Home*.

Guided by the strong arm of her rescuer, she stepped gingerly into the skiff and arranged her possessions about her. The sheriff's man, who had performed this sort of service before, complained wearily, "Why do you people continue to live right on top of the river? You know, as sure as God made little green apples, you'll be washed out each spring."

"I know," the woman patiently agreed, "but it's worth it. When Frank was alive, he used to sit on the bank and catch a fish. The lots are dirt cheap. I make garden in the back yard. It's all right for most of the year, just bad when these floods come. When it's nice, it's such a beautiful valley."

The Iroquois Indians, whose sole domain it had once been, who had subsisted on its bounty and delighted in the grace of its design, and who had fiercely defended it against invasion, had named the country of the Genesee "the beautiful valley." So, too, was it called by the latter-day resident, even as the river that flows through it, insurgent and out of hand, chased her from her home, disorganized her domestic routine, and threatened her investment.

The only river in New York that traverses the state, and the only one of substance in the northeastern section of the country that flows north—that has, in the face of great obstacles, flowed north with a contrariness reflected in not a few of the people who have lived adjacent to it—the Genesee has played a much more vital part in the drama of the white man's expropriation of the North American continent than historians have generally conceded.

How old it is historically has never been exactly determined, but there are ardent and expert regional historians who believe that the river was known to Europeans as early as forty-two years after Columbus kissed the sea-laved sands of San Salvador.

Their story is that Jacques Cartier heard about the Genesee at the time of his first visit to the St. Lawrence in 1534. When he entered the gulf on what was mostly a voyage of reconnaissance, and Indians in canoes swarmed about his small vessel to oh and ah in wonder at the rakehell cut of his European regimentals and the glitter and intricacies of the ship's furnishings, he invited two young braves aboard, kidnaped them, and took them back to France. They were Exhibits A and B of the living wonders of what was later New France.

From these savages, whom he returned the following year to their fellows, Cartier is supposed to have learned about a lake lying west of the St. Lawrence, and of a river, emptying into it from the south, which had its source in the country of the Iroquois.

Marc Lescarbot, a Parisian lawyer, who, by his own statement, fled a corrupt Europe to examine the New World with his own eyes (his desire "to get away from it all" suggests that even in the seventeenth century the pressures of a complex civilization sometimes induced neurosis), later wrote a history of New France in which he extensively discusses Cartier's explorations. Describing in this work the physical features of a lake that is obviously Ontario, he writes, ". . . and a little farther on, on the south shore of the lake, is another river extending toward the Iroquois."

The regional historians feel that this passage confirms their belief that Cartier was cognizant of the existence of the Genesee more than half a dozen years before DeSoto laid eyes on the great father of American rivers, and more than half a century before the *Half Moon,* under Hudson's pilotage, sailed up the stream that bears the name of that celebrated English navigator.

Cartier may have heard of the Genesee, but he never saw it; neither did his illustrious successor on the St. Lawrence, Samuel de Champlain, father of New France and founder of Quebec. Étienne (Stephen, in English) Brûlé, Champlain's interpreter and servant, who is credited with a number of notable "firsts" in North American exploration, was the first white man to see the river, cross it, and perhaps taste its waters. This was in 1615; and the psalmody of the Pilgrim Fathers at Plymouth was not to moan through the bleak New England forest until five years later. The Genesee, historically, is not precisely a "new" river.

Brûlé offered no written testimony to his discovery of the Genesee country and its river. He was not a diarist; he kept no journal. Whether or not he could write is a question; certainly it was not his habit, at the close of a strenuous day in the woods, to record his diurnal activities with a quill pen dipped into a solution of gunpowder and water. That was left to those valiant woodsmen of the cross, the French priests, to whom we are indebted for much that we know of the North American frontier in the period of its earliest penetration.

Two or three short books have been penned about Brûlé; he has been discussed in the writings of the Recollects, the first priests to carry the altar furniture of the Roman Church into the North American woods, and in the *Relations* of their successors, the members of the Society of Jesus. Champlain, in his *Voyages,* makes numerous references to Brûlé, sometimes by name, at other times by such tabs as "my servant," "my lad," or "the interpreter."

Francis Parkman calls him "the pioneer of pioneers," a fitting epithet; but somehow, perhaps because of long periods in his career when almost nothing is known of his activities, or because of his inglorious demise, Brûlé never caught the popular fancy as did such later-day frontiersmen as Davy Crockett and Daniel Boone. Bold and intrepid as Hector, a distinguished explorer, but a queer fish of a Frenchman withal, he lived for many years with the Indians, adopted their habits and customs, consorted with their women, and in the end was killed and eaten by them.

The discovery of two or three of the Great Lakes is attributed to him; he was the first white man to ascend the Ottawa River and to explore the full length of the Susquehanna. But these adventures belong in other volumes; Brûlé's place in this one has to do only with his journey across the valley of the Genesee.

Nothing definite is known of the family background of Étienne Brûlé, but the belief is held that he was born of peasant parents in Champigny in 1592. The "dauntless woodsman of the American forest" was a sixteen-year-old boy when, on a ship commanded by Champlain, he sailed out of Honfleur for the St. Lawrence and the founding, in the summer of 1608, of the tiny colony—Champlain's ultimate Habitation—on the site of the present Quebec.

We have no verbal picture of Brûlé, boy or man. Whether he was short and stocky or tall and thin, lean-faced like his savage companions, or of rotund features, we do not know; no one took the trouble to remark his physical appearance. Obviously, after he had grown out of adolescence, he wore a beard, for a shaving kit was not part of the equipment of the *coureurs de bois,* as the French who wandered in the woods and lived with the Indians were known. (The Dutch, in the Hudson settlements, less elegantly described them as "bush loopers.") And we have been told that at one point in his checkered career the Indians, out of sorts with him, pulled out part of his beard by the roots, which must have left some facial disfigurement. However he looked, Brûlé was a hardy youth, who later proved himself a man of extraordinary stamina and fortitude.

Brûlé readily adjusted himself to the environment and conditions of the primitive land to which he had come. He was enduring on the chase, moving along the trail with swift, silent, pigeon-toed strides; he had at his finger tips the arts of woodcraft, the lack of which, under the taxing conditions of the great, un-tracked reaches of the North American forest, could mean the difference between life and death. And in time, Champlain, eager to have one of his own people examine the Huron country, en-trusted Brûlé for a winter with a friendly Huron chief, who prob-ably took him as far as Georgian Bay and returned him safe and sound in the spring, almost as much of an Indian as the chief's own tribesmen.

He had conspicuously matured during his winter's absence. He had learned to keep from freezing in the woods as a blizzard howled out of the Arctic wastes; he had taught himself to eat half-cooked dog, with the hair still on the meat; to endure the reek of wigwams and bark cabins, and to titillate the Indian women.

Four years after Brûlé had executed his first mission for Cham-plain, he was given a much more serious assignment. This one failed, not as the result of any delinquency on his part, but be-cause of the everlastingly provoking Indian habit of holding a two- or three-day dance festival as preparation for battle. They danced, feasted, sang, and applauded their own prowess, since war to them was still part sport. It was not the grim enterprise of white men, who fought to advance their political or commercial ambitions, or to enforce, by death and disembowelment, rever-ence and oblation to their particular God.

In 1665, Champlain was reminded by chiefs of the Algonquin and Huron Indians of a promise he had previously made to lead them in a full-scale war against their traditional enemies, the Iroquois, the heart of whose domain was that part of the state of New York that extends west from the Mohawk River to the Genesee.

Fierce, proud, ruthless, the bully boys of all eastern Indians, whose raids and incursions often took them hundreds of miles from their villages and hunting grounds, the Iroquois were bound into a confederacy of Five Nations (later Six Nations). Of this Champlain had no knowledge, but he had known of the enmity existing between them and the northern Indians. He had learned this on his first voyage up the St. Lawrence, in 1603, when he had witnessed at Tadoussac the return of a war party bearing a hundred Iroquois scalps, and had been present at a victory feast and celebration at which dozens of Indian maidens, with firm round breasts, had danced naked for the edification of the visiting Frenchmen and the solemn-faced chiefs who squatted at the dancers' twinkling feet.

One of Champlain's salient purposes in New France was to advance the fur trade with the Indians for the glory of France and the profit of a company of merchants to whom he was personally beholden. The Iroquois were a hindrance to this design. They lived in poor beaver country, and beaver was as prized at that time as mink is today. It was the Iroquois habit to ambush parties of northern Indians on their way to the French market, hijack their loads, and sell the furs to the Hudson River Dutch. In these raids murder often accompanied pillage, and the Indians who suffered the attacks, and escaped with their lives, told desperate tales of their encounters with the fierce, swaggering highwaymen from the south. A Huron, on the trail with a pack of peltries, threatened by a party of Iroquois, would drop his merchandise and run like a dog that had stolen a ham.

With trade routes in jeopardy, Champlain quickly acceded to the petitions of the Algonquin and Huron chiefs that he join them in a military campaign to end the Iroquois menace. In the company of Étienne Brûlé and another young Frenchman, and guided by ten Indians, Champlain traveled first some distance up the Ottawa River. Then they went across country to a large Huron cantonment not distant from Lake Simcoe where, if the promise he had been given had been fulfilled, twenty-five hundred warriors would have been assembled. The number was much smaller. The Iroquois stronghold which would be the object of attack, was more than one hundred and fifty miles to the southeast in what is now central New York.

On September 8, eight days after the "army" had left its base,

Étienne Brûlé and twelve Indians were detached from it and sent on a mission to the Andastes, a tribe friendly to the Hurons, whose central town of Carantouan was near the headwaters of the Susquehanna River.

Living south of the Iroquois, but not far enough south for comfort, the Andastes were as eager as the Hurons to smash the military power of the Five Nations. They had promised the Huron chiefs that they would support the attack with five hundred warriors. Brûlé's mission was to advise the Andastes that Champlain and the Hurons were on the march, and arrange to have the Andaste fighters on hand on the day set for the attack.

After leaving the main body of Indians, Brûlé and his companions probably skirted the western shore of Lake Ontario, crossed the Niagara River, and proceeded through the country of the Neutrals to the west bank of the Genesee River.

And at this point they must have trod lightly, must have stepped as daintily as men walking on eggs. There would be no careless breaking of twigs in stride, hallooing, or making anything except the tiniest, mouselike noises. The Senecas, the "men of men," as they acclaimed themselves, and as their performances in combat attested, lived just across the stream. They were the dominant tribe of the Iroquois Confederacy, the champion bush-fighters of the continent.

Although their canton was neither of great length nor of great width, it was a lovely territory of fertile river bottoms, forests of noble trees, and clearings where grass—the famous grass of the Genesee—grew higher than a man's head. These meadows were savannas of ambush. Proud of their exploits and jealous of their possessions, the Senecas wanted no one, unbidden, entering their domain; and those who assumed this liberty often found themselves in a place, for all its beauty, as unwholesome as a charnel house.

Precisely where Brûlé crossed the Genesee is not known, but his guides must have advised him to delay making this move until the party was south of the main Seneca villages. The speculation is that the French adventurer and the Indians passed from the west to the east bank of the river at a point in Livingston County a little south of the present village of Mt. Morris. Their danger, once they had entered the territory of the Senecas, would be intensified; balancing this new threat was the consolation that, barring accidents and attack, these swift and enduring couriers would reach Carantouan, and the end of the trail, in less than two days.

Here fortune gave the palm to Brûlé and those with him. Instead of being surprised by the murdering Iroquois, they themselves ambushed six hostile savages, killed four, and hustled the other two on to Carantouan where, as part of a festival in Brûlé's honor, the poor captives were tortured to death.

The celebration was the undoing of Brûlé's mission, for the Indians did not bring it to a close for several days. They marched, but marched too late. When they reached the scene of battle, Champlain had retired in defeat.

Brûlé returned to Carantouan with the Andastes, passed part of the winter exploring the Susquehanna, and the next spring, with Indians to guide him, started back to the Huron country. As the party was proceeding in the direction of the Genesee River, it was set upon by a considerable body of Iroquois, and Brûlé, running for his life, lost contact with his companions. Alone he was unable to find the trail; hungry, he threw himself upon the mercy of a party of Senecas who were returning from a fishing expedition. They took him to their village, fed and entertained him.

He was a novelty until the village sages, their suspicions aroused, asked him if he wasn't one of the French, who had become anathema to the Iroquois since Champlain's ill-fated attack. The jig was up, Brûlé knew, if he answered truthfully. He pleaded that he was of a different race, and one that aspired to live in everlasting peace with the Five Nations. His dissemblance failed.

The Indians tied him to the torture stake, pulled out part of his beard, pulled out his fingernails with their teeth, put the burning iron to his body, and snatched at a Lamb of God medal that he wore at his throat.

Brûlé was a Catholic, but not active in his religious devotions. The Recollect fathers, who knew of his almost complete adoption of Indian ways, of his trust in superstitions rather than in divine inspiration, and of his promiscuity with Indian women, were often bitter about him, calling him a stumbling block to their pious efforts.

Now, not resorting to prayer, but employing the religious relic as an expedient, Brûlé cried out, "Touch that, and all your race will die!"

It was a hollow threat at first; then a very effective one. The day was sultry; the sun which, a moment before, had been adding its brassy rays to the heat of the burning iron that was smoking Brûlé's flesh, was suddenly clouded over. There was a crash of thunder that seemed to quiver the earth, and the lightnings of an angry God zigzagged through the black clouds that lowered like death and destruction. The Indians, believing Brûlé's threat, ran and hid; in time they came back to him, released him from the stake, and tenderly cared for his wounds.

All of this, at least, is Brûlé's story, repeated by Champlain in his *Voyages*, and credited by Brother Gabriel Sagard, a wise and observing priest, who knew Brûlé well, and speaks of him often in his excellent *Histoire du Canada*. The Iroquois, or Seneca village, in which Brûlé suffered the pains of an aborted execution, and where he remained for some time, is believed to have been in Livingston County, not far from the Genesee River.

Granted by his new friends the privilege of going and coming at will, Brûlé soon quitted the Senecas to return to the Huron country, and did not again meet Champlain until three years later.

Brûlé never saw the Genesee after he crossed it the second time, and never returned to the valley through which it flows after he left the Seneca village in which momentarily he had been in grave jeopardy. He spent most of his remaining years with the Indians, whose freedom and wild, wandering life suited his temperament much better than the restraints and formalities of civilized men. In time he fell into deep disrepute with his own countrymen by serving as pilot for the tiny British fleet which, under command of the Kirk brothers, captured Quebec. He fell later into deadly disrepute with the Hurons, who, for an offense against them of which no record is left, killed him, and ate him in a stew.

Brûlé's visit to the Genesee was not repeated by other Europeans until the second half of the seventeenth century. Those who directly followed him were French, but Frenchmen of a different character, bent on a different mission. They were the Jesuit priests, who courageously entered the Senecas' province in the hope of guiding the idolatrous Indians into the grace of Christ; and one of their number—Father René Frémin—might rightly be called the first white settler in the "beautiful valley." He founded a mission in the Seneca village at Totiakton, at a wide bend of Honeoye Creek, half a dozen miles from the confluence of that stream and the Genesee.

2

THE first impulse of the Genesee River is gained from waters that ooze out of bosky marshes and bubble out of springs high on the Allegheny plateau, in Potter County, Pennsylvania. They run north in several rivulets, most of which a man could spit across, and form into a single stream a short distance south of the New York state boundary. From there they flow in such a tortuous course to Lake Ontario that their channel, observed on a geodetic map, resembles nothing so much as a great writhing snake.

A mile or so south of the hamlet of Gold, Pennsylvania, with a little huffing and puffing, one may reach the crest or ridgepole of a watershed that supplies not only the Genesee, but the Susquehanna and Allegheny rivers as well. Here are found the "heads of the mighty," as someone grandiloquently put it; and so contiguous to one another are the inchoate waters of these three rivers, that some natives boast that a man with a hoe and a strong arm could turn the Genesee into the Allegheny, flood the valley of that stream, and dry up the basin of the other.

This was not the boast, however, of Leon L. Moore, a hardy, solid, slow-spoken man, who has always lived in Potter County, in which Gold is situated, and who once operated a farm high up the slope of the watershed. He later turned to carpentry work, and removed from the farm to a small house in Gold; still later, he retired. When I met him, he was eighty years old, and had quit carpentry two years before, "because my legs got a little tired when I stood on 'em all day." In this rugged section of northern Pennsylvania, men enjoy rugged health at good age.

Questioned about the possibility of diverting the course of the Genesee with a hoe, Mr. Moore smiled indulgently, but offered no direct answer. You knew instinctively that he was a man not given to hyperbole and fantasy. He sat with a purring cat in his lap before a gas burner in the comfortable living room of his home. He stroked the cat's back meditatively.

"I'll tell you what you can do," he said, after a moment. "You can climb up that ridge, and without walking very far in one direction or another, you can throw a stone into the headwaters of the Genesee, the Allegheny, and the Susquehanna. That's how close they are together."

He was asked if the Merle Hosley farm, a little to the south of Gold, wasn't the best place to see tangible evidences of the Genesee's source, and he allowed that that was true.

"But you want to remember," Mr. Moore added, "that there are three streams, the east, the middle, and the west branch, that come together near Genesee, the next village north, to make the river. It's a fact though, you'll see more water at Hosley's place. He's got it stored in a reservoir."

Edwin C. Morley, a farmer, who lives on the road between Gold and Genesee, Pennsylvania, took me to the Hosley place. Morley, like Moore, is a lifelong resident of that section of Potter County. His father lived before him on the farm Ed now owns, and at one time his grandfather also lived there. Back of the house and barn is a mountain brook that originates on the Hosley land, the waters of which flow ultimately into the true channel of the Genesee. Morley half seriously spoke of the brook as the "Genesee River," although a man could step across it, as it passes through his land, without wetting a foot.

Lumber was once the prime industry of Potter County, and the village of Gold, founded in 1857, was given the name it still bears because of the sudden wealth that poured into the tiny settlement when woodsmen first began to decimate the thick forests of hemlock that surrounded it.

Today a state marker at the entrance of the village reads:

GOLD

So named due to early prosperity of village.

Lumbering is still carried on in Potter County, but now maple, beech, and oak are cut, instead of hemlock. Ed Morley, repeating what his father had told him, said that once there was such a thick stand of hemlock on the farm that at four o'clock on a bright summer's afternoon the woods became as dark as midnight.

"When my father was a small boy," Morley said, pointing to a wood lot on the other side of the stream, "that land over there was a hemlock forest. One day he went into the woods to chase out a stray brindle cow. The cow ran out of the woods, crossed the stream and ran up on the road, my father after it. The bright sunshine, after the dark woods, hurt his eyes. He was squinting up the road, looking for the cow, when he saw a man coming toward him, walking slowly and tiredly. He wore an old hat with a floppy brim. A tin water bottle hung from his belt, and he carried a gun. The boy was frightened for a moment. Then the man spoke to him, and told him that he was his father. He was coming home from the Civil War. . . . Morleys have lived around here for five generations, most of them to quite an age."

In the brook back of the Morley house, speckled trout once

Gorsline

abounded; now the streams in the area are artificially stocked with brown trout. The fishing is generally good in several southern tributaries to the Genesee, and the true channel of the river, in its brief course in Pennsylvania, and for several miles north of the New York boundary, is considered good trout water.

Mr. Morley said, "You could do pretty well on food when I was a boy, if you liked fish. My father used to put a potato sack across the stream, and make it taut with a barrel hoop. Then he'd go upstream a little way, and drive the fish down, and take them out of the potato sack. Not sporting, but good eating."

The Pennsylvania History and Museum Commission and the Potter County Historical Society have both erected large signs at the headwaters of the Allegheny River, but no such marker has been put up at the source of the Genesee. Perhaps it is considered a renegade, an apostate, or worse, running quickly away, as it does, from its native soil to put on its gaudiest airs, its most spectacular show, and its handsomest dress, deep in New York State.

There is no booming demonstration of pride on the part of Potter County residents over the fact that the Genesee originates in their shire, though Merle Hosley finds this a convenience. As the water from a spring—one of the prominent sources of the river—rills down the grassy slopes of his large farm, it is collected in a reservoir about the size of a lily pond, and piped from there into Hosley's house. At one time it was also piped farther down the hill to a water tank at the trackside of the Coudersport and Port Allegany Railroad, which operates freight trains over about twenty miles of tracks, and which once filled the boilers of its steam locomotives with water from the Hosley spring. The introduction of diesels ended this service. A Potter County institution, the railroad is spoken of by residents along its right of way as the C and PA; never, triflingly, as the CPA. There is propriety about this.

Morley, telling about the railroad, chuckled.

"Used to be a fellow named McClure, who was superintendent," he said. "One year, while he was still here, we had a very bad winter, and the trains were having trouble getting through the snow. McClure went to a place where they made plows to get some new equipment. There was a little argument about the cost of a plow. McClure was asked how much trackage his railroad had.

" 'Oh, about thirty miles,' he said, swelling a little.

" 'Why don't you build a roof over it, instead of buying a plow?' he was asked."

Morley was not dead sure when the railroad was first put into operation, but his guess was that it started about the same year the church was built in Gold. That was 1899. He drew from a pocket a pamphlet, "The Gold Church," the cover of which showed a picture of a small, frame structure with a belfry that reached only a little above the roof.

"A congregation in which Baptist and Methodist ministers have preached on alternate Sundays since 1899," a line below the picture read.

Before the church was built, the only religious services in Gold were held in the schoolhouse.

Gold once had a couple of cheese factories, a bolt factory, and a hub factory. None of these was a large industry, but each contributed to an economy that gave meaning to the name the tiny village took at its founding. There is no striking evidence of golden prosperity today. The pulse of life beats steadily in Gold, but slowly; the beat is low.

This section of Potter County holds more tightly to certain practices and habits of the past than do most rural communities, and its residents have their roots deep down. They live there, as their parents and grandparents did before them, quietly, a little obscurely, but in good cheer, in good health, and in decent, honest relations with their fellow men. They are kindly, down-to-earth folk.

I thought, since Gold's prosperity was gone, that its distinction should derive from the fact that the headwaters of the Genesee formed about it, but native reaction to this was not impassioned.

"See that stream over yonder," one old fellow said, pointing to a rivulet that was zigzagging down a gentle slope, just outside of Gold. "Well, sir, I used to live up where that stream begins. High up—up near Culver's Summit, south of town. It's part of the water that starts the Genesee, but we never thought a thing about it. We used to pipe it, and use it to flush a privy. If there's anything Potter County's got a lot of, it's water."

Since Merle Hosley takes modest pride in having a source spring of the Genesee on his farm, I asked him why he didn't erect a marker to tell the world of this distinction.

"Oh, I don't know," he said, with a little shrug. "Guess I never thought about it."

"But there's a marker—there're two markers—at the beginning of the Allegheny."

"Well, it's a longer river."

It is a longer river by nearly two hundred miles, to its point of confluence with the Monongahela at Pittsburgh. But length isn't everything. I told Mr. Hosley that I had lived for a total of sixty years never farther than three-quarters of a mile from the channel of the Genesee; that I had paddled a canoe on its waters and swum in them in the summer; skated on its ice, picked chestnuts along its banks, more or less found my wife in it, and yet, until now, I had never taken the trouble to look out its source.

He said simply, "Well, you've seen it today."

"I have," I said, "and I thank you for allowing me the privilege of tramping over your land."

"People occasionally come from up your way, up York State, looking for my spring," he said. "Some of them seem disappointed. Maybe they think a river should be a torrent at the start."

"They forget about the acorn and the oak tree," I said, and thanking Mr. Hosley again, I left, with Mr. Morley still my companion, for further exploration of the watershed.

High up on the ridge, we became bemused by the phenomenon

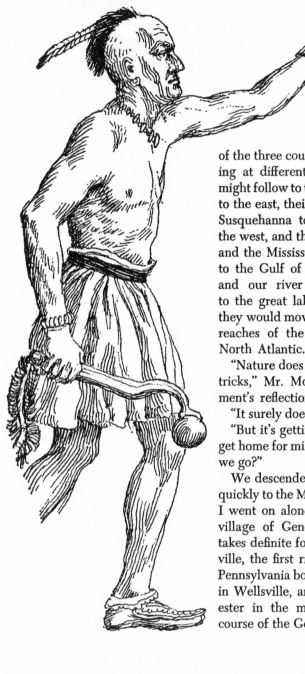

of the three courses that raindrops falling at different places on these hills might follow to the ocean. If they rolled to the east, their way would be by the Susquehanna to Chesapeake Bay; to the west, and the Allegheny, the Ohio, and the Mississippi would carry them to the Gulf of Mexico; to the north, and our river would convey them to the great lake of Ontario, whence they would move through the majestic reaches of the St. Lawrence to the North Atlantic.

"Nature does strange and wonderful tricks," Mr. Morley said after a moment's reflection.

"It surely does," I agreed.

"But it's getting late, and I've got to get home for milking," he said. "Should we go?"

We descended to the car and drove quickly to the Morley farm. From there I went on alone, stopping first at the village of Genesee, where the river takes definite form, and then at Wellsville, the first river town north of the Pennsylvania border. I passed the night in Wellsville, and continued to Rochester in the morning, following the course of the Genesee as closely as the roads adjacent to its banks permitted. I had found the sources of the river; I wanted now to observe its meander, and the physiography of its valley.

My most singular observation, as I drove north, concerned the narrowness of the stream itself, compared with the great flare of its valley. At no time did its waters appear to extend more than one hundred yards from bank to bank, and in many instances they were much more tightly contained. The Genesee has given distinction to its valley; it irrigates it, it fertilizes it; it has helped to make it rich. But during the season of its gentlest flow, it often seems, peered down upon from some fairly distant eminence —little more than a slim, sluggish brook in a crevice of the enfolding hills, or a rivulet curling through encroaching woods and meadowlands. And at such times, the broad sweep of the valley, rather than the river that has given the valley its name, becomes the cynosure in the prospect, the magnetic visual attraction.

Although the "Little River of the Senecas," as some of the pioneers in its valley called the Genesee, is not particularly new historically, some of its more conspicuous physical features are quite new by geological calculation. They came into being at the time that the great ice sheet—that lay a mile thick over the east-west Ontarian River (now the Lake Ontario basin), over all of New York State, and over the northern part of Pennsylvania— began its slow, halting retreat to its arctic provenance.

Originating as a solid body of ice in what is now Labrador, the glacier spread out, under the accumulation and consolidation of snow, much as the perimeter of a mud puddle expands as more mud is dropped into the center of the puddle. But the simile is too soft. The icecap was like a bulldozer of enormous size and inexorable force. It pressed out all vegetation, stanched the flow of streams, razed great forests, solidified lakes and ponds, and pushed before it or dragged on its frozen underbelly vast quantities of detritus or glacial drift.

As animals fled south before its ruthless sweep, the land that had once been their bounteous habitat was transformed into a frigid steppe of desolation and waste upon which, for tens of thousands of years, all life was extinct.

But the time came, as the result of some climatic change, when the icecap failed to receive a sufficient amount of snow to give it growth, and its southern front began to crack and break away. The process of disintegration was slow, and at first marginal. But presently the integument of ice was drawn completely off the Genesee country, vegetation followed the glacial recession, animals returned to the land of their forebears, and forests grew again.

The long-exerted pressure of the ice changed only slightly the general topography of the country, but bulky, high-shouldered moraines and other forms of debris that were left in the glacier's path sensationally altered the course of the Genesee River.

Before the ice sheet had debouched over Western New York, the Genesee had flowed north, as it does today; but it had occupied two channels rather than one in its descent from the hilly country below the New York-Pennsylvania boundary. These streams had come together a short distance south of what is now the village of Mt. Morris, and had continued as one through a broad valley to a point a little distance north of the village of Avon. There the Genesee had turned east, then north, to discharge its waters into the Ontario basin through the valley now occupied by Irondequoit Bay.

This was the ancient channel of the stream, and except for the region of its headwaters, its valley was wide and flaring; there were fewer steep ravines, high cataracts, and other dramatic features. Presumably it was an obese, sluggish river; certainly not one to caper and gavotte. Left to its own devices, the geologists believe it could have been counted upon to pursue unobtrusively the even tenor of its way into the incalculable realm of the infinite.

When its waters again became alive, with the withdrawal of

the glacier, the Genesee appears to have assumed a new character. It was no longer a complacent and tractable river, but stubborn. It was determined to run north in the face of seemingly insurmountable obstacles, and when its preglacial course through the Nunda Valley was dammed by glacial drift, it turned slightly to the west, and fought fiercely for new footing.

Out of the rock strata between the villages of Portageville and Mt. Morris, with pain and attrition, the river cut a deep ravine through which today it plunges over three imposing cataracts and rushes, with high-flung skirts of foam, down a series of intervening rapids. It is bold and beautiful in this sensational display, and wanton as a king's courtesan. It loses within a distance of three miles an altitude of more than three hundred feet. Then, as quickly as its wild mood begins, it ends. Its swooping flight is too swift to sustain long. The waters of the Genesee slow, darken, become even a little sinister; sinking low on the rock floor of the V-shaped gorge, they belly-crawl for several miles over a course that twists and turns and loops like the trail of a fugitive. But this humor, like others of this protean stream, is a passing one. Presently, tiring of its narrow, high-walled confinement, the river emerges into the broad valley of its preglacial channel, dimpling and smiling in the sunlight, guileless as a child.

This, at least, is the way the Genesee formerly escaped from its rock-bound canyon. It did so once of its own will. Now the hand of man is a factor in its flow.

At the Mt. Morris High Banks, a short distance south of that village—and so awesome are these cliffs that one catches one's breath at sight of them, wondering if this is possibly the Colorado—the Federal Government takes the Genesee firmly in hand, and says, "No more of this fancy business, good a spectacle as it has been; you're in my charge now."

And if the waters are at all rampageous, or display a tendency to flood, they are impounded in a reservoir designed to control a drainage area of more than a thousand square miles. Built in 1952, after nearly a hundred years of debate and argument on how best to save the lower part of the city of Rochester and the rural areas south of the city from devastating floods, the $20,000,000 Mt. Morris Dam so far has admirably succeeded in this purpose. The crest of the dam is 790 and its spillway 760 feet above sea level, and these heights the river has not yet threatened.

When the waters of the Genesee are released, at the Government's will, to resume their northern flow, they follow the river's preglacial course to a point a short distance below Avon, and continue from there to Rochester and through the city to Lake Ontario in a channel that the geologists call "recent," since it was formed at the time the ice sheet retreated from this region.

In another day, the run of the river through Rochester was a varied and wondrous sight. It is hardly that now. It offers, to be sure, three cascades, and the first of these, the celebrated Genesee Falls, once attracted visitors from far and near, and caused railroad trains to stop in order that their passengers might alight and exclaim over this splendid natural phenomenon.

The first white man to remark the falls was René Galinée, a Sulpician priest, who landed with La Salle on the shore of Irondequoit Bay in 1669, and pressed through the forest, five or six miles, to the river. He never actually saw the cataract, but he indicated it on an interesting if not very accurate map he made of the "Great Lake Region," and told that large fish abounded in the splashing waters at its foot. In later years the fame of the precipice spread; men of national and international prominence, together with countless thousands of unidentified tourists, visited the "Falls," and those who saw it with eyes that had not previously seen Niagara thought it was a magnificent spectacle.

Today it is no longer a scenic wonder about which native Rochesterians boast, or proudly point out to visiting aunts, uncles, cousins, and in-laws; a junk yard lies near it; it is heavily encroached upon by industry; its aspect, in the dry months of summer, is almost grimy, if the term may be applied to a waterfall.

Observed from a bridge a short distance to the north, the Falls, as a symbol of the Genesee, almost take second place to the painted figure of a long-necked, dark-haired girl on a huge billboard, who, smiling downstream from a riparian brewery, advertises a beer named after the river. With a little planning and foresight—with the employment of a little taste—the city fathers might have preserved as an object of civic pride and beauty this ninety-two foot cataract, which gave the city its first fame, and still made it pull its weight for industry.

In 1959, the Rochester Gas and Electric Corporation, which uses in its various operations large quantities of river water, enlarged its steam plant, once known as Station Three, on the west side of the Genesee, immediately below the Upper Falls. Named after Alexander M. Beebee, a former president of the corporation, and a respected civic leader, the renovated plant is odorless, noiseless, and clean. Its buildings occupy only part of the company's plot of twenty-three acres, and the remainder of the property, turfed and planted with trees, offers a pleasant contrast to the befouled condition of the river basin in most other areas of industrial Rochester.

The Middle Falls, a lesser cataract, stands in the scurf and litter of a neglected area, though a broad pool of water, impounded by head gates, stands just above it. It is a waterfall by an automotive refuse heap, a motorcar graveyard; and often, in dry weather, it is no waterfall at all. At such periods, the water that normally would descend from the verge of the fifteen-foot precipice is diverted into a tunnel and used by the Rochester Gas and Electric Corporation to operate turbines in a nearby hydroelectric plant. There is improvement in the last of the Genesee's cataracts, the one farthest north. As the water tumbles over the craggy, reddish rock face, it flows on through a steep ravine, on the high west bank of which a small but pleasant park makes, during the summer months, a green bower above the coiling river; a flaming tableland of color in the fall.

The palisades fall away as the Genesee approaches the lake,

and on either side of its mouth, as its mud-stained stream mingles with the blue waters of Ontario, is a flare of sandy beach: Charlotte—as it was formerly known—on the west side; Summerville on the east.

Originating at 2,500 feet above sea level, the river loses more than 1,200 feet in its course to the great lake. It is feminine in its moods and caprices during this meander—a spoiled darling, at times. As Shakespeare said of the great lady of the Nile, so too it might be said of the Genesee, "Age cannot wither her, nor custom stale her infinite variety."

The Genesee has an interesting history, which really begins, not on the banks of the present channel, but at its preglacial mouth, Irondequoit Bay, and at a bend of one of its tributaries, Honeoye Creek, where the French priests came and made a mission.

3

E TIENNE BRÛLÉ's double crossing of the Genesee Valley in 1615 neither set a precedent nor started a trend. No further white contact was made with the Seneca Indians in their own province until half a century later. Hooded priests then attempted with the tree of Christ to subdue a savage tribe that other companies of men had been unable to conquer with arquebuses, arrows, war clubs, and tomahawks.

Their efforts failed in the end partly because of the policy of the masters of New France to allow piety to serve the ends of mammon. Although the governors advocated the spread of the gospel, peltries were more important to them than proselytes; and often they and the slick entrepreneurs of the fur trade involved innocent priests in their political and commercial machinations, which nullified the missionaries' teachings and discredited the teachers themselves.

The Jesuits were not the first French priests on the North

American continent. The Recollects and Sulpician fathers had preceded them. These devout and courageous men, who wore gray rather than black robes, had pilgrimaged thousands of miles through the forests before the first disciples of Ignatius Loyola, favored by the powerful Richelieu over their brother religious, disembarked at Quebec, soon to establish missions among Indians who gave their favor to the French.

Their success with friendly savages presently led them to venture among those who were unfriendly to other Indians; and it was not long before their holy zeal took them into the country of the Iroquois, a tribe whose ferocious vitality and ever-growing power made them a threat not only to the colonies of New France, but to all other Indians east of the Mississippi and north of the Ohio rivers.

The Senecas were the dominant people of the Iroquois League, the other members of which were the Cayugas, the Oneidas, the Onondagas and the Mohawks. The Senecas were the fiercest, the most unregenerate, the most likely to scoff at the ministration of a Christian friar; yet it was to this clan that the redoubtable Father Frémin turned his steps, lugging with him through the woods Mass vessels, communion wines, crucifixes, breviary, and portable altar. It was a long journey, first from Quebec to a fort on Lake Champlain, then overland to his apostolic goal—a Seneca village of 120 bark cabins that rested on a rise of ground at a bend of Honeoye Creek, a tributary of the Genesee River, just west of what today is Rochester Junction on the Lehigh Valley Railroad.

Four large Seneca villages stood within a ten-mile radius of one another when Father Frémin opened the mission at Totiakton, which he and his associate priests named La Conception. Totiakton was the nearest of the four villages to the channel of the Genesee, which Indians in a canoe could reach, with a brief portage or two, after seven miles of downstream paddling. Today, in the dry season, Honeoye in many stretches is a sluggish, weed-encumbered stream, too shallow to allow the free passage of a canoe; in Frémin's day it was a swift-flowing, ample waterway with the aspect of a small river.

Father Frémin, who was shortly followed into the Genesee country by a second Jesuit, Julien Garnier, was fortuitously aided by tragedy in the founding of his mission. When he arrived at Totiakton the village was in the throes of a virulent epidemic. Fearing death from pestilence, the Indians gave little heed to the intruder who, advantaging himself of their submissive attitude, nursed the ill and baptized both convalescents and those *in extremis.* In his journal, which was later incorporated into that vast and illuminating work, the *Jesuit Relations,* he wrote of this early experience:

When I arrived here, toward the end of the year 1668, I was well received; but a kind of contagion, supervening at the same time, ravaged the whole country to such an extent that my entire occupation was to visit the cabins constantly, for the purpose of instructing and baptizing the sick who were at the point of death. It pleased God to bless my little labors, so that in a few months I baptized more than six score persons, nearly all adults, of whom more than ninety died immediately after baptism.

The first white man actually to establish residence in the valley of the Genesee, Father Frémin remained three years among the Senecas, after which time he was recalled by the Jesuit superior and given a new assignment. During this period he made innumerable pastoral calls, his bare feet held by rawhide thongs to inch-thick wooden sandals, his body covered by a flowing gown that caught on every prickly bush and soaked up water like a sponge—as ill-equipped, in this habit, for an expedition through the primeval forest as he would be for a foot race. He fraternized with the Indians in the gregarious squalor of their bark houses, prayed with them when they could be induced to pray, and ate with them. And the food that the priests wrote about—the *sagamite* that made the *pièce de résistance* of the Indian meal;

that often, indeed, was the only item on the menu—was dreadful. The bowls in which it was stewed stank; and into the concoction, for seasoning, went flies and other insects, and any small vermin that came to hand. It was often a retching experience to swallow the stuff (one priest compared it to wallpaper paste), and stern resolution was required to keep it down.

Men of delicate tastes and notable culture—many of the Jesuits were academicians—Father Frémin and his priestly associates among the Senecas felt that hardship, mortification, and danger represented a true expression of their faith. And they were often in danger. The Senecas, they discovered, entrusted their destiny to dreams.

A man might dream that he had bought a dog in Quebec, and the next day, to realize his dream, he would set out for that settlement to make the purchase of a dog. If he dreamed that he had been captured by enemies and burned, he would arise and have the torch briefly applied to his flesh in the belief that by satisfying his dream he would avert the infamy of capture and the pain of death. The priest wrote in his journal:

He who has dreamed during the night that he was bathing, runs immediately, as soon as he rises, all naked, to several cabins, in each of which he has a kettle of water thrown over his body, however cold the weather may be.

. . . From this, it is easy to judge in what peril we are every day, among people who will murder us in cold blood if they dream of doing so.

The mission among the Senecas, which continued for nearly twenty years, was hardly a profitable one in the number of converts gathered under the banner of the Roman Church. The Senecas loved to dance, gamble, orate, engage in the chase, torture prisoners, and make war. They were a pragmatic, self-sufficient people, who felt that they needed no outsider to prescribe rules of moral conduct. They had a well-developed social order and considerable political acumen.

Believing that they were the greatest men on the face of the earth, it was their design, in collaboration with the other members of the Iroquois Confederacy, to take command of a good third of the continent. Parkman, the historian, believes that despite the seeming extravagance of this purpose it might have succeeded except for European interference; for at the summit of their career the Iroquois had the military power, the habit of victory, the fearlessness, the enterprise, and the swaggering imperialism that all all-conquering nations possess. Lewis H. Morgan, distinguished authority on the Iroquois, gives support to Parkman's thesis in these words:

No distant solitude or rugged fastness was too obscure to escape their [the Iroquois] visitation. No enterprise was too perilous; no fatigue too great for their courage and endurance. The fame of their achievements resounded over the continent.

The Iroquois were the scourge of the infant church, and the Senecas—of all members of the Confederacy—were its most implacable opponents. The Jesuits who settled in their cantons were vehemently resented by the Senecas' medicine men—the jugglers, as priests called them—who saw in the intrusion of Christian doctrine a threat to their arcana of dream supersititon, mumbo jumbo, and witch doctoring. Often the confrontation of immediate death alone could bring an Indian to the cross.

Torture was an elaborate ritual with the Senecas, as with other Indian tribes. It was an occasion of high celebration; it made a show to which small children were brought to be edified by the writhings and contortions of the victims; it was prolonged for hours, and when death finally released the sufferers from their ordeal, their tormentors fell upon the carcasses with knives, cut them to pieces, and not infrequently made a meal of human flesh.

Frémin tells of the conversion of two prisoners, before they were led to the torture stake at Totiakton. The first of the two consented at once to baptism, and suffered fifteen hours of slow death by burning with scarcely an outcry. The second was obdurate. He resisted the pleas of the priest until shortly before his turn came to be gouged by burning irons, the pain from which would be made more exquisite by water being thrown upon the victim's smoldering flesh. The Indian consented to the Sacrament only at the last minute, "And from that happy, happy moment of his conversion until the last breath of his life," writes the exultant father in his journal, "he sang continually, with an invincible courage: 'Burn my body as much as you will; tear it to pieces; this torment will soon pass, after which I shall go to heaven. I shall go to heaven and forever be happy there.'"

The Seneca village in which Father Frémin had established the mission of La Conception ceased to exist as an Indian habitation in midsummer 1687, when the Marquis de Denonville invaded it with the greatest military host ever assembled, up until that time, on the North American continent.

Appointed governor of New France after Louis XIV had recalled his former appointee, a lawyer named De La Barre, whose administration had been an anthology of errors, Denonville decided, not long after his arrival at Quebec, that the Iroquois had become "exalted to a tone of insolence that must be brought down."

They were still interfering with the French life line of commerce, the fur trade, as they had been doing persistently since the governorship of Champlain; and, besides this, they had arrogated to themselves the right to worship as they pleased. This further aroused the ire of Denonville. He had a strong sense of practicality when it came to saving the Indians' souls. If they refused to accept the sacrament, and its promise of Heaven, bad cess to them; the thing to do then was to run them through the belly with a knife, or put a ball into their head, and quickly and neatly dispatch them to the nether regions.

Denonville passed the winter making preparations for the campaign against the Iroquois. He would have for this adventure about nine hundred habitants of Quebec, who were urged to be done quickly with their spring planting in order to follow their governor to war; a slightly fewer number of professional soldiers, sent out from France; and a considerable body of Indians who had become Christians without abandoning the practice of torture and other barbarities, and whose equipment for the impending encounter included both a scalping knife and a crucifix.

Denonville's army left Quebec in late spring in a fleet of bateaux, laboriously ascended the St. Lawrence River to Lake Ontario, sailed in a southwesterly course across that blue expanse of water to Irondequoit Bay, the old mouth of the Genesee River. At this small inlet, which had long been a canoe harbor and landing place for the Senecas, Denonville's force was joined by a few French from their post at Niagara, and a delegation of Indians, some of whom had come from as far away as the western bank of the Mississippi to help liquidate the terrible tribe of the Iroquois.

The first business after landing at the mouth of the bay, four miles east of the present mouth of the Genesee River, was to erect a redoubt which would be manned by a garrison when the commander's white soldiers and their aboriginal allies moved into the heart of the Seneca country in quest of the enemy.

When all was in readiness, in midafternoon of July 12, the army marched along the beach, ascended a hill at one side of the bay, and soon disappeared into the forest. Its progress, until its formations were broken in order to permit it to defile along the narrow Indian trails, made a spectacle unlike anything previously seen in America.

The regular troops were not accoutered in the fashion of European soldiery of previous centuries, with helmets, beavers, steel breastplates, greaves—the whole inventory of plate armor. They were not equipped for a European campaign. This was to be a siege in the woods, and their uniforms, perhaps for the purpose of protective coloration, were cut from a green fabric. But these men had been trained and drilled in the Old World manner. They were led by the *noblesse,* and they had the precision, the style, the bravura of the parade grounds of their native land. Next came the militia, a formidable company as far as numbers were concerned, but one that lacked the discipline and formal aspect of the professionals; for the civilian soldiers, route-stepping through the sands and disappearing into the woods, were still attired in the nondescript garments they had worn when they had reluctantly abandoned their fields and tillage to press this uncertain assault against the Senecas.

Surrounding the phalanx of trained and partly trained white fighting men, Christian Indians and their heathen brothers from the West, warming up for battle, whooped their hideous war cries and danced their grotesque dances. They were the most spectacular element in this military pageant. They gave it wild and extravagant character. Parkman, who formed his own description of the scene from accounts of eyewitnesses, writes:

. . . they [the Indians] sang and harangued in every accent and tongue. Most of them wore nothing but horns on their heads, and the tails of beasts behind their backs. Their faces were painted red or green with black or white spots, their ears and noses were hung with ornaments of iron, and their naked bodies were daubed with the figures of various sorts of animals.

Denonville's first design was to defeat the enemy in battle, after which he would destroy the Senecas' field crops and burn their villages and the winter food stores that were being gathered in bark-covered pits. The first day of the campaign passed uneventfully. The weather was intensely warm, and no cooling breeze from the lake penetrated the thick forest by which the army was compassed. During the second day's march, the French marquis, governor of New France and commander of this punitive expedition, sweating like the most lathered yeoman in the ranks, stripped down to underwear and boots. He had the look of a caricature, but his leadership was firm and unquestioned; he pushed through the woods, sword in hand, with the élan that had proved his military worth on European battlefields.

On the afternoon of the second day, the vanguard of Denonville's force was set upon by ambushed Senecas. The engagement was brief, but intense. In his professionally calm and orderly report of the action, the commander states that he lost by death on the field five militiamen, one regular soldier, and five Indians. If the fight was the cataclysmic affair represented by some historians, with hundreds of pale- and red-skinned combatants so closely engaged that clubs, swords, hatchets, and knives were employed, one might suppose that fresh cadavers would have strewn the woods like wild flowers.

Different reports of the battle were given by different participants. Baron Louis Lahontan, a young officer in the campaign, who later gained, as a writer, a celebrity far greater than Denonville's fame as soldier and statesman, wrote to a relation in France (the Baron's letters were published in time under the title, *Voyages to North America*) that the French lost one hundred men, their Indian allies ten, and that twenty-two French and Indians were wounded. Lahontan's letter read:

If you had seen, sir, the disorder into which our militia and regulars were thrown, among the dense woods, you would agree with me, that it would require many thousand Europeans to make head against these barbarians.

Our battalions were immediately separated into platoons, which ran without order, pell mell, to the right and left, without knowing whither they went. Instead of firing upon the Iroquois, we fired upon each other. It was vain to call "help, soldiers of such a battalion," for we could scarcely see thirty paces. In short, we were so disordered, that the enemy were about to fall upon us, club in hand, when our savages rallied, repulsed and pursued them so closely, even to their villages, that they killed more than eighty, the heads of which they brought away, not counting the wounded who escaped.

But the day was saved, and not entirely by the "savages." The main body of Denonville's force had a hand in the business, although when it first moved forward to meet the Senecas' assault, panic ran through its ranks and there was a grave threat that the white soldiers would break and run.

This was no formalized warfare such as the French had known in Europe. The foe was not a visible opponent, moving to the attack in orderly formations across a plain; but a naked, howling, painted hellhound, who sprang treacherously out of tall grass, or leaped from the underbrush, or darted from behind a tree, to split a skull with a hatchet and evaporate, in his agile nudity, seemingly into thin air. He was everywhere and nowhere. Holding him in the range of an arquebus, or skewering him on a saber, was as difficult as picking up mercury with a fork. And the deceptive shadows of the woods added by hundreds to his actual numbers.

Denonville was an able and courageous captain. He steadied his wavering lines with a field marshal's charge of duty, caused the drummers to sound the familiar notes of attack. Out of habit the soldiers moved forward. And now it was the Senecas' turn to be frightened by illusion. They thought this fresh battalion represented incalculable reserves. They retreated, hotly pursued by the allied Indians, but not by the French. A victory of sorts had been achieved. The French rested that night, and resumed their march in the morning.

In the next few days they burned four Indian villages, destroyed large quantities of stored corn, ruined field crops, and suffered the taunts of their savage comrades for their failure to follow the routed Senecas to the death. Denonville's explanation that he needed to pause, after the battle, to care for the wounded and bury the dead was considered a craven excuse. The allied Indians were swollen with pride and made arrogant by the part they had played in the defeat of the Senecas. They disparaged the French as womanish warriors, brave enough to fight the beaver, or to attack standing rows of corn, but cowards when confronted by the Senecas; and many deserted, heedless of the white commander's exhortations that they stand by in the event of another assault.

But the Senecas did not attack again, and the tour of ravage and despoilment ended at Totiakton, the largest of the burned villages. There the French celebrated their victory with ceremony; and there, in the same cool manner in which Europeans had been assuming claims to American real estate ever since Pope Alexander VI had handed over to Spain, in 1493, all lands in the western ocean, they announced their possession of the Senecas' valley.

It was an appropriation as supposititious as the Pope's gift. They had scotched the Senecas; they had not killed them. And when, two weeks after its arrival, the invading force left the shore of Lake Ontario in the bateaux in which it had come, the Senecas again were masters of their own domain. They licked their wounds, they built new villages, they grew in strength, and they nurtured for the French a hate that was translated into persistent and ferocious acts of revenge, until they were subdued in the American Revolution, nearly a century later.

4

THE coming of Father Frémin to Totiakton in 1668, with a pure heart, a crucifix in hand, and a burning desire to save the Senecas, and the arrival there nineteen years later of Denonville, with sword, arquebus and torch, to destroy them, mark the extremes of European contact with the Senecas in their large village above the bend of Honeoye Creek.

Before Frémin, no white man had lived within the boundaries of the Senecas' province, and for a long time after Denonville no Frenchman was safe in that territory. In the interim, several men who did not wear priestly robes, as well as a number who did, visited the Seneca villages for one purpose or another. The most notable of these was Robert Chevalier de La Salle.

In his first of two visits to that settlement, La Salle arrived by canoe from Montreal, in 1669, with a small escort of French, two Sulpician priests, and a few Indians. His hope was to discover by the course of the Ohio and Mississippi rivers the Northwest Passage—the quick, easy way to Cathay and the Great Khan—which Champlain before him had sought with diligence and fortitude.

His purpose failed. It was the destiny of La Salle that several of his grand schemes were to fail, sometimes as the result of the disaffection of his followers, at other times because of an evil turn of Fortune's wheel. But misfortune could not divert him from his goal, no obstacle was too formidable to challenge his ambition, and death alone was able to quench his magnificent spirit. At Totiakton he was denied the assistance and guidance he had been led to believe the Senecas would lend him, and after experiencing, for a period of weeks, their dubious hospitality, he and his party moved on to Niagara.

La Salle in part attributed the failure of his visit to the fact that no competent interpreter was available. Neither he nor the Frenchmen with him could speak the Seneca tongue. Father Frémin, who had settled at Totiakton the year before, and whose mission of La Conception was reasonably well established, was attending a conference of Jesuits at Onondaga, a hundred miles to the east. Such, at least, was the advice given La Salle. There may have been another reason for Frémin's absence. Once a postulant of the Society of Jesus, La Salle had found the sacerdotal vocation too confining for his ardent and restless spirit. He had resigned, and apparently his apostasy was never forgiven.

From the time of his arrival in New France in the mid-1660's, until he was murdered in Texas, La Salle was frequently in contact with the Jesuits, but not once does the name of this man whose enterprises and adventures made him perhaps the most conspicuous Frenchman in North America appear in the voluminous *Jesuit Relations*. The singularity of this omission must be attributed, not to chance, but to design.

During the greater part of La Salle's protracted stay at the Seneca village above Honeoye Creek, the Indians were most proper in their relations with him and his white associates. Escorting the Frenchmen overland to Totiakton from the point on Irondequoit Bay where they had disembarked from their canoes, a distance of less than a dozen miles, the red-skinned hosts insisted that their guests pause frequently in order that they not overtax themselves.

When they reached the village, they were welcomed by the solemn-faced, pipe-smoking chiefs and sachems, who had assembled in official conclave. There was an exchange of gifts: pounds of glass beads, hatchets, and kettles from the packs of the Frenchmen; whortleberries, other fruit, and pumpkins from the Indians. There was great feasting, but not the sort appealing to a European.

Father René de Galinée, one of the two Sulpicians with La Salle, a man of scientific learning and keen observation, whose journal gives the best account that has come down to us of the visit at Totiakton, confesses the need of a strong stomach to meet the challenge of the Indians' greatest table delicacy. The priest wrote:

The Senecas rival one another in feasting us according to the custom of the country. But I assure you I was many times more desirous of rendering up what I had in my stomach, than of taking into it any new thing. The principal food in this village, where they rarely have fresh meat, is the dog, the hair of which they singe over coals. After having thoroughly scraped the carcass, they cut it into pieces and place it in a kettle. When cooked, they serve you with a piece weighing three or four pounds, in a wooden dish, which has never been cleaned with any other dishcloth than the fingers of the mistress of the house, which have left the impress in the grease that always covers their vessels to the thickness of a silver crown.

La Salle had been advised that an enemy captive, who was familiar with the Ohio and Mississippi rivers, would be put at his disposal. Instead, the prisoner was given to the custody of three women, each of whom had lost a relative in battle, and whose prerogative it was, by Iroquois custom, to adopt the captive or condemn him to torture. The savage women decreed the latter fate.

A man of good heart and warm sympathies, Galinée was deeply moved by the sight of a "young man eighteen or twenty years old, very well formed," who was to be burned as part of the entertainment for the European visitors. He did not baptize the victim of this tragic spectacle, since he had not had time to instruct him in the Roman faith, but he endeavored to make him understand that God was his only recourse in this dire situation, and that he should pray to him in these words, "Thou who hast made all things, have pity on me."

Galinée thought the contrition displayed by the Indian was enough to save his soul. He was ordered to leave the captive, as the nearest relation of one of the slain Senecas approached with a glowing red gun barrel.

I retired . . . with sorrow, and had scarcely turned away, when the barbarous Iroquois applied the red hot gun-barrel to the top of his feet, which caused the poor wretch to utter a loud cry. This turned me about, and I saw the Iroquois with a grave and sober countenance, apply the iron slowly along his feet and legs, and some old men who were smoking around the scaffold, and all of the young people, leaped with joy, to witness the contortions which the severity of the heat caused the poor sufferer.

Galinée's description of this ceremony, which grows in horror as it progresses, ends when the Senecas stone the enemy Indian to death and hack the scorched and disfigured carcass to pieces with knives and tomahawks. The orgy was intensified by the swilling, by those who participated in it, of quantities of brandy that had recently been obtained from the Hudson River Dutch.

Under the stimuli of blood and brandy, the Indians became so violent in their behavior that La Salle was apprehensive for the safety of himself and Galinée. He proposed, before some assault was perpetrated upon them, that they leave the village and rejoin their French comrades, who were encamped at a place several leagues away.

Their departure was without incident; soon La Salle quit the

Genesee country. Ten years later he revisited Totiakton to obtain permission from the Senecas to build a deep-bottomed sailing vessel on the Niagara River, which had fallen into the province of that conquering tribe. He remained six weeks.

It is inconceivable that a man of La Salle's inquisitive mind and restless humor would be content, during this period, to idle away his days in the banal pursuits of an Indian village. The country around him was virginal, and crying for exploration; and La Salle was an explorer by every implication of his being. He knew Irondequoit Bay, which extended four miles from the lake to the Indians' landing; he had sailed long distances on Lake Ontario. Now he was close to a new waterway, the Genesee River, which made a trade route for the Senecas. It flowed from the south; its source, if discovered, might reveal the way to the beginnings of those mighty rivers he was seeking, which ran in a contrary direction. La Salle must have been impelled to examine this stream, and it may be that he knew it from its mouth to the point below the New York state border where it fans out like the stretched fingers of a hand into mountain rivulets.

But this is conjecture. Father Galinée, annalist for the party during the explorer's first stay at Totiakton, makes no mention of La Salle's interest in the river, and the latter's movements in the Genesee Valley must, for the most part, remain a matter of speculation. During the ten-year interval between his visits to Totiakton, other and lesser men called upon the Senecas, and one of these delighted them with a display of horsemanship.

This mounted voyageur was Wentworth Greenhalgh, who, with several white companions and two or three Indian guides, had ridden up from Albany in 1677 to appraise the military strength of the Iroquois. He was the first English-speaking person to visit the western canton of the Senecas, and the first visitor to arrive on horseback.

The exhibition of equestrian skill by him and his escort so excited the admiration of the Senecas that they transcended the ordinary bounds of hospitality in their desire bounteously to reward the performers. Describing his reception in one Seneca village, Greenhalgh writes in his journal: "Here ye Indyans were very desirous to see us ride our horses, wch wee did: they made great feasts and dancing, and invited us yt when all ye maides were together, both wee and our Indyans might choose such as lyked us to ly with." He goes no farther; he declines, with gentlemanly reserve, to state whether or not the invitation was accepted.

5

I N LATE autumn of 1762 or very early in the year 1763, the
youthful white mother of a half-caste infant struggled down
from the rugged mountain peaks of Allegany County to the lovely
valley of the Genesee.

She was coming home, although she had never before seen the
home to which she had been consigned. Her nine-month-old son
strapped to a cradle board at her back, she had traveled, in the
escort of two Seneca Indians, whom she addressed as "brothers," a
distance of more than six hundred miles to reach her destination.

Weary, footsore, her rough garments rent by the brambles of
the forest through which she had been led, Mary Jemison, teen-
aged Indian captive, had often felt that she would fall on the
path and die from privation and exhaustion. She had been pelted
by autumnal rains; sleet and early winter snows had soaked and
frozen her inadequate clothing; at night only a thin blanket had
covered her and her son as they lay on the naked floor of the
woods.

An early stage of the journey had been made by canoe, but mostly the small party had walked; and at no place along the trail had Mary's brothers, whom she represented as kindly and considerate men, lifted the child from her back. Warriors did not defy the conventions by assuming a woman's burden; it would have been *infra dig*. The child was the woman's charge, and she should carry it.

Favored by the Indians because of her agreeable manner, her light curly hair, her fair skin, and her blue eyes, Mary Jemison had been given the Indian name of Deh-ge-wa-nus, and after her arrival in the Genesee Valley, she was to live nearly seventy years close to the banks of the Genesee, and to make, before her death as a nonagenarian, the river's greatest legend.

Born at sea, the daughter of Thomas and Jane Erwin Jemison, Mary, her parents, her older sister Betsey, and two brothers, John and Thomas, reached Philadelphia probably in the fall of 1743 on the little ship, *Mary and William*, which they had boarded at an Irish port.

By the characterization of his celebrated daughter, Thomas Jemison was a devout man, "given to religious duties." He was a man, too, of resolute purpose and fortitude. Coming to the New World to found a new home, he soon removed his wife and children from Philadelphia to a pioneer settlement a few miles from Gettysburg, in Adams County, Pennsylvania.

There he staked out and cleared a plot of land, worked it for a time; then he resettled his family on a larger farm in the neighborhood. Life was hard in this remote wilderness, but the Jemisons achieved a modest prosperity. Two more sons were born, Robert and Matthew; Mary Jemison matured and grew, though at full growth she was still a diminutive figure, standing no more than a few inches over four feet, with small, delicately designed feet and hands. Neither stalwart nor buxom in the fashion of pioneer women, she nevertheless faithfully performed her domestic duties and helped with farm chores. She learned at her mother's knee, and each day recited her catechism and said her prayers.

One bright spring day, after the Jemisons had been living for some time on their second farm, their quiet, orderly, hard-working routine was shattered by the dreaded war whoop of Indians and shots from the woods.

A neighboring farmer, who had brought to their home his sister-in-law and her three children, two girls and a boy, and who was on his way to procure a bag of grain from another neighbor, tumbled dead from his horse, and a second shot killed the horse.

The events that immediately followed this raid on a frontier farmyard, and those that continued in bloody concatenation for several days, made an unforgettable impression upon the mind of fifteen-year-old Mary Jemison. She was to know many vicissitudes of fortune: want, wretchedness, and interfamily murder. But this was her most shattering experience; years later, at the end of her long life, she described it in vivid detail to Dr. James Everett Seaver, whose biography, *The White Woman of the Genesee* has perpetuated her name, not only in American folklore, but in authentic American history as well.

The incursion occurred before breakfast, which Mary's mother and the visiting woman were preparing, while the smaller children romped about their feet. Her father was shaving an axe-helve at the side of the house; her two older brothers, John and Thomas, were in the barn. They escaped capture and lived, though Mary never saw them again.

The house was surrounded by four Frenchmen and six Indians, for this was during the French and Indian War, and these Indians were allies of the French. Thomas Jemison had nothing except the axe-helve as a weapon of defense. He, his wife, Mary, her sister Betsey, her two younger brothers, and the visiting woman and her brood, were made captives. There was a brief wait while the French and Indians plundered the house, then a march through the woods began. An Indian lashed the children with a long whip when they faltered on the trail. Mrs Jemison, whose strength and courage proved greater than her husband's, did what she could to relieve the desperate ordeal of the other captives, and enjoined them not to renounce their faith in God. From the moment he was taken, Thomas Jemison never spoke. He seemed to know with fatalistic certainty that this was the end, and all heart and hope went out of him.

"To make the Indian a hero of romance is sheer nonsense," Francis Parkman has said; and these Indians were a brutal, blood-stained, ravening lot, and their French cohorts were no better. When the children cried for water, they were offered urine to drink or made to go thirsty; the guides and guards forced the pace, always fearful of pursuit, and no food was given to the captives the first day.

The next day scant rations were handed about, and that night, after a swift march of many miles, one of the Indians replaced Mary's shoes with moccasins. It was an act of transmigration that was radically to change the whole course and manner of her life, and its significance was at once clear to her mother.

Mrs. Jemison said good-bye to her younger daughter, telling her that she would be saved, and that the others would probably be slain.

"Remember my child your own name, and the name of your father and mother. Be careful not to forget your English tongue. Don't forget, my little daughter, the prayers I have learned you —say them often. Be a good child, and God will bless you. . . ."

By Mary's description, the scene of this parting was as foreboding as a place where witches gather in a Shakespearean tragedy. It was at the edge of a dismal swamp in a dark and impenetrable forest. Mary and the youthful son of the woman who had been visiting the Jemisons were separated from the other prisoners. The boy's shoes, too, were replaced with moccasins, and when the march was resumed in the morning only he and Mary remained in the custody of the French and Indian posse. She knew quickly the terrible fate of the other captives. An Indian was preening and prettying the red-haired scalp of her mother. Later she saw the scalps of the other captives stretched on hoops and displayed as ornaments.

The boy who was saved with Mary was consigned to another group of Indians, and she was given to two young Seneca women who had lost a close relation in battle and who adopted her as their sister. Mary says that they were kind, good-natured women. They were entranced by her prettiness and by her small comely body, and when she went with them down the Ohio River, to live in various Indian settlements along that stream, they saw that she was given only light chores.

Longing for the society of people of her own kind, Mary often dreamed of one day returning to civilization. But as time went on, and she adjusted herself more securely to Indian life, she found that its chatty sociability, its lack of exigencies, and its simple routines were not incompatible with her temperament. She dressed like an Indian, she talked like an Indian, for her sisters would not allow her in their presence to employ her native tongue; and except for the fairness of her skin and the light gold of her curly hair there was little to distinguish her from the other women of the Indian villages.

Her sisters presently left, going north to their home tribe of Senecas in the Genesee Valley. Before they departed, they told Mary she must go and live with a Delaware warrior, Sheninjee, who had recently come to the village. Agreeable as she was finding the manner of Indian life, Mary had not expected that miscegenation would be required of her. Her physical being and her instincts revolted at the notion of lying on a couch of skins with a savage, and mothering his progeny. But she was still a captive, if one held in benevolent custody, and an order had been given. Her sisters would not countenance protest or refusal. She went to Sheninjee; in time she gave birth to a girl child, which died in infancy; later to a sturdy little son, named Thomas after her father, and it was he whom she carried on her back to the home to which she had been sent on the Genesee.

6

THE saga of Mary Jemison's life on the Genesee is unique. It has no duplication in the annals of American history. It is the story of a stubborn little woman of civilized birth, who squatted on the banks of a stubborn river, determined to trust her luck with the people of a savage race, whose ways she followed even to the adoption of their pagan religion.

Her captivity was tight at first. Any attempt to escape almost certainly would have failed, and very likely would have been punished by death. However, a time came in early womanhood when she could have left the Indians with impunity, but she ran away and hid from a Dutch trader who wanted to take her to the English at Fort Niagara. She rejected other opportunities to be reclaimed by civilization. She lived three-quarters of a century with the Indians and died among them on an Indian reservation, re-embracing, only as death approached, the Christian faith her mother had urged her never to forget.

Sheninjee, the first man Mary Jemison called husband, and

father of her first two children, was only briefly a factor in her life. He started north with her, then went back to spend the winter hunting with his friends. He would rejoin her, he said, in the spring. Mary pushed on with her "brothers." Their first stop on the Genesee River was at Caneadea, poetically described by the Indians as the place "where the heavens lean against the earth."

The Senecas were the zealous keepers of the Western Door of the Long House, and their council house was at Caneadea. The Long House symbolized the Iroquois territory, which extended east from the Genesee to the valley of the Hudson River; its design the Iroquois felt, resembled the elongated bark houses in which they lived. These were communal residences. Each sheltered several families, and each family had a special area where it ate, slept, kept its chattels, and burned its individual fire. So, too, across Central New York ranged the six tribes of the Iroquois, each supreme in its own canton, but each an integral part of the confederacy.

After resting overnight at Caneadea, Mary and her escorts the next day passed from Allegany into Livingston County, as these districts are now known. The goal of the journey from the Ohio was Genishaw, or Little Beard's Town, on the west side of the Genesee, thirty-five miles north of Caneadea. Here Mary was warmly received by her sisters. And here she learned that besides brothers and sisters, she had acquired a mother, who took her as lovingly to her bosom as if the small, pale-faced girl, with the half-breed papoose on her back, were a natural daughter. Mary actually had come home. Arriving in the Genesee Valley at the age of nineteen, she was to live practically all the rest of her long life close to the river, first—and briefly—at Genishaw, and later on vast lands of her own, a few miles to the south.

Winter had settled over the Genesee Valley. Indian women had few exacting chores at this season. Mary cut firewood for the unpartitioned apartment in the crude house which she, her son, and the members of her adopted family may have shared with

half a dozen other families. She helped fetch the game the hunters killed, bent forward, a carcass on her back, a tumpline pressed across her forehead; she helped dress the meat. She tossed things into the pot for the Indians' supper, pounded samp, made hominy. But she had no beds to make, no parlor tidying to do; probably no sweeping. There must have been a good deal of pleasant chitchat among her and her sisters, who would want to know how things were going on the Ohio; how her brothers had behaved on the journey north. And what about Sheninjee? Where was Sheninjee?

There is a disposition on the part of some who have written about Mary Jemison to picture her as a meek, yielding, pious, sad-faced, little woman, eternally burdened in her long journey through life by the weight of her sorrows.

Actually she must have been as tough as a hickory burl to have survived for more than half a century the privations, hardships, and dangers of Indian life without, as she attests, suffering a single illness. She could not have worn the delicate guise of piety, or for very long the black robes of sorrow, and enjoyed the favor of the Senecas, who, fierce as fiends in war, grave as Roman senators in council, in peace loved to frolic, feast, and wager; who delighted in many forms of gamy entertainment, were apt at the ribald jest, and who made, in their religious ceremonies, a "joyful noise unto the lord," and danced before Him.

When spring came, following the first winter at Genishaw, Mary joined her sisters and other Indian women of the village in field work. This was their expected task. Great in the art of war, the Senecas were also good farmers. They had learned new agricultural techniques from the Albany Dutch and from the English. The women planted and hoed the corn, which grew in prodigious quantity on the rich bottom lands of the Genesee. They grew squash and beans and pumpkins, and gathered in the delectable products of a variety of fruit-bearing trees that stood conveniently at the outskirts of their village.

No great pressures were exerted upon the women laborers in the fields. Their supervision was lax. They were away from their menfolk, who lazed about the village, smoked, fished, speared frogs, repaired traps and nets, and engaged in other warm-weather pursuits. The women enjoyed their daytime hours of freedom. Their laughter and chatter overtoned the chuff of their hoes as they plied them in the loose soil. They may have whispered scandal, even as their white sisters at a quilting bee.

Mary Jemison has extolled the merits of Indian life during its recesses from war. She found its virtues greater than the alleged virtues of civilization, with its avarice, sycophancy, and intrigues. She thought the Indian enjoyed an idyllic existence when uncontaminated by the white man's rum, untutored in his vicious practices, and free from the religious hypocrisy that caused him profoundly to profess a faith that he made no effort to practice.

She waited hopefully through the lush budding of spring for Sheninjee's promised return. Spring passed, and the dog days of summer fell upon the forest village. A short distance to the east the Genesee, fat, truculent, and overflowing during the March thaws, but now placid and shallow, its water made tepid by the hot rays of the sun, crawled north as slowly as the movement of the shadows on a sundial.

There was little stirring in the midday heat at Genishaw. Men slept, women went quietly about their simple tasks, and gaunt curs, tongues lolling from their wet mouths, panted in the shade. The corn grew and fruit ripened on the trees, but Mary Jemison heard no halloo from the woods that would tell her of Sheninjee's arrival. Her concern became active; she wanted near her, for the comfort that even a savage consort might give, the man who had fathered her dead daughter and the sturdy little boy whose blue eyes and fair skin made him an object of mild curiosity as he toddled about the village with tawny, black-eyed children of pure Indian blood.

But Sheninjee did not come; instead, came a messenger with mortal tidings: Mary's husband, as she had called him, had died in the south.

"Strange as it may seem, I loved him," she told her biographer, Dr. Seaver.

"Sheninjee was a noble man; large in stature; elegant in appearance. . . . He supported a degree of dignity far above his rank, and merited and received the confidence and friendship of all the tribes with whom he was acquainted."

All through his fascinating and popular work, Dr. Seaver ascribes to Mary language which, correctly though it may reflect her thoughts and sentiments, can hardly be hers. The paragraph above exemplifies this liberty on the part of the author. What scant formal learning Mary had was acquired as a child. Taken from home at an early age, she spoke nothing but Indian dialect for years, and never, from the time of her abduction to the day of her death, read a book or wrote a sentence. Her school was the woods and the Indian village; her tutors the red-skinned savages.

She tells of mourning Sheninjee's death and wondering how she would manage without his aid and comfort, but time was always the great analgesic for Mary. In a few months Sheninjee was pretty well out of mind. She had simple occupations, and she knew simple pleasures. She seemed to fit into Indian life as neatly as a die into a matrix. She had lost her longing to return to civilization and with it some sense of the niceties of the civilization she had known, even in her crude frontier home. Yet there were some things about the Indians she could not take. She would have no part of their frolics, she refused to drink the liquor they swilled in hogshead lots, and she turned her back on their high festivals of torture.

She had, nevertheless, a high degree of tolerance. Hating the cruel practices of the Senecas, she took for a second husband a man who had refined these practices to an art that may have exceeded the exquisite sadism of a Nero or a Borgia. With or without a pagan ceremony, her marriage to Hiokatoo, a celebrated killer, was consummated at the time her son, Thomas, was three or four years old.

Hiokatoo was good to Mary. By her own telling, he treated her with tenderness, and never offered her an insult.

Parkman has related the incident of Iroquois feasting on the tender flesh of white children, their ghoulish repast made doubly terrible by the forced presence at the board of the children's mothers. Mary does not ascribe cannibalism to her husband, but she does tell how he snatched up white infants at the Cherry Valley massacre and butchered them or bashed their heads against rocks.

He sold women into slavery; he often burned to death, in fires lighted by his own hands, captives he had taken in the field; he tied prisoners to stakes and ordered Indian boys to shoot arrows into their bodies, but not to be hasty in their sport, to draw it out for two days and have good hunting, while the prisoners died slowly.

Mary makes no effort to extenuate the acts of cruelty Hiokatoo practiced "upon everything that chanced to fall into his hands, which was susceptible of pain. In that way he learned to use his implements of war effectually, and at the same time blunted all those fine feelings and tender sympathies that are naturally excited, by hearing or seeing, a fellow being in distress." Yet she bore him six children, lived with him over forty years (except when he was abroad on expeditions of carnage), buried him in his best suit of clothes, laid his ornaments and his lethal tools beside him, and baked a little cake for his journey to the happy hunting ground.

Hiokatoo was sixty when she married him, but vital as a panther, large, lean, the best wrestler among the Senecas, and reputedly—in an earlier day—their best foot racer. He survived innumerable battles, wallowed in the blood of his victims, enjoyed an inordinate amount of luck, and died in bed at the age of one hundred and three.

Killing had been his trade. His predilection for homicide seems to have been inherited by his older son, John, who slew, first his half-brother Thomas, then his blood-brother Jesse, and died himself at the hands of murderers.

John was a polygamist, as were many Senecas. He had two

wives at the same time. His older half-brother, who was putting on airs and assuming some of the customs of white people, taunted him about this, although Thomas himself had taken a succession of four wives to the conjugal couch. He also called John a witch. This was a term of extreme opprobrium. A Seneca thought to be a witch was often killed on sight. Bitter about John, Thomas once flourished a hatchet over his mother's head and threatened to cleave her skull for having delivered him. Always tolerant of the peccadilloes of her children, Mary excused the murderous gesture on the grounds that Thomas was drunk, and thus unaccountable for his words and actions.

He, John, and Jesse, the youngest of the Jemison sons, were all addicted to drink. Their indulgence was a cause of grave concern to their mother. Mary Jemison felt that drink would bring the Indian to utter degradation, and in the end result in the extinction of his race. She was intolerant of the white men's liquor and of his religion. Indians, she said, must be Indians, and they were much better off when no one tried to educate them, when no one supplied them with rum, or attempted to inculcate them with a faith that was not native to them.

One day when Mary was away from home, Thomas, who was in his cups, called at her home and started a row with John. The latter was as forthright as his father would have been under similar circumstances. He promptly pulled Thomas out of the house by the hair of his head and killed him with a stroke of a tomahawk. That was in 1811. The next spring John and Jesse engaged in a drunken quarrel not far from the village of Castile and John, Cain like, stabbed Jesse eighteen times and heard him cry out in mortal accusation, "Brother, you have killed me!"

Mary had been sorrowed by Thomas's death, but had accepted it with some philosophy. The killing of Jesse by the fratricidal John shattered her. Jesse had been her favorite son. He was the youngest and the most comely. There was scarcely a glint of red in his skin, and he had blue eyes like his mother. He did not indulge in Indian barbarities; he was not a warrior; and he did not think, as most warriors did, that he was too strong to work. In violation of Indian convention, he relieved his mother and his sisters of their rightful labors in the fields. To Mary he was an ideal son, except for his addiction to drink. Now, at three score and ten, she would have to resume the heavy tasks of her farm.

Full of sin and wickedness, John lived five years after his murder of Jesse, and died during a drinking bout with two other Indians, who first hit him on the head with a stone and then, seeing that he still lived, finished him off with an axe. He had brought to his mother the full measure of sorrow, but at his death, with a condonation that does honor to her humanity, she partly forgave him. He was a son of her own flesh and blood, and now the widowed mother was left with only three daughters—one, by Hiokatoo, had died in youth—to comfort her in her declining years.

She had holdings that extended along and reached back from the Genesee for a total of nearly 18,000 acres or twenty-seven square miles. She held it in fee simple. How she had acquired this huge slice of Genesee country is a story in itself, and one that begins during the Revolutionary War, at a time when Hiokatoo was away on the warpath, and Mary was left to care for her brood of five children.

7

M ARY JEMISON may have known the most felicitous years of her long life during the interval that marked the close of the French and Indian War in 1763 and the time, two or three years after the beginning of the Revolutionary War, when the Senecas decided to enter the contest on the side of the British.

Her glorification of the simple, wholesome, outdoor delights of Indian life, when free from the stress and violence of war, has almost the character of eclogue. The Indian then was a true child of nature. His wants were few and his anxieties momentary. He knew nothing of prayer, but danced to express to the Great Spirit his delight with any bounty he received. He lived for the day, pleased by a bright prospect, a freshly killed deer, the warm sun dappling through the green foliage of the forest, the blossoming of fruit trees, and the ripening of corn. He counted the seasons by the buds and the leaves and reckoned time by the moon. Habituated to his ways, and remote from the practices of

her kind, Mary Jemison did likewise. Long since she had become an Indian in all but blood.

Although the sovereign quiet of peace lay over the lovely vale of the Senecas, sham battles were occasionally fought in order that the warriors might keep their hands deft and their bodies agile, and that youth might be instructed in the arts of war. These were holiday shows, the best of the Indian spectacles. By instinct the Seneca was a warrior, and no triumph he could achieve was equal to triumph in combat. Champions were crowned in such sports as leaping, lacrosse, wrestling, and foot racing, but the warrior was the great paladin of the tribe. Peace was benign and enjoyed, but its term was limited; and probably, before it ended, the Senecas were bored with it, and spoiling for a fight.

Nevertheless, they and the other members of the Iroquois League sat out the first part of the Revolutionary War, which swirled and bellowed about them with such fierce intensity that they called it the "whirlwind." They had solemnly declared at conferences with Colonial representatives the summer following Lexington and Concord that they wanted no part of this white man's conflict; that they would straddle the fence as neutrals. This was fine with the colonists, who had neither expected nor solicited the Indians' aid.

On the other hand, the British, who had employed savage auxiliaries in their earlier war with the French, very much desired similar help in their struggle with the rebellious Americans. Two years after the Iroquois-Colonial conferences, the British used gifts, bribes, and promises to persuade several of the Six Nation tribes to violate their pledged neutrality, and join the King's forces. The Senecas fell in with the plot.

The English invited them, and fellow members of the Iroquois Confederacy, to attend—as pipe-smoking spectators—a demonstration of British power against the loutish Continentals in the Mohawk Valley; but the demonstration developed into the bloody battle of Oriskany, and before it ended the pipe-smoking spectators were drawn into it, and severely mauled.

Mary Jemison was living with the Senecas at Little Beard's Town at the time. She told Dr. Seaver:

Our Indians went [to Oriskany] to a man, but contrary to their expectations, instead of smoking and looking on, they were obliged to fight for their lives, and in the end . . . were completely beaten, with a great loss in killed and wounded. . . . Our town exhibited a scene of real sorrow and distress, when our warriors returned and recounted their misfortunes. . . . The mourning was excessive, and was expressed by the most doleful yells, shrieks, and howlings, and by inimitable gesticulations.

When their lamentations quieted, the Senecas and others of the Iroquois went back to the wars. Under the command of the great Mohawk chief, Joseph Brant, and in collaboration with Butler's Rangers, led by Colonel John and his son, Walter N. Butler, their raids of forest settlements in Pennsylvania and New York become so terrifying that General George Washington presently sent a military force into the bush to suppress them.

Headed by General John Sullivan, a New Hampshire lawyer, with General James Clinton, second in command, the army of four thousand white soldiers and a detachment of Oneida Indians, who had deserted the Iroquois Confederacy, left Tioga, Pennsylvania, in midsummer 1779, to lay waste the heart of the Iroquois country. Washington wrote to Sullivan:

The immediate objects of the expedition are the total destruction and devastation of their [the six Nations] settlements and the capture of as many prisoners of every sex and age as possible. It will be essential to ruin their crops in the ground and prevent their planting more.

At Newtown, a short distance above the junction of the Chemung and Susquehanna rivers, Brant and the Butlers had assembled a force, predominantly Indian, which engaged Sullivan's army until the Indians saw the flare of linstocks and heard the boom of cannon. They hated the "thunder-logs"; and heed-

less of Brant's rallying cry, they started west through the woods
and never stopped until they reached Canawaugus, an Indian
settlement near the west bank of the Genesee River, not far from
the present village of Avon.

They were a sullen lot. They were mostly Senecas, and the
Senecas for generations had been the leading fighters on the
continent. But the army that had soundly thrashed them at
Newtown, and that was pressing implacably through lands they
had held by right of conquest for an incalculable number of
moons, seemed gigantic—too big to beat.

The Senecas knew the purpose of this army. From reports
brought by runners to Canawaugus they knew also of its early
accomplishments. It was burning their homes, destroying their
stored foodstuffs, and ravaging the growing things in their fields
and orchards.

The Senecas zestfully killed men in battle and gleefully burned
prisoners at the stake. But plant life was sacred to them, and the
violation of it, if not a sin of conscience, was a sin of fact, and one
to outrage the Great Spirit. Nothing that the Sullivan-Clinton
expedition could have done to the Senecas could have been
worse than the despoilment of their lands and homes, particularly at this season, with the bleak, short days and the great snows
of winter in the offing.

A Christian surgeon with the army shared something of the
Indians' animistic feeling about this destruction. Dr. Jabez Camp-
field wrote in his journal under an August date:

I very heartily wish these rusticks may be reduced to reason, by the
approach of this army, without their suffering the extremes of war;
there is something so cruel, in devastating the habitations of any people (however mean they may be, being their all) that I might say the
prospect hurts my feelings.

The skirmish at Newtown—it was hardly a battle—took place
on August 29. Less than two weeks later, havoc and desolation

lying in its wake, Sullivan's army encamped near the eastern verge of the Genesee Valley.

Sullivan's maps were inexact. But, aided by Oneida guides, he had been extraordinarily successful in keeping to his course. Now he was slightly confused. He had heard that a great Indian village, or castle, as the early French called these settlements, lay on the east side of the Genesee, and he knew that he was not distant from that river. But how to put his finger on it and light it with his torch were the problems of the moment. In an attempt to solve these problems he sent out a scouting party.

A bold, impetuous young lieutenant named Thomas Boyd was put in charge of the detail. He was only twenty-two years old, but a seasoned campaigner. He was given verbal orders to take two or three riflemen and an Oneida scout. In violation of the orders he recruited a party of more than two dozen. They crept from the camp after nightfall on September 12. Boyd was to report his discoveries in the morning.

The Sullivan-Clinton campaign was an enterprise to which, before its start, General Washington had given a good deal of thought. It was an important element in the grand strategy of the Revolutionary War, and its success contributed to the ultimate victory of the Colonial army. Oddly, however, its greatest fame derives not from the substantial accomplishments of its main force, but from a tragic episode, involving Lieutenant Boyd's small detail, that was enacted a short distance from the Genesee.

8

GENERAL SULLIVAN's belief that the great Seneca settlement, still unspoiled by his ravaging army, was located on the east side of the Genesee River, was in error. What he was seeking was the Senecas' castle, or Little Beard's Town, a community of more than a hundred houses, set out, if not with the precision of grids on a waffle iron, at least in an arrangement more orderly than the loose and ragged platting of most Indian villages.

This was the staunch Iroquois citadel in the west—the western door of their Long House. It was also the place of Mary Jemison's residence.

Mary knew, of course, of Sullivan's approach and of its awful portent. Hiokatoo was on the warpath. He had fought at Newtown, second to Brant in the Iroquois command, and had run west with Brant and the Butlers and their Indian and Tory cohorts to escape Sullivan's "thunder-logs" and to collaborate in the development of a plan designed to stop the western thrusts of the Town Destroyers. He was probably at Little Beard's Town shortly before Sullivan reached the Genesee, warning Mary of the danger, telling her to take her brood and start west, for the refuge of Fort Niagara.

All mothers in Little Beard's Town had been so instructed. If Sullivan knew of these instructions, the intelligence must have gladdened the commander's heart. It was his purpose not only to punish the Senecas, but to force them to seek shelter and support of the British garrison at Fort Niagara, which, with this extra burden, would soon be hard put to preserve a living economy. And soon he would be laying waste the Senecas' richly cultivated fields in the Genesee Valley, which, since the beginning of the war, had helped fill the Niagara breadbasket. Washington had been prescient in the matter of the Sullivan-Clinton Campaign. He had contrived several uses for it; and there was still another, and a salient one. Sending Sullivan into the Western Wilderness, he was staking out a claim for the conquered territory, and assuring the new nation, if it won the war, that its holdings would not be confined to a narrow strip of land along the seaboard.

It was Sullivan's practice to fire a morning and an evening gun, even in the fastness of the forest. Critics of the campaign later complained about this. Perhaps they felt that touching off a cannon merely to make a noise was a wanton waste of gunpowder. There were those who protested at the cost of the Indian Expedition, though it was hardly favored with luxury items, or overindulged by the commissary. At one point, the marchers were put on half rations; Sullivan's subordinates complained of the scarcity of blankets, and the general himself spoke angrily of those who had been delinquent in supplying his men with shirts.

Sullivan had a variety of critics. Some were venal and false-hearted. They were jealous of his success, and eager, because they were seeking to depose General Washington, to have any scheme Washington advocated fail. There were other, probably honest critics, who felt that some of Sullivan's actions violated justice and outraged decency.

Humanitarians accounted him vandal and unmilitary in destroying the homes and sustenance of a people rather than killing off in fair combat a number of the people themselves. But in scourging the country of the Iroquois, he was merely carrying out the orders of his commander-in-chief. The homeless ran before him, and their plight was a frightful thing. Indians though they were, with their food bins destroyed, with lands that they had inherited through countless generations ravaged, they were as susceptible as white men to the emotions of terror and despair, and to the physical sensation of fatigue.

There was wailing and moaning in Little Beard's Town, for the women could hear, across the valley, the vulcan noise of Sullivan's cannon in its morning and evening salutes. The great blue snake of the colonial army, writhing laboriously through the woods, had crawled close.

On the night of September 12, when General Sullivan sent Lieutenant Boyd on his tour of reconnaissance, the army encamped on the east side of Conesus Lake, not far from the head of that small, pleasant body of water. It had reached the place of bivouac by proceeding through the divide between Hemlock Lake and Conesus, and during the day's march more than one hard-bitten campaigner had remarked the comeliness of the prospect that greeted his eyes. The country of the Genesee, into which these down-East Pennsylvania and New Jersey soldiers were entering, seemed richer in promise than any land they had previously known.

Boyd sent two runners back to the army early in the morning of September 13. They reported that the scouting party had killed an Indian but had not yet located the Senecas' Castle. Lacking the intelligence he desired, Sullivan impatiently marched the army west. It moved before breakfast. An hour later a halt was called at a small Indian village at the head of Conesus Lake.

The village adjoined a cornfield and stood adjacent to one of the lake's inlets. It was not ruled by a red-skinned chief, but by a large, bold, enterprising escaped slave, whose eyes were shot through with iridescent rays, like the eyes of a sunfish. Apt at nomenclature, the Indians called the Negro Sunfish. *Captain Sunfish.*

But he and the Indians had gone. The place was deserted. The army prepared breakfast. The inlet to the lake spread out to a wide, marshy area which prohibited the movement of cannon and supply wagons across it. Sullivan ordered trees felled, a bridge built, and a corduroy approach laid to it. It was a hard, sweaty, cursed job. Before it was finished, several members of Boyd's detail rushed into camp to tell of an ambuscade into which the party had been led, of the killing of more than a dozen of their comrades by an overwhelming force of Indians and Tory Rangers, and of the capture of Boyd and his sergeant, Michael Parker.

What had happened, the army staff chiefs learned, from the fragmentary reports of the refugees, was this:

Leaving the army on the night of September 12, Boyd and his detail, proceeding past the head of Conesus Lake, followed a trail that the lieutenant thought might lead to Little Beard's Town, but which brought him instead to a small Seneca village, abandoned except for four Indians who were riding across its grassy street on horseback.

Midnight had passed. The gleam of dawn lighted the cleared area in which stood the group of bark cabins and heightened the visibility of Indians and white soldiers. The former, aware that they were discovered, beat their heels into the gaunt flanks of their nags and fled for the safety of the woods. All did not make it. A shot fired by one of Boyd's overzealous scouts rang like a tocsin through the silent forest. An Indian tumbled dead from his horse, and the marksman, with no foreboding of the consequence of his rash act, ran gleefully forward to take the scalp of the victim of his aim. And then, before restraining hands could stay his trigger finger, another scout shot a second Indian, but this one did not die.

Nothing was gained from this shooting match except the bloody scalp of a Seneca. Had a prisoner been taken, the knowledge Boyd sought of the location of Little Beard's Town might have been drawn from him. The scouting party cast aimlessly about the woods, searching for the proper trail. Presently an Indian was seen on the path east of Boyd's men, but just out of range of musket fire. Then a second, then a third appeared. The view halloo was sounded. Boyd's people gave chase. Like phantoms, the savages slipped from one tree to another, taunting their pursuers, leading them on.

Hanyerry, a friendly Oneida chief, was a member of Boyd's detail. Although he was unfamiliar with the Genesee Valley, his woodcraft and knowledge of Indian practices were expected to be of value on this midnight excursion. There is reason to believe that he cautioned Boyd about an Indian stratagem. Hell-bent to run the elusive savages to earth, Boyd persisted in his pursuit. Where was the danger? A company of two dozen armed men chasing three or four Indians. And the Indians were running east. If they kept on in that course, they'd bump smack into Sullivan's outpost, and be picked off like sitting ducks.

What is now Groveland Township was the scene of this deadly game of hide-and-seek. Today it is an area of rural homes and hamlets. The cleared land makes excellent farming country. Boyd and his party traversed it along a trail that serpentined through the primeval forest. They were within two miles of their own army, and the Indians were still dodging in front of them when, like apparitions, but armed cap-à-pie, a swarm of Iroquois and Tories rose up, seemingly from the bowels of the earth, and surrounded Boyd and his men. The trap, of which Hanyerry is supposed to have warned his leader, had closed.

There was no hope here of winning, and very little chance of living. The Iroquois could be counted by hundreds; the Rangers reckoned in scores. It was a forlorn cause. But Boyd, short of

some soldierly attributes, was a fighter from toes to teeth. Forming
his men into battle array, he saw them take a toll of Indians and
Rangers before he and his sergeant, Parker, were taken. It was a
brutal struggle. Knives were used, muskets were swung as clubs,
and feet and fists were employed as weapons when the gallant
little company of Continentals and their Oneida ally, Hanyerry,
ran out of powder and shot.

Sixteen of the scouting party died where they fought. A handful escaped. One of these was the nonpareil of Indian fighters,
Tim Murphy. He was swift of foot and deadly of aim. He
carried a double-barreled musket. He scalped, when there was
time for this practice, with the facility and delight of the Indians
themselves. He was as happy in an Indian fight as a sportsman
in partridge cover.

But now, in a sticky corner, retreat seemed the better part of
valor. He shot, clubbed, knifed, and kicked his way through the
constricting cordon of green-shirted Rangers and painted Indians,
and ran for it, and three or four of his comrades followed him.

They reached the army's sentry lines after a sustained sprint,
and their breathless reports of the military action in Groveland,
incorrectly called a massacre (for what rule of war prohibits the
liquidation of a small force by a larger one?), were communicated
to the high command. Light troops were rushed forward. When
they reached the scene of the conflict, the Rangers and the
Indians had gone, the latter leaving their dead upon the field,
a neglect uncommon with them, and one doubtless enforced by
desperate circumstances. They must have felt that the tumult of
the fight would be heard by Sullivan's outpost, and that the
army would soon be about their ears. Why it was not heard, with
the sentries only a mile or two away, is still a mystery.

The Continental dead, and Hanyerry, who had fallen with
them, were buried with military ceremony in the ground where
they had made their last stand. An unsuccessful search for Boyd
and Parker was prosecuted. Their bodies were found next day
when the army forded the Genesee River and pressed in a

platoon front across the flats, which extended back from its western bank. The troops marched over cleared land, ". . . land that can't be equalled," wrote one enthusiastic diarist, who described the grass that grew in some parts of the Genesee flats as being higher than the head of a man on horseback. Little Beard's Town was quickly reached. It was, as Sullivan had been advised, the largest of all Seneca villages.

But the Indians had left, leaving only a horrible example of their capacity to hate and of their unholy genius for revenge.

Parker's stripped body, bearing evidence of having been lashed by heavy whips, lay headless in the middle of the settlement; not far away was found Boyd's cadaver, which had been mutilated almost beyond recognition. He, too, had been beheaded, but before this, he had been subjected to hideous tortures. His eyes had been gouged out, his finger and toenails had been jerked from their fleshy holdings, his genitals had been slashed. In their final and most exquisite gesture of inhumanity, Boyd's captors had pulled his intestines through a hole cut in his abdomen and strung them around a huge oak, which still stands in the Boyd-Parker Memorial Park, near Cuylerville, and which ever since has been known as the "torture tree."

The romantic legends of the noble red men are pretty for children; the men of the Sullivan-Clinton Campaign may never have heard of them.

This (wrote one diarist with the expedition, referring to the discovery of the bodies of Boyd and Parker) was a most horrid spectacle to behold & from which we are taught the necessity of fighting those more than devils to the last moment rather than fall into their hands.

Another, telling about the houses in Little Beard's Town, said that they would have been fairly comfortable, had chimneys been built into them. But the Senecas did not mind smoke in their eyes, nor a stench in their nostrils. The diarist continued: "The Indians are exceedingly dirty, the rubage of their houses, is enough to stink a whole county."

Sullivan corrected this lack of sanitation. He burned the village. It was the fortieth Iroquois settlement he had razed to ashes since his march from Tioga to the Genesee. He had done a great deal of other damage. Isolated Indian homes had been burned, as well as those that stood in clusters in the villages. He had ringed or flattened fruit trees by the hundreds. His official report speaks of the destruction of 160,000 bushels of corn.

Two days after General Sullivan crossed the Genesee, he turned and started back whence he had come. His mission had been achieved. The return march was made without historic incident. He had lost in all forty men.

Time has erased the memory of all but two of these casualties. Boyd, who became a martyr and a hero by disobeying military orders, and his sergeant, Parker, have been enshrined. Two legends have grown up around the former. They have had wide circulation, and may bear repeating; though both, because of their theatric patness, are difficult to believe.

9

THE British fort at Niagara was the operational headquarters and supply center for the Iroquois and Tory bands that terrorized the frontier settlements of New York and Pennsylvania. Brant and Colonel John Butler directed the raiders in the field. On their way to and from some guerrilla enterprise they often passed through Little Beard's Town and stayed with Mary Jemison. Her cabin was a sort of halfway house for the Indian and Tory commanders. She tells of pounding samp for her guests all night long. Next morning she may have filled their pouches with parched corn and dried meat and baked them a little cake for a delicacy. Probably she volunteered this hospitality, or it may have been enforced by Hiokatoo, Brant's lieutenant and prize killer.

In time, Mary learned what had happened to Boyd and Parker. She could not have been surprised. But her congenital humanity never allowed her to accept with equanimity the high Seneca ritual of torture, and she expresses deep compassion for the two white soldiers who fell into the hands of her savage friends and neighbors.

In her biography Mary gives credence to one of the Boyd legends, but she apparently knew nothing about the other. The one with which she is unfamiliar concerns the lieutenant's departure, as a member of General James Clinton's division, from Schoharie, where the division had been stationed long enough to allow Boyd to establish intimate relations with a young woman of that village. She made a scene when the order to march was given. Rushing to her lover in the ranks, she threw her arms about him and pleaded that he spare her the degradation of unwed motherhood.

Angered by the young woman's demonstration, which fell under the stern eye of his superior officer, Boyd threatened her with his sword unless she ceased her theatrical entreaties and took her hands from his person. At this she screamed an imprecation, telling him that if he refused to marry her, she hoped the Indians would "cut him to pieces." The curse implied prophecy; the prophecy was exquisitely fulfilled.

It is probable that Mary Jemison had left Little Beard's Town before Boyd and Parker were taken by their captors across the Genesee River to suffer a terrible prelude to murder. From her own recital, her departure was made with three children walking at her side, one on horseback, and one strapped to her back. She proceeded along one of the great trails that led from the Genesee to Niagara, but she never reached the fort.

She paused at a place called Varysburg, about fifteen miles west of Little Beard's Town, perhaps in the hope that the Sullivan-Clinton forces would be stopped by the Indian and Tories before they invaded the community of her own residence. If cherished, it was a forlorn hope. After a few days, she led and carried the members of her little brood "back home," but her home was gone. The village was in ashes; not enough food could be found to keep a single child alive for a day. Her plight was desperate. Fall storms and chill autumnal nights presaged the rigors of a wilderness winter, difficult under any circumstances, but now stark with the threat of starvation.

Turning from the desolation of Little Beard's Town, Mary and her children followed the Genesee upstream. No plan, only the urge of panic, governed their movements. They stumbled south in the vague hope that, somewhere beyond the wide range of Sullivan's destruction, a place of shelter might be found and food discovered that would give more support to life than the acorns that lay in their path and the grubby roots in the soil along the riverbank.

In the published account of this period of her career, Mary makes no mention of Hiokatoo, who was doubtless too busy with war councils and other affairs of the guerrilla bands to give aid or succor to his children and their mother. At this point, indeed, Hiokatoo seems to have disappeared entirely from her life, and he does not reappear until she has achieved a new and settled position.

Whether it was he who first told her about the torture and death of Boyd and Parker is not known; nor is it known from whom Mary heard the one legend concerning the former that she relates to her biographer. In its general tone, her version of this dramatic but undocumented incident is similar to most of the other reports of it that have been printed.

Brant, the Indian leader, who had adopted many of the white man's ways, without sacrificing his savage craftiness and ferocity, had, somewhere along the line, become both a communicant of the Protestant Episcopal Church and a member of the Masonic order.

He was with Colonel John Butler, his son, Walter Butler, and the Tory and Iroquois forces at the Groveland ambuscade. When the surprise attack ended with the killing of most of Boyd's party, and the capture of Boyd and Parker, the two Continentals were at once exposed to a more dreadful ordeal than the bloody bush fight they had survived.

There were prisoners of the Indians. Inevitably this meant that they would be tortured to death. But as they were being hurried toward Little Beard's Town, prodded probably by sharp weapons and lashed by whips, Boyd, seeing Joseph Brant at the side of the trail, made the Masonic sign, to which the Indian responded.

After this exchange of mystic signals, legend has it that the custody of Boyd and Parker was transferred to Brant, who assured the two men that they would be accorded the decent treatment prisoners of war might expect from a civilized enemy. Brant, however, was dispatched on some military errand, and the captives fell into the hands of Walter Butler, who put them on their knees and demanded that they reveal the secrets of Sullivan's army. When they heroically refused, they were returned to the Indians for torture, mutilation, and murder.

No attempt will be made here to pass judgment on the character and practices of Walter N. Butler. In general, history has stigmatized as a "fiend incarnate" this strange, handsome, half-romantic young lawyer, who followed with a zealot's ardor a cause that led only to early death and dishonor. Brant, who himself defended the Indian custom of murdering prisoners, is credited with the statement that Walter Butler "could outdo my own Indians in diabolic cruelty to white captives."

Brant co-operated with both Butlers in many raids, but curiously escaped the guilt this association might be expected to attach to his name. Contrariwise, he has been acclaimed by many chroniclers as a gallant and noble warrior, a characterization that may have prompted one of Walter Butler's woefully few defenders to remark:

It is one of the mysteries of American history that this savage [Brant], who long after the war murdered his own son, and whose influence over his followers was never sufficient, if indeed it was ever exercised in that direction, to restrain them from atrocities, should be represented as a noble foe, almost, as one historian says, "a saint compared to Walter Butler."

The true story of what happened to Boyd and Parker from the moment of their capture until their mutilated corpses were found by Sullivan's advanced party is lost in the bloody mists of

Groveland and Little Beard's Town. Whether Walter Butler interrogated the lieutenant, as commonly reported, is not known with any degree of certainty. What part Brant played in the affair is equally uncertain. And while it is a matter of record that Brant was a member of the Masonic order, close investigation has failed to prove that Boyd had a similar affiliation. Without this, the incident of the meeting between the two blows away in myth, as airy and insubstantial as tumbleweed.

Not without reason, the tragedy of the Groveland ambuscade has been attributed to Boyd's brash disregard of military orders. Told to organize a detail of three or four men, which could steal about the woods with a minimum chance of detection, he took instead a company that was too large to be subtle in its reconnaissance, but too small to make a stand against the considerable force of Iroquois and Tories believed to be lurking in the area.

But Boyd has become a hero. A monument has been erected in Groveland to the men who fell in the ambuscade in that township, and on the other side of the Genesee a little park has been consecrated to the memory of Boyd and Parker. It makes a pleasant roadside retreat. On summer days it is not uncommon to see picnickers gamboling under the huge tree around which, more than 180 years ago, Boyd's intestines were strung by his tormentors and murderers.

Although the Indians loved torture as a spectacle and show, it is unlikely that Boyd and Parker were treated as they were merely to make a bloody circus for a gallery of whooping, capering savages. Ordinarily the spectators at an extravaganza of this kind wanted time and leisure for the full gratification of their pleasure. In this instance they had no time for a public exhibition; they were jittery with race tension and pressed by a fearful exigency. All that they possessed, lands, homes, food stores, were threatened by Sullivan's ineluctable force. Confronted with the dreadful threat of impoverishment, they struck out, in blind rage, at the handy objects of their hate. These were Boyd and Parker.

Cutting them to pieces, the Indians may have thought that

they were appeasing the manes. And their ferocity may have been further excited by a sense of augury; a conviction that this first invasion of white men would be followed by other incursions until, as indeed happened within a period of less than half a century, white men had gained full possession of all the rich lands of the Genesee Valley and driven from them the great race of warriors that had held them for centuries inviolate.

The close of the Revolutionary War marked the beginning of vast speculations in Indian lands. The dealers in real estate who moved into the Senecas' country found the Indians a hindrance to their operations. The savages entertained an absurd notion that they should be paid for the lands that the white men were trying to take from them. At this period in American history, with new settlements springing up on various frontiers, Indians had become a bother; and the hope of most citizens of the new nation was that they be pushed back to the Mississippi, and beyond; consigned, if this were possible, to limbo. Their interference with the white man's aspirations made them as undesirable as tares in a Biblical grainfield.

But the Federal Government, with wisdom and a sense of decency, insisted that the real-estate operators, before they could own Indian lands, would have to extinguish the Indian titles to these lands; and this often took a good deal of doing.

Councils had to be called and treaties had to be signed. These meetings, by Indian tradition, were rigid with protocol. They often continued to unconscionable lengths. Lacking a written language, the Senecas insisted on elaborate explanations of all matters that came before the council. Their orators served as advocates and interpreters. They were wordy men; they would go on and on like a donkey engine.

They knew the art of the filibuster, and practiced it. The best of the Seneca orators enjoyed a status second only to that reserved for the leading warriors. Red Jacket, the celebrated Seneca Demosthenes—a posey fellow, of enormous self-esteem and a way with words that made it impossible for his listeners to fall asleep during his declamations—was highly regarded, despite the fact that Joseph Brant had branded him as a varlet and a coward on the battlefield.

For the most part, the Seneca orators opposed the monumental land grab that was being schemed up by promoters from New York, Boston, Philadelphia, and even from the far side of the Atlantic. Their protests were unavailing. The rank and file of the Indians seemed resolved to be gulled by men who flashed silver before them and promised that the Senecas' hunting grounds would still be theirs to shoot over even though the titles to these lands reposed in the strongboxes of land agents.

The Senecas "X-ed" in the blank spaces on the treaties, as indicated. They signed away their birthright. Soon they saw pioneers straggling through the bush on foot, coming west on horseback, riding wagon trains that widened out and gave to the narrow Indian trails the aspect of inchoate roads. Forest areas flattened under the axes of stalwarts from New England, New Jersey, lower New York, and southern states that marked the Atlantic coast line. The wonderfully rich lands of the Genesee—as rich, it was said, as the valley of the Nile—were gradually cultivated. Trading posts were established, crude taverns opened their doors along the crude roads, mills were built where fast water ran in the river bed.

Among the first of the pioneers was a picaresque character who had originated in New Jersey, but who had been in and out of the Genesee country during the war. He had served the British cause as a member of Butler's Rangers, perhaps because of principle, but more likely in the interest of profit. He had a spotty past; murder was to be included in his future activities.

He rapped at Mary Jemison's door, during the last year of the war, and she took him in. She was settled then on her own lands—Gardeau Flats—on the west side of the Genesee, and there was work that he could help her with. He was a man of enterprise, he had a glib tongue, he was not unprepossessing, and he had a winning way with women. He was a welcome guest, and presumably Mary's lover. He has been denigrated as a swindler, a ruffian of the first order, and a murderer. He has, nevertheless, a firm place in the history of the Genesee River. His name was Ebenezer (better known as "Indian") Allan, and at different periods in his career he held the land upon which the village of Mt. Morris rests, and extensive property along the river a little east of the village of Scottsville; he built the first mill at the Genesee Falls and, at one time, owned the land that today comprises the heart of the city of Rochester.

Allan's story, during the dozen years of his proprietorship on the Genesee, is closely interwoven with Mary Jemison's. It should be told, however, in proper sequence. To do this, we need first to return to Mary herself, who, when last seen, was struggling south along the riverbank, children at her side and on her back, in search of food and shelter.

10

ONE OF the great things about Mary Jemison was her fortitude. Discouraged, as she often was, she never succumbed to defeat. She had great resilience of spirit, an iron will, and a body of unusual strength despite its delicacy of structure. Now, with two children on her back (apparently she had lost the horse upon which one child had ridden when she had run from her home at the threat of invasion), she came, after trudging six or seven miles south from the ruin of Little Beard's Town, to a cleared area on the west side of the Genesee River.

Here, in a small cabin, lived two runaway Negro slaves to whom Mary hired out. She helped harvest a large field of corn, and received in payment part of the crop which she had gathered. She and her children shared the little cabin with its owners. It must have been a tight fit: five children, two men, and Mary in a shack that had been built for two. Her landlords and employers were kindly men. Without the board and lodging they provided, she and her children might not have survived.

In the spring of 1780 Mary built a shack of her own. The Gardeau Flats appealed to her. The soil of the river bottoms was rich. The prospect from her cabin door was an appealing one. She was industrious, frugal, and forehanded. She cultivated the land; she acquired a few head of cattle. In two years the Negroes left, and Mary had the land to herself. Her tenure continued for half a century.

There is no record that Hiokatoo visited her during the time that she lived with, or neighbor to, the first squatters on the flats. The war had not yet come to an official close, and Hiokatoo was still engaged in guerrilla enterprises at the time Ebenezer Allan first called at Mary Jemison's door.

Allan was still a Tory officer attached to the British Indian Department, from which service he would not be dismissed for another year, and he probably had been sent to the Genesee on an official mission. It is known that he was in the river country in the spring of 1782, for in April of that year he wrote a letter from "Genussio" to Colonel John Butler at Fort Niagara, and Allan may have visited Mary Jemison shortly after this. She attests that he lived with her during the winter of 1782-83, and that he worked her lands until after the peace treaty was signed in 1783. She knew that he was not a paragon of virtue. She says herself that he was a murderer, not once but twice, that he was a seducer of women, and a polygamist. Mary Jemison was not a reformer; she did not attempt to regulate the lives of others. She fed Allan when he was hungry, protected him when he was a fugitive, guarded his treasure for him. When a man was in trouble, or needed shelter, or his belly wanted food, then race, creed, or color meant nothing to Mary. A pagan by choice, she practiced by instinct Christ's simple precepts of charity and forgiveness.

As Mary was the first white settler along the Genesee, so Allan was the second of any conspicuousness. The nickname, "Indian" Allan, was not a misnomer. Like Mary, he had adopted many practices and customs of the Senecas. He was an expert woodsman; he spoke the Seneca language. He delighted in barbaric freedoms. There was, however, one distinct difference between him and the Indians with whom he lived on terms of free association. They were not much given to the lusts of the flesh; Allan was as consupiscent as a Turkish Sultan. He seemed to feel, as a wit of a later day put it, that the way to get rid of temptation was to yield to it.

Part of the time that Allan was a guest in Mary's house, another white man, who had taken a Nanticoke squaw to wife, lived on the Jemison flats. Mary says that the squaw was a "kind, gentle, cunning creature." The husband had several cows, but no hay to feed them during the winter months, and each day he drove them to a place some distance from the house where they could graze on rushes. During the cow owner's daily absence, Allan made a point of visiting his wife, and in "return for his kindness [the euphemism is Mary's], the squaw made him a red cap finished and decorated in the highest Indian style."

The cow man had entertained for some time a suspicion that all was not right between his wife and Allan. When he saw the latter decked out in a fancy cap, fashioned by the loving hands of his wife, his suspicions were confirmed, and he flew into a jealous tantrum. Grasping the little woman by the hair, he dragged her over the frozen ground to the Jemison cabin flung her through the doorway, and, perhaps with a stroke of his boot, announced that he was through with her.

Hiokatoo had returned by this time from his bloody forays and excursions. His war hatchet hung on pegs on the wall of the family cabin. Now the old warrior, who had dashed the heads of babies against rocks, "exasperated," Mary says, "by so much inhumanity," snatched the hatchet from its peaceful resting place and threatened to cleave the pate of the cowherd if he continued to abuse his wife. The man ran away. Mary took the squaw into her house, nursed her wounds, fed and cared for her during the remainder of the winter. Allan, Mary says, also comforted the ill-treated wife. In the spring the lonesome husband decided that being without the services of a spouse was a worse evil than cuck-oldry. He petitioned the forgiveness of the squaw, took her again to bed and board, and the pair lived happily ever after—at least until sometime later when they removed to Niagara, and Mary lost track of them.

The affair with the Nanticoke squaw was the first of a series of scandalous and felonious adventures credited to Allan during the dozen years that he moved up and down the Genesee River. Some doubtless are true; others, as Morley Bebee Turpin, Allan's most conscientoius biographer, has hinted, may have been over-colored if not actually fabricated by his enemies, who were nu-merous. He fell in time into grave disrepute with the British; the colonists did not like him. "A Tory," the colonists said of men like Allan, "is one whose head is in England, whose body is here, and whose neck should be stretched."

He appeared to get along best with the Indians. The regional historians, who have kept Allan's memory alive, have traduced his character with such epithets as "brutal Bluebeard," "scoun-drelly villain," and "bloody picaroon." His "repute," wrote one of this company, "seems to be wholly disrepute."

Oddly, it is Allan's friend, Mary Jemison, who is mostly respon-sible for his evil reputation. Except when they concern her own relations with him, her reports on Allan are as frank as the stories she tells about Hiokatoo's bloody deeds. Allan boasted to her of his crimes and peccadilloes. When he left her flats, he moved a short distance north along the Genesee, crossed the river to the east bank, and settled on land that is now part of the village of Mt. Morris. He farmed this new homestead. He went to Phila-delphia, brought back merchandise by pack horse, and set up a trading post. He was living with a Seneca squaw named Sally. Two girls, Mary and Chloe, were born of this union; and since, among the Iroquois, descent always follows the mother's line, both were considered full-blooded Senecas.

In time their fellow tribesmen bestowed upon the two girls a large parcel of land in the vicinity of Mt. Morris, which, many believed, their father wangled from them and sold for a profit. There is no proof of this. But the alleged fraud became part of the Allan legend. It did new injury to a character which already had been seriously damaged. Close investigation of the matter now tends to indicate that it was not Allan who sold the property from under Mary and Chloe, but the very Indians who had given it to them. It was included in a vast acreage of Genesee Valley lands transferred by the Senecas to Robert Morris, financial backer of the Revolutionary War, and postwar land speculator, at a white and red men's business conference near Geneseo in 1797, known historically as the Treaty of Big Tree.

At that meeting, the title of the Senecas to all lands that reached from the Genesee River to the western edge of the state was extinguished. The transaction bled the Senecas white. Great promises were made to them; what they got were dead cats. For a price of two and a half cents an acre they gave up all they owned. In less than twenty-five years after the Big Tree Treaty they had virtually withdrawn from their paradise in the Genesee Valley to huddle together on small reservations and gloom out from their tepees and huts at the eternal poverty of their prospects.

11

A T THE time of the signing of the Big Tree Treaty, Indian Allan had left the Genesee Valley to live the remainder of his life in Upper Canada. Before that, he had made his residence at three different sites along the river, not counting his stay with Mary Jemison at Gardeau Flats, and had spent ten months, mostly in Canada, as a prisoner of his former associates, the British military.

The Treaty of Paris, which ended the Revolutionary War, left unappeased the enmity British leaders at Fort Niagara and other posts along the lower rim of the Great Lakes basin felt toward the former American colonists, who were now citizens of the fledgling republic. Not wanting peace, they were so actively opposed to the principles of the Paris Treaty, and so disdainful of the boundaries defined by it, that they continued illegally to hold forts within the territory of the United States until the ratification of the Jay Treaty in 1795 compelled their abandonment. It was the purpose of these leaders to prod the Iroquois into revolt, and the Senecas, in the Genesee Valley, seemed susceptible to their incitements.

The Iroquois were still living in their native forest, but the fact that they had chosen the wrong side in the war made their tenure one of grave uncertainty. They felt like pawns in the hands of the victors. They had many times been conquerors themselves. Their policy in victory had been to extinguish the defeated forces and to appropriate their lands. Thus had they dealt with the Neutrals and the Eries. It might now be their turn to suffer, as they had caused others to suffer. There was agitation in the New York legislature to expel them from their canton and confiscate their property. This threat made them surly. They were poised for aggression, and the British were forming at their side, when Indian Allan, with a stroke of genius, quieted the impending tumult, and went to jail for his pains.

He was then living on his lands at Mt. Morris and doing well with his farming and trading post. An Indian uprising, and a resumption of British hostilities, would put his property in jeopardy. He wanted peace in order to pursue his profitable enterprises.

Allan, of course, knew about wampum. It served various purposes for the Indians. It was used as money. It could be given as a ceremonial pledge. He stole a belt of wampum, took it to an American army post, and handed it in as a guarantee of peace from the Iroquois. The Indians were incensed, as were the British, at this deception. But wampum was a fetish with the former, and they would not violate a pledge made with it for fear of bringing down upon themselves the wrath of the Great Spirit.

The peace Allan effected was maintained. It was strengthened in time by various treaties signed by representatives of the United States and sachems from the Iroquois tribes. But before these negotiations were consummated, Allan himself was chased from his Mt. Morris home by a British posse, determined to capture and punish him, not for disturbing the peace, but for the offense of preserving it. He ran south in the hope of finding sanctuary on Gardeau Flats, and for a time Mary Jemison managed to save him from his pursuers. They presently caught up with him. Nearly a year later, when he was released from British custody, he reopened his trading post in Mt. Morris and continued, when opportunity afforded, to engage in the promiscuities for which he was to become notorious.

One of Allan's *affaires de coeur* (if such is the term for them) was accompanied, Mary Jemison relates, by murder. For no readily explainable reason, he moved more than twenty miles north from his Mt. Morris improvements to a 422-acre plot on the west side of the Genesee. The land he obtained adjoins what is now the village of Scottsville. Part of what was once Allan's property lies immediately to the east of three acres owned by this writer; and clearly visible from the room in which these words are being written is the wooded hummock, near the confluence of Oatka Creek and the Genesee, upon which, in 1786, Allan built a comfortable log cabin.

He brought downstream with him the squaw, Sally, who perhaps by then had given birth to one or both of his daughters. He soon had a portion of his new land under cultivation. But Allan was not a man to stand still very long in one spot. If he did not suffer the divine discontent that Kingsley calls the "germ and first upgrowth of all virtue," he had at least a constant itch to engage in new enterprises, and an insatiable zest for fleshly adventures.

He soon moved again, this time a dozen miles north to a 100-acre tract, later to become the very heart of the city of Rochester, where he built, on the west side of the river, first a sawmill, and then a gristmill. The success of these ventures was not notable. The sawmill did little more than cut the boards for the gristmill, and the second establishment, because of poverty of patronage, soon fell into desuetude. Allan, nevertheless, is renowned as Rochester's first businessman, and the earliest promoter of the milling industry, which, in time, brought nationwide fame to the community that straddles the Genesee River, and gave to it the title, The Flour City.

At the time Allan removed from Scottsville to the 100-Acre

Tract, he was loosely involved in one of the first of a series of complex post-Revolutionary real-estate deals that presently were to transfer all lands in the Genesee Valley from Indian to white ownership, and more closely involved in a complex domestic situation.

For a brief period Lucy Chapman, a young woman in her early twenties, lived with her parents, Nathan and Hannah Chapman, near Allan's Scottsville farm. The Chapmans were making their way, by easy stages, to Canada. Allan courted the daughter, who was about half his age; he married her, some believe under vows administered by a cattle drover named Slocum, who posed as a clergyman.

> Till Hymen brought his love-delighted hour,
> There dwelt no joy in Eden's rosy bower.

Whether or not Lucy knew about Sally—or whether, if she did, she thought her a mere bosky divertissement, to be abandoned now that Allan had brought to bed a wife of his own kind—is not known. And no one, not even Mary Jemison, probably the best authority on the life and loves of Indian Allan, explains how he managed to put Lucy under the same roof with Sally and preserve between the two a comity that would seem unattainable except in a seraglio.

In 1789, a year or so following her marriage, Lucy gave birth to a son, who was named Seneca after Allan's Indian friends. It is probable that he was born on the 100-Acre Tract, which would make him the first white child to see the light of day on land that was later to be part of the city of Rochester. He grew up to become an admirable citizen. He was devoted to his mother, who outlived Allan. He moved in time to Michigan, where he became Worshipful Master of the Masonic Lodge, and a warden in the Episcopal Church.

The two wives and their issue lived for a time with their husband on the millsite. The first mill went up with a glorious raising. It sat on a bleak spot near a minor cascade of the Genesee, with nothing but swampland and forest behind it. Allan had managed to procure a cask of rum, which had come off a trading vessel that had turned from Lake Ontario into the mouth of the Genesee, and his neighbors, to the number of fourteen, who lived in cabins at distances varying from within three to fifteen miles of the mill, gathered for a celebration and dance that lasted until the rum gave out two days after the festivities began.

Little progress had been made in settling the Genesee Valley at the time Allan built his mills. The few scattered pioneers who lived in what is now Monroe County, embracing Rochester and its suburbs, had little wheat to grind; and the difficulty of bringing it to the mill further militated against the possibility of Allan's achieving a sensational success.

He did not sell his Scottsville farm at the time he removed to the millsite, and now and then he returned to this property, sometimes proceeding farther south to visit his friend, Mary Jemison. On one of these occasions, by Mary's account, he met a pretty young woman and her elderly husband, who were guests at the Jemison cabin.

Mary says that the young woman "filled Allan's eye." His one staunch defender, Morley Turpin, while not condoning Allan's "offenses in the matrimonial line," feels, nevertheless, that the "awful loneliness of the vast wilderness" may furnish some explanation for them. In any event, with two wives, Allan appeared to desire a third to help relieve the "awful loneliness."

Since the young woman's husband was an impediment to Allan's designs, he led him to the bank of the Genesee River, on the pretext of regaling him with a splendid prospect of the valley, and pushed him into the water. The stratagem was not immediately effective. Sputtering and blowing like a grampus, the old man struggled to the safety of the shore, lived two or three days, and died as the result of exposure and exertion. Allan promptly moved the widow into his home with Sally and Lucy, but the arrangement was only a temporary one. Mary Jemison implies that the third wife became tired of the competition after a year, and left.

The 100-Acre Tract upon which Ebenezer Allan settled for a time, had been given to him by Oliver Phelps, active head of a group of land promoters, who, in 1788 had obtained from the Indians a huge piece of western New York property known ever since as the Phelps and Gorham Purchase. Phelps had stipulated, when the tract was turned over to Allan, that the latter build two mills on the plot for the convenience of the Indians and of the pioneer families the promoter hoped to attract to the Genesee Valley.

But the pioneers came slowly. And when they did come, the river settlements they established were well to the south or some distance north of the millsite. The land given to Allan had never been attractive to the Indians, and white migrants from the east and south showed little disposition to settle on or near it until early in the second decade of the new century. It was a sunken, miasmic area, notorious for the numerous colonies of rattlesnakes that inhabited it and for a fever, supposed to be induced by the swamps, which, at a later date, swept through the small colony at Genesee Falls with the terror of the Black Plague.

The soldiers who had participated in Sullivan's invasion of the Iroquois had returned, many to barren, rock-cluttered New England farms, with glowing reports of the beauty, fertility, and promise of the country that reached back from either bank of the upper Genesee. These reports were heard by moneyed men in the East who, when the war was over, were eager to open up the wild lands of Western New York for white habitation and for quick dollars in their own pockets.

But the impulse of the promoters to exploit the Indian lands was checked by a dispute as to who had jurisdiction over them. Massachusetts claimed them because, in 1629, Charles I of England had granted to the Massachusetts Bay Colony a piece of property that extended full across the continent and included the lands of the present Western New York. New York pressed a similar claim because some thirty years later Charles II, in the cavalier manner in which kings handed about real estate that they had never seen and did not own, had given his brother, the Duke of York, a good-sized piece of land that also included Western New York. The issue presently was settled by a compromise at a convention at Hartford, Connecticut, in 1786. There New York obtained sovereignty over the disputed territory, and the right of pre-emption of the soil, or first purchase from the native Indians, was ceded to Massachusetts.

In the spring of 1788, Oliver Phelps and Nathaniel Gorham, co-heads of a syndicate of Eastern capitalists, induced the Massachusetts legislature to sell them the pre-emption rights to a Western New York territory of about 6,000,000 acres, for which they were to pay, in three annual installments, one million dollars in depreciated Massachusetts securities.

A successful New England businessman, who had served as commissary general during the war, Phelps, with legal certification in hand, was anxious to deal with the Indians. He was the only prominent member of the syndicate, actually to enter the western wilderness. Deeply impressed by what he saw on his first visit, and convinced that this vast forest was the new Promised Land, he in time was to make his home in the village of Canandaigua, to open a land office there, to represent Ontario County in Congress, and to die in Canandaigua, his fortune depleted by a druglike addiction to land speculation.

The Indians with whom he dealt, and who felt that he had paid them only half what he had promised to pay for their lands, thought less of him than did his white admirers, one of whom left this tribute on record:

"Oliver Phelps may be considered the Cecrops of the Genesee County. Its inhabitants owe a mausoleum to his memory, in gratitude for his having pioneered for them the wilderness of this Canaan of the west."

Phelps first attempted to meet with the sachems of the Six Nations at Geneva, at the head of Seneca Lake, which marked the eastern boundary of the territory for which he had obtained the pre-emption rights. But the Indians refused to assemble. Already they had had unsatisfactory dealings with two earlier groups of promoters, one of which, the Genesee Land Company, had obtained a 999-year lease on their property. This was later voided by law. They were chary of rhetorical promises and the jungle of gaudy baubles. Their economy was in a wretched state; they were disgruntled. In Ohio, their red-skinned cousins were in revolt. Under the pressures exerted by these pushing whites—who wanted to expropriate all of their lands, whose words often had two meanings, and whose jugglery baffled their primitive comprehension—they, too, might rise up, hatchet in hand, and go forth on their old excursions of rapine and murder.

But Phelps finally made an arrangement for a treaty, some say through the offices of Indian Allan. He met in the summer of 1788 with the Indians at Buffalo Creek, sixty miles west of the Genesee. A council fire was lighted. Days were passed in high-flown oratory and discussion. Reluctant at first to sell title to any of their property, the Senecas eventually were persuaded to dispose of all their lands on the east side of the Genesee, but refused to part with their forest holdings on the west side of that stream.

The resourceful Phelps still had a card to play. The Indians hewed their logs with an axe; they got their flour by a laborious process of pounding grain with a heavy club. For a slight consideration he would have mills built to cut their logs and grind their wheat. The Senecas perked up at this. What was the slight consideration?

It turned out to be a piece of land on the west side of the river, near the Genesee Falls, twelve by twenty-four miles in size. It was defined as the "mill lot." Included in it was Allan's 100-Acre Tract, upon which the mills actually were built. Perhaps the Senecas gave the mill lot to Phelps as a lagniappe. In all, he had acquired 2,600,000 acres. He had agreed to pay $5,000 in New York currency and $500 annually "forever." The poor Senecas did not realize how short a time "forever" could be.

12

PHELPS and Gorham did not hold on very long to the bulk of the property which they had acquired by successive deals with the Commonwealth of Massachusetts and the Indians at Buffalo Creek. Their land office, the first of its kind in the country, was not a busy place. The promoters found to their disappointment that settlers did not stream into the Genesee Valley like pilgrims to the Kaaba at Mecca.

One check to extensive western migration was the fact that no roads led into the Promised Land, and wagon trains made hard going of the narrow Indian trails. Another deterrent was the disquiet of the natives. They were not accepting with grace and equanimity the expropriation of their birthright; they realized that they had made a bad bargain with Phelps and Gorham. Their smoldering resentment was being fanned into flame by the propaganda of the British policy makers in Canada, who looked upon the peace of 1783 as no more than an armistice. Artful British agents in the Genesee Valley reminded the Senecas that they were still the children of the great king, and assured them that their filial devotion would be rewarded by rich bounty.

Prospective settlers, aware of this tension and of the hair-trigger temper of the savages, were not inclined to seek out a homestead in a wild country where the ordinary hazards of frontier life might be aggravated at any moment by an Indian revolt and the horrors that usually accompanied such uprisings.

The sale of dribs and drabs of real estate to occasional western migrants did little to help Phelps and Gorham meet their formidable obligations to Massachusetts. When the day came for the first of their installment payments, the paper securities that they had pledged had appreciably risen in value, and the promoters were short of funds. To relieve their embarrassment they turned back to Massachusetts about two-thirds of the property which they had not yet freed of Indian claims, but this only temporarily composed their difficulties.

Soon they were pressed again; and, needing cash, they sold most of their remaining holdings to Robert Morris, the greatest land speculator ever to operate in the Genesee Valley, who sent his bright young son, Thomas to administer his affairs on the Purchase.

Young Tom Morris had hardly reached the Genesee county when he learned that his father had sold nearly a million acres of the wild lands, which he had obtained from Phelps and Gorham, for $160,000. The sale had been made to an association of English capitalists, headed by Sir William Johnstone Pulteney, and the dispatch with which it had been accomplished, and the handsome profit resulting from it, may have caused the astute Philadelphia financier to believe that Western New York was the El Dorado of the North American continent.

In any event, Robert Morris's first transaction in these forest properties was followed the next year by a much larger operation, and one that so clearly displayed his acquisitive talents to the Indians that they called him "big eater, with big belly," and pleaded that he not be allowed to devour all of their lands. But this, in point of fact, was what Morris had in mind.

In 1791, he acquired from Massachusetts 4,000,000 acres west of the Genesee River, including the land on that side of the river that Phelps and Gorham had been forced to relinquish, and resold most of this, two or three years later, to a Dutch syndicate known as the Holland Land Company. The price agreed upon was a third of a million dollars, but this sum was not to be paid in full until Morris, at his own expense, extinguished the Indian title to the land. This was not accomplished until several years later, and then with considerable travail, at the celebrated Treaty of Big Tree.

The swift series of real estate transactions, which started with the first sale by Phelps and Gorham to Robert Morris, and which soon resulted in the Senecas' loss of their "beautiful valley," also affected the fortunes of the two foremost white settlers along the Genesee, Mary Jemison and Ebenezer Allan. Mary profited handsomely from the Morris Purchase; Allan, abandoning his mills and selling the 100-Acre Tract to a Morris agent, returned to Mt. Morris. His stay there was brief. The lands that he had held in that place and those that the Senecas had bestowed upon his daughters, presently were gobbled up by Robert Morris and Allan, with his two wives, crossed the American border into Upper Canada, where he lived the remainder of his life.

Always peeping over the hill for a more promising prospect, Allan may have thought that he saw one in Canada. But his residence in the Genesee Valley could not have been entirely without profit. He had made money with his trading post and he had sold the improvements on his Mt. Morris property even before Robert Morris acquired the land itself. The 100-Acre Tract probably was encumbered by mortgages, and his profit from its sale may have been negligible; but he had sold to Peter Sheffer the 472 acres which he had owned at Scottsville.

One of the original white settlers on the west side of the Genesee, Peter Sheffer put his roots so deeply into the soil of Wheatland, the township in which the village of Scottsville is located, that descendants bearing the name Sheffer continued to live there for more than 150 years.

Peter Sheffer, himself, lived half a century on a farm that reached down to the waters of the Genesee. He raised a large family, improved his property, and presently built the first frame dwelling on his side of the river with lumber cut at Allan's mill. He died in this house at the age of ninety.

Backwoodsman though he was until the community grew and he became a civic-minded burgher of the village of Scottsville, Sheffer was not, just because his neck was red and his hands made horny by toil, entirely obtuse. On the contrary, he seems to have been not a little fastidious. Legend has it that after the transfer of the Scottsville property to Sheffer, Allan, his wives and his issue lived one winter with the Sheffers in the cabin near the point where Oatka Creek enters the Genesee. This, Mrs. Munson, one of Sheffer's descendants, has denied. She said that her ancestor could not abide Allan's table habits. The two families did, however, spend one night together in the cabin. When they gathered for the evening meal, Allan, Mrs. Munson said, cooked up "some kind of a snake," which he offered with a flourish to the Sheffers. When the delicacy was refused, Allan devoured it with a relish that made the others, if not green with envy, at least green.

Allan was neither unprepossessing nor uneducated. If he sometimes appeared to have a pathological aversion to the amenities and customs of civilized life, he sounded, on other occasions, like a very civilized man indeed.

Before the British illegally took him into custody and held him ten months for his deception in carrying the dove of peace to the Iroquois, in the form of stolen wampum, Allan visited Philadelphia at the instigation of a Moravian missionary and from that city addressed a letter to Congress that displayed not only considerable wisdom, but a humanity inconsistent with a man to whom murder and other high crimes have been imputed.

The missionary, the Reverend Joseph Bull, had been impounded at Niagara because he, like Allan, had attempted to effect a permanent peace between the Six Nations and the United States. When his good offices were interrupted by his arrest, he managed to get a secret message to Allan. In this he requested the "bloody picaroon" of the Genesee to advise Congress that, if the Six Nations were given some decent guarantees that all of their lands would not be taken from them, they would be well disposed to peace; but if this were not done, the frontier might be turned into a shambles, and thousands of lives sacrificed.

Allan faithfully carried out the missionary's request, and the letter he wrote to Congress closed with this paragraph:

There remain in the Seneca Country about one hundred American prisoners, which prudent commissioners might have delivered up to them immediately. As many of these are young people fast degenerating into savages and forgetting their own language, would it not be wise to draw them out of the hands of the Indians without delay, and restore them to their religion and to their country? In anything I can do, be pleased to command me.

What weight Allan's words carried with the Congress is not known. But the historical fact is that the next year (1784) a treaty that had as its first purpose peace between the United States and the Six Nations was negotiated at Fort Stanwix, and at that time arrangements were made for the surrender by the Indians of all white captives. It was a peace, to be sure, that was often threatened, that sometimes was as tenuously held as the sword above Damocles, but it was not actually violated; and ten years later, when the Senecas learned of Mad Anthony Wayne's smashing defeat of the western Indians at Fallen Timbers, they realized that any aggression on their part against the white usurpers of their land would be tantamount to suicide, and forever after held their peace. If Allan's efforts helped in any way to prevent bloodletting during this interlude, he deserves, it would seem, a better place in the annals of the Genesee Valley than has generally been given to him.

After his removal to Canada, Allan's mills were operated for a time by Christopher Dugan for the Pulteney Association, which had acquired the 100-Acre Tract as part of its purchase of Genesee Valley lands from Robert Morris. But business was no better than it had been during Allan's proprietorship. The swamps, the incidence of fever, and the rattlesnakes combined to make the millsite an undesirable district on the lower river. The situation did not change until, early in the second decade of the nineteenth century, a gentleman from Maryland, who was to give his name to a small community at Genesee Falls and lend his civic genius to its development, bought the property and began to lay out the village of Rochesterville.

When Dugan abandoned the mills, their small usefulness ended. A flood swept the sawmill into the river in 1803, and fire destroyed the gristmill a few years later.

Thomas Thackeray Swinburne, the rhymemaker of the Genesee, dedicating a poem to Indian Allan, sings in his closing lines:

> And when they laid him down to rest
> They placed two millstones on his breast,

but no one knows where Allan is buried in Canada, and the stones from his gristmill, after serving various useful and ornamental purposes, are now embedded in a wall of the Monroe County Courthouse in Rochester.

13

SHORTLY before Ebenezer Allan left the Genesee Valley, a new
entrepreneur entered that country and briefly held forth
along the river. He was a man of entirely different stamp from
Allan. Well-born and well-educated, he wore lace cuffs, a pow-
dered wig, and fashionable New York tailoring in the fastness of
the western woods. He delighted in elegance and sociability;
he brought to the log houses, in which he first lived, imported
wines and other table delicacies; he loved fast horses and beautiful women.

He was a thirty-four-year-old Scot, lean, erect, long-faced,
with the grace of a courtier. He had boundless energy and a bold,
undaunted spirit. His name was Charles Williamson, and he had
been sent out by the Pulteney Association of London to manage
its million-acre estate in Western New York.

With his American-born wife, the former Abigail Newell of
Massachusetts, and his children, Williamson landed at Norfolk,

Virginia, in November, 1791, and quickly acquired American citizenship. This was a vital stipulation in his agreement with Sir William Johnstone Pulteney, head of the syndicate, and its other members, William Hornby, ex-governor of Bombay, and Patrick Colquhoun. All were British; and since New York had passed a law prohibiting alien ownership of state lands, the Pulteney Associates needed an American citizen to take title to their property, and hold it until such time as the obnoxious law could be repealed.

Williamson was eager to inspect the tract that he had been commissioned to settle and sell. Delays he tolerated not at all. Putting off for another day an action that could begin at once was never his policy. He was cautioned against attempting a journey through the wilderness in the dead of winter, but his exuberant spirit could not be repressed by threats of danger or his enterprise restrained by portents of privation and hardship. After establishing his family in suitable quarters, he left the seaboard in February, 1792, and proceeded by sled, by horseback, and by foot to the western border of the Pulteney domain—the Genesee River.

His arduous trek ended near the confluence of Canaseraga Creek and the river, and it was to this place that he returned the following summer to found a settlement that he expected would be the great market town of the river country. He named it Williamsburg after his patron, Sir William Pulteney; and at the same time that forest trees fell on the village site and log buildings rose in their place, Williamson, impatient to advance any project that he undertook, had men at work building a road (later known as the Williamson Road) that led north across the Alleghenies and west across the Southern Tier of New York State to the settlement by the Genesee. A year later, in late summer 1793, the new road was being traveled by persons afoot, on horseback, and some in the carriages of Philadelphia and southern fashionables, all bound for Williamsburg and the first of Charles Williamson's numerous extravaganzas in the interest of land promotion.

Earlier in the summer, Williamson had announced in the Albany *Gazette* that a fair and race meeting would be held in Williamsburg in late September, and during the intervening months he and John Johnstone, a faithful Scot who had come across the seas with him, performed prodigies in their efforts to make the settlement ready for the expected concourse of visitors.

Laborers were withdrawn from their normal occupations to construct a racecourse in the forks between the Genesee and Canaseraga Creek. Captain Elijah Starr, who managed the village tavern, did what he could to improve and expand the accommodations of a hostelry that had gained an early fame because of the dancing school Williamson had organized in its second-floor ballroom. Foods of a kind that had not before been eaten in the wilderness were brought to Williamsburg. Casks of spirituous liquors were stored; imported wines were set aside by Williamson for special guests.

The fair opened on schedule, with all of the attractions that had been advertised. Fat bullocks, working oxen, swine, and other livestock were shown. There were displays of farm products and discussions of agricultural methods. Gentlemen tested the mettle of their blooded horses in a series of races on the newly laid course, for purses up to fifty pounds. There was a public barbecue, wassailing, some wenching. Indians, "well-oiled and limber as snakes," tried their wrestling holds against the white youths of the countryside; there were tests of strength, and foot races.

While the fair and the horse racing made the magnet that drew crowds to Williamsburg, it was the village itself, sprung up almost overnight in a forest clearing, that astonished visitors who had come from distant parts. Its town square was plotted eighty rods from the right bank of the Genesee. Surrounding this were a number of log houses, a store, a blacksmith shop, and a school. There was the two-story tavern; there was a mill on a race that flowed into the river. At the edge of the settlement, on Williamson's own farm, called the Hermitage, was a huge L-shaped barn with a shed for the stabling of dozens of horses. All that the visitor could see gave support to Williamson's proclaimed aspirations for the settlement. But the visitor did not know that revolt seethed below the surface of the village, and that the disaffection of its residents already had given it mortal hurts.

In his early, cursory examination of the Pulteney property, Williamson decided that its development depended upon men to settle it, a market for the produce grown upon it, and roads to allow buyers to reach the market. And the *sine qua non*—the prime and first requirement—was settlers. Williamson had planned from the start to place a host of solid Scots upon the land. Before he was able to execute this design, a considerable company of malcontents and misfits, the off-scourings of the Hamburg slums and docks, descended upon him like the curse of the Biblical locusts, to botch the job of road building he gave them, to malinger, to complain, to rant, to riot, and even to threaten the promoter's life when he attempted to set them to work at Williamsburg.

Williamson had had nothing to do with the selection of these subversive colonists. A German salesman, with a good deal of aplomb, and apparently some charm when he chose to use it, had persuaded Patrick Colquhoun that he had a delegation of stout Germans who would do well on the Genesee lands. Without seeing the emigrants, Colquhoun agreed to ship them overseas. They were eager to escape Europe. Had they remained in Hamburg, they might have been sold into bondage as vagrants. When they landed in Philadelphia, Robert Morris—from whom the Pulteney Associates had bought the western lands, and whose interests were closely bound to those of the British syndicate—sent the Germans rattling off in wagons to join the laborers who were building the Williamson Road.

The immigrants were headed by the man who had recruited them, the salesman (he had sold pictures in Hamburg) William Berczy. He may have pictured to his fellow countrymen that this Canaan of the western world, which they were entering, was a land of milk and honey. Instead, they found that they were expected to cut a swath through the forests of the Allegheny Mountains in midwinter.

They protested at an ordeal which was aggravated by the flabby condition of their city-bred bodies, and angrily proclaimed that the terms of their emigration agreement had been violated. They had been promised houses, cattle, tools, meat, and flour, and none of these was forthcoming. The women among them wanted spinning wheels, flax, and wool. Thirty-nine of the party presently pushed along the half-built road to Williamsburg, where John Johnstone, Williamson's adjutant, with no other accommodations, bundled them into small log cabins. By summer, when other Germans reached the little community, the discontents of all seethed suddenly into mutiny.

The Germans looked to Berczy as their leader, savior, and advocate. He arrogantly attempted to usurp Williamson's authority. There was a clash. The Germans rioted. They drove the Scottish agent into his house, where he barricaded himself behind the furniture. He might have suffered serious physical injury, or have been killed, had not Berczy—perhaps realizing that the law might be evoked even in the wilderness—interceded.

Later, Berczy rode off with three or four of the other malcontents to lay his complaints before Robert Morris in Philadelphia, and Williamson summoned Sheriff Judah Colt from Canandaigua, twenty-six miles away. He arrested several of the rioters, and they were found guilty of disturbing the peace. Fines were imposed, which they could not pay, and they were compelled to work out their penalties. But this was done in Canandaigua, without benefit to Williamsburg.

The Williamsburg fair was abandoned after two or three years, as by that time the village itself was more or less abandoned by its founder, whose interests were widely scattered over the Pulteney lands.

The start of the settlement had been a poor one, owing in large measure to the poor caliber of its first arrivals. The "Hamburg scum," as the Germans were called, gradually slid away, with many of the members of the company migrating to Canada; but Williamsburg never recovered from the wounds caused by their disaffection and revolt. It was a dying village when Williamson, at the order of his principals, surrendered the Pulteney agency in 1801; a dead one a few years later.

When pioneers began to stream into that part of the Genesee Valley early in the nineteenth century, they did not stop at Williamsburg, already "mouldering into ruins," according to the Pulteney agent who succeeded Williamson, but continued a few miles north to the more promising community of Big Tree, now Geneseo, where the Wadsworth brothers had been settled for several years.

Captain William and James Wadsworth had come from Connecticut, each with a fortune in pocket, and title to 2,000 acres of land, and they had come to stay. While their perfumed and bewigged neighbor, Charles Williamson, flew about the Genesee country on a blooded horse, in the prosecution of his spectacular enterprises, his blue, beautifully tailored cape bellied out by the wind like an insignia of squirearchy, the Wadsworths sawed wood, plowed fields, raised cattle, and grew hemp. They were the progenitors of a long line of fine, and often distinguished men and women who were born on the Wadsworth lands, which extend far back from both banks of the Genesee, and which are still owned and managed by men who bear the name of the original proprietors.

But the "diggins," the log cabin in which the two brothers lived during the early days, was without pretense, and, according to one of their guests, without a semblance of sanitation.

The Duke de la Rochefoucauld Liancourt stopped there one night. He had come to America to escape the Terror of the French Revolution, and he had traveled north from the French colony at Asylum, Pennsylvania, to inspect the Genesee country. First falling under the spell of Charles Williamson's charm, he later protested that he was almost overcome by the evil odors of the Wadsworth dwelling, which he described as a "small log-house, as dirty and filthy as any I have seen," and speculated as to whether the "offensive smell . . . proceeded from cats or decayed stores which the Captain (the Duke appears to have met only William Wadsworth, a burly, beak-nosed, blustering man, who kept a Negro wench to comb his hair, and perhaps perform other more personal services) is reported to keep sometimes until they become putrefied. . . . Never," he finally declared, had he "passed the night in a more unpleasant hole."

"Execute your plans and make an immense fortune for your Employers and a handsome one for yourself," Robert Morris told Williamson, when the Pulteney agent first moved to the Genesee, bright with the hope of building a great market city at the forks of that stream and the Canaseraga.

But ten years later, when his principals discovered that rather than making them an "immense fortune," Williamson had spent more than 180,000 pounds developing a property that had cost only 75,000 pounds, they decided that the agent was too rich for their blood, and they let him out. His place was taken by Robert Troup, a Wall Street lawyer, with a talent for the minutiae of account-keeping, but with none whatever for the gaudy entertainments and promotional enterprises that Williamson had used to excite interest in the western lands and that had induced people to travel long distances to see them.

After an official visit to Williamsburg, Troup reported to his employers that the famous tavern, with the dancing school long since discontinued, was without windows or doors, although still encouraging among the "common people" an unholy addiction to "whiskey drams." The great L-shaped barn on Williamson's Hermitage Farm, which was almost as celebrated as the tavern, built, Troup censoriously remarks, "doubtless at the expense of many thousands of dollars," served no purpose whatever. Once it had not only stabled the horses of Williamsburg visitors, but also had been used by a clergyman, who had come to town (not at the solicitation of the agent, who was never very sensible of the settlers' spiritual needs) to hold Sunday meetings.

In the days when his hopes for Williamsburg were highest, the founder of the colony had supplanted with a framed dwelling the log house that had made his early residence in the community. What became of this, Troup does not say. In later years, Williamson used it only as a stopping place on his occasional visits to Williamsburg and never moved his family into it. As a matter of fact, neither Abigail nor the Williamson children, of which there were several, ever visited Williamsburg. They lived in considerable elegance in Bath, fifty miles southeast. There Madame had a serving maid and sometimes a Negro slave for handy work. The house at Bath was one of several Williamson domiciles in that part of the state, and rumor had it that each had a mistress of its own.

Robert Troup ran what a sailor would call "a tight ship," when he took over from Williamson the management of the Pulteney estate. He kept his nose to the grindstone, and he kept a microscopic watch on expenditures. He was known by the settlers as a hard man. After a few years of his superintendency, the Pulteney Associates began to hear the pleasant chink of silver in their coffers. Before the outbreak of the War of 1812, which brought real-estate operations in the Genesee Valley to a standstill, the Pulteney property was showing a profit.

But this wasn't all Troup's doings. Williamson's vision, enterprise, and enthusiasm had combined to open up and settle a wilderness estate that was ultimately to pay off to its owners. His efforts were always heroic; his designs always larger than life. Troup spoke churlishly of what he believed had been the first agent's purpose "to bring the country into an active and prosperous condition as to agriculture and commerce by a kind of *coup de main.*"

Well, the facts are that, a year before Williamson made his first trip to the Genesee and envisaged a colony at the confluence of that stream and Canaseraga Creek, less than one thousand white persons were living in the territory owned by the Pulteney Associates, and land in the Genesee Valley was selling for fifty cents an acre. In the brief decade of his agency, Williamson brought hundreds of settlers into the county, encouraged more productive methods of agriculture, introduced fine breeds of livestock, built towns, schools, roads, and promoted commerce.

He had hoped always to attract to the territory wealthy men who would administer large estates from great manor houses; who would cultivate the arts, give grand balls, patronize theater, race horses, and ride to hounds. And in the autumn of 1800, three Southerners, who at least had the qualifications of breeding and wealth Williamson desired, came riding up from Maryland, a pack horse and a mounted slave trotting behind them, and asked to be shown the country near Williamsburg that the agent's advertisements had alluringly described.

The tourists were Major Charles Carroll and Colonel William Fitzhugh, Maryland natives, and Colonel Nathaniel Rochester, a resident of that state who had been born in Virginia. Before they returned to their Southern homes, they had contracted with Williamson to buy, for the price of two dollars an acre, 12,000 acres near Canaseraga Creek and the Genesee.

Three years later, bound to the Genesee Valley by a considerable investment, they rode north again. This time they were looking out a millsite. Williamson had been relieved of his agency, and had sailed for Europe; but the trio was taken in hand by John Johnstone, the first agent's former factor, who escorted the Southern gentlemen to the 100-Acre Tract at Genesee Falls, once the gift of Oliver Phelps to Ebenezer Allan. The sawmill Allan had built had been swept away in a recent flood, and the grist-mill was falling into decay. The three Southerners nevertheless agreed to purchase the property for $1,750.

The transaction was of historical significance. Several years later, when Colonel Rochester settled permanently at Genesee Falls, the 100-Acre Tract became the village of Rochesterville. Still later, when the village expanded to the proportions of a metropolis, and dropped the last five letters of the village name, it was this area, bordering the west bank of the Genesee, that became the business center of Rochester.

14

I N LATE summer 1797, when the village of Williamsburg was still enjoying its short-lived boom, the hamlet at Big Tree, a short distance north along the Genesee, suddenly became the cynosure of the western wilderness. There, according to rumor that had spread swiftly among the Seneca Indians in the valley, "big kettles would be hung" and a "feast of fat things" enjoyed. There would surely be rum. There would be oratory, which the Senecas dearly loved. There would be, the white propagandists let it be known, rich rewards for the Indians, if only they listened to the white man's "reason."

Soon there was a movement of moccasined feet through the woods, all heading toward the focus of Big Tree, which, in the memory of the oldest tribesman, was more concentrated than any other Indian concourse that had not been inspired by the prospect of war. The Senecas, and an aspersion of other members of the Iroquois race, came on foot, on horseback, and some paddled up the Genesee in canoes. Whole families trailed behind their patresfamilias, sometimes driving a cow, and often with lean, mangy curs slinking at their heels.

Young warriors arrived at Big Tree, not dressed for battle, but flaunting their manliness by displays of strength, by daubs of war paint on their bodies, by their swaggering airs. Old men who had sat at other council fires with the whites, and had come to know that the arts of the Indians were no match for Caucasian guile, moved stolidly through the woods. They would listen again to the parley and palaver, but with little hope that anything beneficial to the Indians would result. The fine promises that they had heard at these conferences in the past often had had no more substance than thistledown. But there would be roast ox to eat; there would be rum to drink. And an old man, with his belly full of food, and his head made giddy by rum, could conjure up illusions; could fancy that the Senecas were still the great power that for moons beyond reckoning had dominated this beautiful valley of the Genesee, this paradise of game-filled woods and fertile gardens, with its lovely, winding river, and the purling streams, abundant with fish, that poured into it.

At Big Tree, the last of the Senecas' lands were to be treated for.

Robert Morris, George Washington's friend, a signer of the Declaration of Independence, and a man who had once been considered the richest man in America, was in a sticky corner. Creditors were about his ears; he was threatened with bankruptcy. Sometime before, he had more or less abandoned his banking and mercantile activities to follow a golden mirage that hung tantalizingly above the western lands. He had become obsessed with the notion of gaining fabulous wealth through speculation in these undeveloped regions, and now, not unlike a compulsive gambler at a dice table, he was going broke.

He had made a fine and quick profit in the sale to the Pulteney Associates of 1,250,000 acres of land on the east side of the Genesee, and he had later sold about 3,500,000 acres on the west side of the river to Theophile Cazenove, American representative for a Dutch syndicate, later known as the Holland Land Company. The deal with Cazenove was made late in 1792. But the money was not laid down in hard cash on the barrel head. A considerable proportion of it was reserved by the Dutch agent until such time as Morris was able to extinguish the Indians' title to the lands, and free them for the syndicate's exploitation. But this, for a variety of reasons, had not yet been done.

Now, deeply involved, pressed on all sides, Morris very much needed the money that had been withheld by the Dutch capitalists, and he had won the grouty consent of the Senecas to negotiate the sale of the title to their remaining lands, which comprised most of New York west of the Genesee. Morris had sent his son, Tom, into the west several years before to act as his intendant; he was a man in his mid-twenties, bright, beautifully educated in schools in England and on the continent, a lawyer by profession, who, liking the western country, made his home in the village of Canandaigua.

Robert Morris, who was unwell, did not attend the council. He had never been on the western lands that he had early believed would make him wealthy beyond his most extravagant fancies, and it was destined that he should never see them. He was sixty-seven at the time of Big Tree; he had five more years to live, and three of these were to be passed in the Prune Street gaol for debtors in Philadelphia.

But he had made elaborate preparations for this conference, which, if it succeeded, might check the precipitant fall of his fortunes. He was a man who had engaged during all of his life in large affairs, who was uncommonly wise in dealing with his fellow men, who was sensible of human weaknesses, and who felt, in this desperate hour, that he must trade on those weaknesses.

"The Indians must have plenty of food, and also of liquor, when you see proper to order it to them," he wrote to his son. And he added in another article of his meticulously worked out instructions, "The business of the treaty may be greatly propelled probably, by withholding liquor from the Indians; showing and promising it to them when the treaty is over."

And he counted on bribes to facilitate his ends.

Since Federal law required that a United States Commissioner be present at all negotiations for the cession of Indian lands, President Washington appointed Jeremiah Wadsworth of Connecticut, a man of large wealth and wide political experience, to represent the government at Big Tree. Wadsworth would serve as arbiter at the conference if the parties concerned were themselves unable to adjust their differences.

Old, touched with gout, not relishing the arduous journey from his luxurious Connecticut home to the Genesee, Wadsworth did not reach Big Tree on the day the meeting was scheduled to open. He was preceded at the settlement by several companies of Indians, some of whose members were so ravenous that they did not wait for the Morris barbecue, but tore apart the carcass of an unroasted ox and ate it with blood dripping from their lips and streaming through their fingers.

Indians were everywhere about the settlement; scores of Indians; presently, hundreds of Indians. At night their campfires spread a pink canopy over the Genesee flats. Some slept in tepees, others lay under trees. They drank milk warm from the udders of the lean cows that they had driven along the trails; they howled, danced, and shook gourd rattles; they chased greased pigs for sport. They competed in tests of strength, and ate themselves out of shape at the expense of a worried old gentleman in Philadelphia, who had written to his son, Tom:

I am to sustain all the expense; this circumstance does not induce a desire to starve the cause, or to be niggardly: at the same time it is natural to desire a consistent economy to be observed, as to the expense of the treaty, and the price to be paid for the lands.

The price to be paid, the Senecas learned a few days after Jeremiah Wadsworth reached Big Tree, and the council fire was in full flame, was $100,000 for approximately 4,000,000 acres. Mr.

Morris's magnanimity was tempered. If his bid was accepted, he'd get the huge tract for something like two and a half cents an acre.

"Brothers," Commissioner Wadsworth had said, on opening the council, "I rejoice with you that the Great Spirit has brought us together, let us so conduct ourselves as not to offend him, lest he withdraw his protection from us."

There was frequent mention by the white speakers of the Great Spirit. He was invoked whenever the Christian delegates at the council felt that use of His name would help accommodate their differences with the superstitious pagans. And the Indians were always addressed as "Brothers," no matter what epithets were applied to them outside of the convention. Robert Morris had prepared a speech, which his son delivered. It began:

Brothers of the Seneca Nation, it was my wish and my intention to have come into your country and to have met with you at this treaty, but the Great Spirit ordained otherwise. . . .

Brothers, it is now six years since I have been invested with the exclusive right to acquire your lands, during the whole of which time, you have quietly possessed them without being importuned to sell them, but I now think that it is time for them to be productive to you. . . .

In council, the Senecas were solemn and mirthless. If protocol had been suspended, they might have roared with scornful laughter at Mr. Morris's suggestion that he was going to make their lands productive for them. The Senecas had had little complaint about the Genesee Valley. They had possessed the Territory for a long time, and they felt that they knew how to use it.

Cornplanter, a noted warrior and a capable orator, in time asked Tom Morris to consult the Book of the White man's Great Spirit and see if he could find anything in it directing white people to intrude on the Indians' property.

He, the orotund Red Jacket, and other sachems and chiefs seemed—until Red Jacket was laid low by drink and several of the others succumbed to venal temptation—irrevocably opposed to the sale of any more land. Morris's appeals, promises, and threats that if the business was not done during the Big Tree meeting his father would never again treat with the Indians, availed nothing. The council was soon as deadlocked as a hung jury. Morris, who was feasting the Indians on roast ox and doling out flour rations, beef rations, tobacco rations, handing about butcher knives and three-foot blankets, saw the money that his father had allowed him for "entertainment" being wasted on a lost cause.

In the early stages of the conference Red Jacket was the greatest obstacle to its success, or at least the success that Tom Morris hoped to achieve through it. All his life Red Jacket had implacably opposed the adoption, by the Indians, of the white man's customs and usages. He had consistently pleaded for race autonomy. He had fought at every treaty council that he had ever attended for the preservation of the Indians' territory, feeling that without this the freedom which the Indian enjoyed, far beyond the liberties of most "civilized" men, would be lost.

The Seneca was not sedentary; and nothing, Red Jacket believed, could make him so. He was a farmer, of sorts; his women cultivated the land and raised squash, beans, pumpkins, and maize. But there was no great permanence to his settlements: no schools, businesses, churches, or expensive houses to hold him in one spot if the whim struck him to leave, if the firewood gave out, if the soil of his garden plot became sour, if the roof of his cabin caved in from climatic rot, if the midden heap around the place became noisome. Then he put his simple chattels on the back of his wife, and she followed him to a new location.

15

AT BIG TREE there were Indian leaders of greater stature than Red Jacket, but none with his eloquence, his skill in debate, his sure understanding of the jobbery and cunning young Tom Morris was employing in an attempt to save the remnants of his father's broken fortune. Red Jacket was a commanding figure whenever he rose to speak at the fire that Morris had kindled in the crude shelter where the council was held, a sort of wilderness convention hall, which lacked walls, but was roofed over with the boughs and branches of trees.

The Indian wore a scarlet coat; it was his insignia, his cachet of distinction. As a youth he had run an errand for an English subaltern and had been rewarded with a tattered military tunic. The color of the garment gave him the name of Red Jacket. When one red coat wore out, he somehow obtained another. A silver medal, given to him by President Washington at an Indian pow-wow in Philadelphia, dangled from his throat.

He was not a warrior. As he said himself, haughtily, when accused of some military demerit, "I am an orator. I was born an orator."

His exceptional talent often served his people well. He was picturesque, theatrical. His mobile face, with its pendulous lower lip, which drooped deeper when he became scornful or sarcastic, was the face of the expert mime. Words flowed from him with little effort. They were heavy, guttural words, for the Seneca language is devoid of labials; but Red Jacket used them with such grace and skill that his periods had a poetic rhythm. Inordinately vain, he was utterly confident of his ability to enthrall his audience.

Speaking in council at Big Tree, Red Jacket suggested that Mr. Morris probably had a great deal of money, but he exhorted him to hold his fists "close" since the Senecas, with part of their ancient seat already gone, preferred retaining what land they still held to any amount of money he might offer them.

It was an artful declaration. The council was adjourned in order to allow Morris and his white counsellors to deliberate on policy. He had hoped to pay no more than $75,000 for the Indian title; now he realized that he would need to increase that amount substantially. When the council reconvened, he offered the Senecas $100,000, and suggested that the money be put into the Bank of the United States, where it would grow, night and day, and produce an annuity of $6,000.

Red Jacket doubtless understood bank interest, but he left to Morris the difficult task of explaining to the Senecas how money would grow if it were properly "planted." They knew about seeds. If one put a seed into the warm earth, it sprouted, pushed to the surface as a plant, and soon was ready to be harvested and eaten. Even trees that bore edible fruit had similar beginnings. But money? Money was hard, like stone. How could that grow in the ground, or anywhere else?

Morris diverted from his exposition on the growth of money to try to impress his hearers with the actual bulk of such a sum as

$100,000 in silver, and said that thirty horses would be required to haul it through the woods from Philadelphia to the Genesee. Impassively, the Senecas shook their heads. They didn't want money, in any amount; they wanted their land. The issue was at a stalemate when Red Jacket, in a fit of temper, leaped up and cried to Morris, "We have now reached a point to which I wanted to bring you. You told us when we first met that we were free either to sell or retain our lands. I repeat, we will not part with them," and to indicate that the council was ended, he covered over the fire around which the debates had been held.

This act of their oratorical champion excited among the Senecas a small riot. The council had gone on for days. The Senecas had had enough of sitting still and holding to legalistic restraints. They leaped up, brandishing their weapons. Morris himself said that anyone unaccustomed to their humors would have thought that all of the whites were about to be tomahawked. But no one was hurt, and the tumult quickly subsided.

Although he had brought liquor enough to provide the Indians with 1,500 "rations," Morris so far had held it in abeyance. To pour it too early would have defeated the purpose which it was intended to achieve. But at this juncture, he must have been tempted to bring it out, allow the Indians to become intoxicated, and hope that in their insensate state they would sign away the title to their lands. The threat, which he had made, that if the Indians did not accept the terms his father was offering them, his father would never treat with them again, had been pure equivocation. Robert Morris's situation was such that the son knew that he could not leave Big Tree without carrying with him the title to the property that the elder Morris so desperately needed.

He waited. He continued to feed the Indians. The entertainment was costing him a pretty penny. But he could not allow them to disperse, and hope to bring them again into assemblage. They played games, did some drinking, chased greased pigs for prize money, as they had done when they had first congregated at Big Tree. Jeremiah Wadsworth protested that he was unwell and ought to be on his way back to Connecticut. William Bayard, agent for the Holland Land Company, was disgruntled by the turn of affairs. He had hoped that the land title would have been transferred before now; that soon the business of surveying the great tract and platting it for sale might go forward.

But these men, and other dignitaries at the council, were not particularly uncomfortable. Robert Morris had been exact in all preparations for this meeting. He had caused pipes of wine to be carted from Philadelphia for the pleasure of the white officials. Their hostel was a new home that the Wadsworth brothers had built, which Morris had rented for the occasion. It was a considerable improvement over the log house which, a few years before, had provoked the profound revulsion of the queasy Duke de la Rochefoucauld Liancourt, first gentleman to the court of the late, guillotined French King, Louis XVI.

16

AFTER a few days of feasting, frolicking, and occasional fighting, the Senecas at Big Tree were in a euphoric mood. Tom Morris had hinted that he was preparing to leave, but of course he had no such intention. He was waiting for what eventually happened. He wanted an invitation to reopen the council. This came presently from Little Billy, Cornplanter, and a fine, staunch old Indian character, Farmer's Brother, a cousin of Mary Jemison's husband, the bloody-handed Hiokatoo. They called on Morris to express their regrets at Red Jacket's unseemly act in covering the council fire. This, they conceded, he had had no legal right to do since, according to their strict ritual, the person who lighted such a fire (in this instance, Morris) alone had the right to extinguish it.

As the result of these friendly overtures, the conference was reconvened. But this time Morris took a new tack. He had failed with the sachems and chiefs. He now brought the women into council. Despite the physical burdens laid upon them, and the menial tasks which they traditionally were required to perform, the Seneca women were not a negligible force in tribal affairs. They and the warriors had a good deal to say about the disposition of the Indian lands, which the former cultivated and the latter defended. But Morris, speaking to the women, did not refer to their prerogative in this matter. Instead, he remarked the hardships and privations of their lives, and dolefully explained how these might have been relieved had the sachems and chiefs seen fit to accept the great sum of money he had offered for the country west of the Genesee.

But now, since the women were everlastingly committed to a life of hardship and toil, he thought it only fair that they should have a little cheer. He had brought presents for them from Philadelphia. His original intention had been to offer these only after the treaty had been signed, but he saw no reason to penalize the women, who had not opposed him in any way, because of the obstinacy and wrongheadedness of their leaders.

And that day, and for several days thereafter, dusky daughters of the woods were preening and prinking themselves like waiting ladies at an elegant court; trying on glass beads and silver brooches, flaunting printed India goods, displaying colored handkerchiefs, swinging vermilion bags, and wearing ornamental combs in their straight black hair. Morris had not been niggardly. Large and small brass kettles, a boon in any Indian cabin, were distributed; and now and then a largesse of utility, in the way of a milch cow, was given to some particularly deserving—or influential—squaw.

A few days after the women had been made happy, the warriors, sachems, and chiefs met again with Morris. Rather grudgingly, they agreed to abandon what remained of their "terrestrial paradise." Red Jacket was not present to arouse the council with his customary salute, "Brothers, lend me your ears," and to offer eloquent opposition to the proposed action of his fellow tribesmen. He was not in the woodsy council chamber. He lay under a tree, some distance from it, sleeping off the effects of a long bout with whiskey which bootleggers had been selling in the woods beyond the hamlet.

He functioned later, however. Before the agreement was signed, a series of debates developed concerning the lands that the natives desired for reservations. These, the elder Mr. Morris had cautioned, ought to be small "as the sum I am paying is very large." The Senecas had different notions about this. Red Jacket, no longer in a coma, violently demanded 900,000 acres for the Senecas living in the neighborhood of what is now the city of Buffalo; Cornplanter, although born and raised in an Indian village on the Genesee, petitioned for a great tract on the Allegheny, which he hoped would be the principal Seneca settlement. In the end, four reservations, each two miles square, and one of sixteen square miles at Caneadea, the western door of the Iroquois, were set aside on the Genesee.

But there was one more reservation to concede. Probably to the astonishment of all—for Seneca women did not plead their own cause in council, but delegated advocates to represent them—Mary Jemison moved toward the fire over which Tom Morris presided. She was known, of course, to the young lawyer and land agent. Her celebrity as the "white woman" who preferred the Indians who had adopted her to the members of her own race extended far beyond the valley of the Genesee.

She was wise in Indian ways; astute regarding the mores of white men. She must have made an arresting figure as she drew near the fire in the council hall. She was fifty-four years old, slightly toil-bent, but a woman of uncommon vigor. Gardeau had been her home ever since, in her despairing search for succor at the time General Sullivan had driven her from Little Beard's Town, she had been taken in by the kindly Negro cabin-dwellers, who had long since departed, and who had relinquished to their former guest the fields that they had cultivated.

Conceding that the land belonged to her, the Senecas had ratified her title to it. Now Mary was lobbying for more property, claiming that to care for her large family she needed extended garden patches for the cultivation of beans, potatoes, and corn.

Lockwood L. Doty, perhaps the best of the Livingston County historians, who was hardly a feminist, wrote caustically of the "white woman's" efforts to promote her own interests, while objecting not at all to Tom Morris's cunning endeavors to promote his.

"Mary Jemison took a part in the deliberations, both in and out of the council-house, urging her claims for an allotment of lands in a manner that was more pertinacious than dignified."

No exact report has been preserved of the speech she made. Morris was tired after a day of debate. He wanted to get the Senecas to "X in" the treaty before they had a change of heart. Mary Jemison was pleading for what may have seemed a rather indefinite property, but surely this strange little character in the odd getup—a short coat tied with thongs rather than held together with buttons, a petticoat and leggings, buckskin moccasins and as a token of her white birth, a hat so hideous no "civilized" woman would have worn it except at a masque—would not need *much* land, and Morris wearily acceded to her claim.

And lo! soon after the grant had been made, he discovered that he had given away nearly 18,000 acres of some of the finest lands along the Genesee River, and that there was no taking back.

The treaty was now ready for the marks of the Indians and they came forward, one by one, to take pen in hand. Bribes in the form of annuities had helped some of the influential tribesmen to come to a decision. The gasconading Red Jacket, who at first had fought the land deal tooth and nail, secretly approached Morris and asked that he be allowed to affix his symbol up near the top of the paper, as becoming one of his dignity and importance.

The deed of conveyance was so handsome in design that it made an Indian proud to sign it. And next to the mark of each Seneca, the white men wrote in both the tribal name of the signer and his English sobriquet if he had one, and some of these were wondrous strange. Hot Bread was listed on the paper, and Hansome Lake, Govenor Blacksnake, Onnouggarhiko, alias The Infant; Big Kettle, Tall Chief, Two Skies of a Length; Oosaukauendauski, alias To Destroy a Town, and Parrot Nose, to name a few of the fifty-two Seneca signatories.

The council broke up after that; the whiskey old Robert Morris had wanted withheld until the treaty was signed was brought forth, and the Indians, briefly, had what they called a "staff." Usually at a "staff" they checked their weapons, and caroused until the liquor was gone, or they gave out physically through surfeit. Their celebration, in this instance, had tragic implications.

The League of the Iroquois had once been the dominant Indian power on the North American continent, and the Senecas had been the most vital element in the confederation. From their log-held seat along the Genesee River they had ranged thousands of miles on expeditions of conquest. They were cruel, but not incapable of loyalties; filthy, but not incompetent home builders; ingenious in all arts of the woods, and good agriculturists. They had a highly developed polity. They were oratorical. In battle, their physical vigor, their enormous courage, and their reputation as inveterate conquerors made them the despair of all red-skinned warriors.

Now, with the scratching of a white man's pen, they had been divested of all of their ancient domain except for a few plots set aside as reservations. These benefices, like the annuities they had been promised, were to continue "forever . . . so long as trees grow and rivers run."

But soon the Senecas along the Genesee felt restive and uncomfortable. White men were crowding in upon them. The ratification of the Big Tree Treaty, which enabled a settler to procure a perfect title to any lands he might purchase, had stimulated western migration. Pioneers surged into the Genesee Valley, where once they had arrived in small, hesitant, widely separated companies. They broadened the Indians' trails to roads. They built bridges over creeks, which the Indians had forded, swum across, or traversed in canoes; and as early as 1804 they were to span the Genesee with such a structure, at a point two miles west of the present village of Avon.

Their axes, wielded like flails in a grainfield, decimated the great forest in a period of two decades. And not long after this the Senecas on the Genesee, saddened by this desecration, and resigned to the fact that their happy hunting ground had become indisputably the province of white farmers, merchants, millers, wool carders, tavern-keepers and such, picked up and left. They moved for the most part to a reservation in the far western section of the state.

There these strong, proud people settled down to a life that was neither fully civilized nor completely Indian. It was a hybrid sort of existence, of sub-Caucasian shabbiness. In their reluctant acceptance of it, they abandoned their old freedoms and former savage dignities. The Senecas, who had made a great deal of American history, had fallen at last before the western course of empire.

17

WHEN Tom Morris, acting for his eminent father, extinguished at Big Tree the Senecas' title to most of what remained of their western lands, he did not turn over all of this great estate to the Holland Land Company. By previous arrangement, he set aside a 500,000-acre tract at the eastern edge of the Holland Purchase, which was known as the Morris Reserve.

This, the elder Morris may have thought, would be a sop to his clamoring creditors, his hedge against a debtors' prison, his ace in the hole. In recent years real estate had been the commodity in which he had put his greatest faith, and the Morris Reserve was a choice piece of real estate. This narrow tract, almost completely crossed and recrossed by the Genesee River, extended from the Pennsylvania border to the shore of Lake Ontario. For a good half of its length, south of the mouth of Canaseraga Creek, it was twelve miles wide; north of that point the lines were irregular. Lying centrally within its boundaries, and straddling the Genesee, was Gardeau Reservation, an enclave in which Mary Jemison had snugly ensconced herself at the expense of the Philadelphia financier and his son. It was a territory that later would yield riches in the form of lumber, farm produce, and oil, and Morris was aware of its great potential.

But this he could not very well exploit. He was deep in a morass of debt. And the years that remained to him were too few to allow him to extricate himself and struggle up to the firm ground of solvency. His Genesee lands, like all of his other properties, were heavily encumbered. One of his creditors was John Barker Church, a high-born Englishman, from whom he had borrowed a sizable sum. As security for the loan, Morris had turned over to Church's brother-in-law (because no alien was allowed to own real property in New York) 100,000 acres in the southern end of the Morris Reserve. This is identified on early maps of the Holland Purchase as the property of "A. Hamilton." It is interesting to observe that on these same maps, a little to the north and slightly to the west of the Morris Reserve, a similar acreage is marked off in the name of "A. Burr."

General Alexander Hamilton never actually owned property in the Genesee Country, and he never visited that section of the state. Colonel Aaron Burr, who, a few years later, was to kill Hamilton in a duel, not only briefly owned land in Western New York, but took an active part in a Machiavellian enterprise that had for its object the secession of that part of the state from its eastern half; and once, in company with his beloved and lovely daughter, Theodosia, he crossed the Genesee at a ford near what is now Avon, or by a rope ferry that Gilbert Barry operated a short distance north of the ford.

The occasion of this visit was an excursion to view the wonders of Niagara. Father and daughter, with suitable entourage, had come to the Genesee over a crude road that followed the old Indian trail from Albany, and that now winds across the state as Routes 5 and 20. Before proceeding to Niagara, they probably put up for a day or two at the tavern that Barry managed in conjunction with his ferry. It was a log structure, an inn of purely frontier character; but it offered to the traveling public the most bounteous hospitality to be found after leaving Canandaigua.

The tavern had been visited by French noblemen, perhaps by Louis Philippe, the future (and last) King of France, who explored a short stretch of the Genesee during his exile in America following the Terror, and by other notables, who sometimes remarked the drunkenness of its Boniface, but complained little about its food and accommodations. Barry had come to the river in 1789 to trade with the Indians at the nearby Seneca Village of Can-a-wau-gus, which means in their language "stinking waters." The reference had nothing to do with the Genesee. That stream, cocoa-colored but pure, was malodorous only at flood time, when rank and rotting vegetation was deposited on its seeping banks.

The "stinking waters" bubbled out of the earth, to form a small pond in a low area a mile or so east of the river. In a later day these sulphur springs were to give to the village of Avon a short-lived vogue as a watering place, a spa, particularly favored in midsummer by the "beauty and chivalry" of the South. During Gilbert Barry's time on the river (he was renowned as Avon's first permanent white settler), the vile-smelling waters were reputed to cure a cutaneous disorder suffered alike by Indians and whites, which the latter diagnosed as the "Genesee Itch," but which may in some instances have been measles. Swine, afflicted perhaps with parakeratosis, also itched, but itched less after wallowing in the sulphur pond and caking their hides with the pale, plasterlike mud of its shore.

During his short stay in Avon, Burr left Theodosia, probably in the care of Mrs. Gilbert Barry, a woman of excellent repute, to visit the falls of the Genesee, twenty miles north, around which the city of Rochester was later to take form. He and his daughter then pressed on to the west, to view the greater cataract at Niagara. Presumably they recrossed the river when they returned to the east, and that probably was Burr's last view of the Genesee

Valley. His contact with the region did not, however, end at once. He retained for some time his 100,000-acre tract on the Holland Purchase. And his ownership of this property was the indirect cause of a duel he fought with John B. Church, whose son later settled on the Genesee Valley lands that were held for a time by the elder Church in the name of Alexander Hamilton.

Burr, who was as prone to get into debt as to get into the beds of various and sundry ladies, owed money on his 100,000 acres in the Genesee country, and decided to sell the lands abroad and meet his obligation. He engaged an agent for this purpose, but the agent's sales efforts were thwarted by the New York law that prohibited ownership of real property by aliens.

The thing to do, Burr then decided, was to bring about the passage of an alien land bill. This was something that the Holland Land Company also desired, and Burr and that organization worked hand in glove to have a piece of legislation enacted which, as an "exhibit of venality . . . stands equal to any in the New York Assembly." Burr's contribution to the success of this effort was the influence he was able to exert upon his fellow members in the Assembly; the Holland Company aided the cause by handing out monies to those it believed would be co-operative and helpful.

Burr himself shared in this bounty. He was first advanced $5,500, euphemistically recorded in the company's book as a "loan," in "compensation for his efforts on behalf of the alien bill." Later, when a creditor to whom he owed $20,000, crudely pressed him for the money, he was provided, through the good offices of the Holland agent, Theophile Cazenove, with a bondsman, and the "teasing" by the creditor ceased.

This was another favor to reward the dapper little colonel for his services rendered in the Assembly to the Holland Land Company, and John B. Church spoke insinuatingly about it at a fashionable New York dinner. When word of this reached Burr, he demanded an apology. He was a crack pistol shot, and some men, at a similar juncture, might have compromised their honor in the hope of saving their skins.

Church was not of this stamp. He was a gentleman-adventurer. Ostensibly he had come to this country to espouse the cause of American freedom, with which, as indicated by his conduct, he genuinely sympathized; it was also believed that he had left his native land to escape arrest for shooting a man in a duel. In the exchange of notes that followed Burr's demands, Church admitted that his remark about the colonel's venality might have been indiscreet, but he refused to apologize for it. The men met, both fired pistols; each missed.

In the reconciliation that followed, Burr, punctilious on all points of the *code duello*, accepted Church's previous admission as satisfactory, on the theory that "an explanation might be received after shots were exchanged that would not be admissible before."

John B. Church did not take full title to the 100,000-acre estate at the lower end of the Genesee Valley even after the passage of the land bill that confirmed his ownership. It was held in Alexander Hamilton's name until, in 1799, Church's son, Philip, bid it in at a foreclosure sale at Canandaigua. By that time Robert Morris, who had given the property in security for the elder Church's loan, was in such straits, in the Philadelphia prison, that he was constrained to advise a correspondent that if he wrote again, to "be kind enough to pay the postage on your letters, for I have not a cent to spare from the means of subsistence."

A year or two after Philip Church had secured for his father the 100,000-acre tract in the Morris Reserve, he made a reconnaissance of the property in company with Moses Van Campen, a famous border fighter during the Revolutionary War, who was then living in a frontier settlement at Almond, now a village in Allegany County, a few miles east of the Genesee River.

Profit was the purpose of this expedition. If Philip would consent to explore the recently acquired property and prepare it for sale and settlement, his father told him that he might have half of the acreage. The proposal was promptly accepted.

Then in his early twenties, Philip Church, at first flush, would hardly seem the person to entrust with a mission into the untracked wilds of the upper Genesee Valley. He was bright, perceptive, personable, a good cricketer, and excellent at other sports pursued by gentlemen. He had courage. But his youth, for the most part, had been the sheltered existence of a son whose parents were credited with the possession of considerable wealth, and whose manner of living, both in New York and in England, was consonant with their reputation. They were able to indulge young Philip, and apparently they had no reluctance about doing so. It might be said that he was born, and raised, with a silver spoon in his mouth.

His birth, incidentally, had taken place, not in England, but in Boston, two years after the signing of the Declaration of Independence.

John Church had come to America during the early days of the struggle between the Colonists and the mother country, under— for reasons that have been hinted, but not clearly defined—the *nom de guerre* of John Carter. He had wealth, talent, and an old-world urbanity, derived from his position in England, which allowed him quickly to meet upon equal footing such leaders of the American cause as Robert Morris, Jeremiah Wadsworth of Connecticut (who was providing subsistence for the Continental troops), Hamilton, Franklin, Lafayette, and even General Washington. He was made a commissary general for the French forces aiding the American cause. He became friendly with General Philip Schuyler, the doughty patroon of the upper Hudson, and married the general's oldest daughter, the sister of Mrs. Alexander Hamilton. A year later, their son was born.

Shortly after the war, Church took his family to Paris, where his wife, a gay, spirited, and intelligent woman excited the attention of many notables in the French capital, one of whom was the frankly enamored Thomas Jefferson, then serving the United States as minister to France. From Paris, after a time, the Churches crossed the channel to England, and took a country place on the Thames. Still a British subject, Church soon engaged in politics, and won a seat in Parliament; not a trivial achievement, for a man who had recently opposed his own nation in a war which cost it half an empire.

During his family's stay in England, Philip Church was enrolled in Eton, of all the fine public schools of that country, the one professedly that excelled in the production of gentlemen. Later, he studied law in the Middle Temple and continued this pursuit in a well-known New York law office, when, in 1797, he recrossed the Atlantic with his parents and made his residence with them in a fashionable house on lower Broadway.

His activities in the brief interim between his return to America and the time, very early in the new century, when he permanently removed to the Genesee Valley, were varied. He was admitted to the New York State bar. He procured a captaincy in the American Army at the time when war with France seemed imminent. He served for a period as secretary to his uncle by marriage, Alexander Hamilton. He acted as second for his cousin, Philip Hamilton, when that youth was killed in a duel on the same ground at Weehawken where his father was to suffer a mortal wound three years later. Church was a prominent member of New York's social "younger set."

Then, suddenly discarding his satin knee breeches, his broadcloth coat, his varnished pumps, his expensive linen, he was espied by the members of Moses Van Campen's family, in the Van Campen corn lot, vigorously shaking wood lice from his rough frontiersman's garments, and picking wood ticks from his flesh.

Philip Church had come to the Genesee Valley to solicit Van Campen's aid in the survey and division of the 100,000-acre tract. The meeting of these two men, so opposite in birth and breeding, developed quickly into a close friendship that ended only with Van Campen's death. It also marked the beginning of a new career for Church, who turned his back upon the refinements of urban living to establish himself as a pioneer citizen of the upper Genesee.

18

P HILIP CHURCH's guide, surveyor, counselor, and good friend, Moses Van Campen, is remarked in the nomenclature of the Genesee. A creek bearing his surname flows into the river at a point a short distance south of Belvidere, a hamlet across the river from Philip Church's house, for which it was named. The recognition is deserved. Van Campen was not only one of the most colorful, but one of the most useful pioneers in the southern half of the Morris Reserve.

He often said that his adolescent education was obtained more from the tomahawk, the rifle, and the scalping knife than from textbooks and the instruction of schoolmasters. Born in New Jersey, he was reared in Pennsylvania's Wyoming Valley. It was a blood-stained frontier. Connecticut and Pennsylvania partisans had fought there over land rights; there the Indians and British had perpetrated one of the bloodiest outrages of the Revolution. Van Campen first saw the Genesee River when he marched up to it, and forded it, as a member of General Sullivan's punitive expedition against the Iroquois in 1779. That was a march of triumph. Three years later he returned to the river, this time as a prisoner of the Indians.

In the interim, the Senecas had tapped him for an unenviable distinction. He had become the object of their greatest aversion, their Enemy No. 1. But they did not know, when they led him captive to their large river village at Caneadea, a few miles north of the slight rise of land above the Genesee where Philip Church later was to build his home, that Van Campen was the quarry they had been seeking for months.

He had been their prisoner before, but had slipped the noose. Following the Sullivan Campaign, Van Campen had gone back to his Pennsylvania home to help protect the Wyoming settlers from British and Indian raids. One day as he stood with his father and small brother in the former's clearing, a party of Senecas came whooping out of the woods, speared the older man to death, and tomahawked the boy when he shrieked an anguished protest at the slaughter of his father.

The incursion was so sudden and unexpected that Moses Van Campen had no time to grasp a weapon or strike a defensive blow. That he was not slain on the spot may be attributed to the vagaries of temper and unpredictable divergencies that often marked the Indians' behavior even while engaged in the most cruel and fiendish enterprises. He was struck, but not with a lethal weapon, bound to one of his captors, and led off through the woods.

As the march continued, the small Indian party pillaged several isolated cabins, murdered some of the occupants, and took two male captives. With one of these, a frontiersman named Pence, Van Campen collaborated on a plan to escape. It succeeded when he cut the cords that bound him and the other prisoners with a knife which an Indian had dropped and which Van Campen had secreted under his foot.

Once free of their bonds, Van Campen slew five of the sleeping

Senecas with a hatchet, and Pence shot four dead with guns that were stacked round a nearby tree. There were ten Indians in all. The lone survivor made a run for it. His name was John Mohawk. Van Campen, as the saying was, "lent him his hatchet," and Mohawk fled through the woods with a deep gash in the base of his neck, which ever after was to put his head awry.

After this sanguinary episode, Van Campen returned to the border wars. His reputation as an Indian killer went with him. John Mohawk's out-of-joint neck was an advertisement of the white champion's prowess; and Mohawk, with an Indian's keen memory for the figure and countenance of an enemy, could be trusted to publish through the Senecas' camps a vivid description of the man who had caused his disfigurement.

Legends that have a Paul Bunyanish quality have been woven round the early career of Moses Van Campen. The extravagant character of some give credulity a stern test. But there is no question of the valor and resourcefulness of this agile, powerful man, whose heavy nose slanted down almost to tip his upper lip; whose mouth, in resolution, was as straight and hard as if it had been cut from stone; and whose eye, at the sight of a hated red man, glittered like a basilisk's. He was the sort of a fellow one would desire to have at one's side if one were in a tight corner. He must have been as durable as corundum; and his weird must have been blessed.

At a time when geriatrics was unknown to medical science, Van Campen achieved the noble age of ninety-two years by meeting a series of pragmatic tests. He outwitted the murderous designs of the Indians, came unscathed through battle, evaded the normal hazards of the woods, and repulsed the insinuating attacks of disease aided only by potions of stewed herbs and the juju of witch doctors.

In the spring of 1782, Van Campen, with the rank of lieutenant, was in charge of a reconnoitering detail of twenty Pennsylvania militiamen that was ambushed by a large Indian party commanded by a British officer. The odds against the Americans were four to one. Three of the civilian soldiers ran away. Nine others were killed, and several wounded, in the short, bitter struggle that ensued.

Encircled, with no chance of escape, and death certain for the remaining members of his detachment if the fight continued, Van Campen chose the alternative of surrender. It was a desperate choice; how desperate he realized when, bound hand and foot, he saw the Indians split the skulls of four of his wounded soldiers, who would have been a bother on the march.

After burying their own dead and scalping the enemy dead, the Indians started west. They had come from Niagara and the Genesee, and there they would return. As he moved along the trail in tight custody, Van Campen had reason to be deeply concerned about his destiny. He could not be sure that some one of his captors would not discover that he was the hated and hotly sought killer who had dispatched five of his keepers at the time of his first capture and "lent his hatchet" to John Mohawk. Indeed, since this was a party of Senecas, he could not be certain that John Mohawk himself was not a member of it. In that event, he would have no illusions about his fate. It would be slow torture.

Reaching the Genesee River near its headwaters, the Indians turned north. Following a path trod smooth by generations of moccasined feet, they soon arrived at a woods on the bank of the stream where a veritable pigeon harvest was in progress. The scene of this phenomenon has never been precisely defined. It probably was a full day's march south of Caneadea. That would place it in present Allegany County, a short distance north of the Pennsylvania border.

Indians had trekked to the pigeon woods, as they were called, from far and near. In many instances they had brought their families, for the killing was a gala. Hundreds of thousands of handsomely colored, long-tailed birds, the now extinct passenger pigeon, had come to roost on the branches of oak and beech trees and to feed on the mast that lay under the matting of forest leaves. Foolish in their gregariousness, they rested on their perches so close to one another that often the branches broke under their weight.

They had no mechanism for defense, but trusted their security to numbers. In this attitude, they were an easy prey. The Indians killed with clubs the birds on the lower branches. They netted them by hundreds. At night, they excited the pigeons into panic by waving burning brands in the air, and knocked them down with long poles when they swirled crazily about the flames in thick, curtainlike flights. Squabs and grown pigeons were roasted over countless fires. In order that the breast meat might not sour, squaws ripped out the crops of birds that were to be packed and taken home. The woods rang with the happy shouts of Indians, whom this feast of plenty had put into a lively humor; they stank with rotting pigeon viscera and the guano that covered the forest floor in layers.

Although the Indians' hostility toward Van Campen had softened during the last stages of the march, the prisoner realized, joining the concourse at pigeon woods, that a new hazard confronted him. Since most of the savages on the grounds were Senecas, Van Campen was fearful, as he had been since he was first taken captive, that if John Mohawk was not present to touch him with the finger of death, some other savage might identify him from Mohawk's description.

Intensely occupied with the killing and eating of pigeons during the daylight hours, the Indians at first gave little attention to Van Campen and the other captives. But at night, in order that all of the savages might closely observe them, they were disposed about the campfire in such positions that their faces and persons were brilliantly illuminated, much as prisoners in a police line-up are placed under pitiless lights for the scrutiny of detectives.

When the inspection was over, Van Campen breathed easier. It had been an ordeal, but he believed that he again had escaped detection. He was mistaken. Before he was returned to the Indians whose captive he was, a young man who seemed an Indian in every aspect, except for a slight variance in facial structure, slipped down beside him. In unaccented English, he whispered that he knew Van Campen was the notorious killer sought by the Senecas, but promptly assured the startled prisoner that only one other person in the pigeon woods (outside of Van Campen's own men) possessed this knowledge. The other informed person was a Dutchman, who had been captured by another group of Indians, and who, until Van Campen's informant had shut him up, had been moaning a threnody, "Van Campen, vot kilt de Enchens is here, and ve'll all be burnt to de stake, every tran bugger of us. Yes ve vill, dat's vot oney way."

The man—or the youth, since he was still in his teens—at Van Campen's side was also a captive. That at least had been his condition at the time he had first come among the Indians. But he had no apprehension that the term of his destiny was near, and little complaint about his fortune. He had achieved the status of an adopted son of the Senecas. They called him Hoc-sa-go-wan, or "Handsome Boy," for his comeliness had not only been feelingly remarked by the squaws, who had never seen a youth of any color with such agreeable features, but by the stolid chiefs as well. Welsh by heredity, Horatio Jones had found so congenial the companionship of the savages, and so suitable to his temperament the hard, free life of the forest, that one might have believed the blood of the French *coureurs de bois,* once the foremost white woodsmen on the continent, coursed through his veins.

"What are they going to do with me?" Van Campen asked, after Jones had revealed his identity, and explained his position.

"I don't know; I can't tell. *But they don't know you,*" Jones repeated with emphasis; and those words, Van Campen often said in later years—when both men were residents along the Genesee, and two of the upper river's most celebrated characters—were the happiest he had ever heard.

19

MOSES VAN CAMPEN's hatred for the Indians did not soften until the vespertine shadows gathered about him and his long life entered its final stage. He was not a man who forgot easily or forgave readily. His memory of the day that he was forced, by his merciless captors, to witness the murder of his father and small brother continued for a long time as a green and living vision. He could not forget the incident of his second capture, when his wounded soldiers were slain in cold blood because the Indians would have found them burdensome on the march. His hate was implacable. Believing that the only good Indian was a dead Indian, Van Campen was dedicated to an effort to effect the extinction of the race. He fought Indians. He killed a quantity of them. He strung their dried scalps on the waistband of his breeches, even as the savages themselves displayed such grisly tokens as symbols of their prowess.

Contrary to Van Campen's attitude, Horatio Jones, who was to live along the Genesee for many years, and become as much a part of the river's legend as Van Campen, held no aversion to the savages. It is unlikely that he ever killed an Indian, and almost from the start of his captivity he enjoyed favors rarely granted by his red-skinned captors to their prisoners. Taken in youth, tutored in Indian ways during his impressionable teens, Jones so readily adjusted himself to his new life that he became in time a figure of importance among the Senecas, serving as their interpreter, sometimes as their counsel, often as the arbiter of their intratribal disputes. His career as an adopted member of the tribe had its grim and tragic moments. There were other times when its baroque and lively grotesqueries gave to it the aspect of a Walt Disney fantasy.

Jones was the son of a Quaker mother and a father who served a small community in southeastern Pennsylvania as a blacksmith and gunmaker. Brought up on the edge of the forest, the boy acquired the habits of the woods, learned to shoot, robbed birds' nests, chased small game, fished in the streams, and so successfully resisted the little opportunity afforded him for formal learning that he could fluently speak the Indian language before he could read or write his own.

Early in the Revolutionary War, when he was fourteen years of age, Jones enlisted as a fifer in a company of minutemen. He saw no action. The company passed the winter in camp, where the youth may have learned the ballads of the barrack's room, and surely heard its bawdries. He found this first taste of military life agreeable. Two years later, violating the stern mandate of his father that he remain home and make guns rather than carry one in battle, he joined the Bedford Rangers, organized in a Pennsylvania county west of his own; and a few months later, serving with a small scouting detail near the Juniata River, some distance northwest of Harris Ferry (Harrisburg), he was captured by a party of Senecas and taken to the Genesee.

The first stages of the march were wicked. Jones saw the

captain of the detail, who had been wounded in the skirmish that had preceded capture, first beaten with a club when he failed to keep up with the other marchers, and then, when his steps still flagged, killed with a hatchet and scalped. Others of the wounded shared the captain's dreadful fate. There was no food until an Indian shot a bear, the raw entrails of which were thrown to the prisoners as the savages would toss bones to a dog.

But in this passage along the wooded trails, Jones was cheerful and often helpful. Captives carried the heavier burdens of their captors. It was part of their vassalage. Jones not only stalwartly managed the pack that had been consigned to him, but he frequently assumed part of the load of some less robust companion. This act of kindness and—more importantly, from the Indians' viewpoint—display of strength, had been remarked by Jack Berry, a halfbreed, who was a prominent member of the Indian party. Berry had taken an interest in the handsome youth from the start, and shortly after his capture he had placed a belt of wampum over Jones's shoulder with a gesture that was almost solicitous. Wondering what it signified, Jones nevertheless had been at pains to preserve the token. When the Indians and their captives trailed down from the hills to the east bank of the Genesee, across the stream from the Indian village of Caneadea, Berry moved close to Jones to warn him of an imminent peril and to advise him how best to meet it.

After the prisoners forded the river, they would be required to run the gantlet. This was a ritual of both joy and hate—the joy derived from beating, maiming, and often killing hated enemies. It was a ceremony in which the prisoners who ran through the lines expiated the offenses they themselves had committed against the Senecas and those perpetrated by their former comrades-in-arms. And for some favored captives, of whom Horatio Jones was one, it was the final trial before adoption.

Berry indicated a long structure at the lower end of a slope on the far side of the river. It was larger and much better made than the ordinary bark dwelling in the village. It had been built by artisans sent out from Niagara by the British, probably at a time when the Indians were hinting at defection, and it served both as the Senecas' council house and as a symbol of the Western Door of the League of the Iroquois.

A white flag fluttered above the building, to identify it as a place of importance, and the house itself marked the goal of the cruel race. Those who reached its door, and passed inside, might be reasonably sure of safety. But the prospect before the captives, as they waded through the shallow waters of the Genesee, and girded themselves for what truly would be a run for their lives, was hardly a promising one.

The return of the band of Indians had been heralded by couriers before Jones and the other white prisoners even knew that they were approaching the Genesee. The warriors had been gone for several weeks. The lack of knowledge of their movements and the uncertainty of their successes had excited fears and apprehensions. But now, as the expedition was returning in good numbers, with several prisoners, there was cause to rejoice and a reason for festivities. The stay-at-homes adorned themselves in their gaudiest raiment; rubbed bear grease in their hair to give it luster; beat kettles, shook gourd rattles, whooped, danced, and brought forth weapons of various sorts to employ against the unfortunate gantlet racers.

There was a trick to gantlet running, and Jones was told about it by Berry. He was not to go off with the first flight, at the starting signal—the cry of "joggo;" but to wait a moment and follow the second last runner. Then he was to scoot along so close to one of the lines of assailants that those who had struck at the runner in front would have neither time to recoil and strike at Jones, nor, because of his closeness to them, room in which to wield their weapons. The trick worked. Jones profited at the expense of the runner directly in front of him, whose head was slashed off with a sword a moment before he reached the threshhold of the council house. Blinded by blood from the victim's severed arteries, but suffering only minor hurts, Jones stumbled into the council house and virtually fell into the arms of a woman who, he later learned, was to be his foster mother. She wrapped a blanket round him and took him to her cabin.

This was to be a new phase in the variable career of Horatio Jones, and one quite compatible with his temperament. The belt of wampum that he still wore had belonged to the Indian woman. She had given it to Berry when the expedition had left the Genesee, with the request that if he found a likely captive, he place the wampum on him and bring him home. Her son had been killed in some recent foray, and she wanted a white youth to take his place in her cabin.

Captured by the Senecas in early summer, 1781, Jones continued in their custody until their Great Spirit—as they believed—spoke to the Whirlwind, quieting it, and the Revolutionary War came to a close. His adoption was a benign arrangement. The Seneca polity was divided into a number of clans, and Horatio was inducted into one called the Hawk, of which his "mother" was a member. Her feeling for her adopted son was as tender as her affection for her natural issue. Jones was called by the Indians "Handsome Boy." He was of medium height, very well formed, muscular, and agile; he had near-reddish hair and a fresh complexion which made him a rare specimen. He was something for his "mother" to pet and cherish. He also must have been a beau of considerable vogue in and around the Seneca village at Caneadea.

The other prisoners who had survived the gantlet were taken to Niagara and given over to the British. They apparently were looked upon as an inferior lot, unworthy of adoption, but good for the bounty the Redcoats were paying for war prizes brought in alive and for the scalps of dead ones.

Jones was honored in captivity. His adoption allowed him much more freedom than a penitentiary "trusty," and he probably had numerous opportunities to escape and return to his own people. But the life of the woods suited him. His most competent biographer related that one night he stole away from the Indian village, intending to return to civilization. Undetected, he had traveled several miles, and his escape was assured. Then his conscience began to worry him like a bogy. He sat down in the woods to debate with himself a moral issue. Was he playing square, he asked himself, sneaking away from his captors, who had trusted him and who had become his friends? He decided that he wasn't. In the morning he went back to the Indians who called him brother.

Even after the momentous news of Cornwallis' surrender at Yorktown had reached the Genesee, Jones, still satisfied with his savage career, remained with the Senecas. He continued as their fellow tribesman, presently with the insignia of chief, until, the year following the signing of the Treaty of Paris, Iroquois leaders and the United States Commissioners signed the Treaty of Fort Stanwix which provided, among other things, for the release by the Indians of all white prisoners.

His escapades during the early stages of his captivity were numerous. Although his adopted mother loved him dearly, Horatio's good looks, athletic skills, and perhaps his easy way with the ladies, made him the envy of some of the younger Senecas; and there were times when they menaced him with tomahawks, attempted to push him over a steep cliff, threw hard objects at him, and practiced other harassments. He had learned very quickly that might, more than pure justice, was the rule of the Senecas; that a strong arm and a bold heart were the qualities most respected in an individual. So, one day when a young heckler threw a foul substance into his soup, Jones grasped by its long, protruding stem a squash that was being roasted in the fire, felled the offending youth, raised his shirt, and blistered his flesh from buttocks to shoulders with the hot squash. That ended *that* nonsense.

He outwrestled the Indians, knowing "civilized" holds that allowed him to flip them on their backs with ease; he outran them.

And the time came when he scored a victory of the heart over a chief, not of his own tribe, but of the allied Mohawks.

Jones by this time had become a man of distinction among the Senecas. The prestige he had acquired by his physical prowess had been enhanced by his usefulness as an interpreter and by his wisdom as a counsel.

His triumph in love, if so it might be defined, was achieved when a white girl who had been taken from her Pennsylvania home, was brought to the Genesee village where Jones was living with the Senecas, by a Mohawk chief, who wanted her for his wife.

Carnal abuse of women was not one of the Indians' common crimes. They were not rapists. But the girl captive, whose name was Sarah Whitmore, was sure that if she did not take the Mohawk chief as her spouse, he would take her scalp as a loving memento. She appealed, in her desperate dilemma, to Jones.

Jones had had an Indian wife, or consort, who had borne him a child. But she had died the year before. He was foot-loose and fancy free. Sarah, who was nineteen years old, had a graceful figure, clear olive skin, dark eyes, and a gentle voice. He would rescue her from the Mohawk chief and take her to wife himself.

The pair was first married in a pagan ceremony in the Indian village. Later, after both had been granted full freedom under the terms of the Treaty of Fort Stanwix, they were married again by the Reverend Samuel Kirkland, Protestant missionary, whose life was unsparingly devoted to providing both spiritual and secular comforts for the members of the Six Nations.

Jones and Sarah settled for a time in a clearing east of Seneca Lake. But the Senecas came for them. They wanted Horatio near their villages on the Genesee, where he could help them, as he had during the days of his captivity, as an interpreter and counsel. They deeded to him in time a large tract of land in the township of Leicester, not far from Little Beard's Town and the pretty, dell-like spot now commemorated as the scene of the Boyd and Parker torture. He never lived again away from the river, but died on his own property at the age of seventy-two years, sound in worldly goods, rich in experiences, commended for good works, and the father of four children by Sarah Whitmore, twelve by a second white wife, Elizabeth Starr, and of at least one Indian by-blow.

20

THE chance meeting of Horatio Jones and Moses Van Campen at the pigeon harvest on the upper Genesee, when Jones was the favored son of the Senecas and Van Campen their captive, developed into a friendship that continued as long as both men lived.

In later life, when the two were prominent and prosperous burghers of the Genesee Valley, they made a point of meeting at least once each year to reminisce on the adventures of their early manhood. They had much to talk about. And perhaps their liveliest discussion was excited by the recollection of their encounter in the pigeon woods, the only adventure which they had shared together, and by corollary experiences after they were separated that briefly put the life of each in jeopardy.

Jones remained with the pigeon hunters after Van Campen was taken to the Seneca village at Caneadea by the Indian party that had captured him upriver. There he received from the

Indians themselves the answer Jones had been unable to give
him to the question, "What are they going to do with me?"

They were going to have him run the gantlet. If he survived
that trial, he might be taken to Niagara and given over to the
British for a bounty.

He survived it handsomely. Despair was an emotion that
Van Campen seemed to think sinful, and he refused to countenance it. He was never more on his mettle than when the odds
were overwhelmingly against him. The gantlet was merely
another challenge made by his hated enemies. He had successfully met others; he would successfully meet this one.

Big, powerful, and swift of foot, he ducked, dodged, shielded
his face with his hands like a boxer, and ran almost to the end
of the bristling lines of Indians without being maimed or dealt a
deadly blow. Then he saw his way to the safety of the council
house blocked by two Indian maidens.

The time was to come when Moses Van Campen, as a regular
guest at the home of Mr. and Mrs. Philip Church, was to cultivate
the graces of polite society. No guest was more welcome at
Belvidere than he. He may have danced the quadrille at the
soirées that were to become common occasions at that elegant
residence. He must have known about fish forks. He probably had
silk hose and lace cuffs for special dinner parties.

But the day he ran the gantlet at Caneadea was before his
contact with the gentlemanly Etonian, Church, and his well-
bred bride; Van Campen was still a rough-and-tumble frontiersman, with gnarled hands, hair in his ears, and little sense of the
exquisite shadings of drawing-room deportment. In his precarious
situation chivalry was not to govern his actions. The two Indian
ladies had not taken their obstructive position with any notion of
playing beanbag or kiss-the-pillow. Each was armed with a stout
whip.

If they stopped him, even momentarily, someone in the line
might have time to deliver a telling blow, or some pursuer to cut
him down from behind with a hatchet. He ran straight at the

ladies. One he felled with a blow of his fist, the other he kicked in the stomach, tumbling her over her fallen sister. Hurdling the pair, he burst into the council house. He had achieved a double triumph. He had saved his own skin, and he had given the Indians a show which greatly pleased them. It was broad farce. They hugged themselves with delight; they guffawed as if their sides would split at the plight of the groaning, pain-laden maidens with the whips.

Shortly after this, Van Campen was taken to Fort Niagara. At about the same time he left Caneadea, John Mohawk arrived at the pigeon woods, excitedly to tell the gathered Senecas that the man who had "lent him his hatchet" and grossly disfigured him, had slipped through their fingers. Mohawk had learned about Van Campen's capture several days before. He had hurried through the forest in the hope of overtaking the party that had, unknown to its members, acquired the Seneca's great enemy.

A hue and cry arose at the receipt of this intelligence. There was a gnashing of teeth. There was a girding on of weapons. Swift runners went forward to Caneadea. But by then, Van Campen was on the trail to Niagara. Jones was brought before the chiefs. He had talked with Van Campen. Why, the furious chiefs demanded, had he not at once identified the hated killer of his Seneca brothers?

During the interview, Handsome Boy was probably in greater danger of losing his life than at any other time since his capture. It required tact, polemics, and a very bold front to convince the Indians that he had not been in collusion with Van Campen. Succeeding in the end, he fully regained the good graces of his fellow tribesmen.

Van Campen, for his part, reached Niagara without incident. There he was turned over to Colonel John Butler, commander of the fort. A few days later a delegation of howling Senecas approached the place. They demanded the surrender of Van Campen. When Butler refused, they attempted to bargain for him. They offered fourteen white prisoners for the one they wanted to

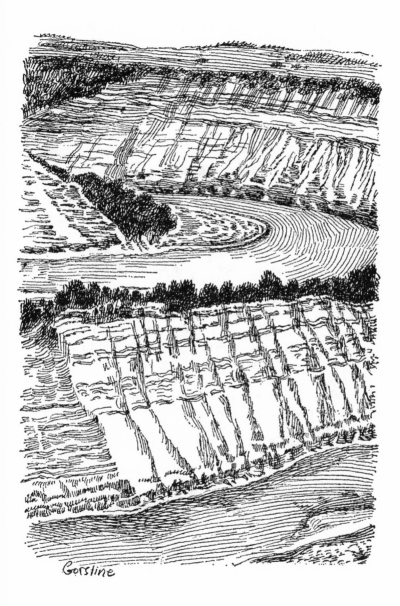

Gorstine

quarter and burn. Butler still refused. Van Campen, so the story goes, was then offered a commission in the British forces, which he declined with a Homeric declaration: "Give me the stake, the tomahawk, the scalping knife sooner than a British Commission."

Instead, he was sent to a military prison in Montreal. He remained there until close to the end of the Revolutionary War, when he and a number of other American prisoners were released upon their pledge not again to take up arms against the British.

Because of his close relationship with Philip Church, Van Campen presently built a fine home in Angelica, a short distance east of the Genesee, on one of the river's affluents, three miles from the Church home at Belvidere. Here, besides practicing the surveyor's craft, he was active in various civic enterprises, and the holder of a variety of public offices which included Excise Commissioner, Judge of the Court of Common Pleas, and County Treasurer.

He left Angelica to live in semiretirement in Dansville, a village still farther east of the Genesee on another of the river's tributaries, and there he died in the autumn of 1849. He was buried in the picturesque little cemetery in Angelica, not far from the grave that was later to be occupied by his friend and patron, Philip Church.

This epitaph, followed by two stanzas of verse dedicated to Van Campen's soldierly career, is graven on a plain marble tombstone:

"A brave officer of the Revolutionary War, An Eminent Citizen and an Enlightened Christian."

Having lived with the Indians as a captive along the Genesee, Horatio Jones continued his close association with them after his release, and his ultimate return, as a free man, to that river.

Early in his post-Revolutionary career, he was appointed an official interpreter to the Senecas by George Washington, with a salary of $400 a year. In this capacity Jones served at several treaties where delegates from the Iroquois Confederacy negotiated alternately with representatives of the United States government and with high-pressure real-estate operators who were trying to gobble up all of the Senecas' lands.

The real-estate operators were not wholly successful. They did not get all of the lands. At the Big Tree Treaty on the Genesee in 1797, and prior to that, at the last general council ever held between the United States and the Six Nations, certain acreages in Western New York were set aside as Seneca Reservations. The general council, held at Canandaigua, in 1794, had been ordered by President Washington, and it was presided over by Timothy Pickering, Washington's friend and deputy. Jones was one of the interpreters.

At Canandaigua, the President—through his deputy—put the national seal to a promise that the "United States will never claim the same [the reserved territory], nor disturb the Seneca nation." It was a pledge given at a moment when the youthful republic very much needed the friendship of the Seneca Indians, who were being urged by the British in Canada to strike again at the usurpers of their western lands. It was made by our first great national leader, whose reputation for honesty was later to be impressed upon every American schoolboy.

Now, in May, 1962, Washington's promise has been shamefully dishonored by the commencement of construction of the Kinzua Dam across the Allegheny River, as part of a flood-control program for the Ohio River Basin. The resultant $100,-000,000 reservoir will extend from Salamanca, New York, into Pennsylvania. When this outrage is consummated, 9,000 acres— most of the good land on the Allegany Indian Reservation—will be inundated and 600 Senecas will lose the homes from which they were never to be displaced. One might expect by now that the trusting, ingenuous Indian would have learned that, when used by his white cousins, the words "forever" and "never" are mere rhetorical terms, adverbs of expediency. After being gulled, fleeced, and lied to by his white cousins for three hundred years, he had learned that the robbery is not yet ended.

Jones was trusted by the Indians. He served them officially not only as interpreter, but as an Indian agent for the United States Government. He had once been a chief of their tribe; now he had the rank of captain in the military. Red Jacket always wanted him at hand when he made a public address. He believed that Horatio effectively translated his sonorous periods and gave proper flourish to his imagery. He called the interpreter "son," and was a frequent visitor at the homes Jones successively built along or near the Genesee.

Addicted to the bottle, Red Jacket occasionally was found in a comatose state in a backwoods tavern, or lying insensible under a tree when his presence—and words—were needed at some conference or treaty signing. It would occasionally be Jones's task to shake the orator out of his vinous lethargy and lead him to the place where he was supposed to speak. He probably understood the Indians better than any other white man on the Genesee. He was genuinely fond of them; his influence with them was considerable, as the following incident indicates.

There was a brave along the river with a malformed great toe. It curled up like a reaping hook. Even when the foot was covered with a moccasin, the toe continually snagged in tough grasses and underbrush, tripping and throwing its owner. He appealed to Jones to correct the disorder.

All that could be done, Jones said, was to cut off the toe. "How do that?" the Indian wanted to know. Horatio told him to get a wooden block, a sharp chisel, and a mallet. When these were provided, the Indian, under Jones's instructions, put the troublesome toe on the block, placed the blade of the chisel against it, struck the head of the chisel with the mallet. And he leaped into the air screaming, "I did what you told me!"

But the toe was gone, Jones reminded him. He'd have no more trouble with *that*.

Although there were times when Jones's career in the Genesee Valley took on the aspect of caricature, his contributions to the development of that region were important. He was not highly thought of by the rigorous and righteous Timothy Pickering, who suspected that Jones's influence with the Senecas was exerted more for his own benefit than for the benefit of the United States Government which was paying him his salary. And there came a time when even his old friends, the Senecas, complained bitterly to President James Madison that Jones and another Indian agent, and former Indian captive, Jasper Parrish, were practicing skulduggery against the Indians. The protest, which was signed by fifty chiefs, with Red Jacket's mark at the top of the list, classified Jones and Parrish with other white-skinned malefactors whose "wickedness and cruelty to the Red Men" would cause their own God to "burn them all up in a great big fire."

But Pickering's suspicions were never proved, and the charges laid against Jones by the Senecas (they specifically claimed that Parrish had abstracted goods entrusted to him by the Government for distribution to the Indians) were sketchy and without support.

Jones was a counselor for Mary Jemison. She liked Horatio. Most women did. She trusted him implicitly. He had helped her to clinch the title to the 17,927 acres given to her by Thomas Morris at the Big Tree Treaty in 1797. Red Jacket had vigorously opposed the gift, probably on the grounds that although Mary was an adopted daughter of the Senecas, her white skin disqualified her from owning such a huge tract of Seneca lands. Jones countervailed Red Jacket's opposition by pointing out that it was not the Indians, but the white Morrises, who were giving Mary the property.

In 1823, Jones was present when Mary Jemison sold to two of her neighbors, Jellis Clute and Micah Brooks, all of her Genesee lands, with the exception of a strip two miles long and one mile wide, which she retained for herself and her heirs. Eight years later, finding the care of real property a burden at her age, she left her beloved Genesee for the Seneca reservation at Buffalo; and there she died, in the autumn of 1833, a pagan until almost the final hour of life, when the Reverend Asher Wright, a Protestant missionary, revived her memory of the Lord's Prayer, which she had learned in childhood. With tears trickling down her worn and wrinkled cheeks, Mary repeated after the missionary the abiding words that Christ had given to his disciples. At death she embraced the faith that she had persistently resisted in life. She was buried with Christian ceremony on the reservation.

Years later, her bones were reinterred in ground high above the Genesee, in Letchworth State Park, a large section of which had once been included in the "white woman's" great holdings along the river. The grave is marked by a marble monument surmounted by a bronze statue which represents Mary Jemison at the time she was brought to the Genesee Valley as a Seneca captive.

She is far better known than Jones, Van Campen, the picaresque Indian Allan, or any other early settler along the river. Her legend is the greatest. Each year thousands of visitors to Letchworth Park read the biographical data carved on the marble monument at her grave and admire the statue above it. In a way, this tiny, untutored Irish woman, personifies the Genesee; and the book-length story of her life, which has gone through many editions and been translated into numerous languages, more than any other medium has spread the fame of the river's lovely, rolling valley.

21

THE elegant land agent, Captain Charles Williamson, was about to quit the Genesee Valley at the time Philip Church, under the escort of Moses Van Campen, first saw the river upon whose bank he was to make his future home.

Had Williamson remained, the two men might have hit it off splendidly. Although the land agent had in no direct way been the cause of Church's migration to the west, the latter was the type of pioneer Williamson had hoped would settle in this opening wilderness. It had been his notion right along to have the country dominated by feudal land owners, who would live in large houses, promote the field sports of gentlemen, and adopt a style of country living similar to that of Merrie Old England. For such a program, Church was well equipped. He had the lands, the means, and the background. He might have been the agent's beau ideal.

Later in the first decade of the new century, Church erected on the east bank of the Genesee a larger and much more elaborate home than any that so far had been built in the river's valley. It looked across the narrow, curling channel of the stream to a vast stand of white pine, the indigenous wood of the region. Church called his new home Belvidere.

Located twenty odd miles south of the site of the village of Williamsburg, Belvidere is as handsome and useful at the time of this writing as it was on the day of its housewarming, more than a century and a half ago. It is occupied by owners who deeply respect its tradition, and who have had the good taste to preserve its character. Fortune, the fickle Gypsy, gave lasting value to the house that Church built; the village of Williamsburg, designed by the flamboyant Pulteney land promoter as the great trading mart on the Genesee River, is now meadowland and a small, fenced-in graveyard.

The upper Genesee Valley country which included the Church estate was more rugged and less inviting to settlers than the soft, rich, sometimes treeless river lands farther north, which the Wadsworth brothers were cultivating with skill and selling, when the fancy struck them, at profit. Land sales were sluggish. But the slow development of the greater part of the Church property was not, in the opinion of Orasmus Turner, entirely attributable to the rough terrain. Turner wrote:

. . . settlements [in the upper Genesee Valley] progressed slowly at first, especially on Church's tract. . . . We know of no reason for the tardy progress of the settlement of Mr. Church's Tract, as the proprietor located himself on the premises in 1804, and expended large sums of money to give it its primary impetus, unless it was that Mr. Church, who was educated in Europe and had associated with the aristocracy, was better qualified to support the high character of his hospitable mansion, overflowing with the substantials, and well stored with all the delicacies and luxuries produced in or imported to this region; than to mete out the hills and dales of the earth by the acre, to the huge-framed axe-men, and long limbed Bill Purdys of the exploring pioneers.

It is true that, as a real-estate operator, Philip Church lacked the vaunting sales techniques and promotional skills that Charles Williamson employed, often at enormous expense, in the exploitation of the Pulteney estate. But there was nothing precious or niminy-piminy about him. Had there been, he and the gnarled, hard-bitten Moses Van Campen would have found little upon which to base their enduring friendship.

Church had no intention of remaining permanently in the Genesee Valley when he first arrived there and met Moses Van Campen. He had come merely to make a reconnaissance of the 100,000-acre tract he shared with his father, John Barker Church, and to arrange for the division and prepare to promote the sale of the property. He returned to his home in New York after being shown over the land, and the next year he sent Evart Van Wickle, an expert surveyor, into the Genesee Valley to lay out a village settlement in the heart of the estate. When Church presently examined the site chosen, he named it Angelica after his mother, Angelica Schuyler Church.

Finding life in the wilderness more agreeable than he had anticipated, Church in time decided to build a substantial abode, not on the village site at Angelica, but at a place on the Genesee River a little more than two miles southwest of there. His intention at first was to erect a large house of native stone, which could be quarried without great difficulty from the bed of a nearby stream (now Van Campen Creek), and from other convenient sources. This idea he temporarily abandoned because, as he wrote to his father in New York, "of the scarcity and dearness of labor. I have been able," he added, "to hire only three men to whom I give $14 a month. . . ."

The house he did build, of white pine, consisted of two rooms and a kitchen. It was coated with white paint. At that time it was the only painted dwelling west of the village of Canandaigua, and at once gained the appellation, White House, which continued to identify it until, a century later, it collapsed in a high wind.

Church was living there in 1804, when word was brought through the woods to him of the shooting of his uncle, Alexander Hamilton, in the Weehawken duel with Burr. He hurried to New York. By the time he arrived, Hamilton had succumbed to the mortal wound given him by Burr, and had been buried, from the home of Philip's parents, in Trinity Churchyard.

Unusual though the circumstances were that took Church to New York in midsummer 1804, the journey itself was not, for him, an uncommon experience. He never completely separated himself from the life of the eastern seaboard, and periodically renewed his contacts with friends and men with whom he had business dealings in New York and Philadelphia. But his roots in the Genesee country were deepening. A small store was being operated under his direction at Angelica. He had built a sawmill and land office, the latter in charge of his agent, Van Wickle. There was no great land boom yet, but Church had hopes. He had many plans for the tract that was under his management. Included in these was the establishment in the White House of his wife.

While attending George Washington's funeral in December, 1799, Church met the Irish-born Anne Matilda Stewart, daughter of General Walter Stewart, a friend of Washington, and it was she whom he married in Philadelphia four years later and took, in the summer of 1805, to his home on the Genesee.

A pretty and personable young woman, who wore the gloss of the fashionable Philadelphia life in which she had been reared, Anne Matilda probably had only a vague notion of the experiences that awaited her when she began, with her husband, her first expedition into the upper Genesee wilderness. The young couple, whose Quaker cook had been sent on ahead, and whose household chattels were following by pack horse, traveled by stage-coach from Philadelphia to Bath, New York.

It was forty miles from there to the White House, and the badness of the trails increased as the small equestrian party, which had been augmented by Tom Morris, who had not yet joined his disgraced and insolvent father in Philadelphia, approached its destination.

In this passage, the young bride may have suffered moments of haunting doubt as she and her companions pressed through the seemingly limitless waste of the forest. The narrow paths were often steep and rocky; there were swift-running creeks to ford, with water reaching to milady's riding boot; there were descents to low, wet swales that needed to be crossed on strips of corduroy, with the chance that a horse, if it misstepped would wallow belly-deep in mire. And here and there a settler might be discovered in his crude log hut, with a blanket for a door, oiled paper for windows, and his scant invoice of necessities: knife, skillet, pot, and a few rough sticks of furniture to give what comfort the woods and his spare economy allowed.

When the travelers were only a short distance from the White House, Mrs. Church's horse stumbled over a hidden obstacle, and she was thrown roughly from the saddle. Sobs of hurt and discouragement rose from her breast as her escorts assisted her to her feet. "This," said Tom Morris, perhaps with a hint of rebuke for his friend, Church, "is too great a trial for a young woman of nineteen."

And the trial wasn't over even when the party reached its goal. Church, in his intermittent residence, had been merely "batching it" in the White House. He had taken shelter there, but had indulged in no luxuries. Now, with the goods that were to furnish their home still some distance downtrail, the Churches slept the first night on straw pallets, with rats nimbling about, and wolf howls outside further to discompose the weary, frightened and disconsolate bride from Philadelphia.

Begun under inauspicious circumstances, the residence of the Philip Churches along the Genesee continued until their career in the river's valley became a veritable triumph. They dominated the section in which they made their home; they gave grace and favor to it; they helped develop it. A year to the exact day of their marriage, the first of their nine children was born, not in the wilderness, but in New York City, where the solicitous young husband had taken his *enceinte* bride.

They returned to the White House with their first-born, a daughter, Angelica, the following summer; and not long after were joined there by the John Barker Churches, who arrived with an entourage. Roads were slowly building. The Churches brought male attendants, serving maids, perhaps a slave or two, and, of all things, a French chef who delighted in the opportunity to prepare for the table freshly killed game and fish that he snatched, alive and wiggling, from the waters of the Genesee.

The elder Churches were enchanted by what they saw of the huge tract of virgin country that bore the Church name. Previously, their experience with country living had been confined to the elaborate seats of the great, parklike English estates, with all that money could provide in the way of service and conveniences. They were a worldly couple; they were cosmopolites. Angelica Church had been one of the liveliest members of what today would be called the "international set" in Paris, London, and New York, and her gay goings-on had not escaped censure. The tastes of John Barker Church were urban, cultivated, and sporting. He was a speculator; he was a gambler whose play was not hedged by limits. He was a member of four New York card clubs. He had, for the elaborate entertainments he and Angelica gave, a solid silver dinner service for two dozen guests.

The dour, the meticulous, the ever-careful Robert Troup, the new Pulteney land agent, had written of John Church to Rufus King, who served twice as United States minister to Great Britain, "There is as little respectability attached to him as to any man among us," and he predicted that Church's gambling would bring ruin to the Hamilton family, to the Schuyler family, and to his own.

Troup's prediction, which had been made sometime before John Church's first visit to the 100,000-acre tract, was not fulfilled. But gaming losses, and land and other speculations, did in time, to some extent, depress the family economy. And partly because of this, the elder Church thought it well that Philip make his permanent home on the Genesee to keep a close eye on the family holdings. The suggestion was not disfavored by the young man. He and Anne Matilda were adjusting splendidly to their new life; and finding in it much that delighted them. But they needed, for a permanent home, a house more in keeping than the White House with Philip's position as patroon of the upper river, and plans were soon devised for the large and impressive stone-and-brick structure which, ever since it rose in a pine clearing close to the Genesee, has been known as Belvidere.

There is some belief that the eminent architect, Benjamin Henry Latrobe, may have provided a loose plan for this mansion, although no mention of it is made in his published journal, and there is little likelihood that he ever visited the site upon which Belvidere stands. There are others who oppose this idea with the argument that the expatriate Englishman was concerned, at that period, only with Greek Revival, while the style of the Church home is definitely Post-Colonial. John and Philip Church probably knew pretty well what they wanted in a house, and Angelica may have interposed her notions. But the general plan seems too good not to have been influenced, to some extent, by a skilled professional, though it may not have been Latrobe.

Only a few alterations have been needed in this large and handsome house to make it suitable for modern living. It now has twenty-seven rooms and seven bathrooms. These latter conveniences were added by the S. Hoxie Clarks, who owned and lived in the house for many years.

The Clarks lived elegantly, perhaps romantically, by candlelight. They refused to permit the installation of electric wires. Desiring to recapture the past, they nevertheless dispensed with slop jars and razed antediluvian outhouses in favor of inside plumbing. They kept one long wing of the house filled with servants, and entertained extensively. They raised squabs and other epicurean delicacies for their own table and, profitlessly, for the New York market. They died. And, after a while, Belvidere came into the possession of Robert B. Bromeley, newspaper publisher, hotel proprietor, a man of a multiplicity of business interests, and Mrs. Bromeley, of Bradford, Pennsylvania.

The Bromeleys may unwittingly have caused a team of workmen, engaged to install an electric-wiring system in the house, to lose their religion. The business of boring conduits through the huge, age-hardened, white-pine beams was as discouraging as the Sisyphean labors. But the wires were ultimately laid. The Bromeleys put in a gas furnace. A gracious lady, with a scholarly interest in the history of the Church family, Mrs. Bromeley has been at pains to inform Belvidere with something of the spirit of its original owners. The decor, the pictures, the furniture are in keeping. She has diligently sought, and sometimes obtained tables, chairs, and other pieces that were used by the Church family. These are choice exhibits; but no guest is allowed to feel that museum ropes restrict his examination of them. As in the early days of the past century, when nine Church children romped through its large, high-ceilinged rooms, and played at hide and seek behind the splendid white columns of its portico, which faces the river, Belvidere is a place today for good living and bounteous entertainment. When the house is open for use, during the clement season, the Bromeleys' children and grandchildren live with them under its spacious and hospitable roof.

Artisans were brought from as far away as Albany to help in the construction of Belvidere. Slaves were employed in the work, for in the early days of their residence on the Genesee the Philip Churches kept several Negroes in benevolent bondage. The stone for the foundation and the outside walls was quarried nearby; bricks were made of clay dug from pits on the property and fired in local kilns; the white pine used for joists, beams, and trim was cut from the forest which reached out in all directions from the clearing where the house was built.

The Bromeley property consists of two hundred acres. This

is a tenth as large as the farm cut out of the 100,000-acre tract by Philip Church for use by himself and his sons. The Bromeleys are not deeply concerned with farming operations. They keep more than half a dozen hunters in the barn at Belvidere, and Mr. Bromeley, his daughter and his son-in-law ride with the Genesee Hunt, whose meets usually form on Wadsworth land, north along the river near Geneseo.

Besides the main house, two other structures that were built by Philip Church still stand upon the property. One is a large, nine-sided brick coach house and barn. The other is an octagonal teahouse, which Mrs. Bromeley has caused to be restored, and which now stands in front of Belvidere, overlooking the river. It is a graceful and feminine retreat in which, on a sunny summer afternoon, one might imagine Anne Matilda Church entertaining house guests at tea, or dutifully consulting with her mother-in-law, the charming Angelica, on matters of domestic management or child rearing; or inquiring shyly about the older lady's fashionable divertissements in London and on the continent; and is it true what they say about the improprieties of the celebrated Madame de Staël, whom "Mother" Church knew very well in Paris?

As another concession to modernity, the Bromeleys have built a swimming pool in front of Belvidere, not far from the teahouse. Beyond is a quite precipitous drop to the river bottoms, and beyond these the actual channel of the Genesee, which has changed substantially since the present owners took over part of the old Church estate, more than fifteen years before these lines were written.

A gentle, cooing little stream in midsummer, the Genesee, in early spring, often gives way to a towering rage. In these paroxysms, it charges straight and fiercely at the high bank that forms part of the eminence upon which Belvidere rests, then rushes on to the north and the great lake, nearly one hundred miles away.

These attacks are alarming to the Bromeleys. They have seen

ten or twelve acres of good pasture lands swept off in spring floods, and only an unsightly congeries of debris left in their place. Riprap deposited by army engineers has failed to contain the stream in its former channel. If the erosion continues, there is always a chance that one day the river may fully undermine the bank and reach back to the foundation of the Bromeley house. It has flooded, to the depth of fifteen feet, the entrance to a root cellar built by Hoxie Clark.

The persistent tendency of the Genesee at Belvidere is to chew away at its east bank. A short distance downstream, at the village of Belfast, the river is cutting so deeply under the property of residents on its west bank that some already have moved to safer ground, and others contemplate doing so.

"This old river," one ancient Belfast native remarked, spitting a stream of tobacco juice through his denture, "she do the damnest things, at springtime. Seems, at that season, she's mad at everbody."

22

HIGH-BORN Frenchmen moved in and out of the Genesee Valley during the late years of the eighteenth and the early years of the nineteenth century. The lame, witty, ex-bishop, lover of Madame de Staël, diplomatist of many casts and facets, and foreign minister for Napoleon Bonaparte, Charles Maurice de Talleyrand, was briefly there; the later-day French king, Louis Philippe—then the Duc d'Orleans—paused, in a sylvan expedition he was making with his brothers, to gaze upon the waters of the Genesee. There were others.

The Terror of the French Revolution had sent many a Frenchman, zealous to keep his head upon his shoulders, to America. The colony of *Azilum*, or Asylum, established on land at a bend of the Susquehanna River, in Pennsylvania, which had once been the property of Robert Morris, was the prime gathering place for these exiles. They had formed a little Paris in the woods, and they had once hoped that the hapless Marie Antoinette might take her titular place among them. Some of the more adventurous members of the colony, made restless by the intramural life of their New World retreat, went forth to examine the frontier to the west. There was no telling whether the noxious political climate of their native land would ever clear sufficiently to allow them to return to France with safety. They were vaguely prospecting for new places of habitation.

The Genesee Valley had been boomed by Charles Williamson, by the Morrises, by agents for the Holland Land Company, and by the Churches, father and son, as an excellent location for persons who were able to envisage a prosperous future in the development of virgin lands. John Barker Church was particularly influential with the French. He had lived in Paris during part of the interval that marked the end of the American and the beginning of the French revolutions. He was a friend of Lafayette, whose forces he had served as commissary during their operations in America. He persuaded several French émigrés, who were seeking American homes, to settle on the Church tract. One of these, who bought five hundred acres, but discovered that he lacked a husbandman's instincts to cultivate them, was Victor du Pont de Nemours, whose younger brother, Irénée founded E. I. du Pont de Nemours & Company.

The son of a distinguished father, Victor du Pont had come to America early in the 1790's as a member of the suite of Comte de Moustier, first French minister to the United States. He was a handsome man, of gallant bearing, six feet three inches tall without his boots. He liked the new country. He had learned its language and had become, by naturalization, one of its citizens. He had vision, energy, and talent; but he had made no great go of several enterprises that he had attempted in America prior to his arrival in the Genesee Valley; and there, too, he was to be something less than a thumping success.

Victor took with him to his new home his French wife, Gabrielle Josephine de la Fite de Pelleport, and their children. The daughter of a marquis, Gabrielle Josephine went under protest.

She had lived as a lady in France, and in suitable residences along the Atlantic seaboard of America. This removal to the backwoods country of the Genesee outraged her sense of the fitness of things and opposed her every inclination. She was supported in her opposition by Irénée du Pont, to whom she refers in her voluminous *Memoirs* as "our good brother," and she states that he "was most unhappy at our departure, but sent with us a wagon loaded with powder worth $1,000."

The du Pont party did not reach the Genesee until the beginning of a severe winter, and it was then too late to clear the land and build a home in the clearing. Instead, using a small supply of gold that Madame du Pont, with the thrift for which French women are noted, had saved, and kept upon her person, the du Ponts purchased a small house in Angelica from Philip Church, and in time erected a store on an adjoining lot.

Irénée du Pont had pleaded that his older brother become his partner in a tiny venture, a powder mill, which was coming to life, with great pains of labor, on Brandywine Creek in Delaware; but Victor thought he saw an easy way to wealth in Genesee land promotions.

"V. will be ruined if he persists in staying on a farm of 500 A. covered with enormous forest trees, for which he has not paid and cannot cultivate," Irénée wrote to his father.

That was early in 1808, and Victor had been gone two years. Later that year, Irénée plodded over the wagon trails, which passed for roads, from Wilmington to Angelica, and during a week's visit with his brother won Victor's promise to join him on the Brandywine as quickly as he could put his affairs in order.

Victor abandoned Angelica the next year. He had been deeply in debt when he arrived and he was in debt when he left. By then, his Genesee property had been assigned to Irénée and other less benign creditors. He had sold a slave, "my black wench named Charlotte," and her four-week-old son, to another French refugee, August d'Autremont, and applied the $200 he received in payment against his debts.

Returning to the East with his wife and family, Victor made the explicit condition that he was to operate, on the Brandywine, a woollen mill which would be independent of his brother's business on the opposite side of the stream. His determination on this point indicates how skeptical he was about the future of Irénée's powder company. Certainly, visionary though he sometimes was, Victor could not have conceived that a century and a half later the assets of E. I. du Pont de Nemours & Company would be upwards of two and a half billion dollars.

Unlike Victor du Pont, some of the other French who moved into the upper Genesee Valley remained there until they died, and their progeny continued to live in Allegany County, of which Angelica was once the county seat. Their graves are marked in the village churchyards, and names of a few of the exiles are recorded on the early rolls of the Angelica lodge of Masons.

Those of the French who permanently settled in the valley, lived on friendly terms with the Church family, whose large house with its bounteous hospitality could be reached from the village of Angelica in a horseback ride of less than fifteen minutes. Owner of an enormous tract of land, Philip Church also felt that he owned that part of the Genesee River that wound through his property; and he imposed upon upriver lumbermen a tax for each log that floated past Belvidere. The tax was paid without demur until Benjamin Palmer, a neighboring land owner to the south, trotted off through the woods to Albany one day and persuaded the legislature to declare the river a public highway.

Although his good works were many, Church had some detractors among his neighbors. He had, as have all human beings, weaknesses. One of these was believed to be a slave girl, Lucy, who worked in the kitchen, and whose natural child, Phoebe, later became the personal maid of the mistress of Belvidere. When Phoebe reached marriageable age, a 500-acre farm was consigned to her and a white farm hand, who took Phoebe to wife, and the pair lived happily thereafter. The issue of this union continued to live near Belvidere for many years, where they were favorites of two generations of the Church family, and highly regarded by other neighbors.

Philip Church was active in all efforts to promote the development of the upper-river country in which his own lands reposed. He introduced an imported breed of sheep, encouraged advanced methods of agriculture, built a church, gave five acres to Angelica for a public park, which is still one of the modest glories of the village. He plumped vigorously for the construction of the Genesee Valley Canal, which, connecting with the Erie Canal at Rochester, proceeded south through the country from which it took its name to a southern terminus, a few miles west of the river's valley, in the city of Olean.

Early in the third decade of the nineteenth century, Church envisioned a railroad with termini at the Hudson River and Lake Erie that would cross the Southern Tier of New York State, and for twenty years he devoted himself to the advancement of this project. He presided at early railroad meetings—or conventions, as they were later called—at which plans for the organization of the New York and Erie Railroad, of which he was one of the incorporators, were formed. One of the first of these was held in Angelica. He opposed, with vigor and sound judgment, proposals to lay the tracks farther north, to the disadvantage of the upper Genesee River country, and his opposition prevailed. In the spring of 1851, ten years before his death, Church saw his dream come true. At that time, he was a member of a party of notables, that included President Millard Fillmore and Daniel Webster, Secretary of State, which ceremoniously steamed across the state in the first Erie train to run from Piermont on the Hudson to Dunkirk, on the eastern shore of Lake Erie.

Philip Church held only one public office during his long residence on the Genesee. In 1807, Governor Lewis Morgan made him the first judge of the Court of Common Pleas of Allegany

County. His judgeship continued fourteen years, during two of which he heard no pleas. In 1811, leaving his wife and family at Belvidere, he made a business trip to England. He arrived there under propitious auspices. He was enthusiastically welcomed by his father's influential English friends (the elder Church was living in America), and prodigally wined and dined. His visit took on a different aspect at the onset of the War of 1812, and Church returned gratefully to the United States, and the Genesee, in 1813. Although he had been delighted with the beauties of the English countryside, his visit, he said, had "a contrary effect from what I expected; it has increased my attachment to Angelica."

Under the joint superintendence of his wife, his father and his mother, Belvidere was completed in every detail during Philip Church's English sojourn. He took up his career there, fully, upon his return; he lived there, with only seasonal visits to eastern cities, and brief departures on business errands, for the remainder of his long and useful life. He died in 1861 and was buried in Angelica Cemetery where, a few years later, his wife was laid in a grave at his side.

At Mrs. Church's death, Belvidere became the property of one of her younger sons, Richard Church, endowed—by courtesy —with the title of "Major." The house contained many objects of historical interest. The walls of an apartment that Philip Church had used as an office, were covered with framed letters bearing the signatures of Washington, Jefferson, Hamilton, and other famous men who had fought for American independence and who had helped found the new republic.

One of the office walls also exhibited the crossed pistols, once the property of Major Church's paternal grandfather, which allegedly had been used in the duel in which Aaron Burr killed his arch rival, Alexander Hamilton. These weapons are now a prized possession of The Chase Manhattan Bank, of New York. The bank explains its ownership of them in a pamphlet entitled, "The Church Pistols: Historical Relics of the Burr-Hamilton Duel," which reads in part:

The particular interest of The Chase Manhattan Bank in these pistols stems from the fact that one of the few common efforts of these two extraordinary men [Burr and Hamilton], so fundamentally antipathetic both politically and temperamentally, lay in the establishment of The Manhattan Company. This company, originally chartered to supply water to the city of New York, subsequently entered the banking business. It provided the original charter, granted by the New York State Legislature on April 2, 1799, under which The Chase Manhattan Bank operates today.

Major Church had the gambling instincts of his grandfather, John Barker Church, but manifested them differently. The card table was not his weakness. He speculated heavily in stocks and western mining lands; lost heavily. When his depressed economy no longer allowed him to maintain Belvidere in its traditional style, he removed to Rochester to live at the home of his daughter, Angelica, and her clergyman husband; and there, at an advanced age, he died.

During his Rochester residence, which continued nearly twenty years, Major Church frequently returned to the upper river country, to poke about Belvidere, to visit the graves of his parents, to reminisce with the older residents of Angelica. He never lost his love for the Genesee lands that had once comprised the Church Tract, or the village of Angelica, which had once been the measured center of the property. For more than two decades after its founding, Angelica had been not only the leading settlement in Allegany County, but one of the most populous and active villages resting upon, or lying adjacent to, the Genesee River. At this writing it has a sawmill with three, and a broom factory with two, employees.

Serene, relaxed, untrammeled, Angelica makes no pretense of hustle, no boast of progress. It is a place from which youth quickly departs, and where elderly men, with an intensity unmarked by other village activities, play croquet at night on lighted, carefully groomed courts on the village green. It has a quaint, past-century charm; it has a main street gloriously alive with trees—in contrast to the denuded main streets of most

Western New York villages—hard maples that stand like handsome sentinels on either side of the broad pavement, and from each of which at sugar time, a sap bucket depends, as in the days when Moses Van Campen was a civil officer in Angelica, and Judge Philip Church held court there. The village has a fine central school.

It had, for a short time, a young woman resident who was later to help make history, and who died as a Christian martyr in the disputed territory of Oregon; and in its graveyard lie the bones of a fiery abolitionist, who once outbid a New Orleans procurer for a beautiful slave girl, offered naked on the block. He was execrated as a "nigger stealer," and suffered, for his many successful efforts to free slaves from their masters, seventeen years' imprisonment and, as supplementary punishment, more than 35,000 stripes from prison whips.

In 1834 or '35, Stephen and Clarissa Prentiss, with their numerous progeny, moved from the town of Amity, which is bisected by the Genesee River, three or four miles north to the village of Angelica. In Amity, Prentiss had erected several farm buildings and built a wooden bridge across the river. He was a man of parts. In Prattsburg, northeast in Steuben County, where the family had originated, he had, among other activities, operated a distillery. He had kept a Bible in the distillery, and there held midweek prayer meetings. He and Clarissa were such profound Christians that it was said of them that they almost never laughed, since laughter displayed lack of piety. Their oldest daughter, Narcissa, was in her mid-twenties when the family settled in Angelica, and she affiliated herself with the Presbyterian church of the village.

Narcissa was unmarried. But she had met, and was soon to become betrothed to a young physician, and religious zealot, Dr. Marcus Whitman. His burning passion was to take the Holy Word to the Indians on the far side of the Rocky Mountains, into the country that was later to become the state of Oregon. He needed money and recruits for such a mission; he needed a wife with a Christian spirit as flaming as his own. Narcissa Prentiss had had two or three religious experiences as a girl; she felt that the "finger of Providence" was pointing the way for her; she was heedful of the command, "Go thou and preach the Kingdom of God."

The question, "Are Females wanted?" on a mission among the western Indians, was asked of the American Board of Missions, but no serious objection was raised against Narcissa Prentiss. On February 18, 1836, following a service in the little Presbyterian church in Angelica, Narcissa, who wore a black bombazine wedding dress, stepped away from the choir, of which she was a member, and joined Dr. Whitman in front of the altar. There the nuptial vows were exchanged.

The congregation then joined the choir in a closing hymn. But a number of the singers, realizing that this might be the last time that they would see Narcissa, whose personality and character had endeared her to her fellow parishioners, were unable to go on. Their throats were constricted by emotion, and sobs choked the words of the hymn. It was the bride's clear, unfaltering soprano that sounded the closing stanza:

> "In the deserts let me labor,
> On the mountains let me tell,
> How He died—the blessed Savior—
> To redeem a world from hell!
> Let me hasten,
> Far in heathen lands to dwell."

The next day, Dr. and Mrs. Whitman left Angelica. They took with them twenty-six dollars contributed to their holy cause by the congregation of the Presbyterian Church. Many months later, after a difficult wagon trek over the Rocky Mountains, that tested the courage and fortitude of all who made it, they reached the Columbia River. Two other missionaries, the Reverend Henry H. Spalding and his wife, were also members of the party. Narcissa Whitman and Mrs. Spalding were probably the first white women to cross the mountains.

Dr. Whitman established a mission in the Walla Walla valley. After a few years, he made a trip east, during which, his adherents believe, he saved Oregon by urging the Government to make it a territory of the United States. Narcissa did not accompany him on this journey. She never again saw her family, her Angelica friends, or even the eastern slope of the Rockies. Four or five years after Whitman's return to the west, he, Narcissa and twelve other whites at the mission were murdered by the Indians whom they were striving to bring into the grace of Christ.

Angelica's other celebrated martyr, who was born in Pike, north of Angelica and a short distance west of the Genesee River, did not take up his residence in the village until after the War of the Rebellion, and by then the cause for which he had grievously suffered had been achieved by the constitutional amendment that abolished slavery.

He was the Reverend Calvin Fairbank. As a boy, he was taken by his devout parents to a Methodist revival meeting in the village of Rushford, two or three miles from what is now the Caneadea dam on the Genesee.

The family stayed at the home of two runaway slaves. Fairbank tells of this experience in his readable autobiography.

One night after service I sat on the hearthstone before the fire, and listened to the woman's story of her sorrow. It covered the history of thirty years. She had been sold from home, separated from her husband and family, and all ties of affection broken. My heart wept, my anger was kindled, and antagonism to slavery was fixed in me.

"Father," I said, on going to our room, "when I get bigger they shall not do that;" and the resolve waxed strong with my growth.

A few years later, when he was a theological student at Oberlin College, in Ohio, Fairbank took a slave on a raft from the West Virginia side of the Ohio River to the free state of Ohio.

That was the beginning of his private campaign to manumit the Negroes of the South, whom he persistently and vociferously protested were held in illegal bondage. In all, he guided nearly fifty slaves to the North Star and freedom before his second and longer incarceration in a brutal Kentucky prison, from which he was not released until 1864.

A man of powerful stature, Fairbank was reduced during his prison term from a normal weight of 180 to 117 pounds. He insists that his report of the number of lashes he received is approximately correct (in the end, the floggings were sometimes administered by a charitable keeper, who tempered their severity), and attests that his great strength alone allowed him to survive them. If he fell insensible, and lost count, other prisoners kept the grim score. Each week a tally was scratched on the cell wall.

When Fairbank finally gained his freedom, he married a Massachusetts schoolteacher to whom he had become engaged before his sentence. The marriage ended with Mrs. Fairbank's death in 1870. The widower then returned to the Genesee Valley, where he had been born, and settled in Angelica; and there, in peace, after the good fight he had made for an ideal, he passed the twenty odd years that remained of his life.

23

THE War of 1812 did not end until more than a year after Philip Church had returned from England. He took no part in the contest. He was thirty-five years old. The "captain" that had first been prefixed to his name at the time that he served, rather ornamentally, as aide-de-camp for his uncle, Alexander Hamilton, had been dropped for several years. He was Judge Church now.

By a crow's flight, the Church home was only seventy-odd miles from the bitter fighting and the scenes of military devastation on the Niagara Frontier. But the inhabitants of Belvidere felt only faintly the pinch of war, and the actual hostilities must have seemed remote from their forest clearing on the bank of the upper Genesee. At the small settlements close to the mouth of the river, the war caused consternation and panic; and it was not remote from Judge Church's neighbors (if, in the sparsely populated countryside, men living thirty miles downriver might so be called), the Wadsworth brothers, at Geneseo. William Wadsworth, the older of the two, left home to lead troops in battle, during which, as one observer remarked, he "was extremely cautious to keep his breast toward the [enemy] balls, saying 'he had no notion that a Wadsworth should be shot in the back.'"

William Wadsworth had held the rank of brigadier general in the state militia for some time. But this had prepared him only slightly for actual warfare. The governor of the state summoned him to duty, and he responded promptly. Not ordinarily a humble man, he displayed in this situation the humility of *noblesse oblige*. He did not believe that he was up to the job of leading a command in battle, and he explained his apprehensions in a letter written from his Geneseo home to Governor Daniel D. Tompkins. It read in part:

Sir: . . . I take command of the troops at Black Rock and its vicinity in obedience to your Excellency's order with the greatest difficulties, having had no experience of actual service. My knowledge of the military is limited; indeed, I foresee numberless difficulties and occurrences which will present themselves to which I feel totally inadequate. I have been ambitious that the Regiment and the Brigade which I have commanded should be distinguished at the reviews, but I confess myself ignorant of even the minor details of the duty you have assigned me, and I am apprehensive that I may not only expose myself but my Government. Any aid which your Excellency may think proper to order will be received with thanks. . . . Permit me to add that every exertion in my power shall be made to discharge the duties of my office and to merit the approbation of your Excellency.

This was late June, 1812. In mid-October, the "parade" general, who in the interim had striven mightily to bring his command to battle efficiency against odds made by lack of camp equipment, short rations, and even a scarcity of military weapons, found himself in a desperate fight to hold possession of Queenstown Heights, on the Canadian side of the Niagara River, which he and part of the forces under General Stephen Van Rensselaer had valiantly scaled.

And the Heights might have been held had the troops on the far side of the river displayed any stomach for battle. They refused to cross the short stretch of water, perhaps under the notion that their tour of duty committed them only to engagements within the boundaries of the United States, and the maddest exhortations of their officers failed to budge them. Wadsworth's performance in the field at this critical juncture, later caused General Van Rensselaer, commander of the New York State Militia, to commend him to Governor Tompkins, in these words:

"Brigadier General Wadsworth proved himself an officer capable of commanding with promptness, coolness and decision in all the vicissitudes of battle, and though he was fortunate enough to escape wounds scarcely a garment he had on but bears more than one mark of honorable testimony."

Wadsworth may have commanded with "promptness," and his battle decisions may have been sound, but there were moments during the heat of the strife when he was anything but calm. At one point, approaching the brow of the steep cliff, he made furious cuts of the air with his sword, and delivered such a purple Philippic against the skulkers across the river, who were allowing their comrades-in-arms to be cut to pieces, and pushed over the precipice, that one auditor later declared that the general's language was the "worst in the whole American army."

"I think it was old General Bill," said the present William P. Wadsworth, half seriously, "who was responsible for the army regulations that prohibit officers from cursing their men. But what else could a man do in a spot like old Bill's? It was said that his declamation at Queenstown was not merely accomplished; it was inspired!"

Toward the end of the engagement, active leadership of the American forces on Queenstown Heights was transferred from General Van Rensselaer, who had been seriously wounded, to Colonel Winfield Scott, who was later to achieve fame through his brilliant campaign in Mexico. By then, the command was hopelessly beleaguered. To save it from total extinction, Scott surrendered. General Wadsworth was one of the prisoners taken.

When word of his brother's plight reached Geneseo, James Wadsworth set out at once for Lewiston, across the Niagara River from the Queenstown battleground. What artifices he employed in an attempt to effect the release of his brother are not known. But the fact is that the general was paroled. He was soon back in Geneseo. He was permanently out of the war. His sword was hung upon the wall of the good, four-square cobblestone house that he had built several years before. In the future, the general's sword would be flourished only in peace-time parades and at other military pomps.

But the war did not end with William Wadsworth's withdrawal from it, and neither he nor his fellow citizens in the little village on the east bank of the Genesee were relieved of the threat made by its hovering horrors until the signing of the Treaty of Ghent.

During the winter of 1812-13, Geneseo was swept by an epidemic that took more lives than might have been lost had the village been besieged by the enemy. The disease, which may have been a virulent form of influenza, had been spread among the members of the civilian population by returning soldiers, who attested that they had contracted it from the British. It was accompanied by a racking cough, high fever, violent chills, and a horrid crimson bloating of the features. The fear of it hung over the village like the scythe of death. As fresh earth mounded up in the cemetery, the living, who stumbled about burying the dead, wondered dolefully who might be left to bury them. Men, who had engaged unflinchingly in battle, were terrorized by a spectral enemy that could not be repulsed by musket fire or stopped by the thrust of a bayonet. The usually undaunted General Wadsworth wrote to a friend that he was "not well and not without apprehension that the epidemic may lay claim to me."

The "Cold Plague," as the epidemic was commonly called,

lost its severity with the coming of warm weather. It was followed not many months later by new trials for the residents of Geneseo and a fresh fear that the war might soon be at their doorsteps.

In a night assault on Fort Niagara in December, 1813, which met with little resistance after two detachments of pickets had been bayoneted, the British regained the historic bastion on the American side of the Niagara River. They were to hold it until the end of the war. This reverse, which the exercise of proper military vigilance might have averted, was a grievous loss both of face and of property for the Americans. The news of it, quickly conveyed to Geneseo and other settlements along the Genesee River, aroused among the residents of these places a sharp sense of impending disaster. A few days later, other British forces crossed the Niagara River, routed the opposition, and burned several frontier villages, including Buffalo.

The scenes that followed were tragic. In a panicky exodus men, women, children and retreating soldiers pushed pell-mell over all arteries of travel that led away from the British. Their homes gone, impoverished, and often inadequately clad for a winter's pilgrimage, the residents of the burned settlements in many instances pursued the crude, snow-covered roads that led to the Genesee.

Some of the refugees crossed the river and found succor in settlements well to the east of the Genesee. Others remained in Geneseo where, during the remainder of the winter, they occupied every available foot of shelter and ate their hosts out of pantry and cold cellar.

It was well known in the village that hundreds of American militiamen had disappeared like wraiths of smoke in a fog at the time the British had attacked Buffalo and the adjacent American settlements; some of them, in retreat—as one writer put it— "hugging . . . 'as spoils of the vanquished' the arms they had neglected to use." Now, with Fort Niagara in the hands of the British, there was no assurance that the red-coated hordes, with their shrieking, savage auxiliaries, would not proceed the short distance from the reclaimed fortress to the rich, fertile, and immensely desirable lands of the Genesee; indeed, on the contrary, there was a very real likelihood that such an action would be put in train.

But nothing of the sort actually happened. And later on, in subsequent engagements on the Niagara Frontier, at Plattsburg, and at New Orleans, American forces displayed both on land and on water a valor and effectiveness in battle that the militiamen who had failed to oppose the British at Buffalo notoriously lacked. Their dereliction in that instance, as in others, might be attributed in part to the fact that they were woefully short of training, that they were inadequately equipped, that many were ill, and that there was confusion in their minds as to the merit of a war openly disfavored by many of their countrymen and used by others, who were selling vital supplies to the enemy, as a scheme to get rich quick.

Although the residents of Geneseo worried continually during the War of 1812 that the enemy might at any moment pounce upon them, he was never actually as close as a day's march to their village. At the mouth of the Genesee, forty miles north, there was more genuine cause for alarm. There, on three occasions, a squadron of His Majesty's ships paused for several hours at the point where the cocoa-colored waters of the "little river of the Senecas" debouched into the blue expanse of Lake Ontario; and at the time of the first of these visits the captain of the squadron, Sir James L. Yeo, ordered seamen ashore to plunder a riverbank warehouse.

This was in mid-June, 1813. Yeo had been sent out by the Royal Navy the preceding autumn to command a fleet of fighting ships on the smallest of the Great Lakes. If he had heard the dictum of the great Duke of Wellington that naval superiority on the lakes was a *sine qua non* of success in war on the Canadian frontier, he little heeded it. Neither he nor his American opponent, Captain

Isaac Chauncey, who had previously fought the Tripolitan pirates, seemed eager to engage in a decisive collision; and their maneuvers on Lake Ontario often had more the aspect of a long-distance yacht race than naval warfare. Their official reports were redundant with denunciations of the "enemy" for refusing the gage, but the prime tactic of both was to "edge away."

Historians have scarcely deigned to mention the operations of the enemy's ships at the mouth of the Genesee. But Yeo's visits were not lightly regarded by the residents of the tiny settlement at the junction of lake and river, or by pioneers at Rochester-ville, seven miles upstream, who, at the alarm, "The British are coming!" packed their wives and children into carts and sent them rattling over the new, roughly made roads to villages farther from the lake.

Reporting his shore raid to the Secretary of the Admiralty, Yeo wrote: . . . "On the 13th June 1813 we captured two schooners and some boats going to the enemy with supplies; by them I received information that there was a depot of provisions at Genesee River. I accordingly proceeded off that river, landed some seamen and marines of the squadron, and brought off all the provisions found in the government stores; as also a sloop laden with grain for the army."

Contrary to Yeo's report, the place plundered was not a government depot, but a private business establishment—a store and trading center—owned by Frederick Bushnell. The raiders were unopposed. After they had cleaned out all of the provisions, all of the salt and whiskey, they presented (perhaps with tongue in cheek) to Bushnell's clerk a receipt for the goods abstracted, bowed politely, and proceeded to transfer the booty to the ships, which did not depart until the following day.

During the twenty-four hours that the squadron lay off the river's mouth, no one was harmed except Bushnell, who was hurt in pocket. But the alarming fact that the enemy had been able to land at will, without anyone to oppose or harass him, excited residents of the lower Genesee to appeal frantically to the state militia for protection. Militiamen in material numbers were not, however, easy to come by, since most of those who had any genuine feel for fighting, already were on the Niagara Frontier. And three months later, with the little port at the mouth of the Genesee still without guns or a garrison—on September 11, the day following Commodore Oliver Hazard Perry's brilliant victory on Lake Erie—Yeo's ships were again discovered in easy cannon range of the lake shore, and the frightening tiding of this —and a call to arms—was rushed south to Rochesterville.

Men girded on their bucklers—or grabbed up a scythe, a bludgeon, or a musket, and started for the river's mouth. There was only a handful of them. When they reached the port, and joined the residents of the place, they saw—and cheered the heartening spectacle—part of Chauncey's fleet rounding a bluff westward along the lake shore, and all were sure that this day the British would not essay a landing. The Americans had a slight breeze; Yeo's ships were becalmed. Immobile, sailcloths limp in the dead air, they reposed upon the flat, glistening waters of the lake, as fair a target as sitting ducks.

This shaped up as one of the rare naval engagements on Lake Ontario. With the advantage of maneuverability, Chauncey was moving in to attack at close range, when Yeo's sails bellied out with a sudden breeze, and off he went. In his official report the captain stated that he had been chasing the enemy for some time, but had been unable, owing to his heavy-sailing schooners, to come to grips with him "until the 11th September 1813 off the Genesee River; we carried a breeze with us while he lay becalmed, to within three-fourths of a mile of him, when he took a breeze, and we had a running fight of three and a half hours; but . . . he escaped me and ran into Amherst Bay. . . .

"I was much disappointed that Sir James refused to fight me, as he was so much superior in point of force, both in men and guns. . . ."

Before Yeo ran away, a broadside was delivered against one of his vessels. Others were lightly hulled in the running down-lake fight that followed. A midshipman and three sailors were killed. Yeo officially admitted damage to his ships and loss of personnel; attested that his force was far inferior to the enemy; and deprecated Chauncey's failure to display the "least spirit." He explained that, on leaving the Genesee River, "I steered for the False Duck Islands near the foot of the lake, under which the enemy could not keep the weather-gauge, but be obliged to meet me on equal terms. This, however, he carefully avoided."

The gasconading of the captains in their reports, and their strangely pacific attitudes afloat, are vaguely reminiscent of the abortive encounter between two hesitant schoolboys, one of whom (it was said) was afraid, and the other dassen't.

Yeo returned to the Genesee for the third and last time, May 14, 1814; discharged a few harmless shots from a gunboat; sent details ashore to parley with the Americans; and departed after lying more than a day at anchor without stealing even so much as a keg of whiskey. This was the most notable incident of the war at the river's mouth. It has been fully covered by local historians, and a state plaque marks the spot where a scratch detail of homespun soldiers, the "valiant thirty," met the enemy, not to fight and conquer him, but to bluff him to a fare-thee-well.

The Port of the Genesee had been created by an act of Congress in 1805, and a short time later the settlement at the mouth of the river took the name of Charlotte, in honor of some lady who has never been precisely identified. Business at the port was slack the first year, and Samuel Latta, the collector, didn't make his keep. His receipts were $22.50 against expenditures of 24.30. Things soon picked up. In 1808, $30,000 or $40,000 worth of wheat, pork, whiskey, and potash was shipped from river wharves to down-lake ports. But the threat of war ended the little boom, as it checked the expansion of the village of Charlotte. By 1812 there was a scattering of half a dozen houses on the high ground overlooking the river, a couple of stores and a tavern. There were rattlesnakes in such numbers that a boy with a sharp hoe could keep busy killing them from dawn until sundown.

Swamplands, which were believed to be the cause of the dreaded Genesee Fever, reached back from the soggy bank of the river. The village had no great appeal to persons from other parts seeking a new place of habitation, though its handful of boosters were confident that, if peace came, Charlotte would become the most important community on the Genesee River.

But the peace seemed long in coming, and the hope of it was shattered with particular force the May day in 1814, when Yeo's ships were seen riding at anchor off the river's mouth. They had come early in the evening, and the news of their presence was carried swiftly south to Rochesterville, which could recruit more able-bodied men than Charlotte. By two o'clock the following morning, Colonel Isaac W. Stone, a tavern-keeper, who had been made head of the local militia, had all available musket-bearers standing at attention before him. Or all but two. One, a poltroon—or a conscientious objector—refused to answer the call to arms; the other was left to lead the women and children into the woods in the event that the British overwhelmed the opposition and raided the village.

The command to march was given. Colonel Stone rode a white horse. The night was rainy. The foot soldiers slogged and slipped over the miry, wooded roads that led north seven miles to the lake. Thirty reached the port settlement. They were of various crafts. Among them was Rochesterville's first tailor, Jehiel Barnard, who was so eager to fight the British squadron that he was willing to attack it from a rowboat; there were two millers, Francis Brown and Elisha Ely, each raised to the rank of captain; there was a left-handed fiddle player.

The lake was calm and shrouded in a mist that gave the vessels, standing half a mile off shore, the unreal appearance of phantom ships. Stone called for volunteers to reconnoiter the squadron in a boat manned by oars. Captains Brown and Ely were given charge of the detail, and tailor Barnard was one of the militiamen who lay, with loaded muskets beside them, out of sight below the gunwales.

The fog lifted as the small American boat was creeping about the lake, shots were fired over it, and the British sent a twelve-oar barge in pursuit. As a hasty decision was taken by the leaders of the scouting party to turn and flee, Jehiel Barnard rose from his secreted position. "I hope," he pleaded, "you will let us fight first."

Wiser counsel prevailed, however, and the boat reached the shore in safety. During this episode, Colonel Stone had militia-men marching in military formation in and out of the woods near the lake. It was a ruse that worked. From shipboard, the British appeared to see an endless column of armed men. Presently a small party with a flag of truce was sent toward shore, and Brown and Ely were ordered to treat with it. "But don't let them come into the river," Stone instructed his soldiers. "Don't let them land at all. Their feet shall not pollute our soil."

The American captains met the officer in charge of the enemy party accompanied by a small detail of men with loaded muskets at the alert. This was hardly *de rigueur*. "Is it your custom to receive a flag of truce under arms?" loftily inquired the Britisher. An apology was offered. Brown and Ely explained that they were ignorant of the finer points of military etiquette. But the detail was not dismissed, and negotiations went on in its presence.

The British officer made known the purpose of his visit. He had come to offer protection to private property provided the Americans peacefully surrendered the government stores at the Port of the Genesee. Various versions of the meeting have come down through the years. One reports that Captain Brown answered the Britisher's insulting proposal with a fiery declaration, "Blood knee-deep first!"

Years later, Elisha Ely, writing of the incident at the lake shore, said that he and his fellow officer took the British proposition to their commander, Stone, who sent them back with a soundly heroic answer, if less epic than the one attributed to Brown. "Go back and tell them," said the colonel, "that the public property is in the hands of those who will defend it," and he signaled his handful of troops to continue its illusion of multitude.

Sometime after the British party returned to the ships, other militiamen arrived at Charlotte. They gave substance to Colonel Stone's phantom legions. To the British, the woods seemed filled with troops. Another parley under a flag of truce was held. It failed, as had the first one. The British then fired a few balls, one of which did slight damage to a warehouse on the riverbank. The Americans retaliated as ineffectually with two or three cannon they had set up along the lake front. When this brief exchange ended, Yeo's squadron weighed anchor and sailed off down the lake.

"We saved the town and our credit by fairly outbullying John Bull," an exultant higher-up in the militia, who had brought the reinforcements to Charlotte, wrote to Governor Tompkins. It was a boast of merit.

Later in the year, three thousand troops disembarked at the river port, but these were Americans. Bound for the Niagara Frontier, they had been brought by Captain Chauncey's ships from Sackets Harbor. They encamped three nights near the mouth of the Genesee, while wagons to carry their supplies were collected from the adjacent countryside, and then marched west.

This was the last demonstration of armed force at Charlotte during the war.

24

THE ending of the War of 1812 had a vitalizing effect on several of the inchoate communities that were struggling for life and recognition along the lower Genesee. With the threat of a British invasion removed, energies that had been cramped and stifled by the war were released for peacetime enterprises. Hopes were revived. A population surge started, as migrants, again moving west across the state in search of homesites, often found what they were seeking on the northern banks of the north-flowing river in Western New York. There was a general upswing; a boom was forming.

And there was evidence of this even at Rochesterville—at the "Falls," as it formerly had been called—which, a few years before, a visitor had described as a "tangled wilderness, a fever-infested swamp, the abode of wild beasts, savages and rattlesnakes," and had declared that it would be difficult to find anywhere "a more dismal or unpromising spot."

For a period of twenty years after Ebenezer (Indian) Allan

had abandoned the 100-Acre Tract at the head of the first cataract on the lower Genesee, no concentrated effort had been
made to develop the plot. The mills, erected by Allan in 1789,
had had only a slight term of usefulness in a forest community
that numbered less than half a dozen families within a day's
journey of their location. They fell quickly into disrepair.

The millsite itself changed hands several times after Allan
quitted it, before coming into the possession of Nathaniel Rochester and his two Maryland friends, William Fitzhugh and
Charles Carroll, who bought it in 1803. With its potential of hydraulic power, the Falls interested these astute gentlemen.
They recognized a location which others had seen only as a
gloomy patch of primordial slime, but they did nothing about
their purchase for several years. Then, in 1811, after Rochester
had removed from his Maryland home to Dansville, forty miles
southeast of the 100-Acre Tract, he rode a horse up to the
Falls one day and started laying out town lots on those areas of
the property that he could tread upon without sinking hip-deep
in muck.

This, in a sketchy way, marked the beginning of the settlement. The next year the first permanent settler moved into a log
cabin, which was raised on a site now occupied by the Powers
Building, which adjoins Rochester's oldest hotel. Later in the year
a bridge was opened to traffic across the Genesee at a point about
a quarter of a mile south of the highest of the lower river's cataracts.

The bridge was the second to span the Genesee. The first, on
the old Mohawk-Niagara trail at Avon, had been built in 1804.
When the proposition to erect such a structure at the Falls was
discussed in the Legislature, one member, familiar with the proposed location, spoke vehemently in opposition. Who would use
such a bridge, he wanted to know, at a "God-forsaken place, inhabited by muskrats and visited only by straggling trappers, and
through which neither man nor beast could gallop without fear
of starvation or fever and ague"?

Other persons shared the legislator's sentiments. But the act to build the bridge was passed, and its opening, in 1812, was properly celebrated. It would have been an immediate boom to Rochesterville except for the war. The war temporarily checked any material expansion of the place, although by the end of 1812, ten or twelve families were settled in makeshift homes on firm land above the fever-infested seeps and bogs that constituted more than a negligible portion of the 100-Acre Tract.

The newcomers must have been joyfully welcomed by the first settler, Rochester's No. 1 Citizen. He was Hamlet Scrantom. In the spring of 1812, before the outbreak of war, and before the new bridge was completed, he had come lumbering down from the Black River Country, 175 miles northeast, in a horse- and ox-drawn wagon, with a linen tentlike covering to protect his wife, his six children, and himself, en route.

A New Englander by birth, Scrantom had briefly tried living in northern New York. He was discouraged by the rigors of the climate. He wrote to his father at the family home in Connecticut that he was leaving the Black River Country, which was "too cold and snowy," for the promised land of the Genesee.

Scrantom had contracted the year before to have a cabin ready for the reception of his family. He reached the east side of the Genesee on May 1. Snow was falling. He put his wagon on a scow that served as a ferry and crossed to the west side of the river at a place called Castle Town, two miles south of his objective, the 100-Acre Tract. When he struggled downriver to the site of his new home, he found that the cabin was roofless.

Frontiersmen, who knew nothing of the welfare state or the phenomenon of the push button, had a dogged way with difficulties. Self-reliance was ever their stock in trade. Scouring the immediate countryside, Scrantom found on the east side of the river a settler who offered the family shelter of a sort until their own home was ready. He recrossed the stream with his wagon, his wife, and his children. In the morning a foot of snow covered the ground.

At that point, he may have questioned the wisdom of his judgment. To escape a country that was "too cold and snowy," he had made a long wagon-trek over tortuous trails to find that the region of his hopes was still held, in early May, in winter's chill embrace.

When the Scrantom cabin was ready for occupancy, it was hardly adequate for a family of eight. Hamlet's means of livelihood were limited at first. But he possessed the virtues of thrift and ingenuity of his New England heritage. Somehow he managed to make do. "I have built a house the summer past and supported my family but how I cannot tell any more than this, by prudence and industry," he wrote to his father in February, 1813. Scrantom prospered. He raised a fine family. He took part in all good works in the village of Rochesterville and in the city that grew out of it. He died an esteemed and honored burgher in 1851 at the age of seventy-eight years. His progeny carried on in the city that he had helped to build.

Hamlet Scrantom has a place of some distinction in the early history of Rochester. It is not correct, however, to honor him as the first settler of the 100-Acre Tract, which is tantamount to calling him the city's earliest citizen, unless the adjective "permanent" is employed to distinguish him from others who lived on the millsite before 1812, but failed to fix their roots in the soil.

Ebenezer Allan was, of course, the first of these transitory residents. He made his home at his mills, on and off, for two years. He was followed by his brother-in-law, Christopher Dugan; Dugan by a family named Sprague, who were living in a shack that adjoined one of the mills when the Pulteney land agent, Charles Williamson, who had bought the tract for his principals, sent Colonel Josiah Fish there to serve as caretaker of the property.

A New England native, who had served as a colonial officer in the Revolutionary War, Fish first visited the millsite in 1795, in company with one of his sons, Libbeus, who recorded the experience in a journal. Father and son were put up by the Spragues.

The fare was not much to young Libbeus's liking. It consisted of raccoon, morning, noon, and night, with the variation of an occasional cake, "shortened and fried in raccoon oil."

The Spragues left the next year, and the Fishes moved in. Libbeus wrote in his journal that his father then built a new shack, but one that was neither particularly commodious nor remarkably convenient. One of the refinements it lacked was a chimney. According to which way the wind blew, the smoke escaped through an opening in the roof or lay so densely under it as to threaten the occupants of the house with suffocation.

During the few years that the Fishes lived on the millsite, two events worthy of remark occurred. The family's numerous children were added to by one when a son, christened John, was born in a cradleland of miasma, rattlesnakes, fever, and ague. He survived infancy. And long after Josiah Fish had died, and the family had moved from the Genesee, a claim which seems well-founded was made that John Fish was the first white child born on the site upon which Rochester was founded.

The other, and perhaps less notable event, was a visit paid to Colonel Fish and his family by the Count de Maulevrier, Royal refugee from the French Terror. The count, who had served with Admiral de Grasse's fleet during the Revolutionary War, on this occasion was making a horseback journey from the seaboard to Niagara Falls. Leaving Canandaigua on a fine October morning in 1798, he reached the east bank of the Genesee in early evening, crossed the stream on a rocky ford that was only two feet deep, and applied to the colonel for fodder for his horse and board and lodging for himself.

In his Journal, the count attested that Fish was an "excellent man," but he thought less of his accommodations.

"At nine o'clock he took me to a room in the mill where there was a bed, the appearance of which attracted my attention because of the many fleas which I found there and which were sure to keep me awake all night. Besides, there were eight in that room, both men and women, all sleeping close together on feather beds on the floor."

Some of the count's bipedal bedfellows, he explained, were transients like himself. They were stopping only for the night. The count also quit the colonel's hospitality after one fling in the communal bed. The next day, he rode south along the west bank of the river to the home of Peter Sheffer, in what is now Scottsville. The fleas there were as numerous as they had been at the mill, and he philosophized about this in his journal.

"I slept a few hours [at Sheffer's] despite the fleas. I have noticed a rather strange thing: during the two and a half years I have been in New York, Philadelphia, Baltimore, and a hundred other smaller towns, I have been devoured by bedbugs and have been surprised not to find a flea. In the region I have been travelling . . . I have encountered all the fleas I had previously missed, and they are just as bad companions in America as in Europe."

The Count de Maulevrier made one other river stop, at Berry's tavern at Avon. He then turned west, following the road to Niagara. A few miles from the Genesee, he came to a rather large log hostel where "nine young ladies in their best attire" were engaged, with a number of young men, in a feast, frolic, and dance. The count was asked to join the festivities. Exhausted by the vigor of the frolic, he left it at eleven o'clock for bed. Sleep eluded him. This time, however, it was not fleas, but fancies that disturbed his repose. "Having doubtless had my imagination moved by the charms I had seen," he confessed in his journal, "I slept but poorly."

25

THE village that grew out of a swamp at the edge of the lower Genesee, and which was destined to become the greatest community on the river, by hundreds of thousands, had rivals for prestige and population before it got firmly on its feet and started to walk off with all of the honors.

Some of these rivals had substance and solidity; others had little more than a name and a May-fly's existence. Those that lasted any time at all, in time were absorbed by the city of Rochester. The most notable of these was Carthage: the first of any importance was King's, or, as it was later and more enduringly known, Hanford's Landing. The evanescent colonies were Castle Town, Frankfort, McCrackensville, Athens. Charlotte, at the mouth of the river, grew modestly, knew a modest prosperity, and continued its autonomous village life for more than a century before being lured into the city's embrace and incorporated as a lakeside ward.

In its meander of 159 miles, the Genesee had, at the time white men began seriously to settle its lower valley, three separate stretches of navigable water, and the shortest of these—the six-mile flow from the foot of the river's last cataract to Lake Ontario —was commercially the most important.

On this short stretch of navigable lower river, the depth of which was sufficient for the passage of lake schooners, men with foresight saw the chance to establish a port, which would serve the lake trade, and they came early to the west bank of the Genesee to execute the project they had in mind.

In 1797, Oliver Phelps, of the land company of Phelps and Gorham, who had bought a huge tract of land from the Senecas on the east side of the Genesee, and a lesser acreage, twelve by twenty-four miles on the west side of the stream, sold part of the second property to several men from his home town of Suffield, Connecticut.

Three of these purchasers—Gideon King, Zadock Granger, and Elijah Kent—had made a trip to the Genesee late the year before to examine what they had been told was a country of fabulous fertility and promise. They were men of substance and repute in Suffield. They were impressed with what they saw. A few months after their trip of inspection, King, putting hard cash on the barrel top, bought 3,000 acres of Genesee lands, and Granger gave a land mortgage for a plot of similar extent. Kent did not become a proprietor on the Genesee, but he removed there to live, and there at last he died.

The land purchased by King and Granger reached back from the west bank of the river, about a mile below the Genesee's last cataract, at a point opposite what today is the giant Kodak Park plant of the Eastman Kodak Company in the northwest section of Rochester. The river here flowed through a steep-walled channel, which it had carved out of a rock stratum of considerable variety after the great ice sheet retreated to the north. The walls were rugged, and timber grew in their interstices. At the river's edge was a firm, flat area of land, which the Indians had used as a landing place. It was this that particularly attracted the prospectors from Suffield. They envisaged great wharves and warehouses on the river's bank, a prosperous settlement at the crown of the bold cliff above it.

King was a successful contractor and builder in Connecticut. He had been a Minuteman at Lexington. His position, and his enterprise, gave him leadership of a small party that set out again for the Genesee, with cattle, wagons, and building tools in early spring 1797. His two oldest sons, Thomas and Simon, accompanied him. Zadock Granger and Elijah Kent also went along, the former with his grown son, Eli. They cut a clearing, threw up shacks, made a road, planted seeds.

Charles Williamson once boasted in the public prints that "No man has put a plow to the ground [in the Genesee Valley] without being amply rewarded." Eli Granger, who kept a sketchy journal during his early days on the Genesee, wrote under date of July 18, 1797: ". . . Dined on the first Green Beans that ever was eat or rais'd in this town before—Mr. Kings work on their house rais'd their Ridge." Five days later he again mentioned the colony's garden products: "Very clear and pleasant day & warm wind northerly & light—Major Kent pick'd the first cucumbers that has been eat hear among us."

Before this, he told in his journal of less pleasant matters. The river country was infested with rattlesnakes. Killing them was not sport, but an enterprise of deadly seriousness. In April and early May, Granger kept a tally of the rattlesnakes killed in daily snake hunts. On one occasion a total of fifty-four was destroyed, with nine black snakes, which are harmless to human beings, thrown in for good measure. No hunt that he reported accounted for less than twenty rattlers.

After the Kings, the Grangers, and Elijah Kent had made a fair start of a settlement, they returned to Connecticut to organize a third expedition to the western frontier, which would include their families. Thomas King and Eli Granger each had a wife and child. Kent had a wife. Besides Thomas and Simon, Gideon

King had a third adult son, Bildad, and a teen-aged daughter. These were the children of his first wife, who had died. Later he had married Ruth Graham, who was considerably his junior. The fruit of this union was two small boys.

The second Mrs. King was the daughter and granddaughter of well-known clergymen, noted for the eloquence of their sermons and their ability to flay the souls of their parishioners. The younger of the pair seemingly had other talents. He was the father of seventeen children. It was said of Ruth, that she was "reared in a deeply religious atmosphere and in strict discipline," and was thus prepared to meet difficulties with patience and fortitude.

One of her brothers, Daniel Graham, lived in Suffield. He had a business association with Gideon King. On a sudden, he and his wife, Lydia, decided to share their fortunes with the others who were going to the Genesee; and when the wagon train moved on, they, their children and their household goods were part of it.

Presumably the caravan reached the river at Avon, and crossed to the west bank of the stream at a nearby ford. Two families lived between Avon and the lands purchased by King and Granger. The Peter Sheffers were settled ten miles downriver. Twelve miles farther north, Colonel Fish, his wife, and his ten or twelve children made their home at Allan's mills, on the 100-Acre Tract. From there, the King party needed to proceed another three miles to reach its destination.

There is no record that the wagon train stopped at Sheffer's, but some of its members met Fish, and learned from the colonel that his wife was ill with fever and ague. They saw no portent in this, which was well for their morale. They were as yet ignorant of the dreadful mortality of the disease that they came to know as the Genesee Fever. Blithely, they continued on their way.

Hope for the new colony was based on the notion that as the country in the upper Genesee Valley opened up, great shipments of lumber, pearl ash, and farm produce would be sent out from the river wharves to the ports of Lake Ontario. Until the year before King's Landing was begun, the lake had been tightly controlled by the British. The signing of the Jay Treaty in 1794 had prepared the way for the ending of this insolent domination; the surrender in 1796 by the British of the forts at Niagara and Oswego had made it a fact.

The first winter, the winter of 1797-98, was, for the migrants from the east who had come to the Genesee, a period of intense activity, of hardship, and of accomplishment. There were not enough cabins to go around when the King party arrived at the incipient settlement; snow was in the air; and some of the hardier adults were required to find shelter under upturned wagon boxes until more suitable accommodations were provided.

As the accepted leader of the colony, King, with the assistance of his sons, would have charge of the building of the village itself; the Grangers would attend to matters on the flat river land below. Eli Granger had been a shipwright in Connecticut. His project was at once the construction of a sailing vessel.

In this he was handicapped at first by lack of lumber, a deficiency which also restricted King's operations on the village site. The settlers had hoped to cut boards with the sawmill Ebenezer Allan had vacated. But the mill was in a woefully dilapidated condition. The builders could not await its repair, and the houses that were hurriedly thrown up against the coming of winter were made of logs.

Allan's sawmill in time was put into fair working condition, and Eli Granger got dressed planks for his ship. It was a sailing craft of forty tons, and was launched with jubilation and the high hopes of the residents of King's Landing in the spring of 1798. Granger named her *Jemima* after his wife. She was the first of a number of sailing ships to be dropped from stocks into the lower Genesee.

A trial run proved the *Jemima* seaworthy, and Granger went up the Genesee Valley to tell the promoter, Charles Williamson, that he was in the shipping business. Williamson was enthusiastic about what he heard. He vigorously supported every scheme and enterprise that promised to expedite the development of the Genesee country. He sent business to Granger; he wrote in a Philadelphia newspaper of the new transportation service on the lower Genesee. And in this, as in all of his promotional announcements, he made use of the license granted poets, and assumed by advertising copy writers, as a prerogative of their craft.

He told that, after launching the *Jemima* in April, Granger made a trip in May to Niagara with "two hundred barrels of provisions and there were then lying on the beach two hundred barrels more, ready to be put on board at his return. If we calculate on what has been experienced in other settlements, the port on the Genesee River [King's Landing] bids fair in a very few years, to be a place of considerable importance."

Granger's shipping business was neither so large nor so pressing as Williamson had represented, and the land agent's prediction that King's Landing would become a port of importance was not, in strict truth, fulfilled. The failure of this expectation was not, however, owing to any geographic disadvantage in the site chosen for a port, but the result of a combination of fortuitous circumstances that were beyond the control of the colony's courageous and energetic founders.

In early spring of 1798, the residents at the Landing were saddened by the intelligence brought to them through the woods that Mrs. Fish had succumbed to the fever that was indigenous to the lower Genesee. Stricken the autumn before, she had lingered through the winter and died as the first warm days of early spring raised up the virulent miasma of the marshlands and bogs that surrounded Colonel Fish's shack at the millsite. Among her numerous brood, Mrs. Fish left children who were scarcely out of infancy. Her husband brought her body to King's Landing. Although she had not been part of the colony, she had been a neighbor to the new arrivals from New England, and neighbors were cherished in that sparsely populated country. Building a new settlement for the living, Gideon King had given little thought to the dead. Now he realized that a plot of land should be set aside as a cemetery, and in this, with proper ceremony, Mrs. Fish was laid to rest.

The high spirits and enthusiasm of the colonists could not be damped for more than a moment by the obsequies in the new graveyard. There was so much to do, with the snow gone from the land, and so few hands to do it. The energies of the colonists seemed bursting, even as the buds on the trees. There was the continual noise of hammering; the sibilant sound of saws. Men could be heard shouting commands to the oxen that drew away the felled logs from the steep and difficult road that would connect the settlement on the high ground with the river flat. By early summer the wharf was ready, and a start had been made on a warehouse. Eli Granger's sailing ship was frequently on the lake, bearing to Canadian and American markets produce that had been transported by wagon from the upper river country.

Daniel Graham's wife gave birth to a daughter—the first child born at the settlement—and Daniel himself, having had experience as a merchant in Connecticut, was busy assembling goods for a store that he hoped soon to open. Four newcomers —the Rowe brothers: Ebenezer, Daniel, Abel, and Asa—bought land from Zadock Granger and cleared it for farming.

By midsummer, matters were going boomingly forward at the Landing, which was sometimes called Fall Town. In the brief period of the dog days, the heat was often intense, and its enervating pressure was increased by the humidity in the air, which was greater near the lake than farther up the valley. Men sweat through their clothing at the slightest exertion, but kept unceasingly at their tasks. The ponds and marshlands, which extended back from the river, were scummed over with putrefying vegetation and hidden by rank, high-growing grasses. Frogs croaked on rotting logs, and mosquitoes swarmed over the stagnant water. In time, the clearing of the forest would dry up these infectious areas; now they were pestilent sinkholes of nature.

Suddenly, mysteriously, one by one, the residents at the Landing fell ill. "This day catch'd fast to the ague," Eli Granger wrote with a shaky hand in his journal. He survived. The Rowe brothers, whose farm shack was a short distance from the cluster of houses occupied by the original settlers, were all stricken. One who was still ambulatory struggled to the little settlement for help. His brother Asa, he said, was desperately ill. What help was possible was given, but it was ineffectual. Asa died. And a few weeks later first Daniel Graham, the prospective storekeeper, and then—to deal the colony a staggering blow—Gideon King succumbed to the sickness that became notorious as Genesee Fever.

After that, the little graveyard that Gideon King had marked off, seemed to become more populous than the village itself. Bildad, Gideon's third son by his first marriage, was fatally stricken two months after his father's interment; and Zadock Granger, who recovered from an infection in 1798, died of a second attack of fever the following year. Elijah Kent was also a victim.

The spreading news of the plague discredited the early reputation of King's Landing as a settlement of opportunity and promise. Suffield neighbors of the Kings and Grangers, who had intended to join their friends on the Genesee, abandoned the idea of a western migration. The place seemed no more promising to persons, who had formerly been inspired by Gideon King's leadership and enthusiasm, than a leper's colony. Thomas King, Gideon's oldest son, removed his family from the settlement and cleared a farm some distance west of the Genesee and the mephetic bogs that he believed had caused the death of his father and brother. His prudence was rewarded. He alone, of the King men, survived the plague.

When Thomas left King's Landing, Simon, the second son took over the leadership of what was left of the settlement, and became head of the King household. He also took unto himself a wife. Ruth King found her position in a house that was dominated by a stepson and his wife untenable; and she, together with her widowed sister-in-law, Mrs. Daniel Graham, returned with their small sons and Mrs. Graham's baby girl to Suffield.

Eli Granger, fearful, as was his friend Tom King, of the deadly disease that was decimating the colony, in time sold his sailing ship and moved to a location that he thought more healthful than the Landing. Simon King remained in the house that his father had built until 1804 when he died of Genesee Fever. With his passing, neither a King nor a Granger was listed as a resident of the settlement, which languished until the arrival there in 1809 of the seven Hanford brothers, who had come from Rome, New York.

Frederick, the leader of the Hanford clan, erected a tavern, which seemed to give a new spirit to the place. And the hard spirits he sold may have been considered a prophylaxis against Genesee Fever, for new settlers came to what was now called Hanford's, rather than King's, Landing, and from the river wharves which the Kings and the Grangers had hopefully built late in the preceding century, a lively shipping business was carried on for a short time before, and for a few years after, the War of 1812.

A year after the opening of Hanford's tavern, DeWitt Clinton, as a member of a commission that was exploring a route for a canal that would extend from the Hudson River to Lake Erie, stopped at the Landing. He and the other commissioners had crossed the Genesee at Avon and proceeded north along the west side of the river until they reached its mouth. Clinton had a keen eye and an attentive ear for facts and figures. With the party's arrival at Rochesterville, he remarked in his journal that "An excellent bridge of uncommon strength is now erecting at this place." Later his journal had this notation:

We dined and slept at Hanford's tavern, who is also a merchant, and carries on a considerable trade with Canada. There is a great trade between this country and Montreal in staves, potash, and flour. I was informed by Mr. Hopkins, the officer of the Customs here, that 1000 barrels of flour, 1000 ditto of pork, 1000 ditto of potash, and upwards of 100,000 staves had been already sent this season to Montreal. . . .

At Charlotte, where the Genesee enters Lake Ontario, Clinton observed four sailing ships in the channel. He took note of the fact that village lots were being sold for $10 an acre, "on condition that the purchaser erects a house in a year." The Pulteney syndicate owned a fair share of the property near the mouth of the river, and their agent, Robert Troup, hoped to make Charlotte the most flourishing and populous settlement on the lower Genesee. He succeeded in this, briefly; for a time the place had more residents than Rochesterville, and it went well ahead of Hanford's Landing.

The impetus given the Landing by the arrival of the Hanford brothers was not long sustained. The lake shipping presently went to Carthage, a new port on the east side of the Genesee, which enjoyed a mercurial rise under the sponsorship of wealthy and energetic promoters. Hanford's tavern, later called the Steamboat Hotel, was favored by the traveling public, and a couple of stores at the Landing prospered from a transient trade.

While these establishments appeared to flourish, the settlement itself sank into an obscurity from which it was not lifted until Rochester drew the area that constituted Hanford's Landing into its corporation, and dedicated a narrow strip of land at the crest of the river's gorge as a municipal park. Today the fallen stones of a neglected graveyard and a bronze plaque embedded in a huge boulder on Hanford Landing Road, commemorate the brave efforts of the Kings and Grangers to found, as the plaque reads, "the first white settlement and lake port west of the Genesee." Both a headstone in the cemetery and the plaque on the boulder attribute the failure of these efforts to the deadly disease of the region, Genesee Fever.

26

THE founder of the settlement at Genesee Falls, three miles (and four cataracts) upriver from Hanford's Landing, who gave the place his name and lent it his prestige, did not become a resident of Rochesterville until 1818, and by that time the village had several hundred inhabitants.

Born in Virginia, Nathaniel Rochester removed in his youth to North Carolina and later to Hagerstown, Maryland. In Hagerstown he was esteemed by his fellow townsmen and highly regarded by men of national prominence, including Thomas Jefferson and James Madison, with whom he was in occasional correspondence. After living there more than a quarter of a century, he decided in 1810 to migrate to the Genesee country, where—in the preceding decade—he had acquired a third of the 100-Acre Tract, purchased a parcel of land at Dansville and a farm on Canaseraga Creek.

Rochester was not a swashbuckling frontiersman, and his decision to leave Hagerstown for the wilderness of the Genesee Valley was not taken at the prompting of any love of adventure. He was a man of fixed habits. For the most part, his pursuits were sedentary. He was one of the founders and president of the Hagerstown bank. He had prospered in various commercial and business enterprises. The people of Hagerstown had frequently attested their trust in him by electing him to public office, though politics was not much to his liking, because of the "intrigue and management" he had discovered among officeholders. At Hagerstown he had a splendid home; there he had married; and there eleven of his twelve children had been born.

From this settled way of life, with its prospect of a felicitous, latter-day retirement, Rochester suddenly, and rather wrenchingly, displaced himself. At the age of fifty-eight years, he organized a caravan of Conestoga wagons, pack horses, riding horses, and with his wife, his nine living children, his slaves, and his household chattels, he began a three weeks' journey over abominable roads to the Genesee country.

Rochester's objective was not the 100-Acre Tract, which at that time was forlorn of inhabitants, but his property at Dansville. Several reasons may have urged the bold experiment that he was undertaking. But his prime purpose in leaving what he called "an old settled country" was to provide, in a new and virtually untrammeled section of America, a fuller opportunity for his numerous progeny to develop and express themselves. Besides this, he abhorred the injustice of holding human beings as chattels, and he felt that the economy of the Southern states, depending as it did upon the institution of slavery, reposed upon weak and impermanent supports. He wanted to escape to a land where *all* were free.

"A man whose schemes of life," as one of his admirers wrote, "were well and wisely planned," Nathaniel Rochester had full confidence in his talents to succeed. These had been demonstrated at the age of twenty-one, when a North Carolina merchant, for whom he worked as a clerk, sensible of the young man's business aptitude, took him into the firm.

At Dansville, Rochester freed his slaves. He remained in the village five years. He farmed a considerable acreage, ground corn, made paper, operated mills that sawed logs. His friends, Carroll and Fitzhugh, who shared with him ownership of the 100-Acre Tract, followed him to the Genesee Valley in half a dozen years. They were men of somewhat different stamp from Rochester. They had been born to the purple. The Rochester family had come early to America from England, and its blood lines were good. But Nathaniel did not possess the inherited wealth of his Southern compatriots. He had to make it on his own. Carroll and Fitzhugh erected large homes on the broad lands they held, close to the upper Genesee, and lived in the elegant manner of Southern gentlemen.

Rochester was the active member of the three-way partnership, and to him his two associates more or less consigned the superintendence of the property at the Falls, as Rochesterville was known at first. During his residence at Dansville, he frequently rode a horse to the 100-Acre Tract, to lay out town lots and offer them for sale.

But he made at first no large sales; and presently, discouraged by the slow development of the tract and weighted with pecuniary obligations as the result of his various improvements at Dansville, he offered his share of the millsite to the two other joint owners. Major Carroll declined for both. "Hold on," he wisely counseled, "and you'll have an estate for any man."

Not too many years later, Rochester's portion of the 100-Acre Tract was valued at $100,000, not an inconsequential fortune in the first quarter of the nineteenth century.

When Rochester left Dansville, he lived three years on a large farm at Bloomfield, which was several miles east of the Genesee, but much nearer the 100-Acre Tract than Dansville; and in 1818 he removed from that place to Rochesterville, which the year before, owing largely to his own petitions to the Legislature, had become an incorporated village.

He was in his sixty-seventh year, a tall, spare, slightly stooped patriarch, whose habits were modest almost to the point of austerity. Rochester was a conservative of the first rank, and the city of his founding still bears, in this regard, the stamp of his character. All his life he had worked hard, saved, eschewed high jinks, and made opportunities for himself without compromising his notable integrity. Not given to expedient practices, he was known, however, on one occasion to sacrifice principle to a cause of merit. The story is told that once, on moral grounds, he caused one of his sons to return to the loser an election bet the young man had won, but before he moved north, Father Rochester himself had helped manage a lottery that raised several thousand dollars for an Episcopal Church in Hagerstown, which he served as vestryman.

When Colonel Rochester settled in Rochesterville, the swamplands of the 100-Acre Tract were drying up, as the forest receded under the ringing axes of woodsmen. Six years before, this plot and the adjacent area on the right bank of the Genesee had appeared to Edwin Scrantom, Hamlet's articulate son, as a "wild and desert place . . . cheerless in daytime, and doubly dark at night . . . a thick jungle of dogwood, alder, birch, and chokeberry, brambles and blue-beech" under the "tangled canopy" of which "wild beasts crouched and serpents innumerable crawled."

But the dens of the rattlesnakes were being destroyed by the tools of men, and the snakes themselves killed off. The howl of wolves was heard no longer at the village gates. Indians occasionally pattered into town on moccasined feet, to excite a mild curiosity, rather than the terror they once caused. They came to sell skins, to buy goods, to get drunk in the taverns.

Rochesterville would soon have a thousand inhabitants. The mud-chinked log shacks, with their stick chimneys, which had provided makeshift shelter for the original settlers, were giving way to framed houses, some two stories high. Three or four mills had been built and others were building; and those already in operation were busy day and night sawing logs and grinding wheat. A tannery had come into being, a brickyard, and a weekly newspaper. A dam had been built across the Genesee to provide water for a mill flume on the east side of the stream which was to be known for more than a century and a quarter as the Johnson & Seymour Race. The wooden bridge, just below the dam, was being crossed by hundreds of westbound migrants on foot, on horseback, in oxcarts, in stage wagons, and in fancy horse-drawn dearborns, with curtains to protect the passengers against the elements or, if privacy was desired, from Peeping Toms along the road.

Thrice weekly a stage, which operated between Lewiston, on the Niagara River, and Canandaigua, the county seat of Ontario County, clattered into town. All who were within the vicinity of its stopping place paused in their labors to speculate as to whether the alighting passengers were transients or persons who intended to settle in the swift-growing community on the west bank of the Genesee.

The Genesee River was the very heart of Rochesterville, the reason for its being; and it was fitting that, when Colonel Rochester came with his family to reside for the remainder of his life in the village, he should take a house overlooking the river.

He was the oldest resident of a community that was vibrant with youth and bursting with an energy that would help soon to make it the most booming boom town on the American continent. But he was not, in his sixty-seventh year, antediluvian or outdated. Even when he had lived a day's horseback ride from Rochesterville, he had kept in touch with the affairs of the village. Now, as an actual resident of the place, all of his interests were concentrated there and his best efforts were directed to its development.

He had obtained the property upon which he lived from a physician who was not practicing his profession. There were several doctors in Rochesterville, but most of them had renounced the Hippocratic Oath to try to get rich as quickly as possible. They were engaged in the real-estate business, in the mercantile trade, one had opened a pharmacist's shop, another, Dr. Matthew Brown, with his brother, Francis, had dug Browns' millrace on the west side of the Genesee, which was to endure as a Rochester landmark as long as the Johnson & Seymour Race on the opposite side of the river. The medical men were too busy exploiting the expanding opportunities of the village to find much time for pill-rolling and bedside diagnosis.

Colonel Rochester had bought into the 100-Acre Tract because of the hydraulic potential he saw in a series of waterfalls that began at the eastern extremity of his property. Today there are three cataracts on the lower Genesee, the southernmost of which has a height of ninety-two feet. When Rochester first saw the river there were four, and the first of these—nearly half a mile south of the celebrated Upper Falls—descended only fourteen feet over the jagged floor of the stream.

The fourteen-foot cascade disappeared early in the nineteenth century, when workmen, to facilitate the construction of an aqueduct across the Genesee, leveled by blasting the rocky bed of the river. Before that, the swift run of water had turned the wheel of Ebenezer Allan's nondescript mill, and convinced Nathaniel Rochester that here was a place where the flour industry might prosper. But he had no notion how greatly it would prosper; or how, during his residence in Rochesterville, the cataracts of the lower Genesee would power a dozen mills, which would produce more flour than any other milling center in America.

A year before Rochester settled in Rochesterville, the destiny of the community for the next seventy-five years was more or less decided (without benefit of the counsel of its founder) by the passage of a state law authorizing the construction of a Grand Canal from the Hudson River to Lake Erie.

The idea of such a waterway was not new. It had been discussed long before the Revolution. But it was not until 1808 that an official survey of a canal route was made. This, and a second survey eight years later, indicated that the most feasible place for the great trough of water to traverse the Genesee was, if not at water level a short distance south of Rochesterville, by aqueduct spang through the heart of the village.

Several reasons decided the latter course, and one of these was a rambunctious display the Genesee put on the very year that Rochesterville gained the dignity of an incorporated village. After a week of heavy rains in November, 1817, the swollen stream, boiling down from the upper valley hills, hit the community at the Falls the first of a series of devastating blows that were to continue intermittently until, more than a hundred years later, a flood-control dam was built fifty miles upriver at Mt. Morris.

The turbid, bullying waters spread wide over farmlands south of the village, and brought down in their angry torrent drowned pigs, farm sheds, an occasional cow, and now and then a small river craft that had been moored at a bank of the stream's natural channel. They inundated part of the village of Rochesterville, carried off several small buildings, and threatened the wooden bridge that spanned the river. They ripped out a dam.

After this display, the engineers abandoned any notion of having the canal cross the Genesee, behind a dam, at river level. If the river could take out one dam, it could probably—if its dander were up—take out theirs, and the decision was made to span the stream by aqueduct, in the center of Rochesterville. It was a fortunate choice for the village that Nathaniel Rochester had founded.

Before the first spadeful of dirt was turned on the first section of the canal, Rochester recognized the merit of the project and lent it his active support. His attitude was contrary to that of the Virginians, whom he greatly admired and who had been top dogs in Washington for years, with a triple run of presidents. They voted not a penny of Federal money for the undertaking, and most of them seemed to concur with Jefferson's expression that Clinton's Big Ditch was "little short of madness."

But the digging of the canal went forward in the face of all opposition, and despite the volleys of invective directed at its great projector, Clinton, whose "folly" some believed would ruin the state, if not indeed, the nation. The Big Ditch reached the east bank of the Genesee in early summer 1822, and late that year boats were being towed from Rochester (the last syllable in the village name had been elided by usage and official decree) as far east as Little Falls. The aqueduct, which would raise the waterway above the river, and allow it to continue, uninterruptedly, to its western terminus, was building.

This was a monumental structure. It was ready for use in September, 1823, though its formal opening was delayed several weeks in order to allow the Canal Commissioners to approve the work. It gave importance—even an architectural grandeur—to a community which, less than a dozen years before, had seen its first permanent resident settled in a log shack on what was now a populous thoroughfare.

The aqueduct had required two years to build. It had cost $83,-000. There had been interruptions and contretemps. There had been trouble about the poor quality of stone taken from a nearby quarry. River ice had knocked out one of the aqueduct's piers. An early contractor, William Brittin—who had built the State prison at Auburn—had persuaded the authorities to lend him thirty convicts to break rock. The forced laborers needed goads to keep them at their tasks. They were resentful of the free workers, mostly newly arrived Irish, with muscles that enabled them to lift dumpcarts on their backs, who were paid the munificent wage of fifty cents a day, with found. One day the convicts took a notion to bolt from their chains and from their keepers. Several gained their liberty. Fears of rape and murder were rampant among the village women, but the guards quickly apprehended all but a couple of the escapees.

When Brittin died, before completing his contract, the impressment of prison laborers was abandoned. The job was finished by a new contractor, and 400 workers, who helped swell the village population to an estimated 3,700. Some—particularly some of the Irish drudges—remained permanently in Rochester. They

founded on the east side of the river a colony that was known for years as Dublin, where whiskey was said to "run like water," where squalor often prevailed, and where a man, to be cock of the walk, needed to be as tough as two shillelaghs.

"The bridge that carried water," as some who came to marvel at the massive gray stone structure described the aqueduct, was 802 feet in length. The river passed under it through a series of Roman arches; canalboats passed over it in a trough of water seventeen feet wide.

It was dedicated October 6, 1823, when two gaily decorated packet boats, bearing canal officials, village officials, and sundry

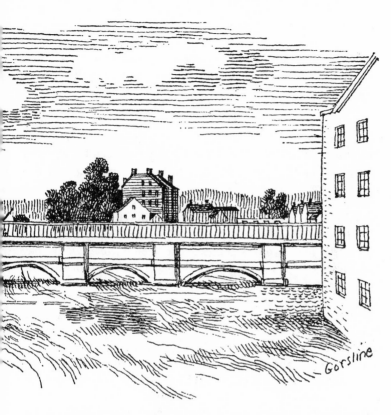

other badge wearers, careered at the breakneck speed of four miles an hour from the east to the west side of the structure. There the dignitaries were greeted with loud huzzas, a salvo of musketry, and the blare of a brass band. There were speeches, of course, when the boats were moored in the turning basin on the west side of the Genesee; there were more speeches that evening at a sumptuous celebration dinner, presided over by the venerable Colonel Rochester, in the leading tavern of the village. There were toasts far into the night. At the twenty-fifth toast, the boys began to think of their loved ones, and they made it "to the ladies." After that, some got up and went home.

The opening of the aqueduct did not mean that the entire

length of the Grand Erie Canal was navigable. Two years were to pass before cannon boomed full across the state to signalize the completion of the great inland waterway. That day DeWitt Clinton began his historic voyage from Lake Erie to the seaboard in the packet, *Seneca Chief*. He carried with him a jug of lake water to empty into the briny expanse of the Atlantic and effect the "wedding of the waters." His second day out, October 27, 1825, he and his party were honored with high ceremonies when the *Seneca Chief* reached the Genesee.

After the celebration, and after the governor's vessel had moved east across the aqueduct to continue its triumphant pageant, it was followed by a Rochester packet, *Young Lion of the West*. This maxim on its burgee, if it flaunted one, would have symbolized the brawny growth of the village which now straddled the Genesee and which soon would achieve, by law, the status of a city.

Perhaps it is true that Rochester was more advantaged by the Erie Canal than any other seat of population along its route. It was not the canal, however, but the cascading waters of the Genesee that gave the first great impetus to the village and started its phenomenal growth. The cataracts powered the mills that were forming chockablock along both banks of the stream; and the mills, as they increased in number, ground the wheat— brought by river boat, by cart, and by pack horses from the enormously fertile growing lands east, west, and south of the village—into incalculable bushels of fine-textured flour.

The canal, when it came, provided means of wide distribution for this snowy product. It carried it, at greatly reduced shipping charges, not only on its first run to remote points on the American continent, but also started it on its way to foreign markets. But the Genesee antedated the canal by a million years, and the mills, whose function depended upon the river's precipitant waters, were, to a limited number, going concerns a dozen years before Clinton's Big Ditch was dug.

And it was the mills that gave Rochester, when it reached the dimensions of a metropolis, its far-flung and honored title, Flour City; that made it, with an assist—to be sure—from the Grand Canal, the breadbasket of the nation.

27

With the routing of the Erie Canal through Rochester, the hopes entertained by neighboring settlements on the lower Genesee, of outdoing the village at the Falls, withered and died on the vine. Some died more slowly than others. Carthage, which was situated on the east side of the river, at the Lower Falls, gave up stubbornly. Its aspirations had been high. It was prideful and challenging; and its promoters had a style—a flamboyance—that attracted attention and brought settlers to their colony.

The promoters came in 1817, after a large tract of land had been partly cleared by an earlier settler, from whom they purchased a thousand acres. Their leader was Elisha B. Strong, a Yale blue out of Windsor, Connecticut. He was young, spirited, and chuck-full of bright ideas.

Strong had previously made a sightseeing trip through the western wilderness. Liking what he saw, he decided to make his home in Canandaigua. There he studied law in a local office. But

Canandaigua was already a well-established community, and the zestful young man had a desire to found a settlement of his own. He chose for this enterprise a site at the head of Genesee shipping, and he and his associates, who had formed a land company, soon had village lots staked off, houses under construction, and a wharf and warehouse built at the river's edge.

Half a mile downriver, on the opposite bank, Hanford's Landing had fallen into disrepute owing largely to the ravages of Genesee Fever. But lake schooners still unloaded there; and early in the very year that the Carthage promoters inaugurated their ambitious building program, Hanford's Landing gained a brief new fame when the *Ontario*, the first steam vessel to part the waters of the lower Genesee, put in at that port.

Carthage had several advantages over the diminishing colony at Hanford's. It seemed to have escaped the endemic disease of the river country which had swept through the latter settlement like the scythe of death. The descent to its landing place at the river bottoms was not as precipitant as the approach to the low plateau where boats docked at Hanford's; and leading from Carthage Landing, north along the border of the stream, was an Indian trail which was broadened—as more and more shipping bypassed the older for the newer river port—to form a towpath. From the towpath, oxen hauled up and down the narrow channel of the Genesee sailing vessels that were becalmed or vexed by adverse winds.

The Carthage promoters had imagination, great enterprise, and a feeling that they were divinely touched—that the "God of nature has fitted and destined our place to become . . . one of the principal establishments in the western country." They ardently petitioned the United States Bank at Philadelphia for permission to establish a branch bank at Carthage, but failed in this. They strove to command the lake shipping that passed up and down the Genesee, and succeeded in obtaining the greater part of it. They desired that the Erie Canal cross the river at their village, but the Canal Commissioners gave this advantage to

Rochester. They hoped to connect the eastern and western sections of a famous highway, the Ridge Road, which were separated at Carthage by the Genesee River, and briefly—for fifteen months—achieved this design.

The bridge which they built to span the wide gorge of the river at the Lower Falls was the boldest project undertaken by Elisha Strong and his associates, and for a time it made Carthage the scene of one of the structural wonders of the continent.

Begun in 1818, by builders who were said to have given a warranty that their work would hold up for a year, the bridge was ready for use in February, 1819. To obtain funds for the undertaking, some of the Carthage proprietors had heavily mortgaged their real estate. They were badgered about this. A correspondent for the New York *Spectator,* observing the bridge in the process of construction, called it a "monument of folly" built by "bankrupts and adventurers without capital."

Nevertheless, the "bankrupts and adventurers" must have swelled with pride when the last bolt was screwed into place and wagoners started lumbering across the bridge, showing—to the world—a brave demeanor, though the icy sweat of fear might have been oozing through the pores of their skins.

The Carthage bridge was a direct challenge to Rochester, the booming village upriver, where, as one perceptive young resident wrote to his betrothed in Connecticut, "froth and puffing is the order of the day." Rochester might in time have its dirty old ditch, which Clinton was building; but where else in America was there such a bridge as the one at Carthage? Indeed, there was nothing quite like it in the world.

Its span was awesome; its height was even more so. From bank to bank it reached 718 feet and its floor was more than 190 feet above the river that it crossed. It was only a little shorter than the famous bridge at Schaffhausen, in Switzerland, which had stood (until its destruction twenty years before the erection of the Carthage bridge) as an engineering phenomenon. The curious came from many miles to see the bridge at Carthage;

traffic across it was heavy, and carters—made bold by their famil-
iarity with the wooden span—asserted that the structure stood
firm and tremorless under loads of twelve and fifteen tons.

The bridge had a Gothic arch, the chord of which measured
352 feet; it was 30 feet wide; hundreds of trees had been felled
to supply the lumber for its construction; and it was held
together (the statistical-minded chroniclers of the day boasted)
by 800 large iron bolts. The number was insufficient. In May,
1820, with a great death groan, the arch buckled under the
weight of its framework, and the pride of Carthage plunged
shatteringly into the gorge of the Genesee.

With the destruction of its monumental edifice, Carthage suffered a major catastrophe. Until this accident, its optimistic
proprietors believed that the place would soon gain ascendancy
over its rival at the Upper Falls. Some of the proprietors now
abandoned their aspirations for the colony and moved upriver to
Rochester. Others persisted in a brave determination to reclaim
the broken fortunes of the settlement. Their bridge had come
apart like something made of playing cards; but they had built
half a hundred houses on the heights above the Genesee, they
had stores and a couple of mills doing business, land set aside
for a public park, a school in prospect, and a church (later to
suffer from the fierce competition of four or five taverns) was
being organized. And, most important of all, they had the
Genesee at the foot of the Lower Falls and wharves and warehouses to cater to the shipping trade.

In 1820, the year that the Carthage bridge fell, 316 visits were
made by merchant vessels to the Genesee, and the greatest
number of these calls took the schooners and the single steamship that was then in the lake trade, as far south as the busy
wharves at Carthage. In all, 67,467 barrels of flour were carried
out of the river in Canadian and American bottoms; and the
total valuation of exports from the time that the Genesee was
navigable in early spring until it became ice-locked in late autumn, was a respectable $375,000.

In a dozen years, exports from the Genesee tripled in value, and Carthage continued as the dominant river port. The steamship *Ontario* now passed Hanford's to make weekly calls at Carthage Landing. She was a convenience because of the dependability of her schedule, and a curiosity because of the oddity of her design. She was a hybrid craft. Built by American shipwrights at Sackets Harbor, she was propelled under steam by port and starboard paddle wheels and had, for occasions of "engine trouble," masts for the spread of sails. Seven years after the *Ontario* first visited the Genesee, a second steamship, the *Martha Ogden,* cautiously moved through the breached sand bar at the river's mouth, and made her noisy way upstream to Carthage. And it was not long after this, now that the practicability of steamships for the lake trade had been demonstrated, before a fleet of five of these vessels was making Carthage a regular port of call.

Schooners, however, still carried the greater amount of tonnage. One day an observer counted seventeen vessels of this type lying off the Carthage docks. Lake shipping increased, rather than diminished, with the opening of the Erie Canal at Rochester. The canal was a stimulus to all activities in that village. New industries were springing up, and the products of some of these were carried on their way to distant markets by canalboats and lake vessels. But the place was still predominantly a flour-milling town, as it would continue to be until well after mid-century. At the time of its incorporation as a village, Rochester had two or three mills within its precincts. Seventeen years later, when it was granted a city charter, it had twenty mills, with a run of more than ninety stone, and an annual output of nearly half a million barrels of flour.

As the village of Rochester boomed, so boomed the river shipping at Carthage. But Carthage was not growing swiftly enough for the promoters who still remained there and cherished the dream of metropolitan grandeur. They felt that something novel was needed to attract attention to the place, now that their spectacular bridge had fallen into the chasm of the river. They envisaged a railroad. It would not, of course, be a steam line; that would have been premature. It would be a horse railroad. Nevertheless, it would provide a much more convenient and rapid way of transporting freight to and fro between Rochester and Carthage than the haul over a corduroy road that wound widely around the three cataracts of the lower Genesee.

The cost of the railroad was estimated at $30,000. The capital was quickly subscribed, and the organization that projected the work was known as the Rochester Canal and Railroad Company. Elisha Johnson—who had previously replaced the first Rochester bridge to span the Genesee with a new structure of greater serviceability and more impressive design; who had built a dam across the river which supplied the Johnson & Seymour millrace; and who had given to the state the eastern half of a strip of river bed it needed for the canal aqueduct—was called upon to build the railroad.

Johnson was not a Carthage resident. Like the first Carthage promoter, Elisha B. Strong, he had migrated from New England to Canandaigua, and removed from that village to the Genesee, where, on the east side of the stream, he owned a considerable acreage. A former student at Williams College, he was a surveyor, an engineer, and a builder. He had abounding energy. Elisha Strong, a handsome six-footer, of elegant tastes, carried a gold-headed cane and wore a ruffled shirt. A ruffled shirt gave a man in early Rochester the brevet of aristocracy and marked him as a glass of fashion. Johnson also carried a gold-headed cane, wore an impressive silk topper, but eschewed the ruffled shirt. He often worked out of doors in the mud during his surveying and building operations.

Strong served for a term in the State Legislature; was made a county judge when the county of Monroe, of which Rochester is the seat, was created in 1821; and over the bitter opposition of Colonel Nathaniel Rochester, who denounced him as a "malignant, black-hearted rascal," was made president of Rochester's first bank. But he had overextended himself in his Carthage operations, and never recovered from the pecuniary losses which he suffered at that time. Late in life, he left Rochester for Detroit, Michigan, where he died in straitened circumstances.

Johnson, whose activities will be dealt with more extensively in later pages of this work, experienced no such fate. He was a go-getter of the first rank. His acquisitive talents seemed never to dull; he turned from one enterprise to another, as easily as he might change partners in a square dance; and though at times he was given to lavish displays and bizarre extravagances, he appeared never to allow his indulgences to threaten his sound financial position.

The building of what was popularly known as the "Carthage Railroad," despite the wordier title given it by its founders, was begun in 1831, and the greater part of the three-mile "system" was opened to the public in September, 1833. The Rochester terminus was at a canal basin at the east end of the aqueduct, and the line, when completed, extended north to the settlement above Carthage Landing.

Rolling stock of the railroad consisted of numerous freight cars and two "elegant, double-decked pleasure carriages," which vaguely resembled stagecoaches. The train was pulled by horses in tandem hitch. The rails were four-by-six wooden timbers, covered with iron plates. This was Elisha Johnson's first experience as a railroad builder. He was later to patent a method of laying railroad tracks and, still later, to build the first steam railroad to enter Rochester.

For a mile and a quarter before the Carthage Railroad reached its northern terminus, its cars were drawn over tracks that were laid at the crown of the river's gorge. From this vantage point, the deep, wooded, winding chasm of the Genesee, as yet unspoiled by the grimy hand of industry, offered an enchanting prospect. The railroad's "elegant pleasure cars" were often crowded with sightseeing tourists and, on holidays, with local excursionists.

Although both passenger and freight business were profitable for a time, the Carthage Railroad continued as a going institution less than a decade. And the year after it was completed it ceased to be an interurban line, since, at that time, the village of Rochester, granted a city charter, promptly made Carthage part of its corporate body.

With the loss of its autonomy, the settlement lost some of the zest it had displayed during the period when its promoters were striving to give it distinction as a municipal entity. Carthage Landing, however, continued for several years as an active lake port. There was a tannery at the river bottom; there were mills just above the Lower Falls, and the Roger brothers, shipwrights, dropped from their stocks several schooners which entered the lake trade.

But the time soon came when the bulk of the lake traffic left what was now the city district of Carthage for the left bank of the Genesee, where it had originated late in the preceding century. The new port was known as Kelsey's Landing. Its promoters made a winning bid for the steamship and schooner trade by first cutting a winding road in the rocky wall of the river gorge, and then by instituting an omnibus service. The omnibuses appealed to steamship passengers; the road to the wharf facilitated the movement of export and import freight.

Kelsey's vogue was brief. It ended with the opening, in 1854, of a steam railroad, which connected the city of Rochester with the village of Charlotte. Wharves and warehouses had been built at Charlotte (Sha-lót, as the name is pronounced by natives of the region); piers had been extended from the river into the lake to give definite lines to the harbor; and a lighthouse long since had taken the place, as a point of reckoning for lake mariners, of a giant elm tree on the riverbank, once known as the "pilot tree."

People continued to move into Carthage even after the shipping business began to dwindle. They tried other industries. The mills still operated; the tannery prospered; there was a distillery in the neighborhood, which dumped its refuse into the river.

There were three taverns on the high ground above the Landing and two at the water's edge. One of the latter was managed by Adonijah Green, who had given up farming to try the life of a Boniface.

Arriving at Carthage at a time when the settlement was at the peak of its glory, Green took over an inn called the Pavilion. It was a popular resort for fresh-water sailors, passengers on lake vessels, dock-wallopers, and carters who hauled freight to and from the Landing. Adonijah Green provided his patrons with strong grog, substantial table fare, and hearty hospitality; but these excellencies alone would not have preserved his name in the Carthage annals. Posterity knows him as the father of Seth, a "notional" lad, sometimes called the "laziest boy in town," who was destined to achieve, in a specialized field, an international celebrity.

28

WHEN Adonijah Green removed to Carthage Landing from the farm a few miles east of the Genesee, where Seth was born, the boy was two or three years old. He was not an only child. Adonijah and his wife had a considerable brood. Busy for long hours each day providing entertainment for their patrons, the Greens, good Christian parents though they were, had little time to dote upon or indulge their children. Young Seth was quickly free of his mother's apron strings. His education, under the tutelage of authorized pedagogues, was limited; but he had other less formal teachers.

Sailormen who came up the Genesee on schooners became his friends; the trappers who got furs along the riverbank and in the woods that reached back from it, were his guides; and he also learned about woodcraft—the calls of birds, the tricks of reptiles, the habits of wild beasts—from a small group of Seneca Indians who grew corn on a patch of land they owned just north of the

Carthage settlement, and who came to the Carthage stores to trade.

But Seth Green was largely self-taught, and the river—or that short stretch of the Genesee that flows from the Lower Falls to Lake Ontario—was his study hall and laboratory. There he made the early observations and prosecuted the early experiments that were the genesis of scientific formulae, which in time were to bring him honors from foreign countries, rewards from his native land, and acclaim as a "benefactor of mankind." He was also to be designated the Father of Fish Culture, a title which Seth, who was not afflicted with modesty, could wear with aplomb and bravely flaunt to the world.

At times during his long, lusty, and useful life, Green contributed, to newspapers and various other publications, articles which touched on aspects of his youth and early manhood; but his out-of-door activities allowed him little time for sedentary pursuits, and perhaps because of this—and lack of inclination—he never wrote his memoirs, and no one, more's the pity, has done a full-blown story of his life.

As a boy, he would lie long hours in a flat-bottomed boat, and people ashore would remark that "the lazy Green boy" was sleeping on the water in order to avoid the chores that a good Christian lad should perform on land. But Seth was not asleep. Stretched prone on the thwarts of his small boat, his head dangling over the stern, he might be watching the wallowing of a carp on the surface of the water, or studying a school of bullheads feeding on floating refuse from the Carthage distillery, which he had discovered was a favorite food of these large-headed fish.

He was alert, keen, and intensely perceptive. He was quite as sensitive to the phenomena of natural history as Henry Thoreau, who shared his natal year of 1817. His observations of the behavior of fishes were perhaps as minute as the ornithological studies which the famous clergyman-naturalist, Gilbert White, reported from Selborne, in scientific detail and in beautiful language, to the Honorable Daines Barrington and Thomas Pennant, Esq.

When Seth saw the Kelsey people blasting out the rock that was to make the road to their landing much more accessible than the one at Carthage, he decided that it was high time for him to buckle down and help eke out the family's income which, he correctly surmised, would be drastically reduced if the lake traffic moved to the new port on the opposite bank of the Genesee. Brought up on the river, his obsessing interests had been the study and catching of fish, but these pursuits had been a hobby and a sport. Now they would become a vocation.

He had made ingenious hooks out of pins, and with these he had caught strings of fish while others fishing near him had had only nibbles. He knew every hole where the finny monsters lay between the Falls and the lake, and monsters then existed in the lower Genesee.

Large bass, pike and muskelunge were plentiful. Catfish, which often weighed 50 pounds were taken, and in the spring fishermen frequently speared or, if more sportively inclined, played with hook and line sturgeon heavier than their own bodies. A sturgeon weighing from 100 to 150 pounds was known as "Albany beef." It made solid food. Its roe was a delicacy. Its air bladder could be processed into isinglass.

Seth Green bought a big net, caught a large number of fish, opened a store in downtown Rochester. The store was located on what is now Front Street. In those days Front Street was little more than a sandy beach on the west bank of the river, and part of it was always under water at floodtime. It is still, while awaiting a promised civic face-lifting, something of a "beach," because of the numerous derelicts who live in its mission and squalid lodging places. It once had a haymarket and a notorious concert hall. It now has emporiums where chickens are dressed and sold, meat markets, fish markets, secondhand stores, hobo lunchrooms, and cheap saloons. Green added a small restaurant to his store, and his clam chowder was described as "supreme." Besides fish, he sold partridge, woodcock, wild duck and other game, for he was a crack shot as well as the most expert fisherman on the river.

As a market hunter, he shot everything that moved and was edible; as a fisherman, his river and lake catches were prodigious, and he had other commercial fishermen bringing the spoils of their creels and boats to his store.

Today, by a proclamation on a bronze plaque erected by the Izaak Walton League at the State Fish Hatcheries at Mumford, New York, Seth Green is commemorated not only as the father of fish culture, but as a "world famous pioneer in conservation."

When he entered this phase of his career, he remarked that since he had been as "responsible as anyone for depleting the streams of fish," he felt it his duty to restock these barren waters; and he spoke, at the same time, and in a tone as near to sadness as one of his euphoric humor could assume, of the deplorable waste of wild life in the woods, and particularly of the slaughter of native songbirds, to complement women's vanity. Women of the period seemed to believe that they attained the height of fashion only when they resembled an ornithologist's specimen case.

"I am sorry the songbirds of our country have so many enemies," Seth said. "Their worst enemy is the ladies, next the skunk, next the cat, next the ladies, next the snakes, and last the ladies. I met a lady in Rochester the other day who had the breasts of six birds on her hat."

One day, while fishing for salmon in a Canadian river, Seth became so fascinated by their actions that he laid aside his fishing gear and climbed a tree at the side of the stream better to observe what was going on below its surface. He had turned from killing fish to make an academic study of their habits and behavior, which wasn't an unusual practice of his. What he saw in a vigil, which continued two days, convinced him that, with proper cultivation, the waters of lakes and rivers might become as productive for man's estate as soil that was plowed, fertilized, and seeded.

As he watched, he saw the female salmon preparing nests for their eggs. They did this by fanning out, by the vigorous use of fins and tail, small holes in the bed of the stream, which they later covered over with sand and fine gravel. But once deposited and mixed with the milt of the male, the eggs were ravaged by the male salmon, who gobbled up all that the female was unable to hide. This seemed to Seth a dreadful waste of natural resources. When he climbed stiffly down from his arboreal perch, at the conclusion of his studies, he made up his mind that one day he would learn to save millions of fish that were now, in embryo, being sacrificed to cannibalism.

Upon his return home, he began to experiment with fish culture in his natural habitat, the Genesee River. Although he had never heard of fish being artificially propagated, knowledge of the rudiments of the science may have antedated by millennia the discoveries Seth Green was later to announce. There is a belief that, while Europeans were still using stone axes, Chinese nobles were competing with one another in the improvement of the breed of goldfish, much as millionaire horsemen compete today in improving the breed of the thoroughbred. In Green's time, two Frenchmen and a Prussian army officer had made advances in the science of fish culture; Seth was the American pioneer.

But the development of his theories was delayed for more than a quarter of a century. During this period Green married and raised a family of six children. His domestic obligations required that he attend closely to his business. It was not until 1864, when he purchased a stretch of land on Spring Creek, which flows into Oatka (once named Allan's Creek after the notorious Ebenezer) and thence into the Genesee River, just east of the village of Scottsville, that he was able fully to devote himself to research and experimentation.

He knew very well the principles of artificial insemination of trout eggs; what he had not perfected were the techniques and apparatus needed for a practical demonstration of his principles. Now, with his entire time devoted to the science, these were soon developed; and the news that Seth Green was artificially growing hundreds of thousands of trout fry, was displayed on the front pages of newspapers which were largely devoted to the final episodes of the Civil War. Overnight, the former Front Street fish dealer had become famous.

The wide publicity given to Green's successful experiments in artificially inseminating the eggs of brook trout brought to his Mumford Hatchery, among other interested persons, Robert B. Roosevelt, whose nephew, Theodore, was later to become President of the United States. Roosevelt and Green were poles apart in background and breeding. The former was a wealthy aristocrat; the latter, the son of a tavern-keeper. The distinction was no hindrance to a close friendship which, once formed, was severed only by death. The two men were among the leading sportsmen of the day. They often competed against each other in fly-casting tournaments. In this delicate art, Green had few superiors; and by Roosevelt's asseveration, no one had Green's all-round competence as a bird shot, trap shot, pistol marksman, and fly-caster.

Fascinated by what Green was doing at Mumford, Roosevelt spent a good deal of time observing his friend's experiments. The fruit of these studies was a book upon which the two men collaborated, *Fish Hatching and Fish Catching*. With another collaborator, Green wrote a book on trout culture, which was translated into the French; and a third, by himself, *Home Fishing in Home Waters*.

In 1867, at the solicitation of New England authorities, Seth succeeded, after several tries, in artificially propagating shad in the fished-out waters of the Connecticut River. He later restocked the Hudson River with millions of shad, and still later, in an epic expedition, he carried shad fry clear across the continent, and dumped them, wiggling and full of life, into the Sacramento River, where shad fry had never swum before.

After these accomplishments were publicized, Green received medals from fishing and scientific societies in France and Germany, and similar recognition from this country. He was credited by some enthusiasts with developing more edible fish life than any other man alive. A London newspaper, in an expansive tribute, said in part: "Seth Green . . . has done more toward producing good wholesome food for the toiling masses of the United States than all the peers of the United Kingdom rolled together."

Green did not back away from any honors that came to him, but his head was not turned by fame. He was something of a showman. His many exploits, boy and man—and a fat book would be needed to recount all of them—always, with his telling, made "good copy." He announced that he wanted to make every lake in America a fish pond. When asked to go abroad to propagate fish in European waters, he begged off on the excuse that there was still too much to do in his native land. He was a hearty, gregarious, physically powerful man, who delighted in masculine companionship and a variety of outdoor pursuits. In his youth he had been a wrestler of such skill that he had won money prizes at the sport. An expert yachtsman, he won numerous sailing races on waters adjacent to Rochester, where he lived most of the seventy-one years of his life. He raced trotting horses in matinees.

He sold the Mumford Hatchery, which is three miles west of the Genesee River and nineteen miles south of Rochester, to the State of New York. It is known as the first state-owned hatchery in New York. It was established in 1870. Green was its first superintendent. He introduced from Germany brown trout, which he found thrived in water warmer than that of streams normally inhabited by native brook trout.

Seth Green died in 1888. Although he was not the most distinguished Rochesterian of his time, he may have been more widely known, outside of Rochester, than any other contemporary resident of the city. He left the heritage of conservation, which had been little thought of before he advanced the idea of restocking barren waters with fish, and a trout fly that bears his name. Besides the plaque erected in his memory at the State Hatchery at Mumford, his name has been given to a Rochester street which winds along the crown of the Genesee River gorge at the place where the village of Carthage was founded with such high hopes and bold aspirations.

29

Probably its crossing by General John Sullivan and his Continental army is the most notable historical event in the long saga of the Genesee; but it was a traveling stunt man, full of braggadocio and brandy, who leaped over the Upper Falls—and didn't live to leap another day—who first brought the river into national prominence.

The career of Sam Patch, whose fatal jump was made November 13, 1829, has been examined with almost the care and minuteness biographers might employ in investigating the life of a poet a few cuts below the immortals or of a general who had won battles, but not a war. He was known prior to his arrival in Rochester as the "Jersey Leaper," though the probability is that he was born either in Massachusetts or Rhode Island; and before his body was exhumed from an ice cake at the mouth of the Genesee four months after it had disappeared in the turbulent waters below the Falls, he was to become a legend, the pet of poetasters, a subject of sermons, a martyr, a hero—even a genius, in the fancy of one journalist, who solemnly declared that had Patch lived, he "might have astonished the world, perhaps for years, with the greatest feats ever performed by man."

Sam Patch sought the "bubble reputation." But his fame continued after his death as a green and living thing throughout the remaining seventy years of the nineteenth century, and it persists, in narrowing scope, even today. In recent years, a bronze plaque set in a granite stone has been placed at the long-neglected mound in Charlotte Cemetery where lie his bones; and efforts, which so far have failed, have been made by persons interested in the preservation of historic landmarks to induce the state to erect one of its blue and yellow markers in Sam's memory, and to persuade Rochester authorities either to give the name "Sam Patch" to a small city park or to a bridge that spans the Genesee some distance north of the "Jersey Leaper's" final performance.

What figure of a man Patch was, posterity may never know. The bills that advertised his exploits gave no indication of his lineaments. No portrait of him has been uncovered. He has been variously described. Some who met him, represented him as a squat, thick-chested fellow, ignorant, loutish, and addicted to the bottle; others described him as a lithe and graceful athlete, debonair in the face of danger, who was temperate in his habits and devoted to a widowed mother. One man reported that Patch was begging for his bread, that he was no better than a tramp and a panhandler when he arrived in Rochester. It is more reasonable to suppose that a bit of pageantry attended his arrival. Sam was a showman. He traveled with a trained bear on a chain and a pet fox on a rope.

In his late teens, Patch gained local fame as a daredevil in Pawtucket, Rhode Island, where he was employed in a cotton mill, by dropping feet first into the Blackstone River from the top of a high building. He first appeared as a professional leaper in Paterson, New Jersey, and moved from there to Niagara Falls,

where twice he jumped into the white and agitated waters below the cataract. His second jump was made in mid-October, 1829.

Since his occupation was a seasonal one, he would need to act promptly if he were to fill other engagements before ice began to form on northern rivers. Rochester was less than a hundred miles from Niagara. It was a boom town. It had a picturesque falls, ninety-two feet high, a short walk from its teeming trading center. It was an ideal place for Sam's last exhibitions of the season.

When he arrived in Rochester with his bear and his pet fox, he lost no time in getting out handbills and posters. The facts and fancies printed on these were composed into news stories by the press.

ANOTHER LEAP!
SAM PATCH AGAINST THE WORLD

the *Rochester Daily Advertiser* announced in its October 29 issue.

Then followed one of Sam's maxims which soon got into the idiom: "Some things can be done as well as others."

The paragraphs below explained that since Patch had jumped over Niagara Falls, he was determined to show the citizens of Rochester that he was the "real 'simon pure'" by jumping over their falls on the afternoon of November 6; that "there was no mistake about Sam Patch. He goes the whole hog—and, unlike too many politicians, he 'turns no somersets' in his progress! He goes straight as an arrow!"

The newspapers suggested that "gentlemen who felt disposed to witness the spectacle" leave their subscriptions with the landlords of the various taverns who, in the event that the "Jersey Leaper" failed to leap, would return the money. But Sam's boast that "there was no mistake about Sam Patch" was confirmed. He "performed according to promise, the feat of jumping over the Falls of the Genesee," the *Rochester Daily Advertiser* reported. The *Advertiser* added that the exhibition was "all that could be anticipated," and that it was witnessed by between six and eight thousand spectators, who were held in "breathless suspense."

But the gentlemen who had left subscriptions had not left enough. Sam profited only modestly from a performance which had exposed him to double jeopardy. Added to the hazards of the actual leap, was the threat that the November waters of the Genesee would freeze not only the "genial current of his soul," but his body as well. He had had the homage of a vast crowd; now he wanted money. His bills were soon again in circulation. In a new format they announced—prophetically, as it developed— "SAM'S LAST LEAP!"

And this leap was to be "Higher Yet!" Sam proposed to erect a platform twenty-five feet above the head of the Falls, and he hoped that this time all who witnessed the performance, which was designed to "astonish the world," would contribute something to remunerate the performer. He would jump at three o'clock, Friday afternoon, November 13, to flout the superstitions —although this the announcements did not say—and, as the moralists later pointed out, an "outraged Deity."

The fact that the second leap was to be considerably higher than the first quickened a new interest in the advertised performance. On the day of the exhibition thousands of persons congregated in the village. Farmers abandoned their labors to see the wonder jumper. They drove into town in oxcarts, rode lumbering work horses, or trudged over the roads on foot. The packet boats on the canal were crowded. The stage lines did a land-office business. Some of the curious came by steamships and sailing vessels from distant lake ports.

The emotions of the huge crowd that lined both river banks long before Patch was scheduled to appear were mixed. Some of the spectators were like persons waiting excitedly to see a horse race; others had the ghoulish aspect of men and women anticipating an execution.

Sam was ten minutes late mounting the platform. He lacked his usual poise. There were those in the crowd who, claiming to know his habits, were sure that he had failed to put the stopper in the brandy bottle. He wore a close-fitting jacket and a pair of fancy white pantaloons, part of a band uniform which he had borrowed from an innkeeper, who doubled as a horn player. He seemed to want to delay. He tested the staging. He wrapped a silk sash round his waist. He made a short speech. His voice, like his legs, was not quite steady.

"Napoleon was a great man and a great general," Patch said. "He conquered armies and he conquered nations, but he couldn't jump the Genesee Falls. Wellington was a great man and a great soldier. He conquered armies and he conquered nations, but he couldn't jump the Genesee Falls. That was left for me to do, and I can do it, and will."

The November day was gloomy and exceedingly cold. The spectators, who had been waiting for hours, were chilled to the bone. Sam still hesitated. He stepped presently to the edge of the platform and peered down. He appeared unenchanted by the prospect. But a moment later, he took his jumping stance, and leaped.

As he left his high perch, a sibyl in the crowd screamed shrilly, "If there is anything in dreams, the man is dead!" And so great was the tension that one prominent citizen, in a front row position, bit off the tip of his thumb.

Sam had a practiced technique. In true form, he had complete control of his body in flight, and his descent, as he himself boasted, was as straight as an arrow.

But this day, his body was out of line. Ordinarily, his arms were held tightly at his sides, and his feet were kept close together. Now his arms flapped crazily, like the wings of a bird that had been disabled by a sportsman's shot, and his feet were widespread. He did not strike the water in a perpendicular position, but at an angle that exposed a wide area of his body to the impact. The shock must have been as severe as the trauma that he would have suffered in falling from a lesser height to solid ground.

A great plume of white water rose as his body sank. The spectators waited with held breath for his head to bob to the surface. They waited a minute, another minute; then a low murmur of horror, suddenly penetrated by hysterical cries, "He's dead!" swept through the crowd, and almost all of its thousands of members, as though they had been descried at some unholy spectacle, crept furtively from the scene.

The next day threnodies were sounded in the press; frank reports were printed that Sam was drunk on brandy when he jumped; bets were made that he had hidden under the falling waters of the cataract, and would soon reappear; the Patch Legend began to take shape; and the moralists had a field day.

A writer in *The Observer*, who shamefully confessed that the sensational promise of Sam's leap had caused him to join the throng at the Falls, dissertated at length on the sinfulness of circus riding, tightrope walking, cataract jumping, and other hazardous performances; and avowed that all who witness or encourage these exhibitions "offend against the Majesty of Heaven, and are daring the Vengeance of an offended Deity."

The clergy preached in similar tone. And Josiah Bissell, pious and prominent citizen, who himself had resisted the spectacle at the Falls, told the little children of his Presbyterian Sunday School that they verily stood at the verge of Hell since each, by watching Sam leap to his death, had been an accessory to his murder.

Two weeks after Patch's final leap, a notice was posted in Reynolds Arcade in Rochester that he would appear that day at the Eagle Tavern and recount his experiences. There were constant rumors that he had been seen in villages on the route to New Jersey. Even after his body was found in the ice of the Genesee River on St. Patrick's Day, 1830, and unequivocally identified by the sash round its waist and the fancy pantaloons which Sam had borrowed from the hornplayer-tavern-keeper, belief in his existence persisted.

The actual character of Sam Patch was soon lost in myth and glossed by the patina of romance. The rhymesters took him to their hearts, and some took him seriously. Mother love got into the maudlin doggerel that was written about him. He was supposed to have jumped over the falls for the dear little mother back in Pawtucket. To some poets he became a hero in Byronic mold. A Newark, New Jersey, doctor told, in lengthy narrative verse of "The Great Descender, Mighty Patch—Spurner of Heights—Great Nature's Overmatch"; and with no hint of tongue in cheek, likened him to Columbus, Galileo, Franklin, Lord Nelson, and Newton. Humbly born Patch, the poet proclaimed, "half dust, half deity" was one of the immortals who combined "The heroic body with the inventive mind," and died a "true martyr to science."

The place from which Sam had leaped became the cynosure for all who passed through Rochester. The natives of the village escorted out-of-town relatives and visiting firemen to the scene of the fatal leap, and the further the day of the tragic event receded into the past, the more heavily they embroidered their descriptions of it with fancy.

Like other tourists who passed through Rochester, Nathaniel Hawthorne, on his way to Niagara Falls, visited the Falls of the Genesee to observe the scene of Patch's leap.

"How stern a moral may be drawn from the story of poor Sam Patch," he later mused in print. "Why do we call him a madman or a fool when he has left his memory around the falls of the Genesee more permanent than if the letters of his name had been hewn into the forehead of the precipice? Was the leaper of cataracts more mad or foolish than other men who throw away life, or misspend it in pursuit of empty fame, and seldom so triumphantly as he?"

The caustic Mrs. Trollope, mother of the celebrated Anthony, told in her widely discussed *Domestic Manners of the Americans,* of her visit to the Upper Falls "renowned as being the last and fatal leap of the adventurous madman Sam Patch." Mrs. Trollope also saw Sam's bear, which she said was kept on display at a Rochester hotel, whose manners she seemed to believe were less gross than those of many Americans she had met in her tour of the country.

For many years Sam Patch, posthumously, was Rochester's and the Genesee River's greatest press agent. In his semicentennial history of the city, W. F. Peck suggested that the city fathers erect a monument to the "Jersey Leaper," since he was inextricably a part of Rochester's history. The Rochester Press Club, many years later, urged a similar memorial, since Patch had furnished Rochester with its first sensational news story. There was a Patch bit in the city's centennial celebration.

But only in recent years has his grave been marked by a stone and a tablet, and the identification was made without any help from the city. The memorial was paid for and erected by students of Charlotte High School, who were led in this enterprise by a youthful Patch enthusiast, fourteen-year-old David Coapman.

Patch's name still occasionally bobs up on the pages of local newspapers. All of the verses about him probably have never been collected. One rhymester denominated him, "Samuel O'Cataract," and closed his long poem with these lines:

> Napoleon's last great battle prov'd,
> His dreadful overthrow,
> And Sam's last jump was a fearful one,
> And in death it laid him low.
>
> T'was at the falls of Genesee,
> He jumped down six score feet and five,
> And in the waters deep he sunk,
> And never rose again alive.

30

At a fairly early date in the development by white settlers of its valley, as early as 1813, a section of the upper Genesee River was designated by the State Legislature as a "highway," and warnings were issued that persons obstructing it would be fined —and stiffly fined. Five dollars! Fifteen years later the Legislature passed another law which extended the "highway" all the way from the village of Rochester to the Pennsylvania state line.

But with that the state rested, as though on the honors of a notable achievement. It did nothing to facilitate the movement of traffic over the watercourse it had proclaimed a public thoroughfare. North of Rochester, at the mouth of the Genesee, government monies were spent to breach a sand bar which, for years, had troubled Lake Ontario mariners who called at the lower river ports. Piers that defined the harbor were built at a cost of many thousands of dollars; a lighthouse was erected. The "mariners" of the upper river were favored with no such expensive improvements. Like waifs, they were left to make their way up and down the stream as best they could, and their best was often poor going.

The upper Genesee was navigable in parts, but not for the full extent of its course from the Pennsylvania border to Rochester. Halfway between these two points there were (and still are, of course) three large and well-spaced cataracts. Today these falls, and the spectacular gorge through which the water that foams over them flows, constitute the prize natural showpieces of Letchworth State Park.

Before the white man's expropriation of the Senecas' beautiful valley, the falls had been for an inestimable period of time a famous Indian carrying place. Bound north, the voyageurs would lift their elm-bark canoes from the river at a place, now the appropriately named village of Portageville, and return them to the water at a point a short distance below the Lower Falls. From there they would have fair sailing until they reached the Rapids, two miles south of the first of the triple falls which once informed with scenic grandeur the river's course through what is now the city of Rochester.

Beginning at a point opposite the present River Campus of the University of Rochester, the Rapids made navigation impracticable for even a lightly burdened Indian canoe except at times of high water. If an Indian party was continuing to the lake, it carried its canoes over a long-traveled trail from the first breaking of white water to the natural launching place below the last of the three falls, which was later known as Hanford's Landing.

Although the elm-bark canoes of the Seneca Indians were neither as graceful nor as pliable as the birchbarks used by their Canadian cousins, they nevertheless had considerably more maneuverability than the river scows and Durham boats of the white men. Manned by native paddlers who understood the crotchets of the upper Genesee, and who were familiar with the stream's snags, shoals, sudden turns, and frequent alterations of course, a journey of thirty or forty miles up or down its channel was scarcely a momentous undertaking. When white men began to use the river for commerical traffic, they rarely found it benign or helpful to their enterprises; and the time came when they urgently appealed to the state to improve it as a navigable stream by removing flood debris and other obstructions and by deepening its channel. The appeals went unheeded.

When the mood strikes it, the Genesee is capable of shortening or lengthening its flow by cutting new channels, often to the dismay of persons whose riparian rights are affected by these perverse whimsies. At its bullying worst, it drives nearby residents from their homes, drowns pigs and sometimes cattle, uproots great trees, and slices away from its banks huge pieces of good arable land.

One flood day in early spring, when the raging Genesee, with the effectiveness of a motorized earth mover, was gouging out the banks of the property of the Robert Bromeleys, at Belvidere, the late Charles Whitcomb, a friend and neighbor of the Bromeleys, observed the river's assault with philosophical resignation.

Deep into his eighties at the time, a tinker of clocks, a philosopher, a historian of local repute, a lover of good whiskey, and a man who had lived virtually all of his long life no more than a few minutes' walk from the river, Mr. Whitcomb spat, and spoke a truth known only too well to his neighbors along that stretch of the Genesee.

"A man owning bottom land on this river," said he ruefully, "hasn't any more real estate than buckwheat."

Mary Jemison had never, of couse, heard Whitcomb's maxim. But she would have appreciated the meaning conveyed by it.

One night, in the spring of 1817, after the Genesee had been swollen by several days of rain, the banks two hundred feet above part of Mary's land on Gardeau Flats, gave way and slid down to the stream's level. The noise before the slide actually started was something like the grumbling of an earthquake; and the crash, a few minutes later, resounded for a great distance, as the descending earth was heavily timbered with huge trees which were part of the original forest.

The loose soil, boulders that were freed from it, and broken uprooted trees choked the river channel. The displaced earth spread twenty-two acres over the Jemison bottom lands. For a time, these acres had the desolate aspect of an area that had been swept by a tidal wave. But as the soil settled, vegetation took root and trees, which had not been broken or flattened in descent, found viability and strength in the rich earth of the river flats. The Great Slide, as the phenomenon became known, occurred on the left bank of the Genesee, the flow of which was only momentarily stanched. Angry, black with mud, but indomitable, the stream quickly cut a new bed considerably east of what had formerly been its right bank and pressed on to its ultimate destination, Lake Ontario.

The scene of the cataclysm was about five miles north of the last of the triple falls, which display their beauty in that part of the river that now flows through Letchworth State Park, and a short distance above Mary Jemison's cabin. The slide was perhaps the river's most radical aberration since a record has been kept of its history.

For years, the Great Slide attracted the curious to the part of the river where it had occurred. It provoked scientific speculation. It was used to explain a Biblical miracle. A geologist from Oberlin College, who presently visited the scene, made the exegetic pronouncement that a landslide similar to the one at Gardeau Flats had parted the waters of the Jordan long enough to allow the Israelites to walk, dry-shod, across its bed.

Commercial boating on the upper Genesee began shortly after the close of the War of 1812. The village of Rochester was soon to boom, and the country south of it was to be opened wider by pioneers, mostly from the East, who by the pragmatic test of clearing and cultivating the lands of the Genesee Valley would decide whether they merited their far-flung fame of wonderful fertility.

The cleared acreage was constantly expanded by the toil and sweat of men whose working hours seemed endless, and who knew nothing of the ingenious tools which later were to lessen the drudgery of farm work. Great trees of the forest fell, and were burned to ash (and the ash, if the farmer had iron pots and time for the process, was converted into potash and sent to market), but the stumps and the roots of the trees remained. The roots broke the shares of the wooden plows; the stumps required that a farmer plowing a field follow a course as tortuous as a labyrinth.

Wheat was the chief market product of the upper Genesee Valley. Rich and productive as were the lands of the Genesee, formidable difficulties confronted a man trying to get a start on them. And one of his greatest trials was moving his produce to market. Wheat that was lugged to Rochester mills from a distance of twenty miles might be twelve or fourteen hours in transit. The secondary roads were dreadful. At certain times of the year, they were little better than quagmires. Oxen were more effective on these journeys than horses. They could wallow through the mire or pull a loaded wagon out of a pothole without falling spent and wind-broken in the traces.

What was needed to exploit the potential of the river country was improved transportation facilities, and Abraham Hanford, who had successively operated a store at Scottsville and a mill on Oatka Creek, which flowed through part of the village, was one of the first to take practicable measures to this end.

One of the seven Hanford brothers, Abraham, who had succeeded to King's Landing on the lower river after Genesee Fever had taken the lives of the original proprietors, knew something about lower river shipping. Deciding to use the upper river for commercial transportation, he built a scow called the *Skimmer*. She was scarcely as light and airy as her name implied; she "skimmed" only on downriver trips when the water was high and fast. Returning to her home "port" of Scottsville, the *Skimmer* was propelled upstream by men with setting poles; and since she had no running boards, this work was disadvantageously performed from the bottom of the boat.

Launched in 1817, the *Skimmer,* which had a carrying capacity of twenty loaded barrels, may not have been the first commerical craft on the upper Genesee, but she was the first recorded by name in the river's history. She did well for a time, so well, indeed, that Hanford found it practicable to build a warehouse on the Scottsville side of the stream to store produce awaiting shipment. Soon other craft, of better design than the *Skimmer,* were employed in the river traffic.

By 1820, nearly a dozen boats were engaged in a lively and highly competitive river trade which was to continue until the opening, twenty years later, of the Genesee Valley Canal. The crews of these scows and Durham boats, all of which floated down and were poled upstream, were typical rivermen. They were inured to unconscionably long hours of cruel toil. Sometimes they survived an upriver voyage, that logged no more than three miles in a working day, on what was known as "river cakes," a species of hardtack, and quick draughts of grog. They were a raffish lot. They were loyal. They were colorfully profane. They drank like all two-fisted mariners. They fought men from rival crews and later (their particular anathema) canalers whom they encountered on the Erie Canal feeder at Rochester.

With such boats as the *Lady,* the *Asia,* the *Shove-ahead,* the *Boxer,* the *Independent,* the *Northumberland,* the largest in the river traffic—a huge craft, manned by eighteen polers, a cook, and a captain—rivermen went as far south as Geneseo if the water was high, and occasionally even to Mt. Morris. Warehouses were built at various shipping points along the river. There were three in the vicinity of Scottsville, the first important river stop; one at Avon; others at Geneseo and Mt. Morris. Numerous taverns dotted the better-than-fifty-mile route of navigation from the Rapids south of Rochester to Mt. Morris.

Today, in this regard, the upper Genesee is quite pristine and pure. There are no low-ceiling resorts, with battle-scarred serving tables, and sawdust on the floor, such as the rivermen knew a century and a quarter ago; no dainty little *boîtes*, such as one might discover in the pastoral course of a winding stream in France. There would be scant patronage for either type of retreat.

Pleasure boating on the upper Genesee is limited to a few not very enduring canoeists, an occasional angler puttering about in a battered skiff, and infrequent trippers in motorboats who, fortunately, always seem eager to escape the solitude and quiet of the lovely, winding summer stream, which their noisy and smelly contraptions briefly violate. What commerical navigation this part of the river knows is confined to a stretch of water between a state dock near the heart of Rochester and the Barge Canal, which crosses the Genesee at water level two miles south of the dock.

During the years that river traffic was at its height, a tavern-keeper named William Tone did a rousing business at Dumpling Hill, ten miles upriver from Rochester. Today much of the Dumpling Hill area is part of the vast parklike estate of Rochester's millionaire brewer, Louis A. Wehle, who has no feeling that money is going out of style, but who disperses it with an abandon that sometimes conveys this impression to gape-mouthed observers of his extravagances. The Wehle plantation, which skirts the left bank of the river for a considerable distance, is a show place for blooded horses and cattle and purebred sporting dogs. It is enclosed by miles of white rail-fencing. Within the enclosure is a tennis court, a swimming pool, a riding ring, a training track, a skeet range. There are elaborate kennels and stables, and several family houses with rumpus rooms. But one couldn't buy so much as a bottle of beer within a mile of this delightful domain, and even then one would have to leave the river to make the purchase.

Before the inauguration of formal river traffic, poor squatters in the Genesee Valley sometimes eked out their spare incomes by floating downstream white-oak staves, which were caught in a boom at the Rapids and carted from there to the lower-river lake ports. A more substantial lumbering trade developed on the Genesee with the opening of the Erie Canal. Soon to become a city, the hustling village of Rochester included among its numerous thriving industries several yards in which canalboats were manufactured. The builders favored the fine oak timber of the upper-river country. Stands of this wood were notable in the vicinity of St. Helena, once a fairly flourishing river settlement on the left bank of the river, south of Gardeau Flats. Today St. Helena is inhabited by birds, small beasts and, to attest to its utter abandonment by man, rattlesnakes.

31

ONE DAY, late in the first decade of commercial boating on the upper Genesee, a penny-whistle toot was sounded near Avon bridge and, wonder of wonders, a steamboat hove into sight. She was the *Erie Canal*, Captain Bottle, of Utica, in command. She was seventy-seven feet over-all, with a twelve-foot beam, and a very shallow draught. She was a side-wheeler. Her upstream passage had been a halting one. Her crew had been hard put to warp her off reefs, snags, and sunken logs. In free water, her captain proudly asserted, she was capable of a speed of four miles an hour. She was a glorious innovation; almost *en masse*, the village of Avon turned out to welcome her.

> "Cheer up you lusty gallants
> With music sound the drum,
> For we've descry'd a steamboat
> On the Genesee hath come,"

the Avon correspondent for the *Livingston Register* (published in Geneseo) wrote under date of July 28, 1824.

After his lyrical outburst, the correspondent continued his dispatch in prose. He pointed out that, since this was the first time the Genesee had been navigated by steam, a celebration seemed fitting and proper. It was held aboard the *Erie Canal.* Bottled refreshments were served quantitatively. Good, free-loading newspaperman that he was, the correspondent remained until the last of nearly twenty toasts had been drunk. Captain Bottle, his ship, George Washington, Robert Fulton, the Genesee River (from whose borders "solitude fled affrighted" at the approach of "the genius of industry and enterprise") were included in the tributes. The correspondent reported to his newspaper the number of cheers that followed each toast.

In time the refreshments were exhausted, the cheering voices wearied, and Captain Bottle prepared to sail on to Geneseo, his southernmost port of call. He left before any of the celebrants fell from the deck of the *Erie Canal* and drowned.

By road, Avon and Geneseo are separated by nine miles. Owing to the radical convolutions of the Genesee, the distance by water is considerably greater. The *Erie Canal* reached the latter village the day after she had left the former. There another celebration was held. Captain Bottle took a party of leading "ladies and gentlemen" from the village on a short cruise. It was a delightful excursion. The captain was quoted in the *Register* as saying that, if the state cleared the Genesee of flood debris, it would be one of the most navigable streams in New York.

But the state seemed singularly obtuse in this matter. The petitions of the press and the prayers of influential land owners in the Genesee Valley made scarcely any impression upon the legislators. They were not insensible of the need of opening up back areas of the state by connecting them by watery highways with the Erie Canal, but for this purpose they seemed to favor lateral canals over natural streams.

The success of the Big Ditch which DeWitt Clinton had envisaged and built had generated throughout the state something like a canal mania. The steam locomotive was yet too embryonic a thing to excite the hope that one day it would dominate the country's transportation system. Canals were what were wanted, and groups of residents in various parts of the state were clamoring for them.

In the meantime, nothing was done by the state to improve the navigability of the Genesee, crying need though there was for improvement. The crooked, twisted channel of the stream was as encumbered as ever by fallen trees and other refuse. It would be deep beyond the head and fully raised hands of a tall riverman standing on its bottom at one stretch of its erratic course; so shallow at the next that to move a laden scow half a mile upriver might require a full afternoon's labor by men on shore with a windlass.

For a couple of seasons, the "steamship" *Erie Canal* huffed and puffed upstream and down, exposed to a variety of hazards and harassed by innumerable obstacles. Then Captain Bottle decided that the sport was not worth the candle, and he left the river, and the *Erie Canal* disappeared into limbo. Several years later a stern-wheeled steamboat christened *Genesee,* which was larger than her predecessor, briefly operated on the river. Her speed was advertised at eight or ten miles an hour; and in good water, she was reputed to have gone racketing downriver from a dock at Geneseo to the Rapids in six hours.

She could do well in high water, but almost nothing in low; and when her owners found that she could not make her keep, they retired her from service. From then on, the quiet and solitude of the upper Genesee were no longer broken by the belching and thumping of a steam engine, but only by rivermen calling down imprecations upon the canine mother of a stream whose fitful temper, whose cluttered channel, and whose general cussedness were enough to break the spirit of a saint.

In 1836, after years of listening to the pleas of residents of the upper Genesee Valley for an improved waterway for the conveyance of their goods to market, New York legislators, displaying their practiced indifference to the potential of the Genesee River, passed an act authorizing the construction of a canal through the river country.

The course that the engineers finally decided upon would take the new artificial waterway from a basin of the Erie Canal at Rochester to a point far south in the Genesee Valley, where it would veer to the southwest and join the Allegheny River near Olean. Thus, the canal advocates urged, a shipment made at an Erie Canal port might be transported entirely by water, via the Allegheny, the Ohio, and the Mississippi Rivers, to the mouth of the last-named stream. It was a grandiose scheme; it had something of the gaudy promise of the Northwest Passage, which had beguiled the fancies and animated the exertions of early continental explorers. It was a river route familiar to La Salle, who, two centuries before, had attempted to persuade his sovereign, Louis XIV, to set up fortified trading posts along its banks; it was the old canoe trail that the Seneca Indians had followed, in the days of their greatest pomp, when prosecuting expeditions of conquest and imperial aggrandizement.

In their long-ranged southern excursions, the Senecas took advantage of the waters of the Genesee. They would paddle upstream to the first of the upper river's triple falls, portage around these cataracts, and continue by water to a point near the present New York-Pennsylvania boundary. From there they would carry their canoes a few miles cross country to the head of the Allegheny. The canal engineers found no use for the river except to supply their narrow ditch with water. They would run their waterway parallel to it for a considerable distance; they would cross it twice; but no boats from their canal would move up or down the river's channel.

The work of digging the Genesee Valley Canal was begun in June, 1837; twenty-one years later it was completed to what the engineers had designated as its southwestern terminal, Millgrove Pond on the Allegheny River. Nearly $7,000,000 had been spent on the project; a great deal of what was considered expendable

Irish immigrant labor had been grossly exploited; a number of men had been killed by accidents; and enormous stealings, frauds, and malefactions had been perpetrated by engineers, contractors, and canal employees. Moreover, by then the railroad had pretty well nullified the practicability of the canal; and sixteen years later, when its operating costs were shown to be several thousand dollars in excess of its revenue, it was closed by state edict.

Noble E. Whitford, in his authoritative history of the canals of New York State, wrote in 1906, "The whole history of this Genesee Valley Canal reveals a series of unfortunate events; the numerous delays were costly; the time for building, most inauspicious; and even the advisability of beginning the project at so late a date is not sustained by results."

But though the measure of its utility, as Mr. Whitford adds, "was out of all proportion to its cost," the canal did contribute greatly to the economy of the territory through which it passed and the economy of its termini. It stimulated industry, increased agricultural wealth, quickened a new interest in the advantages of the Genesee country. It brought to Rochester large quantities of lumber needed in the construction of houses and the building of Erie Canal boats (an important Rochester industry) at an annual saving of $150,000. It carried farm produce to market. And it provided, as did other early canals, a practical school of engineering at a time when very little formal instruction in this science was available in America.

Many men were corrupted by the canal—and many men who were employed in its construction, and who were susceptible to corruption, profited from their wrongdoings; and the frauds and stealings by contractors, engineers, and others, helped to double and then to triple the first estimate of the canal's cost. But slowly, interruptedly, expensively, the waterway was completed.

In September, 1840, the first thirty-six miles of the little ditch, as compared with the big ditch of the Erie—a stretch between Rochester and Mt. Morris was opened with ceremony. The next year the canal crossed from the left to the right bank of the

Genesee behind a dam at Mt. Morris, which provided a reasonably quiet pool of water for this purpose; and presently, in its progress south, it was raised by a series of sixteen locks, set so close together that their entire chain extended a distance of less than two miles, to a high ridge which separated the valley of the Genesee from the valley of the Cashaqua, a long, winding stream, whose waters ultimately entered the Genesee by way of Canaseraga Creek.

One hundred and six locks were required, when the waterway was in actual operation, to raise the main line of the Genesee Valley Canal to its summit level and drop it down to the basin of the Allegheny River; and the Deep Cut started just south of Lock 60. From that point the canallers had smooth sailing for the next nine miles—the Nine Mile Level, as it was called—and the cry "Hoor-ay-lock," which signaled lock tenders that a vessel was approaching their water gate, was silenced, for the Nine Mile Level was without a lock.

The plan of the engineers was to have the waterway recross the river on a wooden aqueduct just above the Upper Falls. But before the crossing place was reached, the canal would have to traverse what was virtually a small mountain, which rose sheer above the bed of the river to a height, in places, of four hundred feet.

To save cutting the mountain down to meet the Nine Mile Level, the engineers boldly—injudiciously, as it turned out—decided to bore through it; and the contract for the tunnel job dropped, perhaps like a ripe and juicy plum, into the lap of Elisha Johnson, a man who had performed many public works, who sometimes displayed a commendable public spirit, but who never allowed tangential interests to divert him from the first purpose of making an honest, or a nearly honest dollar.

32

THE tunnel job, or Section 57, as it was known on the engineers' work sheets, was the most momentous undertaking along the entire 124-mile canal route. It was also an expensive experiment: it was never completed, and the state's money spent on it was wasted. But it did very well by Elisha Johnson, according to Colonel George Williams, prominent upper Genesee Valley resident, who sold to the state the land through which the tunnel was to be dug.

Deposing before a special Assembly Committee, which had been organized to inquire into canal graft, Colonel Williams said that he regarded Johnson, when he took the tunnel contract, "as a bankrupt in property," and added that "he could scarcely be worth less than $50,000 or $60,000, at the time he suspended work. This was made out of work done, and does not include damage for stopping the work."

The deponent estimated the amount of damage paid Johnson,

after work on the tunnel was stopped, as between $22,000 and $23,000. This the committee discredited as hearsay. The committee admitted, however, that the tunnel job had cost the state $188,-334.27; and it took occasion, "even in the absence of the evidence of fraud," to point out to the Legislature and the people various irregularities in Johnson's performance of the work.

Three times president of the village of Rochester, and mayor for one term after the village gained the status of a city, Johnson left the last-named office to take the canal job; and left the canal for Tellico Plains, in East Tennessee, where he lived most of the remainder of his long life in a place called the Mansion, which from all accounts was not misnamed. When he left, and faint shadows of suspicion were cast by the manner of his departure, the presumption was (and Colonel William's deposition was not needed to support it) that he did not leave empty-handed.

After the tunnel contract had been given him, Johnson's first move was to build a log cabin atop the mountain range, which offered a stunning prospect of the area which is now Letchworth State Park and the country adjacent to it. Broken only by the deep gash of the river gorge, with its thundering, mist-clad cataracts, a timberland which dipped into wooded dells and rose to imposing wooded eminences, reached out from every angle as far as the eye could see.

Called Hornby Lodge after William Hornby, who with Sir William Pulteney had once owned a vast territory in the Genesee Valley, Johnson's log cabin was no workman's hovel. It could better be described as an early nineteenth-century country club. Its motif was elegant rusticity. It had a dozen and a half rooms and a grand salon large enough for a ball. It was topped by a solarium, four stories above the ground. A winding staircase, which offered access to the upper stories, was fixed to a large, unbarked oak tree, which rose from the center of the grand salon. The furniture and appointments of the "cabin" were in keeping with its sylvan location.

Johnson was an expansive host during the few years that he

lived at Hornby Lodge. The numerous guest chambers were frequently occupied and elaborate dinners were served in the grand salon. There is no record that he entertained canal engineers at champagne parties, a practice of some contractors which the Assembly investigating committee associated with bribery and fraud. But one of Johnson's guests, whether treated to champagne or to liquid refreshment of a less sparkling character, was Hiram P. Mills, a discredited resident engineer, who, his pockets stuffed with gold, left his state post to repose, benignly, among admiring fellow townsmen in Mt. Morris.

This was the lighter side of Elisha Johnson's canal project. The task that he had contracted to perform required that he bore a tunnel 1,082 feet long, 27 feet wide, and 21 feet high through a mountainous ridge that was soon found to be composed of shale so frangible that it continually fell from the walls and ceiling to clutter the path of the diggers. Headings were made at each end of the tunnel area and a lateral drift, which faced the river, was cut between them. Laborers, who could be counted in the hundreds, carried broken rock in their leather aprons from the drift and headings and dropped it over the precipitous wall of the river gorge. Hand digging a tunnel through rock was brutal work. Men died at it. It went on and on, with ever-mounting costs until the state enacted what was known as the Stop Law, in 1842, which put an end to all public works that were not considered vitally necessary.

When the Stop Law was rescinded, and public works were resumed, the Legislature decided against throwing good money after bad; and the tunnel project was abandoned in favor of an open cut, which ran along the curving rim of the river gorge. Begun in 1846, the digging of the Open Cut was a spectacular engineering achievement. It fixed the channel of the artificial waterway so close to the dizzy periphery of the Genesee that a person could toss a biscuit into the river, three hundred feet below, from the deck of a canalboat. The towpath was on the river side of the canal, and the mules and horses, and the men who drove them, were separated only by a low curbing of loose stones from the river's perpendicular wall.

A short distance after it had passed the Upper Falls of the Genesee, the canal was returned to the left side of that stream on a wooden aqueduct. A few years later—and five years after work on the Open Cut had begun—an army of busy diggers, grubbing like ants into the earth, had excavated the channel to a point just west of the river village of Belfast, in central Allegany County. From there the canal moved gradually away from the Genesee Valley to achieve, in 1861, its terminus on the Allegheny River.

In full operation, the Genesee Valley Canal was a quaint, Currier & Ives sort of institution. It had its brief day of glory, it performed a brief service (at enormous expense) for the communities that adjoined it and were close to it, and it gave issuance to an anthology of legends. But nine years before it was completed, a portent of its end appeared in the form of a huge railroad bridge which spanned the little ditch and the Upper Falls of the Genesee River just north of Portageville. Known as the Portage High Bridge, the structure stood more than 250 feet in the air. From this eminence, trainmen may have amusedly observed the slogging, mule-hauled little boats below, and speculated as to how soon their own mighty iron horses would render obsolete these toylike instruments of public transportation.

By a state order, the operation of the Genesee Valley Canal was discontinued in 1877. The railroads had done it in; and as though to mock its passing, the state sold the canal property to the Genesee Valley Railroad, and steam trains were soon speeding noisily over the route of what once had been a quiet waterway. Trains still operate between Rochester and Olean, now under the aegis of the Pennsylvania system; but their movements are less frequent than formerly and their traffic is limited to freight.

Fourteen miles south of the wooden aqueduct at Portageville, upon which the Genesee Valley Canal crossed from the right to the left bank of the Genesee River, the canal, paralleling the river, reached a settlement once known as Houghton Creek. It had another name during the canal days. It was then called Jockey Street.

Ensconced below a high cliff, which rose like an escarpment from the river bottom lands through which the canal channel had been dug, Jockey Street had become a favorite resort for canallers during the months when their boats were locked in ice and their season's earnings, bulging their pockets, itched to be spent. The settlement had three rough taverns where steersmen, deck hands, and mule skinners caroused and brawled to their hearts' content; it had, inevitably, since it was a gathering place for men unrestrained by domestic ties, a full quorum of soiled doves; and there was a race track where auction pools were sold and where the jugglery of horse trading was practiced.

But this rake-helling, these Saturnalian goings-on, had made the place so infamous in that part of the Genesee Valley that one pious ex-canaller, who lived across the river, prayed on bended knees each night that liquor cease to flow in Jockey Street, that evil women be driven from it, that wagering end, and in time the prayers of the petitioner (his name was Edmund Palmer) were categorically answered.

Just north of the northern boundary of this once raffish and riotous community, a roadside sign which hints at the new character of the village and identifies it by its present name greets the southbound motorist:

CHRIST DIED FOR OUR SINS
Houghton Gideons

A little farther on, a second sign gives the dates of Houghton's annual revival meetings, and a third—smack in the center of town—announces that the place is the seat of Houghton College, an institution under Wesleyan Methodist sponsorship.

The village is all college except for a small company, owned by a Houghton alumnus, which employs twelve workers to manufacture minnow traps in a barn. No beer or hard liquor is sold in Houghton. Neither vending machines nor store clerks dispense cigarettes. There is no dance hall; no cinema.

A scant, starveling, little backwoods seminary when it was founded in 1833, the school at Houghton now has an enrollment of 900 young men and women and full college accreditation. Its founder was not an educator or an ordained clergyman. Willard Houghton was the farmer son of a Vermont pioneer, who had moved into the Genesee Valley in the second decade of the nineteenth century. He was born in a cabin on an eminence, now the Houghton College campus, which overlooks the Genesee River and the old canal bed.

When the Genesee Valley Canal began to operate through the village that was first identified by a small stream named after his father, and he observed the infamies of the canallers, the younger Houghton joined his neighbor, Ed Palmer, across the river in asking the Lord to exorcise Satan from the newly christened Jockey Street. But he did not wait in idleness for the granting of his pleas; he was continually occupied in spiritual endeavors.

In a spring buggy, he traveled about the countryside organizing Sunday schools, promulgating the Word, pleading with the unregenerate to follow him to the "mourners' bench," passing out ornamental scripture cards, and putting his hand on the heads of children. And always, with this gesture, he asked the same question, "Does this little child love Jesus?"

"The touch of his hand on a child's head was like a benediction," said Dr. Frieda Gillette, who has taught history at Houghton for many years. "I know. As a child, I experienced that touch."

In the early 1880's, one of the leaders of the Wesleyan-Methodist connection suggested to Willard Houghton, a devout communicant of the denomination, that the former Jockey Street —no longer a benighted community, since the canal had ceased to operate, and the canallers, and the offscouring of the saloons, the bawdyhouses, and the race track had moved out—would be an excellent place to start a school, "free of the evil influences of large cities."

This was a challenge Houghton had been waiting for. His heart and soul went into the job of raising money to erect a school building on a site a short distance south of the present Houghton campus. The second graduate of the "Old Sem," as its alumni affectionately termed the little school, was James Seymour Luckey, a neighboring farm boy, whose determination was to preach the gospel. His unwilling departure from this course is part of the Houghton College legend.

" 'Call me to the ministry,' he prayed, but God answered, 'I want you to be an educator.' "

After devoting several years to advanced studies, Luckey returned in 1908 with a Harvard degree to the little school overlooking the Genesee River which had first given him a taste for education, took over its presidency, and in a long and consecrated career in that office built Houghton into the solid institution of higher learning that it is today. He annealed its character in the furnace of his own idealism. Houghton is intransigently dedicated to the principles of fundamentalism.

President Luckey wanted nothing to divert the young people from intellectual pursuits or to lure them from the narrow path of righteousness. Houghton is co-educational, but no mating ground.

The code of student conduct issued during the Luckey regime insisted that young women not leave their rooms after 6 P.M., and sternly enjoined students not to use the fire escapes unless they heard the clang of the fire gong. Viewing with alarm "the modern trend of fashion that exposes the body to the gaze of the public," the president ordered young women to wear dresses "with sleeves extending at least to the elbows" and skirts "extending four inches below the knees." The card table, the dance hall, and the theater were denounced as the "devil's triangle," and were ruled out. In substitution for these tabooed divertissements, a course was offered in the Major Prophets or a student might study cello on the side.

Today the relations between male and female students are more fluid than formerly, and concessions have been made by the college proctors to "the modern trend of fashion." There is evidence of this in the current (1961-62) catalogue. A photograph shows a group of young men and women on a hiking expedition, and the young women—enough to cause the late President Luckey to twirl in his grave—are wearing ski pants!

There is a commendable earnestness about the attitude of Houghton students. They are not diverted by such anti-intellectual antics as two-day football rousers and Junior Prom weeks. Sixty per cent of those who earn baccalaureate degrees go on to graduate schools. A third of all graduates become teachers, and more than a third enter full-time Christian service as ministers or missionaries.

Six years after the strict evangelican teachings of the newly formed Wesleyan Methodist Seminary began to exert their influence on the reformed village of Houghton, the neighboring village of Belfast, six miles upriver, gained fame from the visit of a huge, besotted, swaggering bully and notorious adulterer, who was also the idol of half the English-speaking world.

He stumbled into Belfast in the spring of 1889, and was laid out, stiff as a board, in a back room of a quiet house on a quiet street, and from the hour of his arrival until he departed—with the exception of one or two abortive revolts—he was subjected to a monastic routine which enraged his soul, and which put his body into a finer physical condition than it was ever to know again.

The visit of the celebrated voluptuary and brawler established a point of reference in the history of Belfast. From then on, old graybeards, attempting to fix a date for some village happening, would pull their whiskers, spit in the general direction of a brass cuspidor, and speculate: "Let's see, was that before—or after— John L. was here?"

"I don't see why everyone who comes to Belfast asks about Sullivan," said a lady who has lived all her life in the village, and who is the custodian of its historical records and relics. "After all, he was here only six weeks. There wasn't anything epic about it."

"If Sullivan's visit wasn't, what was epic?"

"Well, they built the bridge," she said. "In 1910."

The Erie Railroad viaduct, just north of the village, is 1,321 feet long and its tracks stand 140 feet above the Genesee River. It was built as a "cut-off" to save heavy freight trains from struggling over the formidable elevations traversed by the railroad's main line in Southern Allegany County. The bridge was an imposing structure when it was built, as it is today; but no one talks very much about it. The legend of John L. Sullivan is still lively in Belfast.

Famous on two continents as the "Boston Strong Boy," Sullivan was taken to Belfast by the Iron Duke. The Duke was an ex-cavalryman, who had ridden with Phil Sheridan through the Shenandoah Valley. Before the Civil War, he had lived contentedly on the small farm near Belfast where he had been born in 1845; after the war, farm life held no appeal for him, and ambition took him far afield and led him into a variety of pursuits.

By 1889, when he returned with Sullivan to his natal place, William Muldoon himself was something of a celebrity. A mighty muscle monument, who had posed in public as The Quoit Thrower, world's champion Greco-Roman wrestler, Muldoon also had appeared as Charles the Wrestler in *As You Like It* with such top-drawer Shakespearean mimes as Helena Modjeska and Maurice Barrymore. In a later day he was to consort with Presidents, with powerful captains of industry, and to criticize sharply the negligent manner in which Secretary of State Elihu Root washed his toes in a shower bath.

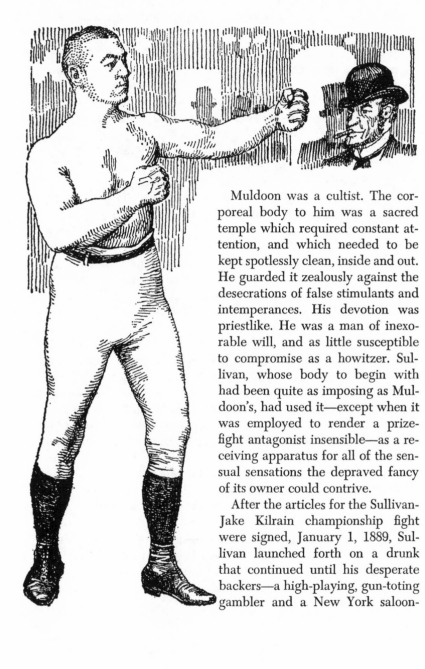

Muldoon was a cultist. The corporeal body to him was a sacred temple which required constant attention, and which needed to be kept spotlessly clean, inside and out. He guarded it zealously against the desecrations of false stimulants and intemperances. His devotion was priestlike. He was a man of inexorable will, and as little susceptible to compromise as a howitzer. Sullivan, whose body to begin with had been quite as imposing as Muldoon's, had used it—except when it was employed to render a prize-fight antagonist insensible—as a receiving apparatus for all of the sensual sensations the depraved fancy of its owner could contrive.

After the articles for the Sullivan-Jake Kilrain championship fight were signed, January 1, 1889, Sullivan launched forth on a drunk that continued until his desperate backers—a high-playing, gun-toting gambler and a New York saloon-

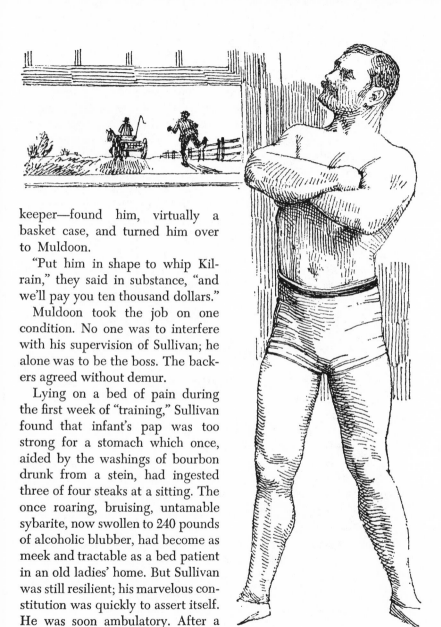

keeper—found him, virtually a basket case, and turned him over to Muldoon.

"Put him in shape to whip Kilrain," they said in substance, "and we'll pay you ten thousand dollars."

Muldoon took the job on one condition. No one was to interfere with his supervision of Sullivan; he alone was to be the boss. The backers agreed without demur.

Lying on a bed of pain during the first week of "training," Sullivan found that infant's pap was too strong for a stomach which once, aided by the washings of bourbon drunk from a stein, had ingested three of four steaks at a sitting. The once roaring, bruising, untamable sybarite, now swollen to 240 pounds of alcoholic blubber, had become as meek and tractable as a bed patient in an old ladies' home. But Sullivan was still resilient; his marvelous constitution was quickly to assert itself. He was soon ambulatory. After a week, he was taking short walks and eating solid food; in a few more days the short walks had become runs; he was lifting weights in a barn (which still stands) next to the Roman Catholic Church in Belfast, punching the heavy bag, wrestling with his mentor. By the end of the second week, the Iron Duke's regimen was in full force, and the steaming pig flesh of the champion was turning into solid muscle.

And now the battle of wills was on, and Muldoon's was to prove the stronger. Sullivan hated to run on the roads, and Muldoon took him eight and ten miles at a lick. He abhorred the weight-lifting, the wrestling (at which Muldoon was his master), the getting up at 6 A.M., the retiring at 9 P.M. There were two saloons in town, and all Sullivan had had to drink, he shouted vehemently, was "that stuff that flows under bridges."

Muldoon slept in the same room with his charge, ate with him, rarely let him out of his sight. But one night, as the Iron Duke slept, Sullivan escaped from his keeper. Drawn, as if by a lodestone to the nearer saloon, he was on his second drink and had ordered the terrified bartender to set up a third, when Muldoon arrived. Knocking glass and bottle to the floor with a sweep of his big hand, he plunked $25 on the strip, and ordered the bartender to close the place for the night.

After that, all amiable relations between the pair ended. Muldoon gave orders, and Sullivan gruntingly obeyed; but there was no conversation. Denied drink, Sullivan sent for Ann Livingston, the "$10,000 [burlesque] beauty," with whom he had lived openly for years. She was a woman with a will of her own, and a strong feeling about her sovereign claims on the champion. She was traveling with the Forepaugh Circus at the time, but she wired John L. that she was quitting the show to go to Belfast. Muldoon wired back that if she came, she wouldn't be allowed to leave the train; and there is no purple passage in Belfast history to indicate that she disobeyed the Iron Duke's mandate.

In late June, Sullivan, his backers, and Muldoon left Belfast for a place near Richberg, Mississippi, where, on July 8, 1889,

John L. defeated Kilrain after seventy-five rounds of bare-knuckle fighting (London Prize Ring Rules), and rose to greater heights of popularity than he had ever known before.

Muldoon deservedly received $10,000 for his efforts, but that was not the extent of his profit. The public knew that he had transformed a helpless wreck of a man into a world's champion athlete. He was acclaimed a miracle trainer, a "Professor of physical culture"; and in time millionaires, cabinet officers, leading actors, professional men, and the heads of great corporations were to flock to his celebrated health resort at White Plains, New York, where, for a substantial weekly fee, they were to be as subject to the Iron Duke's will as John L. Sullivan had been at Belfast.

33

Next to the city of Rochester, the village of Wellsville is the largest municipality bordering on or straddling the Genesee. Situated eleven miles from the New York-Pennsylvania boundary and eighty miles south, by the flight of an airplane, from the gash in the coastal sands through which the river flows into Lake Ontario, the place has more the aspect of a prosperous little city than that of a village. It has attractive residential areas, solid industries, a smart country club, and a bustling business section. Wellsvillians look neither woebegone nor down-at-heel. If the village economy is not quite as flushed and rosy as it was before the Sinclair people dismantled their refinery (once the largest in the land for the refining of Pennsylvania crude oil), it is still not wan or anemic.

Many believe that Wellsville derives its name from the fact that the buckled terrain adjacent to it is as pierced with oil wells as the steppes of the Mississippi Valley are with gopher holes. The inference is incorrect. Long before oil gushed from the first man-drilled well in Allegany County, Gardner Wells, the largest landowner in the area that now comprises Wellsville, remained snug against his fire one squally autumn night when his neighbors assembled to give the tiny settlement a name.

"Let's call it after Gardner Wells; he owns most of the land," they said in substance, after some discussion; and the thing was done. That was in 1832. Nineteen years later, when the Erie Railroad finally reached the hamlet—and touched and crossed the Genesee River—Erie officials named their station "Genesee," and stamped that pleasantly musical word upon their tickets and schedules; but the natives were obstinate. They clung to the name Wellsville, and the railroad in time deferred to popular clamor.

Back country—so far back, indeed, that the Indians themselves used the high, rugged peaks of southern Allegany County only as a hunting ground—the section of the county that is now Wellsville failed until well after the Revolutionary War to attract white men, though by that time numerous villages had formed in the northern reaches of the Genesee Valley. It was not until 1795 that the first white settler, a Connecticut native, struggled along the bank of a brawling affluent of the Genesee to clear land and build a cabin at a place five miles northeast of present Wellsville.

Legend has it that Nathaniel Dyke was an aristocratic son of old Eli, that he all but wore a whacking big "Y" on his buckskin shirt; and legend also distinguishes him as a member of General Washington's staff during the Revolution. The investigations of modern historians have discredited these claims; and today Dyke is commemorated as a courageous, resolute, hard-bitten pioneer, without social, military, or scholarly pretense, who materially helped to open up a country which, before his coming, had seemed to white migrants as forbidding as one of Dante's Circles. His memory is perpetuated by the stream upon which he settled, now identified as Dyke's Creek, which joins the Genesee River in downtown Wellsville.

Dyke remained on the land where he first settled, and the place now has the name of Elm Valley. Early in the new century, he erected a sawmill and a gristmill; presently built a tannery, which presaged an industry that later, with lumbering, gave Wellsville its first taste of affluence and its earliest sense of commerical importance. But the settlement of Wellsville itself was delayed well into the second decade of the nineteenth century, and growth was slow until the early 1840's. By that time, Dansville, in Livingston County—thirty miles northeast—had become the lumber mart of the region; and Wellsville lumber, taken there by wagon, was transshipped, over an eleven mile spur, to the main line of the Genesee Valley Canal, and thus made accessible to Rochester, to Erie Canal ports, and to the lake port at the mouth of the Genesee.

At successive periods in its history, Wellsville annually shipped 60,000,000 feet of pine lumber and turned 500,000 sides of hemlock sole leather in its several tanneries. These achievements came after the arrival of the railroad, and the railroad came in 1851; years later, when the lumber business began to flag, and shortly before the tanneries began to peter out, the village economy was stimulated, as if by a shot of adrenalin, by the discovery of a new source of wealth.

On June 12, 1879, Orville P. Taylor, a former Confederate cavalryman, who had been urged by friends to quit his profitless monkeyshines and "try to make an honest living for his family," after twice drilling dry holes, struck oil on a farm four and a half miles southwest of Wellsville.

A Virginian by birth, Taylor had been impoverished by the Civil War, and had moved North, with his Yankee wife, after the war, to try his fortune in the cigar business in Wellsville. Industrious and well-liked, he had made a modest success, when tantalizing visions of wealth induced him to gamble all that he had saved on the proposition that oil lay deep in the sands below the surface of Allegany County.

To support Taylor's hope, there was a history of oil in the region. As early as 1859, Edwin L. Drake, a New York, New Haven & Hartford Railroad conductor, had achieved an epochal oil strike near Titusville, Pennsylvania, about one hundred miles southwest of Wellsville; and long before that, in 1627, Joseph de la Roche d'Allion, a Franciscan monk, who was exploring the Western (New York) Wilderness in the company of friendly Indians, wrote back to France of a "good kind of oil which the Indians call Anonontons."

The "good kind of oil" Father de la Roche d'Allion remarked may have been displayed to him in some small Indian receptacle, and there is no certainty that he ever visited the place where it was obtained; but the presumption is that the oil had issued from the Seneca Oil Spring near Cuba, in Allegany County, a dozen miles west of the Genesee River. Later, several French priests definitely visited the Seneca Oil Spring, and one indicated it on a crude map drawn in 1670, which was reproduced in *Histoire de la Colonie Française* in Paris nearly two hundred years later.

The Seneca Oil Spring is not unique. There are other places in Western New York where oil, without the implementation of man, issues from the ground. The Seneca Oil Spring is distinctive only in that it was the first oil spring on the North American continent to be recorded in writing. The Indians believed that it had been created by a fat and greasy squaw falling into a hole, and that the oil was her liquefied blubber. They used it for medicine, and poured it on their tribal fires. White men found the oil insufficient for commercial purposes, and those who drilled in areas contiguous to the spring, in the expectation of discovering a paying stratum of oil sand, had only dry holes for their pains.

Orville Taylor first put money into what was called the Bottom Dollar Oil Well. It was dry, and it took practically *his* bottom dollar. He persisted, financing his explorations with money his wife had obtained from the sale of her jewelry. A second well proved a "duster." The third, famed as Triangle No. 1, produced six or eight barrels a day, and aroused intense excitement. Soon hundreds of men were drilling for oil in Allegany County. Many came to Wellsville. The village boomed. A score of new saloons came into being; houses with red lights on their porches burgeoned forth. Thimbleriggers and three-card monte men lent their insidious skills to the animated scene. In the meantime, Taylor opened other producing wells. But his dream of riches was never realized. He died less than five years later after Triangle No. 1 had vindicated his faith in the subterranean wealth of the region. Posterity commemorates him as the "Father of the Allegany Oil Field."

Although no oil has been produced in its environs, much of Wellsville's wealth derives from oil, and the village has been for more than eighty years the administrative center of the Allegany field. Four large companies are still producing oil, but the zest has gone from the industry, and it may end in another decade. Oil leases are continually being abandoned. There is still oil in the ground; perhaps twenty-five per cent of the original deposit.

"But the trick is," explained Knight Thornton, of the Thornton Company, which has been producing Pennsylvania crude oil for more than three-quarters of a century, "to get it out, and profit from the operation. It can't be done by methods we used in the past. They are too expensive."

The Sinclair Refinery, the largest single employer of labor in Wellsville, went out of business in 1958, the year after the *Daily Reporter* had cautiously predicted, in its Wellsville Centennial issue, that the refinery would continue as a local institution indefinitely. The shock of this stoppage was severe, but far from fatal to the Wellsville economy. And while the remembrance of things past is hardly rewarding in such a situation, the fact is that the Sinclair plant had done very well by the village in the years that it operated there. Built during the depression of the 1930's, it had immunized Wellsville from the distress suffered by other villages and cities in the United States. And it had made a Wellsville hero of Harry F. Sinclair, ex-drug clerk, former wildcatter, owner of the Derby horse Zev, and the man who had been investigated in the Teapot Dome scandal, and who had gone to jail for contempt of court.

Today, besides the oil companies that are still doing business in Wellsville, the village has—more importantly to insure its future economy—several industries that are neither related to nor dependent upon the diminishing oil field, and which employ more than two thousand workers. It boasts of such plants as The Air Preheater Corporation, the Worthington Corporation, and Capital Plastics, Inc. And the place has other distinctions. . . .

It is the birthplace of Reverend Charles Monroe Sheldon, whose religious novel, *In His Steps*, first read in installments to the congregation of his Topeka, Kansas, church, later outsold by hundreds of thousands such mighty best sellers as *Uncle Tom's Cabin* and *Gone with the Wind*; one of the young men of the village, George (Gabby) Hayes, ran away with a burlesque troupe, ultimately to be apotheosized by the youth of two continents, and to be voted the fifth most popular cowboy in motion pictures; it had a quiet and orderly bookkeeper, who embezzled $22,000 from a Wellsville bank, not to lavish on scarlet women or dissipate in other lush entertainments, but to fund the debt of his insolvent fraternal order; it was the lifetime home, despite long absences from it, of William Duke, who for many years trained race horses in Europe for William K. Vanderbilt and the Aga Khan, and who, during one of his periodic visits to this country, trained Flying Ebony, winner in 1925 of the Kentucky Derby. It has—to cause the Wellsville visitor to blink, and blink again at its rococo lace valentine-like architecture, and to wonder about its color and the veracity of the stories told about it—its Pink House.

In color, the Pink House *is* pink—or mauve, or lavender, or magenta, according to the lights that fall upon it. Built by a Wellsville druggist, ninety-odd years ago, the house stands imposingly on a large lot in a section of the village on the west side of the Genesee River.

"Since the Pink House is one of Wellsville's outstanding landmarks, it is amazing—and disappointing—to find that very little printed information is available on the subject," Mrs. Milton Sweet wrote in the *Wellsville Daily Reporter*, several years ago; and thereupon she described the house, inside and out, but said not a word concerning its legend, which is this:

Many years ago, the petite blonde daughter of a wealthy lumberman, who lived a short distance away from the site upon which the Pink House now stands, was enamored of a dreamy-eyed youth from the wrong side of the tracks. He had become, as the romance progressed, anathema to the girl's father. The lumberman saw the young man as nothing more than a beggar, and desired his pretty daughter (her name was Mary Frances) to marry a prosperous druggist, who also sold paints and engaged in other money-making pursuits; who was a solid, God-fearing citizen, and the pretty blonde's senior by more than a dozen years.

The boy and girl continued to meet, however, and love was having its way, when, desperate to save his daughter from what he believed would be a dreadful mistake, the father forged her name to a letter that told the young man that Mary Frances wanted nothing more to do with him; and during the estrangement that ensued, a day was set for the girl's marriage to the druggist.

Meeting by chance, the day before the wedding, the young couple learned of the father's perfidy; and the next morning, Mary Frances' dead body was found in a millrace that ran through the lumberman's property.

In 1873, a long narrative poem by Hanford Lennox Gordon, a poor boy from the wrong side of the Wellsville tracks, who had left the village to seek his fortune in the west, appeared under the title *Pauline*. Pauline's betrothed was a young man named Paul, and the story of how their romance was blighted by a letter forged by the girl's father, and how Pauline, rather than marry an older man whom she did not love, flung herself from a bridge and drowned, on the morning of her wedding day, is vividly told.

There was in Wellsville, before the Civil War, a Mary Frances Farnum, who died in young womanhood, and whose sister, Antoinette, married E. B. Hall, Wellsville's first druggist. Hall is reputed to have made a good deal of money during the Civil War through the sale of whiskey which, on the advice of political friends in Washington, he bought before the war, when the excise tax was low. After the war, he and Mrs. Hall made the Grand Tour. Hall was beguiled by the pink-washed stone castles in the Italian lake country, and upon his return to Wellsville he built a house which he painted pink. And the Pink House ever since has been pink—or a shade fairly close to pink—some say by a stipulation in the Hall will.

34

THE most notable area of scenic beauty in the Genesee Valley was saved from the ravages of power companies, in a day when power companies were about as sensitive to scenic beauty as the horsemen of Ghenghis Khan, by William Pryor Letchworth, a gentle-mannered bachelor of Quaker heritage, who is aptly called "the good genius of the Genesee."

One day, three or four years before the outbreak of the Civil War, Letchworth left an Erie Railroad train on the right bank of the river, after the train had crossed the High Bridge at Portage Falls, walked out on the wooden trestle, and saw, from this eminence, a prospect that enchanted him.

Below the bridge upon which he stood was the first of the three falls of the upper Genesee, and the beginning of a great, rock-walled canyon through which the river, with many loops and turns, continued seventeen miles to the village of Mt. Morris, without once leaving its steep defile.

Although not the greatest of the three cataracts, the Upper— or Portage Falls—made a brave display, as the river waters tumbled, like a billowing white panache, from a rocky upper ledge to a narrow basin below; and hurried on, once their agitations quieted, in a broad, velvety stream to the next descent— the Middle Falls, where the drop was 107 feet; a phenomenon, of its kind, outmatched in the northeastern section of the United States only at Niagara.

The Middle Falls were clearly visible to Letchworth, but the third cataract, more than a mile beyond the second, was hidden from his eyes, and he may not have known of its existence, as he gazed from the bridge. Besides the river gorge itself, and the far sweep of the country that his high position brought into view, he saw on the left bank of the Genesee, not far below the Upper Falls, a blighted, slum-cluttered area upon which stood a small tavern and two or three huts. There was a dilapidated sawmill below this, at the edge of the stream. For years lumbermen had worked over the area, and had worked it out. Here, it seemed to the solitary observer, paradise had been profaned.

William Letchworth was definitely in search of a country estate. He had come from his Buffalo home on an Erie train to reconnoiter the upper Genesee, and his first look made him feel that here was what he was seeking. He was not, however, a man who acted on impulse. He needed time to explore the proposition of purchase that was forming in his mind, and it was not until early in 1859 that several hundred acres on the left side of the river, which were soon to become a plot of a thousand, and compass all three cataracts, fell into his hands.

Thirty-six years old at the time of his purchase, Letchworth already had made a rousing success of the saddlery and carriage hardware business. His success would continue, and grow; and at the age of fifty he would retire from business, not to idle in the luxury of his country home, but to strive unceasingly during the remainder of his long life to salvage pauperized and forsaken children, to promote more humane care for the insane and the epileptic, and to improve the deplorable conditions of nineteenth-century penal insitutions.

Once he had acquired the deed to the Genesee lands, which included the blighted area he had seen from the bridge, Letchworth systematically set about restoring them. In the end he planted more than ten thousand trees to take the place of those that had been lumbered off. He effected many other improvements. The small tavern, although high above the river level, reposed in a glen a short distance from the Middle Falls, the mist from which often formed a rainbow in the sun. Expanding the tavern into a splendid country home, its new owner gave it the happy title, Glen Iris, and so the building—which now serves as a place of public entertainment—is known today.

For the superintendent of his property, Letchworth built a chalet, which still stands. He erected large barns, put blooded cattle on the land, caused paths and drives to be cut through the woods. A large house, with wide verandas, spacious downstairs rooms and numerous upper chambers, each identified by some forest tree—larch, maple, hickory, birch—Glen Iris often housed, when Letchworth's career became one of philanthropy, men and women who were interested in the same causes to which their gracious host was implacably dedicated.

His first philanthropic labors were prosecuted in the field of child welfare. He had discovered in visits to county poorhouses in New York State that hundreds of pauperized and parentless children were inmates of these institutions. The conditions under which they lived were unspeakably depraved. Letchworth inaugurated a campaign, which was often opposed by political blocs, to have the poorhouse children removed to suitable asylums, or placed out with private families.

In later years, his efforts in the interest of the mentally ill, the epileptic, and the confined felon, took him to many parts of this country and to Europe. His work in these fields was acclaimed on two continents. He wrote two books, *Care and Treatment of Epileptics,* and *The Insane in Foreign Countries.* He was a member of the State Board of Charities for twenty-three years and for nine of these years he served the Board as president.

Letchworth was a man of cultivated tastes, whose interests were numerous and varied. Fascinated by the Indian lore of the region, he caused the Iroquois council house at the old Indian village of Caneadea to be transferred to a high plateau on his estate, placed there also a log cabin Mary Jemison had built for one of her daughters, and in time had Mary's remains removed from their distant grave and reinterred in land that she had once owned.

Standing between the two log houses in Letchworth State Park today is a bronze statue of Mary Jemison, rendered, during Letchworth's ownership of the property, by the sculptor, Henry K. Bush-Brown. It surmounts the "White Woman's" grave, and shows Mary, as a teen-aged mother, on the long trek from her first place of bondage to her ultimate home on the Genesee.

Letchworth lovingly maintained his estate on the Genesee for half a century, and the beauty of the lands increased with the passing years. The fame of Glen Iris spread; and its master, desiring others to share its glories, opened the property on specified days to the public. Trees grew in an area once ravished by the lumberman's axe. The grounds surrounding the owner's house, which stood less than half a minute's walk from the Middle Falls, the crowning ornament of the river gorge, were richly landscaped. At night, guests of the house were lulled to sleep by the ceaseless diapason of the falling waters. Here was peace, serenity, and gracious hospitality.

But the Arcadian delights of Letchworth's residence at Glen Iris were threatened in time by a syndicate organized to convert the water power of the upper Genesee into electric power. The building of a dam above the Upper Falls was contemplated. Letchworth strove to prevent this desecration, which would limit to a trickle the flow of water over the three cataracts and turn the river gorge into an arid waste. His efforts were enfeebled by ill health. He was an elderly man and he had suffered a stroke. If what was proposed by the power syndicate was effected, he wrote to a friend ". . . I shall 'lay me down and die.' Glen Iris will only remain a

> Bright summer dream of white cascade,
> Of lake and wood and river."

But the "desecration" was not perpetrated. In 1906, Letchworth offered his property to the State of New York with two provisos: he was to retain life use and tenancy, and his thousand acres was to be consecrated "forever" as a public park.

Early the next year the Legislature passed an act providing for the acceptance of the gift. Three years later, Letchworth died at Glen Iris in his eighty-eighth year. His one-time property forms the nucleus for what is one of the most beautiful recreation areas in the state. Composed of 13,750 acres, Letchworth Park lies on both sides of the Genesee gorge and includes, on the river's right bank, a tableland once famed as a training ground for Civil War soldiers from Livingston, Wyoming, and Allegany counties.

"In 1961, nearly six hundred thousand persons, from every state in the union and from every province in Canada, visited Letchworth Park," said Gordon W. Harvey, the extremely able and completely dedicated park manager and chief engineer. "Our attendance has quadrupled in a dozen years. We have to look ahead. At the cost of a million and a quarter, we are developing a park within a park at the northern end of our property."

Extending the full length of the river gorge, Letchworth Park offers from its northern overlook, a spectacle to excite exclamations of wonder and surprise. For here, at the Mt. Morris High-Banks, the gorge not only broadens out to proportions that inspire, perhaps without too much hyperbole, the appellation, "Grand Canyon of the East," but also contains, within its steep, shaley cliffs, an impressive artificial prodigy in the Mt. Morris Dam.

In its isolated position, the dam, at first sight, gives the impression of a border fortress. The windows of its turret might be embrasures for cannon; the bulwark of its sloping outer wall might resist siege howitzers. And to carry on the military analogy, the dam is operated by the United States Army Corps of Engineers, which built it. Into its construction went 1,600,000 tons of stone and 3,500 carloads of cement. Behind the dam, the canyon's high walls provide a flood-control pool of 337,400 acres. In the ten years of its operation (1952-62), Miles J. Freeman, superintendent, estimates that the dam has saved lower Genesee Valley property owners $8,000,000 in flood damage.

Besides the dam at its northern extremity, Letchworth Park has a man-made wonder at its southern end for sight-seers to exclaim over. When the Erie Railroad first spanned the Genesee at the Upper Falls, it did so on a wooden bridge 800 feet long which rose to a dizzy height above the cataract. Built in 1852, the trestle was destroyed by fire twenty-three years later, and replaced by a wrought-iron bridge which still stands, an enormous, webby-looking structure, held aloft by a dozen towers that rise up from the river gorge.

At a time when the public was more ingenuous than it is today, the High Bridge was considered so wonderful a thing that excursion trains were run to Portage, a hamlet on the right, and to Portageville, on the left bank of the river, and taverns at these places did a bang-up business entertaining bridge gazers. No longer the cynosure it once was, the bridge is still more than an incidental attraction at Letchworth Park, and a person on the ground, gazing up at it as a train moves across its long, lacy span, knows the tingle of apprehension one experiences watching a man ride a bicycle on a high wire in a circus.

The first bridge has more history than the second. Besides the spectacular fire that destroyed it, a workmen's riot, which required the threat of a militia company's cannon to quell, attended its building, and several persons died from eating roast ox at a barbecue that celebrated its opening.

With one exception, the taverns that formerly catered to bridge crowds are gone. At Portageville still stands the Genesee Falls

Hotel, a small, gracious hostelry, with a nineteenth-century air, which attracts Letchworth Park visitors, young people who ski on the Genesee Valley slopes, and tired businessmen (and their wives) who desire, for a few days, "to get away from it all."

In an earlier day, the hotel boasted of its upper-story ballroom. There, many years ago, Yussiff Mahmout, the "Terrible Turk," wrestled Ed Atherton, a Portageville protégé, purportedly for the world's championship and a $250 side bet. Shortly after the encounter, the Turk jumped from the taffrail of a ship that was stricken in the mid-Atlantic, and went down like a plummet, weighted by thousands of dollars in gold that he was carrying back to his native land in a money belt.

35

WHEN residents of the northern reaches of the Genesee Valley speak of "The Valley," the reference usually has a parochial sense. Those who use the term are not thinking of Letchworth Park or of such far upriver places as Belfast, Belvidere, or Wellsville. By "The Valley," they mean only those broad and rolling lands adjoining and adjacent to the village of Geneseo, thirty miles south of Rochester, which have been for many years the domain of the Wadsworth family.

Wadsworths first came from England to the North American continent in 1632, and late in the next century members of the family had penetrated the Western Wilderness to the Genesee. They quickly acquired land, land galore. In 1800, ten years after hawk-nosed, blustering General Bill, and his younger, more elegant brother, James, had reached the river, they held between them more than 35,000 acres, and the core of this tract is still in Wadsworth hands. Today, the two branches of the family,

William Perkins Wadsworth, and his cousins, James J. and Reverdy Wadsworth, own, in total, about 20,000 acres, and William and Reverdy—in the tradition of their forebears—cultivate the land.

Unlike many other prominent American families, the Wadsworths have provided no scandalous headlines for the tabloids; and though occasionally, during the centuries that the clan has lived in America, a Wadsworth has turned up who drank to excess, who dissipated his heritage, who divorced his wife, or who engaged in some rascality, such aberrations have been far from the general behavior of the family. The women have been singularly gracious, and often beautiful. The men have contributed notably to the development of the Genesee Valley, taken leadership in civic affairs, fought gallantly in their country's defense, and distinguished themselves as statesmen.

Perhaps the rural economy under which earlier Wadsworths lived made the farming of Genesee lands a more rewarding enterprise than it is at present, and it may be because of this that now and then a parcel of the family land is sold to a neighboring farmer. But Wadsworths still dominate "The Valley"; they have preserved its character. Their fields have not been stripped and gouged by earth movers to fit them for factory sites; their wood lots have not been flattened; their smiling pastures have not been transformed into subdivisions, for the spawning of hundreds of depressing little cheesebox houses, each as similar to its neighbor as one block in a child's set of blocks is like another. Now, as a hundred years ago, dirt roads, shaded by great trees, wind in and out of the property, inviting neither snorting trucks nor racing motor cars. Here the sometimes dubious thing called "progress" has been restrained; here a blessed peace and a pastoral quiet prevail.

Today the two branches of the Wadsworth family are separated by the length of Geneseo's Main Street. William Perkins Wadsworth lives in the ancestral seat, The Homestead, at the southern end of town; and Reverdy occupies what is known as Hartford House, which his great-grandfather built, at the northern end of the village.

Left to their own devices, the cousins might have chosen smaller houses. Instead, they followed a Wadsworth tradition. As a sole heir, Bill Wadsworth took over The Homestead at the death of his widowed mother; and Reverdy—since his brother and sister had left "The Valley"—became the occupant of Hartford House when his parents, the James W. Wadsworths, died in the mid years of the century.

In an age when valets are no more, when footmen in livery are mere figures from Victorian novels, and butlers often steal the family silver or leave to drive taxicabs—with the complete passing of the obsequious domestic servant—a house as large as The Homestead must at times be something of a white elephant.

The James Wadsworth who came with his brother to the Genesee in 1790 built The Homestead for his bride, Naomi Wolcott, whom he married in 1804. The house has been continuously lived in by Wadsworths. But the first James would not know the place today, with the additions that have been made to it by succeeding generations. It is a great, wide-flung wedding cake of a house, three stories high, which offers from its windows a fine prospect of gently rolling meadows, ornamented by splendid trees and pasturing jumping horses. It is so vast that the present master was stumped when a visitor inquired the number of its rooms.

"I can't tell for sure, but I know this," said William P. Wadsworth ruefully. "There are nine servants' rooms. When I was a boy, every one of those rooms was occupied, and other help came in by the day. The one servant here now is the little old woman who let you in through the door."

A Yale graduate, who had briefly taught school in Montreal, the builder of The Homestead was a man of refined tastes and scholarly interests. He raised a family of five children under conditions that were greatly different from the rough woodsman's life that he and his brother had known when they first reached the Genesee. Even in its original design, The Homestead bore no resemblance to the squalid hut that had been for a time the frontier home of Bill and James Wadsworth. It was stoutly constructed, spacious, tastefully furnished, and it soon became the center of the social life of the countryside.

As the wilderness receded under the pressure of thousands of new settlers, James Wadsworth decided that the residents of his "Valley" should be educated, and he earnestly devoted himself to the establishment of a common-school system, and spent, in the advancement of this purpose, $90,000 of his own money. He died a widower in 1844, and left a daughter, Elizabeth, and two sons, William Wolcott and James Samuel Wadsworth, the oldest of the trio, a vibrant, devil-may-care youth, who was dropped

from Harvard, who studied law under Daniel Webster, who married a celebrated eastern beauty, and took her to Europe on a honeymoon.

Beguiled by the manner in which the English aristocracy lived, James Samuel Wadsworth decided to make the style of their life the pattern of his own. He built, in Geneseo, Hartford House, which he named after Lord Hertford (pronounced "Hartford"); he took a town house in New York, maintained a splendid stable and a notable wine cellar. He entertained lavishly. His father had left him a huge fortune which the son, extravagant though he was, managed to increase.

Although he indulged himself in the luxuries made possible by his wealth, and delighted in the fripperies of society life,

James S. Wadsworth was no social fop. He was a man of unusual talents, high principles, and physical and moral courage. He had many interests that transcended the levees, the cotillions, the twelve-course dinners of New York fashionables, and the genteel sports of Geneseo. He took leadership in agricultural movements; lost, as a Republican candidate, a gubernatorial contest of New York; spoke loudly and persistently against slavery, when many persons of his class were hush-hush on the subject, or definite antiabolitionists. And when the tensions caused by the issue of slavery precipitated the Civil War, James, as General Wadsworth, fought valorously at Bull Run, at Gettysburg, served for a period as military governor of Washington, D. C., and died, every inch a hero, from wounds suffered in the Battle of the Wilderness.

There has been a succession of James Wadsworths in the Genesee Valley since the arrival there of the first James, who is sometimes credited with "creating The Valley," and one of the successors bore the full name of the general who died in battle, though he was far better known by the dimunitive, "Jim Sam." A Falstaffian character, though his belly was less ponderous than Sir John's, Jim Sam backed a musical comedy, raced a stable of horses, took a second wife after his first marriage ended in divorce, fought a war, lost his heritage, and all along the way of life to his terminal illness had a whale of a good time.

A member of the "Pork"—Harvard's swank Porcellian Club—and the younger brother of the courtly beau, Craig Wadsworth, who, Jim Sam avowed, had been fifth on the list of men to be shot by Harry Thaw—this impoverished scapegrace was the liveliest wit in The Valley, and a man no more impressed by rank, wealth, or royalty than he was by the village barflies who were his friends, or by the grooms of the Wadsworth stables, who adored him.

The Valley is horsy country. The English blood sport of fox hunting was introduced there in 1876 by Major W. Austin Wadsworth, whose son, Willian Perkins Wadsworth, is the present

MFH. The Genesee Valley Hunt is the third oldest in the country. Its history is distinguished; its traditions are as well preserved as a ladybird in amber. The male members ride in uniforms of blue and buff, not unlike the uniforms of the Continental Army, since the founder, and first master of the hunt, opposed on patriotic grounds the "pinks" of British hunt clubs.

The hunt came upon lean days after the death of Major Wadsworth, was briefly suspended, and was revived under the mastership of a dapper little swell from Tuxedo Park, and other eastern resorts, Winthrop (Winty) Chanler, who, by his own admission, had "fallen in love with The Valley." He was the great great grandson of John Jacob Astor. His wife was the niece of Julia Ward Howe, and the talented author of *Roman Spring* and *Autumn in the Valley*. His brother, Bob, had married (for a week or two) the beautiful and notorious opera singer, Lina Cavalieri, and was to be identified, thenceforth, by the comic strip caption, "Who's Looney Now?" which one of his brothers, who had suffered a slight mental derangement, wired him at the time of his nuptials.

Under Winty Chanler the hunt prospered. But his tenure was brief. At his passing, there was need of new financial support, and this was provided by Ernest L. Woodward, from the nearby village of LeRoy. He was the son of the man who had bought the formula for manufacturing JELL-O for $400, and it was Ernest Woodward, as Jim Sam used to say, who "parlayed the prescription into forty million dollars"—the sum paid for the little LeRoy company by a national food syndicate.

A genial, gracious man, and an ardent horseman, Mr. Woodward had more enthusiam for the hunt than knowledge of how to direct it: Jim Sam had a good deal of knowledge, but no means, no horses, no uniform. A deal was made. Mr. Woodward would take the mastership, and "do things for the hunt," and, incidentally, for Jim Sam, if the latter would serve as joint master. The arrangement was ideal. The two masters made a brave show when they took the field behind the chevying pack, except that

Jim Sam, re-exposed to high living, suffered gout in one of his great toes, and rode most of the season, beautifully accoutered down to his left foot, which was cossetted by a carpet slipper.

One December morning during the season of the Wadsworth-Woodward mastership, the Princes Gustaf Adolf and Sigvard Bernadotte, sons of the Swedish crown prince, who had been guests of George Eastman in Rochester, arrived in Geneseo to ride with the Genesee Valley Hunt.

In the past, many figures of prominence, including the first Roosevelt to occupy the White House, had galloped over the rolling lands of the Wadsworths in pursuit of the bushy-tailed, crafty vermin, and all had been held rigidly to hunting protocol. In the field, they were subjects, not the peers of the Master of Fox Hounds. But royalty perhaps needed to be dealt with differently. The proposal was made that the princes be allowed to ride up with the masters. The issue, however, was still in debate, when Jim Sam, a fine figure of a sporting squire, in his resplendent regimentals, started—as a gesture to royalty—to fit his gouty foot into a lustrous leather riding boot.

This painful operation was being undertaken in the kitchen of Jim Sam's small house on the Avon-Geneseo road, and was witnessed by this writer. The boot was partly on and Jim Sam was groaning with the pain of it, when the question was put to him:

"What about these princes? Are they going to ride with you and Mr. Woodward, or be put back in the field with the ordinary hunters?"

Jim Sam tugged again at the boot. This time it went full over the sore foot. "Ouch! Christ!" he cried. Then he answered, "We're going to put numbers on the sons-of-bitches like football players," and rising from the chair, he tenderly tested the newly booted foot on the floor.

The late W. Austin Wadsworth was considered one of the great masters of fox hounds in America. He was a perfectionist. Fox hunting with him was an art, not an excuse for a casual canter over hill and dale to blow out a jumping horse and provide exercise for the rider. He lived for the sport, and he lived alone until middle life in The Homestead, which he had inherited from his mother. Shortly after the turn of the century, he married Miss Elizabeth Perkins, from Boston, who complemented his own interests; and from then on The Homestead, with its many rooms and a staff of servants that would have been adequate for a small hotel, became the most hospitable dwelling in the Genesee Valley. The doors were unlocked night and day during the hunting season, and often only footmen, stealing through the silent house at night, collecting shoes that had been left outside of bedchambers for polishing, knew how many guests might be expected for breakfast.

Austin Wadsworth's era was the great era of the Genesee Valley Hunt. He owned the pack. He owned much of the land that was hunted over. An autocrat, who believed that The Valley was the valley of the Wadsworths, and that the other residents were there under sufferance, he countenanced no defiance of his authority. His closest friends were men and women of wealth and station, but he enjoyed, because he was sternly protective of their lands and property, complete rapport with neighboring farmers; and a farm boy, in ratcatcher's clothes, provided he had a good seat and a pair of good hands, was as genuinely welcome in the hunting field as a Roosevelt, a Belmont, a Chanler, Devereux Milburn, the ten-goal polo player, or Arthur Brisbane, the famous editor.

A subscription pack today, the Genesee Valley Hunt still provides a colorful autumn spectacle in The Valley. It is a more democratic institution than formerly. Among its riders in recent years have been bankers, lawyers, farmers, wealthy sportsmen from Rochester, Buffalo, and East Aurora, a couple of undertakers, a village priest, and a state trooper. And during the season, following a precedent of nearly ninety years, the doors of The Homestead are flung wide, for guests who come a-hunting, though footmen no longer carry the guests' shoes backstairs to buff.

General James Samuel Wadsworth and his grandson, Senator James W. Wadsworth, Jr., are the most distinguished members of the Wadsworth clan and the great men of The Valley. Between the two was the General's son and the Senator's father, James W. Wadsworth, Sr., a rollicking, full-blooded, mustachioed farmer and plutocrat, who dressed like a Mississippi-steamboat gambler, who loved baseball, harness racing, and the rough and tumble of political contests. Once, during a vote count at a Republican National Convention, he slugged a man who had shouted out that Wadsworth's beloved son, James, Jr., was a crook; once he fired a farm hand who presumed the ostentation of owning a T-model Ford. And when his neice, Mrs. Porter Chanler, remonstrated with him about this, telling him that feudalism was a thing of the past, he shouted at her fiercely, "Mary, you talk like a goddamned Bolshevik!"

Known as the Boss—and the title fitted him as neatly as a pinchback coat—James W. Wadsworth, Sr., was generally liked by the rural commonality despite his occasional antic flights into suzerainty and his amusing assumption of the role of a three-tailed bashaw. The tenants on his farms and his farmer neighbors delighted in his appearance, his forthrightness, his peppery eccentricities. They were entertained by the crack baseball teams, composed of proselyted college stars—young Jimmy, at first base, was the only native player—that he put into the field in Geneseo uniforms. He had an air of bravura. At the age of eighteen, he had come out of the Civil War a brevet major; after the war, he had been a quasi-Indian fighter with Buffalo Bill. He had no timidity, whatsoever, and an old-fashioned kind of honesty.

The Boss had married a New York Travers, whose cousin was the mother of Winston Churchill, and whose father had made a great fortune in Wall Street; and the pair had a daughter and James W., Jr., whom the old man hand-tailored for the tripartite role of gentleman, farmer, and politician. Young Jimmy was brought up with a silver spoon in his mouth and a hay fork in his hand. He worked summers as a field laborer on the Boss's vast farms. He went, of course, to the proper schools: the Fay School, St. Mark's, and on to Yale, where most Wadsworth men have gone, when they haven't gone to Harvard.

Very early he learned from the Boss that true gentlemen tell the truth despite the consequences; and the lesson in time brought him defeat in politics and tributes from men of rank, who saw what many voters failed to see, that here was a candidate whose special merit was his refusal to covet political popularity at the expense of conviction.

He left Yale to go bounding off, as a private, to the Spanish-American War, which ended before he saw any fighting. He went later, as a civilian, to the Philippines, where he observed, and never forgot, the mess his country was making of its military establishment. Upon his return he married Alice, daughter of the great John Hay, diplomat, historian, and President McKinley's Secretary of State, whose older daughter had previously married the many, many times millionaire, Payne Whitney.

To the delight of the Boss, young Jimmy's political career began early. Before he was thirty, he was elected to the New York State Assembly; before he was forty, he began a two-term career in the United States Senate. When he ran for a third term the "drys," who were determined to poleax him into political obscurity, because of his persistent advocacy of the abolishment of the Eighteenth Amendment, defeated him, but failed in their full purpose. Seven years after he lost his seat in the Senate, he returned to Washington as a freshman in the Lower House, and remained there until poor health caused him to quit, nine terms later.

Remembering what he had seen of American military botchery in the Philippines, he fought unceasingly in both the Senate and the House for better military preparedness. He served for a time as Chairman of the Senate's Military Affairs Committee. During the deceptive lull between the first and second World Wars, he strongly advocated a Defense Act which would include universal military training. The Act was passed with this vital element elided, which later caused General George C. Marshall to remark:

"If Congress had passed the original Wadsworth bill I do not believe even Hitler would have dared to provoke a second World War. . . ."

And at the time that Wadsworth spoke in favor of holding drafted men in the army—three months before the strike at Pearl Harbor, and in the face of violent public disfavor and the opposition of leaders of his own party—the *New York Times* characterized his plea as "one of the half-dozen speeches in the whole history of Congress which really swayed opinion and changed the course of history."

There were times when Senator Wadsworth appeared to suffer political myopia, notably when he staunchly supported the presidential candidacy of Warren Gamaliel Harding, and when he intransigently opposed women's suffrage. He always stood on his principles, right or wrong; he spoke out for his beliefs in ringing tones, without equivocation or the mincing of words. It was said of him that he did not have integrity; he *was* integrity! He died in 1952, leaving, besides his widow, a daughter, Evelyn—Mrs. W. Stuart Symington, wife of the United States Senator from Missouri; and two sons, James Jeremiah Wadsworth, former American Ambassador to the United Nations, and Reverdy, of Geneseo. For many years he served truly, and often brilliantly, what his father was fond of defining as "This beloved country of ours"; and the old Boss, lying in the Geneseo cemetery, might well have been proud of his only son, the splendid product of his handiwork.

36

Scientists, engineers, poets, and scholars have written informatively and sometimes eloquently about the Genesee. The scientists have discussed the river's geology and physiography. The engineers have dealt expertly with such matters as hydraulic power and flood control. The poets and scholars have told of the history and romance of the river. They have extolled its beauties and lamented the abuse it has suffered from industry and from the gross untidiness of persons who live along its banks.

But the scientists and engineers mostly couch their disquisitions in the cold and academic language of their specialties, and their studies are confined to those areas of the river that are suitable for the employment of their peculiar talents. They take small account of the river's personality, its vibrancy, its humors; to them it is purely an object of professional inquiry. And the poets and scholars often leave one with a feeling that they are familiar only with certain conspicuous features of the stream. They have glorified the gorge and falls at Letchworth Park. But they appear not to have traveled isolated reaches of the Genesee in a small boat, which is the best way to learn about the river's ambages, its shoals and holes, the frequent alterations in its riparian contour, the flora and fauna of its banks, its crotchets and moods; the places where bass, and pike and pickerel may be had. The poets and scholars are a little like tourists enchanted by the hugeness and beauty of the Jungfrau, who know nothing of the bewildering little paths, with their variety of interests, that wind up its slope.

A canoe is the proper craft for use on the upper Genesee, as the Seneca Indians, who first ruled the river, very well knew. Their reign ended; their elm-bark canoes disappeared, and for a time white men prosecuted a crude river trade, poling flatboats upstream and floating them down with wheat for the Rochester mills. This traffic ended when the Genesee Valley Canal penetrated the valley from which it took its name. After that, the ribald shouts of boatmen ceased, the river taverns disappeared, and the upper Genesee reverted to a pristine quiet, which still prevails during much of the river's meander from Mt. Morris to Genesee Valley Park, Rochester's southernmost purlieu.

In earlier decades of the century, before we succumbed to the domination of the combustion engine, the quiet, leisurely pastime of paddling a canoe was popular on the Genesee. Several boat clubs and a boat livery stood on the left bank of the stream in Genesee Valley Park, Rochester's spacious and most beautiful public playground. Stuffing duffel under the scant decks of their craft, canoeists often went upstream for a night, a weekend, or a week. There were pleasant camping sites all the way to Avon. A favorite springtime stunt was to ship a canoe in a railroad express car to some upriver station and come booming down in floodwater to the park.

I had enjoyed these excursions in the past. Recently, curious to know whether the physical aspects of the river had materially changed since my last long paddle on it, I essayed another excursion in the company of Donald F. Southgate, of Geneva, New York. Our journey was not, however, confined to the upper river. We went all the way from Mt. Morris to Lake Ontario, with a motor portage around the river's three cataracts in Rochester. The trip was made in four stages, of a day each, each stage separated by several weeks.

Don Southgate and I chose a warm, sunny, early April day for the first leg of our expedition. In mid-March, there had been a good deal of snow in the valley. Rains and soft weather had followed. The Genesee's tributaries were gushing water into the main stream. Tiny rivulets, whose narrow beds are practically arid during the summer months, were brawling torrents. The river was swollen almost to its brim. But it would not spill over its banks to steal away good top soil from adjacent farm lands, to sweep into the living rooms of houses in small river settlements, and to make a mess of low-lying streets in downtown Rochester. The Mt. Morris dam, its huge reservoir still unfilled, was capable of preventing any such mischievous caper as that.

Carefully placing our light wooden canoe into the water, which strove angrily to tug it away from the muddy bank, we gingerly crawled into the narrow craft, each wearing a ridiculously large, red life jacket. The Rochester police had warned that persons using pleasure craft on the river would be arrested. But we were well south of their jurisdiction. Nevertheless, we were not without qualms; there was no bravado in our attitude. We are men well beyond our physical prime, and we had been told that our undertaking was foolhardy, if not actually suicidal. We trimmed the boat. We released our hold of a stout twig, which served as a mooring line, and felt at once as if we were spinning down a steep slope of glass-smooth, mud-stained ice. It was a momentary sensation. It ended as quickly as we got the feel of the swift-running water, and found that we could handily manage the boat in it.

We set Avon Bridge as our first day's goal. With the aid of the swift current, we calculated to reach it in four or five hours. We never saw the welcome outline of the structure until dusk, and by then we had been at our task a straight seven hours. Moving always with the current, we discouragedly found ourselves on several occasions proceeding due south on a river that gains much of its distinction from the fact that it flows north into Lake Ontario. When we later traced our course on a geodetic map, we discovered that we had looped, backtracked, followed enormous oxbows, and wandered over half of Livingston County. In laying out the course of the Genesee, Mother Nature took no account of the geometric axiom that a straight line is the shortest distance beween two points.

In our journey of more than thirty miles, we remarked half a dozen automobiles crossing the three or four bridges under which we passed, and we saw two fishermen. Beyond that, for the most part, we seemed remote from human intercourse. There are areas along that part of the Genesee that I am sure have not changed very much in the hundred-odd years since the last rivermen abandoned the river and left it to an occasional angler, or to men who might trap or hunt along its banks. Our boat was the only one on the scene.

We were about two miles downstream from our launching place and had rounded a hairpin turn, when Southgate, kneeling on the bow thwart, exclaimed sotto voce, "Boy, oh boy, oh boy!"

"What is it?" I whispered.

Before he had time to answer, the flat, cocoa-colored water, seventy yards beyond, was churned into small white waves; there was a great flapping of wings, an angry honking, and not ten, or twenty, or fifty, but two or three hundred Canada geese rose into the air. They spread out in a long, waving echelon that reached full across the stream, and flew over our heads. Those at the lower tip of the line seemed so close, that I half believe, had we stood up in the boat, we might have knocked them out of the air with our paddles.

"I've been a goose hunter for years," Southgate said wonderingly. "I've traveled long distances looking for geese. I've never seen anything quite like this."

Half a mile farther, another flock, which had been feeding some distance back from the river, was startled into flight by the noise of our approach. Long before we reached Avon, we must have seen thousands of geese. They became so commonplace that I lost interest in them, and turned my attention to a great blue heron, which flew ahead of us like a scout reconnoitering the country through which we were to pass. We were diverted by a variety of wild life. We saw black ducks, wood ducks, teal, mallards; two deer, a fox running back from the river, mud turtles, muskrats. I was beguiled by a tiny, swift-darting little bird, which was teasing the life out of an owl.

Twice we stopped and mounted the riverbank, hoping to find some landmark that would give us our bearing, for the mazelike course of the river had destroyed our sense of orientation. Nothing we saw was familiar. There was no road or farm building in the prospect. If there is blessedness in solitude, wide areas of the Genesee Valley are blessed.

Our feeling of isolation lifted as the buildings of the State Teachers College at Geneseo loomed up, high above the stream's right bank. We had a good view of the lower part of the village. Five minutes later, when we rounded a bend in the river, we might have been five hundred miles in the bush, so quiet was our watery trail, so undisturbed the stands of beech, cottonwood, quaking aspen, and sycamores that flanked it.

The village of York, which reposes two miles back from the west bank of the river, some distance below Geneseo, was invisible to us. During the years of commercial navigation on the Genesee, the landing at the water's edge—York Landing, as it was known—was a lively port. It was above York that navigators had their greatest difficulty at times of low water. To overcome this, a dam and a lock (the only lock on the river) were built at the Landing. From then on boats were able to proceed south as far as Geneseo, even during periods of drought.

When the Genesee Valley Canal was routed through the Landing, the place enjoyed a prosperity even greater than it had known as a river port. Mills were built, large warehouses were erected. There was a turning basin next to the canal prism, which today is a scum-covered pond. Passing in our canoe what formerly had been a busy river and canal stop, Southgate and I saw only a desolate cluster of swamp timber, the crumbling foundations of a warehouse, and a straggle of refuse from a village dump.

We were tired when we reached the Avon Bridge. Our ancient muscles ached from an unconscionably long spell of paddling. With considerable effort we raised the canoe to the crest of the river bank. We had covered the longest stretch of the Genesee that we would paddle in a single day in our several excursions. Our next voyage, undertaken after the river had fallen several feet, took us uneventfully from Avon to Scottsville; the third from Scottsville to the river terminal of the Barge Canal, which is close to the heart of Rochester.

The Genesee becomes a river of considerable substance a short distance south of the point in Genesee Valley Park where the Barge Canal crosses it at water level. Dredgers have lowered its floor. A dam at Court Street, two and a half miles north, has broadened it and provided a channel fourteen feet deep for heavily laden canalboats, though they no longer proceed downriver to the Rochester terminal. Commercial traffic on the canal is dying. It has been dead at Rochester for several years.

As a boy and young man I lived in Rochester, and the canoe in which Southgate and I made our voyage was then kept in the summer quarters of the Rochester Athletic Club, on the left bank of the river, in Genesee Valley Park. In those days, the boat livery was a short distance downstream, and beyond that was a string of small canoe clubs. The athletic club is gone, the boat livery has moved farther south, and the canoe clubs are boarded up and unused. Boating on the upper Genesee is largely confined to motorboats, and most of these turn quickly from the river to the safer waters of the canal. What few canoes one sees are rented by their occupants from the boat livery. Before World War I, canoeing was extremely popular on the river. Competitions in the sport were held. And each year a gigantic water carnival, with a procession of decorated floats, attracted between seventy and eighty thousand persons to the park.

In its reach from the canal to the Rochester canal terminal, the physical character of the Genesee has changed greatly since my youth. Once the lower half of this flow was a rapids, so shallow at certain places during the dry season that a boy could traverse the rock-cluttered channel on foot. The new depth and breadth, acquired at the time the stream became a spur of the canal, gives the river new dignity. Its bends are gradual. One would expect to see its ample surface alive with traffic. It would make an ideal course for eight-oar crews to race the Henley distance. But there are no oarsmen on the upper Genesee; cargo vessels have no purpose there. And pleasure craft rarely pass the northern boundary of the park to explore an area of the river that offers a splendid view of the Rochester sky line.

The changes which I remarked in the channel, as our canoe drifted north on a stretch of river unnavigable in its native state, were no more pronounced than some of the alterations I observed on the banks of the Genesee. I was very young, and had just become acquainted with the river at the time that a hilly piece of farm land surmounting the stream's east bank, immediately north of the park, was seeded, graded, landscaped, and given over to the new-fangled game of golf. Under the ownership of the Oak Hill Country Club, the property continued to be used for this purpose until the second decade of the century. Then another transition took place.

George Eastman, founder of the Eastman Kodak Company, overcoming a long-held prejudice against educational institutions that stressed the humanities over scientific studies, began with calculated munificence to hand over to the University of Rochester millions and more millions; and soon this lean and hungry little institution (begun, legend has it, in a tavern that the owner thought might do better as a college) bought up the country club's property and removed from its near-downtown location to what is now known as the River Campus. And there it began an expansion that still continues, aided and abetted by a better than eighty-million-dollar endowment.

The river bows gently around the River Campus, and goes on from there in a fairly straight course to the Court Street Dam, which Southgate and I reached after twenty minutes of paddling. On this stretch it is flanked by concrete walls, which prevent it from flooding the depressed areas adjoining its banks, as it did during periods of high water in the past. Engineers call the Genesee a "flash" river because of the speed with which it rises under the impulse of rains and melting snows. It has caused many disastrous floods. The most memorable of these were in 1865 (at that time, the Rochester city fathers unavailingly petitioned Abraham Lincoln to exempt Rochester men from the draft, in order that they might help repair the flood damage), and in 1916.

When we reached the lip of the dam, our canoe stood a few rods east of the river border of the old 100-Acre Tract, once a place of pestilence, fever, and rattlesnakes, upon which the city of Rochester was founded. The spot where Ebenezer Allan's mills were erected was a quarter of a mile north, a short distance from the stream's left bank. We raised our canoe from the water at the canal terminal, on the right bank, and on foot took cognizance of our surroundings.

37

THE heart of Rochester lies on the Genesee, and swift running water is the reason for the city's being. In its earliest character it was a milltown, whose economy depended upon a double service from the Genesee. The river made a highway for the flatboats that carried wheat to the Rochester mills and river water turned the mill wheels that ground the wheat into flour. But the business was of limited promise. The early millers produced good flour, but the trick was to get it to good markets. These were in the East. Days were required to move a barrel of flour even as far as Albany, and wagoners were expensive.

When the Erie Canal reached Rochester and crossed the Genesee by aqueduct less than a dozen years after the village was founded, there was great rejoicing. Here was the dreamed-of outlet for the product of Rochester mills. Profits soared. Industry was immensely stimulated. New mills sprang up along the river. They stood cheek to jowl in the vicinity of the Upper Falls, and there were mills at the Middle and Lower Falls as well. Rochester's boast that it was the breadbasket of the nation was not pure puffery, and its title, the Flour City, was widely flaunted. Before mid-century, its twenty-one mills were producing more flour than any other milling center in America, a condition that prevailed until the opening of the vast Western wheat fields, when millers moved West to accommodate the growers. But by that time, Rochester had become the home of the largest commercial nurseries in the world, the "u" in Flour was replaced by "w," an "e" was added, and it was then known as the Flower City.

Today, it has a third and still more famous sobriquet: the Kodak City. It derives from the colossal Eastman Kodak Company, without which, as some wit perhaps not inaptly remarked, a huge sign might be laid flat upon the runways of the local airport: *This* WAS *Rochester.*

The economy of Rochester has been sustained for many years by the Eastman Kodak Company, and the late George Eastman stands out indubitably as the city's greatest benefactor and most distinguished citizen. There is a small group of intellectuals who protest that the second insignia should be attached to the memory of Lewis H. Morgan, father of American anthropology and author of a monumental work on the American Indian, *The League of the Iroquois;* there is a steadfast group of women worshipers who militantly contend that Susan B. Anthony was Rochester's most eminent personage, and they tell with considerable truth how the shadow of this small, utterly uncompromising crusader for women's rights has lengthened until it stretches around the world.

Both Morgan and the secular saint—Saint Susan—were outstanding Rochester citizens. But the contributions of Eastman to industrial and medical science and to education; his efforts to help the lowliest in their struggle toward the light; his brilliant demonstration to American industry of an ideal management-labor rapport, conceived out of his desire to have his workers share with management the profits and benefits of his company; his glorification of his city and country, give him status as the greatest Rochesterian, and place him among the eminent Americans of his time.

He was a man who eschewed personal publicity and detested flamboyance. Once he gave ten million dollars to the Massachusetts Institute of Technology under the pseudonym, "Mr. Smith." His personality lacked that sometimes dubious thing called "color." He was a bachelor. He raced no horses, he maintained no steam yacht; he did not turn to blonde women for diversion. Dedicating his early life to his industry, he devised in his later years a scientific plan for the distribution of the great wealth that he had gained from his industry to causes and institutions that promoted the health, the culture, the education, and the pleasure of his fellow men. He gave away ninety million dollars, more than half of which went to the University of Rochester, and other local institutions. He died by his own hand when he felt that he had exhausted his usefulness, leaving this note next to his dead body: "My work is done, why wait?"

When Southgate and I left the full, fine sweep of the Genesee above Court Street Dam to peer into the channel immediately below the dam, we remarked an abrupt and depressing change in the river's aspect. It was here that the Genesee, no longer enshrined in its "beautiful valley," began to lose caste, and its degradation—resulting from Rochester's shameful neglect of its greatest natural heritage—continued through the center of the city. The stony walls and rocky floor of the river's bed resembled nothing so much as a hard-worked quarry. No water was falling over the dam, though a slim stream, released through a lower sluice, flowed along the right wall of the channel. The stream passed first under the old Erie Canal aqueduct, now Broad Street, and then under Main Street bridge, a structure unique in American cities.

Built more than a century ago, the bridge offers to passers-by no view of the river. It has no wall, no parapet. Each side is solid with buildings. An earnest and imaginative committee, the Arts Council of Rochester, has designed elaborate plans for the beautification of the Genesee River in the Rochester area. If the plans should materialize, the bridge may be revamped somewhat in the style of the Ponte Vecchio, in Florence; but this is for the future. In its present state, the bridge is a shabby structure from any angle, though there are some who would preserve its "picturesqueness."

Gazing from east to west across the river, my companion and I could see, rising on a plot of twenty-seven acres, Rochester's new Civic Center which, when completed, will give a handsome new look to a decadent, down-at-heel area on the west side and complement an impressive new development on the east side of the city. One of the buildings in the Civic Center scheme was completed in 1955. It is a splendid, seven-million-dollar auditorium known as the Community War Memorial, which occupies a full block along the river, with an esplanade overlooking the channel. Beyond, a little to the west of the War Memorial, several buildings of a group that ultimately will house the courts, the police station, the sheriff's office, and various other components of the city and county governments, were in advanced stages of construction.

After our brief survey of this project, Southgate and I turned our steps to the heart of the east side of the city, where two Rochester merchants with great vision and an abundance of courage have caused to be created a mercantile plaza that has excited the admiration of city planners from coast to coast.

Gilbert J. C. McCurdy and Maurice R. Forman had suffered the endemic disorder of most downtown merchants in America. They had seen business running away from their stores to suburban shopping centers. The desertion was serious. They decided to gamble high and hope to check it. They engaged the Viennese-born architect, Victor Gruen, to design a business and shopping center, Midtown Plaza, which is the most exciting innovation in downtown Rochester since George Eastman built what was then considered the finest theater in the country, put a sixty-piece orchestra in its pit, live shows on its stage, and leading motion pictures on its screen.

The heart of the shopping area is a covered central mall, a spacious plaza which is heated in the winter and cooled in the summer. Along the three thousand feet of enclosed frontage are two major stores and more than forty other shops, restaurants, and commercial agencies. There is a novel "Clock of the Nations" in the center of the mall which daily attracts thousands of visitors. The decor includes fountains and growing plants. There are benches for weary shoppers.

Directly below the mall is a three-level municipal parking garage, with a capacity for nearly two thousand cars; above it are thirteen floors of offices. And above these are four hotel floors, with a restaurant on the lowest that offers a spectacular view of the city, the adjacent countryside, Lake Ontario, and the Genesee River. McCurdy and Forman have surpassing faith in the city. In their efforts to revitalize its downtown area, they have gambled thirty million dollars.

On the last leg of our intermittent voyage on the Genesee from Mt. Morris to Lake Ontario, Southgate and I put our canoe into the river just below the Lower Falls, from which, that day, scarcely a trickle of water was falling. The blight of the stream, which began below the Court Street Dam and continued three miles through the city, ended below the Lower Falls. There the Genesee again assumed the character of a river. It had depth and breadth. It flowed. It was in its natural element, under open skies, not hidden in a tunnel to provide power for the turbines of the hydro-electric plant of the Rochester Gas and Electric Corporation, which was just behind us.

Our launching place was a shale bar, which had once been Carthage Landing, a river port for lake vessels. Later it was called Brewer's Dock. A short distance to the south, Driving Park

Avenue Bridge, so named because it formerly served as an approach to a Grand Circuit track, spanned the steep gorge at what seemed from our low position a terrifying height.

The walls of the gorge were Queenstone shale, and the left one was surmounted by Maplewood, one of Rochester's many pleasant parks, which followed the curving crest of the escarpment for a considerable distance. The timber at the verge of the gorge was heavy, and trees grew in the interstices of the shaley wall. Here the Genesee had not been despoiled. It seemed pristine in its rugged, arboreal beauty. I was struck by the notion that this river scene which my eyes were delightedly taking in was, with minor alterations, the same scene that lake mariners had come upon, many years ago, as they tacked upstream to Carthage Landing.

We had followed a gentle eastward leaning of the Genesee, which had taken us out of sight of the falls, the bridge, and the power plant. We were in the midst of a populous city, but free of its turmoils, out of earshot of its cacophonies, and out of view of the works of man. Ensconced in our watery course by the wooded, unascendable cliffs of the gorge, we were quite as isolated—or so it briefly seemed—as we had been during our descent of the remote reaches of the upper river. Thick beds of cattails (employed by early settlers to calk beer kegs) stood near the shore. Now and then, in small clearings of intervale, we saw clusters of pink and white flowers, which neither of us could identify, but which might have been attractively displayed in a florist's window. Muskrats slipped into their watery caves at our approach; a black-capped tern, outraged at our intrusion, flew angrily about our heads. Large carp, which curiously reminded me of swine, wallowed lazily on the surface of the stream; and I recalled that in Seth Green's time, catfish weighing as much as a half-grown boy were often taken from these waters; that Green had speared sturgeon weighing as much as a man.

Any illusion we might have entertained that we were pioneering the river left us as we passed under an arch of the Veterans' Memorial Bridge, a large and impressive structure in the northern section of Rochester. A few minutes later we saw, perched atop the west wall of the gorge, the new research laboratory of the Eastman Kodak Company, the gates of whose 1,000-acre Kodak Park plant stand a couple of hundred yards from the river.

We had been paddling about an hour when we came opposite the river docks of the Baltimore & Ohio Railroad. From this point coal from the bituminous fields of West Virginia and Pennsylvania has been shipped by lake boats to Canada for many years. For a time the trade slacked. It is coming back. The ever-growing city of Toronto has exhausted its hydraulic potential and from now on will need large quantities of coal for the development of electrical power. In anticipation of this, the B. & O. is planning to replace its outmoded coal tipple with a four-million-dollar device which will load three thousand tons of coal an hour. Perhaps the railroads are not quite finished.

On our way from the B. & O. docks to the lake, a distance of a mile and a half, we passed Rattlesnake Point, a promontory notorious in the early development of the region for the dens of poisonous reptiles found there. We were well out of the gorge; the banks were flattening. The river widened. Dozens of small yachts and motor cruisers were moored along the shore.

Soon we were opposite the Rochester Yacht Club, on the east bank of the Genesee, very close to its mouth. Our voyage had been undertaken on a bright, late-spring afternoon. The water was dotted with pleasure craft which were sailing out past the long piers to the lake or returning to the yacht club's basin or to upstream slips and mooring places.

The yacht club represented the lighter, the sporting character of the lower Genesee; the warehouses of the Port of Rochester, diagonally across the river, offered evidence of the stream's utility. Moored to the dockage that paralleled the warehouses was a large freighter that flew the Union Jack. She was out of Glasgow, Scotland. Her chief cargo was seventeen hundred tons of Scotch whisky, a consignment to provoke the covetousness of the amateur shellbacks across the stream, who traditionally have associated hard liquor with hard sailing. The freighter was only one of many foreign, ocean-going vessels that have sailed from the lake into the Genesee since the opening in 1958 of the St. Lawrence Seaway.

In 1961, sixty-two such vessels visited the inland seaport of Rochester. That number increased the following year. Now freighters from London, Glasgow, Antwerp, and Rotterdam make scheduled monthly calls. Other ships come less regularly from other countries. If they are able to traverse the Seaway, they will be able to turn in the basin of the Port of Rochester.

Recently a Japanese freighter of more than five hundred feet put into the "Little River of the Iroquois" to discharge a burden of steel, plywood, and Mandarin oranges. Although this was the first visit of a vessel from the Orient, no one in Rochester seemed excited by the event. It might have been a novelty to Ed Morley, down in Potter County, Pennsylvania, whose father used to stretch a potato sack across the breadth of the Genesee, as it flowed through the Morley farm, and catch a mess of brook trout for supper.

ACKNOWLEDGMENTS

The author of a work of this sort needs the help of many persons. This help was given to me with great willingness. In some instances, those who assisted are mentioned in the text of the book, and my thanks to them is implied. The names of others are printed below. But more persons than those named in the text or catalogued in these paragraphs contributed to the total effort. Unfortunately, a list of these secondary coadjutors would be too long to print.

I am particularly beholden to Miss Emma Swift, head of the Local History department of the Rochester Public Library; to her assistant, Mrs. Thelma C. Jefferies; to Miss Gladys E. Love, a former member of the library staff; to George B. Selden, Jr., a profound student of certain areas of early Genesee River history; to Mr. and Mrs. J. Hayward Madden, authorities on the Genesee Valley Canal; to Dr. Edward J. Hoffmeister, professor of geology at the University of Rochester, and to Howard Harding, who for many years made exhaustive engineering studies of the river for the Rochester Gas & Electric Corp.

I am also indebted to Mrs. Katherine Barnes, the late George S. Brooks, Miss Margaret Butterfield, Arthur B. Donnan, Mrs. Marjorie C. Frost, Dr. Frieda A. Gillette, Dr. Eric S. Green, Sen. Cartter Patten, Mrs. Annie O. Peet, Mrs. Marie C. Preston, Walter B. Sanders, Carl F. Schmidt, the late George J. Skivington, Sr., and Knight Thornton.

Mrs. Frank H. Kaiser, who has typed the manuscript for every other book of mine, again did a handsome job on the manuscript for this one; and George H. Chapman patiently read my text for error. I am grateful to both.

HENRY W. CLUNE
Scottsville, New York

BIBLIOGRAPHY

A Biological Survey of the Genesee River System (*Supplemental to Sixteenth Annual Report of the Conservation Department, State of New York*). Albany, New York, J. B. Lyon Co., Printers, 1927.

Adams, Henry, *The War of 1812*. Washington, D.C., Infantry Journal, 1891.

Alexander, Holmes M., *Aaron Burr, The Proud Pretender*. New York, New York, Harper & Brothers, 1937.

Anderson, Mildred Lee Hills, *Genesee Echoes*. Castile, New York, 1956. Privately printed.

Anderson, Mildred Lee Hills, and Willey, Mrs. Marian Piper, *St. Helena— Ghost Town of the Genesee*. Castile, New York, 1954.

Babcock, Louis L., *The War of 1812 on the Niagara Frontier*. Buffalo, New York. Published by the Buffalo Historical Society, 1927.

Bailey, Ralph Edward, *An American Colossus: The Singular Career of Alexander Hamilton*. Boston, Massachusetts, Lee & Shepard Co., 1933.

Bartlett, Charles E., *The Boyd-Parker Story: Groveland Ambuscade*. Castile, New York, Castile Historical Society, 1956.

Bishop, Morris, *Champlain, The Life of Fortitude*. New York, New York, Alfred A. Knopf, 1948.

Bliss, Hubert D., *Peaks of Allegany*. Wellsville, New York, Angelica Advocate Press, 1940.

Brush, Edward Hale, *Iroquois Past and Present* (Sketch of Mary Jemison). Buffalo, New York, Baker Jones & Co., 1901.

Buell, August C., *Sir William Johnson*. New York, New York, Appleton & Co., 1903.

Butterfield, C. W., *History of Brulé's Discoveries and Explorations, 1610-1626*. Cleveland, Ohio, Western Reserve Historical Society, 1898.

Carmer, Carl, *Genesee Fever*. New York, New York, Farrar and Rinehart, 1941.

Carmer, Carl, *Listen for a Lonesome Drum*. New York, New York, William Sloane Associates, 1936.

Chalmers, Harvey, 2nd., *West of the Setting Sun*. Toronto, Canada, The Macmillan Co., 1943.

Chambers, Robert W., *The Hidden Children*. New York, New York, Appleton, 1914.

Chandler, Mrs. Winthrop, *Autumn In The Valley*. Boston, Massachusetts, Little, Brown, & Co., 1936.

Chapman, Frank M., *Handbook of Birds of Eastern North America*. New York, New York, Appleton, 1895.

Charlevoix, Pierre François Xavier de, *History and General Description of New France*. Volume 1-2, New York, New York, Francis P. Harper, 1900.

Chidsey, Donald Barr, *John the Great: The Times And Life Of A Remarkable American*. New York, New York, Doubleday Doran & Co., Inc., 1942.

Clarke, Thomas Wood, *Emigrees in the Wilderness*. New York, New York, The Macmillan Co., 1941.

Conover, George S., *The Birthplace of Sa-g-ye-wat-ha, or The Indian Red Jacket*. Waterloo, New York, Waterloo Library and Historical Society, 1884.

Conover, George S., *The Genesee Tract*. Geneva, New York, 1889.

Cook, Frederick, *Journal Of The Military Expedition Of Major General John Sullivan Against The Six Nations*. Auburn, New York, Knapp, Peck & Thomson, 1887.

Cowan, Helen, *Charles Williamson*. Rochester, New York. Published by the Rochester Historical Society, 1941.

Craighead, The Reverend J. G., *The Story of Marcus Whitman*. Philadelphia, Pennsylvania, Presbyterian Board of Publication and Sabbath-School Work, 1895.

Cranston, J. H., *Étienne Brulé, Immortal Scoundrel*. Toronto, Canada, Ryerson Press, 1949.

Devens, R. M., *Our First Century: One Hundred Great and Memorable Events In The History of Our Country*. Springfield, Massachusetts, C. A. Nichols & Co., 1876.

Dibble, R. F., *John L. Sullivan: An Intimate Narrative*. Boston, Massachusetts, Little Brown & Company, 1925.

Doty, Lockwood L., *A History of Livingston County*. Geneseo, New York, 1876.

Doty, Lockwood R., *History of Livingston County*. Jackson, Michigan, W. J. Van Deusen, 1905.

Drury, Clifford M., *Marcus Whitman, Pioneer and Martyr*. Caldwell, Indiana, The Caxton Printers, Ltd., 1937.

DuPont de Nemours, E. I. & Co., *The Autobiography of an American Enterprise*. In commemoration of the 150th anniversary of the founding of the company, New York, New York, Charles Scribner's Sons, 1952.

Eaton, Elon Howard, *Birds of New York*. Albany, New York, University of the State of New York, 2 volumes, 1910-1914.

Edmonds, Walter D., *Mostly Canallers*. Boston, Massachusetts, Little, Brown, & Company, 1934.

Elwood, Mary Cheney, *An Episode of the Sullivan Campaign and Its Sequel*. Rochester, New York, The Post Express Printing Company, 1904.

Evans, Paul Demund, *The Holland Land Co.* Buffalo, New York, Buffalo Historical Society, 1924.

Fisher, Edwin A., *Report On Flood Conditions In The Genesee River.* Rochester, New York, 1937.

Fiske, John, *New France And New England.* New York, New York, Houghton Mifflin Co., 1902.

Fiske, John, *The American Revolution.* Volume 1, New York, New York, Houghton Mifflin Co., 1891.

Fiske, John, *The Critical Period of American History.* 1783-1789, New York, New York, Houghton Mifflin Co., 1888.

Hanford, Rear Admiral Franklin, *Notes on the visits of American and British Naval Vessels to the Genesee River,* 1809-1814. Rochester, New York, The Genesee Press, 1911.

Hand, H. Wells, 1808-1908, *Centennial History Of The Town of Nunda.* Rochester, New York, Rochester Herald Press, 1908.

Hatch, Alden, *The Wadsworths of the Genesee.* New York, New York, Coward-McCann, Inc., 1959.

Headley, Joel Tyler, *The Second War with England.* New York, New York, Charles Scribner, 1853.

Herrick, John P., *Empire Oil: The Story Of Oil In New York State.* New York, New York, Dodd, Mead & Co., 1949.

Holthusen, Henry Frank, *James W. Wadsworth, Jr.* New York, New York, G. P. Putnam's Sons, 1926.

Hough, Franklin B., *Proceedings of the Commissioners of Indian Affairs For The Extinguishment of Indian Titles In The State of New York.* Albany, New York, Joel Munsell, 1861.

Howland, Henry R., *Voices of the* [Letchworth] *Glenn.* New York, New York, J. Mooney, Printer, 1876.

Hubbard, John Niles, *Sketches of Border Adventures in the Life and Times of Major Moses Van Campen.* Bath, New York, R. L. Underhill & Co., 1842.

Hungerford, Edward, *Men of the Erie.* New York, New York, Random House, 1946.

Hutchins, S. C., *Civil Lists and Forms of Government of the Colony and State of New York.* Albany, New York, Weed, Parson & Co., 1870.

Jones, Louis C., *Things That Go Bump in the Night.* New York, New York, Hill & Wang., 1959.

Kelly, Thomas, *The Big Tree Treaty.* Geneseo, New York, Published at Mt. Pleasant Farm, 1909.

Lahontan, Louis Armand de Lon d'Arce, *New Voyages to North America.* Chicago, Illinois, A. C. McClurge & Co., 1905.

Larned, J. N., *The Life And Work Of William Pryor Letchworth.* Boston and New York, Houghton Mifflin Co., 1912.

Lenski, Lois, *Indian Captive: The Story of Mary Jemison.* New York, New York, Stokes, 1941.

Lobeck, Armin K., *Things Maps Don't Tell.* New York, New York, The Macmillan Co., 1956.

Lossing, Benson J., *Centennial History Of The United States, From The Discovery Of The American Continent, To The End Of The First Century Of The Republic.* Hartford, Connecticut, Thomas Belknap, 1875.

Marshall, Orsamus H., *LaSalle Among the Senecas in 1669.* Buffalo, New York. Published by Buffalo Historical Society, 1874.

Marshall, Orsamus H., *Narrative of the Marquis Denonville's Expedition against the Senecas in 1687.* (Translated from the French), New York, New York, Bartlett & Wellford, 1848.

Marshall, William I., *Acquisition of Oregon and the Long Suppressed Evidence about Marcus Whitman.* Seattle, Washington, Loweman & Hanford Co., 1905.

Mau, Clayton, *The Development of Central and Western New York.* Dansville, New York, F. A. Owen Publishing Co., 1958.

McKelvey, Blake, *Rochester: The Water-Power City: 1812-1854.* Cambridge, Massachusetts, Harvard University Press, 1954.

McKelvey, Blake, *Rochester: The Flower City: 1855-1890.* Cambridge, Massachusetts, Harvard University Press, 1949.

Merrill, Arch, *River Ramble.* Rochester, New York, Seneca Book Binding Company, 1956.

Merrill, Arch, *The White Woman and Her Valley.* Rochester, New York, Seneca Book Binding Company.

Milliken, Charles F., *A Biographical Sketch Of Mary Jemison, The White Woman Of The Genesee.* Rochester, New York, 1924.

Minard, John S., *John Barker Church.* Belmont, New York, Fuller-Davis, 1916.

Minard, John S., *History of Allegany County.* Alfred, New York, W. A. Fergusson & Co., 1896.

Mitchell, Margaret Knox, *The Passenger Pigeon in Ontario.* Toronto, Canada, University of Toronto Press, 1935.

Morgan, Lewis H., *League of the Ho-de-no-sau-nee of Iroquois.* New York, New York, Dodd, 1901.

Murray, Elsie, *Ezilum: The Story of a French Royalist Colony.* Athens, Pennsylvania, Tioga Point Museum, 1937.

Parker, Jennie Marsh, *Rochester: A Story Historical.* Rochester, New York, Scrantom, Wetmore & Co., 1884.

Parkman, Francis, *The Jesuits of North America in the Seventeenth Century.* Boston, Massachusetts, Little, Brown & Company, 1867.

Parkman, Francis, *Pioneers of France in the New World.* Volume 3, Boston, Massachusetts, Little, Brown & Company, 1865.

Pearson, Henry Greenleaf, *James S. Wadsworth.* New York, New York, Charles Scribner's Sons, 1913.

Peer, Sherman, *The Genesee River Country.* Ithaca, New York, 1954.

Peer, Sherman, *William Pryor Letchworth and Glen Iris.* Castile, New York. Published by Genesee State Park Commission, 1956.

Pound, Arthur, *Lake Ontario.* Indianapolis, Indiana, Bobbs-Merrill Co., 1945.

Preston, Marie C., *Avon Heart of the Genesee Country*. Avon, New York, Avon-Herald News, Inc., 1958.

Roosevelt, Theodore, *The Naval War of 1812; or The History of the United States Navy During the Last War with Great Britain*. New York, New York, G. P. Putnam's Sons, 1910.

Sagard, Théodat Gabriel, *The Long Journey to the Country of the Hurons*. Toronto, Canada, Champlain Society, 1839.

Scudder, Horace E., *Men and Manners in America One Hundred Years Ago*. New York, New York, Scribner, Armstrong, and Company, 1876.

Seaver, James Everett, *A Narrative Of The Life of Mary Jemison, The White Woman of the Genesee*. New York, New York, The American Scenic & Historic Preservation Society, 1932.

Slocum, Helen Edson, *Kings Landing: First White Settlement West of the Genesee River*. Rochester, New York, Published by the Rochester Historical Society, 1948.

Smith, James Hadden, *History of Livingston County*. Syracuse, New York, D. Mason & Co., 1881.

Stewart, Alexander M., *French Pioneers in North America*. Albany, New York. Published by the New York State Archaeological Society, 1938.

Stillwell, L. L., *Angelica Collectanea*. Angelica, New York, The Angelica Advocate, 1955.

Stone, William Leete, *The Life And Times of Sa-go-ye-wat-ha, or Red Jacket*. Albany, New York, J. Munsell, 1866.

Stone, William Leete, *Life of Joseph Brant—Thayendanegea: Including The Border Wars Of The American Revolution*. 2 Volumes. Cooperstown, New York, H. E. Phinney, 1845.

Swiggett, Howard, *War Out Of Niagara: Walter Butler and the Tory Rangers*. New York, New York, Columbia University Press, 1933.

Thwaites, Reuben Gold (editor), *The Jesuit Relations and Allied Documents. Travels and Explorations of the Jesuit Missionaries in New France*. Volumes 52, 54, Cleveland, Ohio, The Burrows Brothers Co., 1896-1901.

Trollope, Frances, *Domestic Manners of the Americans*. New York, New York, Dodd, Mead & Co., 1927.

Tucker, Glenn, *Poltroons and Patriots: A Popular Account of the War of 1812*. Indianapolis, Indiana, The Bobbs-Merrill Company, 1954.

Turner, Orsamus, *History of the Pioneer Settlement of Phelps & Gorham's Purchase*. Batavia, New York, LaVerne C. Cooley, 1946.

Turner, Orsamus, *Pioneer History of the Holland Purchase of Western New York*. LaVerne C. Cooley, 1946.

Van Every, Edward, *Muldoon the Solid Man of Sports*. New York, New York, Frederick A. Stokes Co., 1929.

Whitford, Noble E., *History of Canal System of the State of New York*. Albany, New York, Brandow Printing Co., 1906.

Winkler, John Kennedy, *The DuPont Dynasty*. New York, New York, Reynal & Hitchcock, 1935.

Winsor, Justin, *Cartier to Frontenac*. New York, New York, Houghton Mifflin Co., 1900.

Wright, Albert Hazen, *The Sullivan Expedition of 1779*. Ithaca, New York, 1943.

Articles, Letters, Reports:

Annis, H. K., "Fifty Years of Fishing and Studying Fish." Rochester, New York, *Rochester Gas & Electric News*, December, 1929.

Ayrault, Isabel, "The True Story of Mary Jemison." Rochester, New York, Rochester Historical Society, Pub., Volume VIII, pp. 193-218.

Barton, W. H. H., Scrapbook, Newspapers, 1853-1892, Rochester, New York, Rochester Public Library.

Black, Sylvia R., "Seth Green, Father of Fish Culture." Rochester, New York, *Rochester History*, Volume VI, No. 3. July, 1944.

Clapp, E. P., "The Travel, Trade & Transportation of the Pioneers." Rochester, New York, MS; 463 pages, in possession of this writer.

Douglass, Harry S., "The Immortal Mary Jemison." Arcade, New York, *Historical Wyoming*, January, 1958.

Fairchild, Professor Herman LeRoy, "The Physical Causes of Rochester's Prosperity." Rochester, New York, Rochester Historical Society, Pub., Volume X, pp. 83-101.

Harris, George H., "Early Shipping on the Genesee: Reminiscences of Capt. Hosea Rogers." Rochester, New York, Rochester Historical Society, Pub., Volume IX, pp. 92-111.

Harris, George H., "The Life of Horatio Jones." Buffalo, New York, Buffalo Historical Society, Pub., Volume VI, pp. 387-504, 1903.

Holton, Gladys, Reid, "The Genesee Valley Canal." MS, Rochester, New York, Rochester Museum of Arts and Sciences.

Hubbard, Elbert, "In Re Muldoon." East Aurora, New York, *The Philistine*, Volume 25, No. 3, pp. 65-83, 1907.

McKelvey, Blake, "Indian Allan's Mills." Rochester, New York, *Rochester History*, Volume I, No. 4, October, 1939.

Moore, Crary, "The Genesee Valley Hunt." New York, New York, *Harper's Bazaar*, September, 1958.

Motley, Maude, "The Romance of Milling: With Rochester The Flour City." Rochester, New York, Rochester Historical Society, Pub., Volume X, pp. 141-234.

Olds, Nathaniel S., "From LaSalle to Indian Allan." Rochester, New York, Rochester Historical Society, Pub., Volume X, pp. 61-82.

Perkins, Mrs. Gilman, Scrapbook, Newspapers, 1890-1915. Rochester, New York, Rochester Public Library.

Report of the Select Committee of the Assembly of 1846 Appointed to Investigate Certain Frauds Committed on the Canals of this [New York] State. Assembly Documents, Volume 3, No. 100, Albany, New York, 1847, C. Van Benthuysen & Co., Public Printers, 1847.

Rogers, Fannie, Rochester, "Col. Nathaniel Rochester." Rochester, New York, Rochester Historical Society, Pub., Volume III, pp. 321-326.

Scrantom, Edwin, "Reminiscences of Col. Nathaniel Rochester." Rochester, New York, Rochester Historical Society, Pub., Volume III, pp. 315-320.

Selden, George B. Jr., "Étienne Brulé." Rochester, New York, Rochester Historical Society, Pub., Volume IV, pp. 83-102.

Selden, George B. Jr., "The Expedition of the Marquis de Denonville Against the Seneca Indians." Rochester, New York, Rochester Historical Society, Pub., Volume IV, pp. 1-82.

Selden, Henry R., "The Genesee Valley Canal." MS, 1940.

Troup, Robert, Letter Book. No. 7, MS, pp. 8-9, 189-190.

Truesdale, Dorothy S., "Historic Main Street Bridge." Rochester, New York, Rochester History, Volume III, No. 2 April, 1941.

Turpin, Morley B., Ebenezer Allan in the Genesee Country. Rochester, New York, Rochester Historical Society, Pub., Volume XI, pp. 313-338.

INDEX

New York Classics, a series devoted to reprinting regional literature of lasting value.

Frank Bergmann, *Series Editor*